ATLAS INFERNAL

CZEVAK NARROWED HIS eyes, searching both his mind and his surroundings for possibilities. Belphoebe had been snatched away by her rangers and his retinue were smashed. Snarling through the stabbing throb of broken ribs, Czevak slipped the *Atlas Infernal* into his coat and rolled over. Crawling arm over arm across the collapsed canvas of the marquee, away from the Thousand Sons Space Marine, away from certain death, the High Inquisitor heard Klute's shotgun run dry. Craning his neck, Czevak saw the Rubric Marine batter the inquisitor mindlessly aside with the sweep of one ceramite arm. Czevak knew what was coming next. He willed it on.

A WARHAMMER 40,000 NOVEL

ATLAS INFERNAL

An Inquisitor Czevak Novel

Rob Sanders

BLACK LIBRARY

For TC, Jonah and Elliot - you know why...

A BLACK LIBRARY PUBLICATION

First published in Great Britain in 2011 by
The Black Library,
Games Workshop Ltd.,
Willow Road, Nottingham,
NG7 2WS, UK.

10 9 8 7 6 5 4 3 2 1

Cover illustration by Stef Kopinski.

A CIP record for this book is available from the British Library.

ISBN13: 978 1 84970 070 2

Distributed in the US by Simon & Schuster
1230 Avenue of the Americas, New York, NY 10020, US.

See the Black Library on the internet at
www.blacklibrary.com

Find out more about Games Workshop
and the world of Warhammer 40,000 at
www.games-workshop.com

Printed and bound in the US.

IT IS THE 41st millennium. For more than a hundred centuries the Emperor has sat immobile on the Golden Throne of Earth. He is the master of mankind by the will of the gods, and master of a million worlds by the might of his inexhaustible armies. He is a rotting carcass writhing invisibly with power from the Dark Age of Technology. He is the Carrion Lord of the Imperium for whom a thousand souls are sacrificed every day, so that he may never truly die.

YET EVEN IN his deathless state, the Emperor continues his eternal vigilance. Mighty battlefleets cross the daemon-infested miasma of the warp, the only route between distant stars, their way lit by the Astronomican, the psychic manifestation of the Emperor's will. Vast armies give battle in His name on uncounted worlds. Greatest amongst his soldiers are the Adeptus Astartes, the Space Marines, bio-engineered super-warriors. Their comrades in arms are legion: the Imperial Guard and countless Planetary Defence Forces, the ever-vigilant Inquisition and the tech-priests of the Adeptus Mechanicus to name only a few. But for all their multitudes, they are barely enough to hold off the ever-present threat from aliens, heretics, mutants - and worse.

TO BE A man in such times is to be one amongst untold billions. It is to live in the cruellest and most bloody regime imaginable. These are the tales of those times. Forget the power of technology and science, for so much has been forgotten, never to be re-learned. Forget the promise of progress and understanding, for in the grim dark future there is only war. There is no peace amongst the stars, only an eternity of carnage and slaughter, and the laughter of thirsting gods.

I

The Dance Without End: The Ruins of Iyanden

'…befell the mighty eldar craftworld of Iyanden in the Galactic East. During my days as guest and observer in the shattered halls I came to learn the tragedies of the Second Tyranid War and the alien eldar's part in the defeat of the tyranid foe.

Our hosts also shared with us a rare gift, an experience of which few humans have been deemed worthy. We were present while the Iyanden craftworld received an unexpected visitation from a troupe of their Harlequin brethren. Farseer Iqbraesil arranged our inclusion in the audience, in no little way, I suspect, to impress upon us the solidarity of their ancient race. The Harlequins, as you may or may not know, are a faction of the eldar race to whom the responsibility of remembrance falls. They travel from craftworld to craftworld, keeping the legends and ancient history of the eldar race alive through their dance, drama and martial performance. The Harlequins are both servants of the Laughing God – the only deity of their race to survive the mighty Fall – and custodians of the hallowed Black Library of Chaos. The Black Library is a dark craftworld hidden within the webway and is the eldar's shrine and repository of forbidden lore regarding the Ruinous Powers of the universe.

For the Harlequins there is no distinction between art and war; they are the archetypal warrior poets, travelling the labyrinthine expanses of the webway, bringing enlightenment to their audiences and certain death to the servants of darkness. The Harlequin troupe presented for the Iyanden the *Dance Without End*, which I'm told dramatises the inevitable Fall of the eldar civilisation. While the Mimes performed the roles of the epic piece, Shadowseers launched hallucinogenics about the chamber and unleashed their potent tele-empathic abilities upon the audience. What the words and actions of the Harlequins suggested, the hallucinogens and psycho-emotional manipulations of the Shadowseers realised. We were completely immersed in the actuality of the piece, in a way no human work of art could hope to reproduce. We were one with the tale.

The Harlequins' works are myriad and diverse, however, and afterwards Farseer Iqbraesil told me that the events depicted in the Harlequins' performances – events significant to the destiny of their race – were not always historical. Some were actually happening as performances unfolded and some, he said, had yet to happen at all.'

Inquisitor Bronislaw Czevak
Letters to the Casophilians

I

PROLOGUE

*Uthuriel craftworld crash site, Darcturus proto-world,
Moebius subsector*

CHORUS

'PERHAPS IF YOU spent more time studying the xenos and
less time burning them, Inquisitor Malchankov, you
would be better equipped to understand the import of
my meaning, sir,' Interrogator Raimus Klute heard his
master suggest.

Dipping his hand in the stoup and with his fingers
moistened, Klute made the sign of the aquila. Adjusting the line of his Manteau cloak about his immaculate
carapace, the young interrogator pulled the thick curtain
aside, passing through the black-out canvas of his master's improvised chambers. His ancient lord was holding
conference in the centre of the vaulted tent, surrounded
by a small crowd of dead-eyed servitor nexomats. Each

monotask drone stood flesh-plugged into the next,
nests of vox-lines and cables dangling between their
automatronic bodies. Through each, a dread member of
the Holy Inquisition spoke. The Moebius Conclave was
in subsector-spanning congress.

Czevak stood at the pulpit, ancient and irascible, as
if daring the frayed and knotted thread that was his
artificially elongated life to snap. The plasglass of his
blister-helmet clouded with light breath, obscuring the
bruised sockets of his eyes. The hairless crimp of an age-
spotted scalp and the deep lines of his collapsing face
marked an eternity of study and engagement. The bulk
of his cryogenic suspension suit sighed and hissed nitrogen from under the liver-brown shag of his Fenrisian
mastodon-hair coat.

A nexomat stood before him crucified – his tormented,
vat-cultured frame shot through with aerials and
antenna, the telescopic tips of which extended from his
fingers and the base of his neck. Into his chest was crafted
a system of loudspeakers and from these Inquisitor
Malchankov's savage syllables reverberated.

'And if you spent less time searching for corrupt wisdom in the embrace of the alien and more time searching
your soul, High Inquisitor, then you would come to realise how far from the God-Emperor's true path you have
strayed.'

Klute watched his master erupt in an apoplectic storm
of brittle words and confounded curses. The interrogator
shook his head. Before he had been Bronislaw Czevak's
acolyte, Klute had been the venerable High Inquisitor's
chirurgeon. Klute had advised Czevak a thousand times
to keep his anger in check. At over four hundred years
old, the inquisitor's rising choler alone could kill him.

Cynthis-Six dutifully approached the interrogator,
more spindly machine than woman, handing him scroll
after data scroll, which Klute unravelled and handed
back to the calculus logi with disinterest. Unwilling to

disturb the High Inquisitor during the lengthy congress, she presented Czevak's acolyte with the logistical nightmare of the High Inquisitor's manpower and operation. As part of his duties Klute routinely waded through a daily mountain of minutiae and force management. The God-Emperor might be in the detail but this little interested Bronislaw Czevak and the High Inquisitor left his young apprentice to handle the strategic and organisational reality of running the Ordo Xenos operation on Darcturus.

'Take this down,' Klute instructed her. 'Send messengers to Confessor-Militant Caradoq and Lieutenant Colonel MacGrellan. The good confessor needs to order his frater digteams in Zones Omicron through Omega East back to the camp perimeter. Colonel MacGrellan needs to do likewise with his engineers. Have him organise Gorgons for the transportation of the Death Korps and frater militia alike and riders to escort. Make sure that the colonel is aware that eurypterids have recolonised the abandoned trenches on the peninsula. If they try to walk out of there, they'll be cut to pieces.' The calculus logi simultaneously scribbled messages for both men, before skittering away to summon messengers.

In the background, Czevak continued to spit venomous accusations while the unfortunate nexomat vox-relaying his message bore the full brunt of the High Inquisitor's ire.

'How long?' Klute put to a pair of figures standing in the shadows of the tent-chamber. They were watching their inquisitor in debate with the Moebius Conclave.

'Sixteenth hour,' Sister Kressida confirmed. She was wreathed in the spectral smoke of her lho-stick, its tapered holder clasped between her perfect teeth. The medicae devotions of her hospitaller order – that of the Eternal Candle – were plain to see on her slender vestments. She leaned on Czevak's ornate walking cane – a ferrouswood stick with an eldar spirit stone decoratively embedded in its pommel like a sceptre. She was holding it for the inquisitor during the subsector conference. 'I've tried to get him to rest, but he won't have it.'

'You impudent cub…' Klute heard the High Inquisitor shout between torrents of heated words. While Czevak and Malchankov raged at one another, the chatter of servitor vox-traffic and garbled static filled the chamber; the Moebius Conclave in uproar.

Arch Magos Phemus Melchior towered beside the sister – his hairy arms and hunched back glistening with the forge-sweat of his labours. He looked like some kind of chthonic deity, with his beard of mechadendrites and his remaining eye magnified to grotesqueness through the lens array bulging out of the side of his face. He had been with Czevak ever since the inquisitor's tour of the Iyanden craftworld – the Xenarite Diagnostic Coven at Vulcraetia volunteering the arch magus's services as a gift to a kindred spirit. Melchior had been a gift indeed to Czevak, assisting the High Inquisitor with his many techno-spiritual projects and designing for Czevak the cryogenic suspension suit that not only preserved his body, but allowed the movement of muscle-wasted, decrepit limbs through the aid of a mind-impulse link in the back of the inquisitor's skull.

'He's been hammer and tongues with Malchankov for a while now,' Melchior boomed, '– that Monodominant hellraiser. The High Inquisitor won't appreciate the interruption, lad.'

'He'll appreciate this,' the interrogator insisted, flashing a data-slate at them. Taking the ferrouswood cane from Sister Kressida he strode out across the conference space.

Cabled to the antenna-wracked servitor in the fashion of a chain gang was another nexomat, from which another inquisitor had intervened in the war of words crossing the chamber. The drone had a crate torso and no legs and was built into a half-track chair. His box-body was a bank of sockets into which the nexomat compulsively plugged vox-cables, while extracting and exchanging others. Half of his head was dominated by a bell-box and cradle arrangement upon which sat a manual vox-unit.

'Perhaps what our Ordo Hereticus colleague is suggesting,' a voice rattled through the nexomat, 'is that before we authorise further resources, you take some time – may I suggest Saint Ethalberg of Bona Phidia – praying for guidance in this matter. Utilising the spiritual technologies of the xenos, even in the Emperor's good name and interest, is not to be undertaken lightly – if undertaken at all.'

Klute heard Grand Master Ephisto Specht's brazen diplomacy through the servitor's grille speakers, cutting through the dissent and discussion in the chamber. Specht was an Amalathian to the core. If it were not for Czevak's more radical views, his clear seniority would have made him subsector Grand Master long ago, Klute reasoned, and he wouldn't be debating details with conservatives like Specht.

'Ephisto – is this really what you think the Emperor would want?' Czevak asked his master. The inquisitor didn't wait for a reply. 'For us to wait – to maintain a deteriorating status quo? Should we not do everything – everything in our power to ensure his return, back where he belongs, leading his Imperium, not only spiritually, but physically in these uncertain times?'

'The God-Emperor has already shown us what he wants,' Malchankov interrupted. 'The Great Crusade was his Holy Mandate to claim the galaxy in humanity's name. He did not bargain and ally himself with the xenos, as faith-traitors like you do, Czevak.'

'I think it unwise to debate what his Beneficent Majesty would want in such circumstances,' Grand Master Specht called out.

'The eldar are an ancient race who have forgotten more about ressurrective incarnation and soul transference technologies than humanity is ever likely to know–' Czevak said, his insistence a grizzled wheeze.

'Heresy!' Malchankov screamed.

'Especially if Puritan anarchists hold court with their own self importance,' the ancient Czevak seethed. He turned on the crucified nexomat. 'You – witchslayer and propagator of thaumaturgicide – your tyranny would put to flame those who feed the Astronomican and the Navigators that guide the ships of the Imperium by its light; you would end half your brother-inquisitors for their talents and the telepaths that carry your own authority across the stars. Malchankov – I have no doubt that your brand of lunacy would have put our beloved Emperor to the stake, for his own burgeoning, superhuman abilities.'

'Monstrous schismatist,' the Monodominant called back.

'Inquisitors, please!'

'I claim your blood, Czevak. Do you hear? I'm coming for you, High Inquisitor…'

Malchankov's nexomat servitor suddenly gave a violent shudder before reporting in a flat voice, 'The vox-link is broken.'

Nobody in the chamber doubted that the nexomat on the other end of the communication was dead.

'Gentlemen, please!' Grand Master Specht insisted. 'This is not how the Holy Ordos conduct themselves.'

Bowing before the pulpit and beneath Czevak's crabby eyes, Klute passed the inquisitor the data-slate. Snatching it irritably, Czevak peered through a magnified section of his blister-helmet at its contents.

'He's gone, Ephisto,' Czevak told the Grand Master, and then, satisfying himself as to the contents of the slate, said to himself, 'and so am I.' Slicing a suited finger across his neck at Arch Magos Melchior, Czevak climbed down from the pulpit. The congress was at an end. For a moment,

Klute thought he saw his master betray a giddy excitement.

'Captain Quesada?' the High Inquisitor asked, handing back the slate.

'The Deathwatch are on site and await your orders, my lord.'

Czevak strode out of the canvas chambers, tearing the curtain aside, his fur coat hunched around him. As he followed, he tossed Sister Kressida the data-slate.

'They found it?' Melchior asked, ready to follow.

'Omega West,' Klute told them. 'Arch Magos, ready your team; you'll go in with the second wave. Sister Kressida, we have no idea what we are going to find in there, a eurypterid nest if we're lucky. Report to the sanitarium station and ready the High Inquisitor's personal surgical bay.'

'Be careful,' Kressida cautioned, sliding Klute's medicae satchel from her shoulder and hanging it on the young interrogator's own.

'Klute!' Czevak called from the Death Korps Salamander Command Vehicle waiting outside.

'Send for the Idolatress,' Klute said to Kressida and Melchoir, 'and be ready.' With that he disappeared through the curtains after his master.

Klute held on tightly to the guardrail as the Salamander blasted between the tents of the Ordo Xenos encampment. Slipping on a plas-mask, the interrogator breathed deeply.

Darcturus was a young world. Although its atmosphere could support human life, the air was thin, reedy and low in oxygen. Without the mask, Klute would be fatigued within seconds and on his knees within minutes, not to mention the splitting headaches that seemed to incapacitate anyone attempting to walk unmasked between their billets. The skies were the yellow of old bruises and the surface largely covered by an inky, black ocean. Czevak had had the 88th Force Engineer Regiment of the Death Korps of Krieg make camp on one of the miserable, featureless archipelagos that reached out into the dark sea. When Czevak had discovered the ancient crash site of the Uthuriel craftworld, spread out across the sink-sands of the archipelago and shallow ocean basin beyond, he had Confessor-Militant Caradoq from the nearby cardinal world of Bona Phidia raise a frater labour militia. The Lesser Procta Cenobists, as they were called, all wished to do good, simple work in the Emperor's name. They were rewarded for their faith with the task of digging the expanse of archaeological trenchworks – under the professional eye of MacGrellan's Death Korps engineers – which Czevak required to locate fragments of the colossal crashed eldar craftworld. The physical effort alone was worthy of legend – not to mention the shifting wet sands and mud holes that cursed the frater militia's efforts and the eurypterids that scuttled onshore to tear Death Korps Guardsmen limb from limb.

As the Salamander blasted along the sandy mire that was the track to Zone Omega West, Guardsmen in gas-masks and muddy trench wear bled from their billet tents. They were joined by off-shift Cenobists, away from their prayers, all of whom went down on one knee in the waterlogged sand in the presence of the High Inquisitor. Czevak seemed not to notice them, his mind elsewhere.

'Where's Joaqhuine?'

'The Idolatress is on her way. Was that wise, my lord?' Klute put to Czevak over the din of the Salamander's struggling engine.

'Was what wise?' Czevak answered, having already forgotten the previous episode.

'To alienate the Ordo Hereticus.'

Both men smiled at Klute's choice of words, a crooked smirk somehow finding its way through Czevak's crumpled face.

'Valentin Malchankov is a monster: a Puritan, a Monodominant, a maniac. Unfortunately, the Holy Ordos have need of such men.'

'But, he threatened your life, sir.'

'What's left of it.'

'Can we afford such enemies?' Klute asked, driving the point home. 'I mean, my lord, presumably we lost the extra manpower you were requesting.'

'If we have truly discovered the Kaela Mensha shrine chambers then we shall not need the extra resources, nor need to worry about Malchankov and his idle threats.'

The Salamander finally moved out of the Ordo Xenos camp and headed across the quagmire which served as a road. As the vehicle passed across an improvised embankment, they came upon a skirmish. Klute saw gas-masked Death Korps Guardsmen on horseback, attempting to rescue several of their hardy steeds as the screeching animals were dragged below the surface of a sinkhole. The Death Riders proceeded to dismount and hammer the sand with las-blasts from their Lucius-pattern rifles. Several granular explosions later, the Guardsmen and their steeds were set upon by three hulking eurypterids, freshly emerged from the dunes-cape. The sea scorpions were top of the food chain on Darcturus and the only species of the myriad of proto-world creatures that ventured onto land.

The clinker-plated monstrosities looked like giant lice – all razored pincers and primitive stingers, with underbelly cilia-spines constantly embedded in the sand, tracking the vibrations and movements of their prey. Since the arrival of Imperial forces on their blood-ied shores, they had developed a particular taste for horsemeat, but mainly feasted upon Confessor-Militant Caradoq's frater labourers. As the Guardsmen slipped and sank in the moving sands, the eurypterids sliced up the terrified, Krieg-bred steeds. Las-bolts bounced from the alien beasts' armoured shells and in the end it took a grenade launcher to knock one of the horrors onto its back and a Death Korps sergeant to go to work with his chainsword on the monstrous underbelly of the thing.

As the other two were joined by a third and then a fourth, crawling up out of the sinkholes, Klute drew Czevak's attention to the scene.

'Should we assist?' the interrogator asked, placing a hand on his medicae satchel.

'Drive on,' the High Inquisitor told the Death Korps driver without a second thought. The Inquisition's business was too important to be delayed by the death of common Guardsmen. 'If we can unlock the secrets of eldar soul transference, their spiritual mechanism of divine incarnation, then imagine what those that follow us could achieve?' the High Inquisitor continued, picking up his previous line of enquiry. 'We could pave the way for the resurrection of the God-Emperor, for surely if a mortal man can become a god, then a god may indeed become a mortal man?'

'My lord?'

'We could transfer the spirit, the very being of the God-Emperor into the body of another. A pulpit in flesh, from which the Emperor can guide the Imperium once more, lead from the vanguard of humanity and complete his glorious Great Crusade. The hands and lips of another delivering the words and deeds of a god.'

'My lord, forgive my questions – but I have many. If such a thing were possible, what would happen to the Astronomican under such circumstances? A mortal man could not sustain such a wonder – a wonder upon which the entirety of the Imperium relies. And what of the dangers of corruption? If such a being were mortal, would it not be susceptible to the temptations of within or without, as all mortal men are? We would, after all, be using the warp practices of an ancient and alien race to achieve this.'

'You sound like Grand Master Specht.'

'No, my lord. I believe in what we are doing here. To have questions is not to disbelieve. I believe in the God-Emperor but, be assured, I'd have plenty of questions for him should I meet – be praised – his mortal incarnation.'

'My boy – all I know is this,' Czevak preached, 'in those precious few years running up to and during the Great Crusade, more progress was made by humanity than in the thousands of years that followed. Many of the evident truths we have come to live by and rely upon in the 41st Millennium were established in those times. The Imperium and its manifest purpose became more than just an idea in that golden age, it became the very fabric of reality that we take for granted here and now. Everything between the dark days of the Heresy and this very hour has been a hiatus. Men like Specht and Malchankov – fearful in their different ways – are like maggots in the decaying flesh of the Imperium, living off the promise of history but never to be instrumental in the realisation of its future potential. Today, Raimus, we shall be part of that realisation. How big a part remains to be seen.'

The Salamander hurtled down into the artificial shallows of Zone Omega West. Jutting up from a flooded excavation area was part of the shattered remains of the Uthuriel craftworld. The osseous fluidity of the architecture was unmistakably eldar in origin and the crystalline darkness of its wraithbone surface matched the other excavated remains that Czevak had had his forces uncover and investigate. Curvaceous towers and arches dominated the structure, bearing the bold swirl of alien runes and glyphs, all marked out in a different shade of darkness. The Death Korps engineers had been instructed by the High Inquisitor to search for a very specific set of markings, which up until now they had failed to find on any of the remains. Markings in the eldar's ancient tongue that signified the part of their vast city-vessel dedicated to Kaela Mensha – the Shrine of the Bloody Hand.

As soon as the find had been confirmed, the frater labour force excavating it had been evacuated and the only evidence that a small army of pious workers had been there were the abandoned shovels and buckets littering the flooded pit into which the Salamander descended. Planks of sodden wood demarcated pathways and fortified archaeological trenchworks. Platoons of Death Korps Guardsmen fought in the shadow of small mountains of excavated, wet sand that sagged at the pitside. Up to their thighs in the black, tidal shallows, the Guardsmen waded in their sodden trenchcoats, firing volleys of las-bolts into the agitated waters. The dig site had displaced a nest of eurypterids; they had no intention of surrendering their territory to the Imperials, and the Death Korps had been forced to fortify the excavation with heavy weapons teams along the flooded coastline. To prevent the excavation site from becoming damaged, Czevak had forbidden the use of artillery, and this meant that the Lesser Procta Cenobists had slogged to the constant chatter of heavy bolters tearing up the shallows and the pincered monstrosities emerging from them.

The echo of such activity filled the air as the Salamander reverse-tracked and skidded to a halt outside of the dark structure. Deathwatch Space Marines stood nearby like ominous pieces of architecture in their own right, their armour gleaming like tenebrous beacons of certain death. Only their shoulder pads bore any trace of colour – on one side the insignia of their varied parent Chapters and on the other the markings of their Ordo Xenos calling.

A group of Death Korps engineers was gathered at an elliptical arch that was the seeming entrance of the derelict structure, garrisoned by a lieutenant and his infantry platoon. The lieutenant came forward as Klute and the inquisitor stepped down from the vehicle and saluted – the only feature distinguishing him from his fellow masked Guardsmen were the stripes on his sand-spattered coat. Like his men, he bore a thirteen digit designation on his chest rather than anything as personal as a name.

'Melta charges are in place, High Inquisitor; ready on your order,' the lieutenant called through his mask. 'Excellent work, lieutenant. Continue in your efforts to secure the perimeter. Colonel Magrellan has reinforcements on their way from the eastern zones,' Czevak informed them.

The Deathwatch approached in silence. At first Klute thought he was sinking in the sand, but in reality it was the sheer size of the Space Marines, growing with every step, that disorientated the young interrogator.

Captain Hektor Quesada of the Aurora Chapter took off his helmet, fixing the High Inquisitor with a single eye of gunmetal grey. The other was tightly bandaged and spotted with blood. His hair was cropped short and shone like freshly wrought steel.

'Inquisitor Czevak.'

'Captain. You and your team are a most welcome addition to our endeavour.'

'As I understand it, we are to safeguard your person and neutralise any alien threats,' the captain confirmed with words that rumbled from somewhere deep inside his reinforced chest.

'The inquisitor's security is of prime importance during this mission,' Klute added with an emphasis that disintegrated in the presence of the Deathwatch. Quesada neither ignored nor acknowledged the interrogator, instead turning to his team with a nod. They proceeded to chamber rounds in their boltguns, bless their weapons and check the seals on their power armour. As they moved about one another, Klute was privy to their Chapter insignia. An Excoriator cradled a brute of a belt-fed heavy bolter, flanked by a member each of the Crimson Consuls and Scythes of the Emperor. The Scythes of the Emperor warrior's right arm had been replaced with a thick-set bionic appendage, rippling with bunches of telescopic tendons and hydraulic pistons. The remaining Space Marine reared up to full height, after checking the

Excoriator's helmet seals. He was tall, even by the standards set by his Deathwatch brethren and bore a clenched, silver gauntlet on his shoulder pad, identifying himself as a member of the Astral Fists Chapter.

The roar of an engine preceded the appearance of a Death Korps Chimera bouncing over the summit of a nearby dune. Locking off its tracks, the Imperial Guard transport skidded down the slope raising its dozer blade in time to hit the bottom and tear across the dig site toward the ruins. Even before the Chimera sand-spat to a stop, its side door had rolled open.

Klute was dazzled as a lithe figure disembarked. The reflective surface of the chest-hugging breastplate and the heavy, jangling aquila hanging about her neck caught and magnified the light of the dismal Darcturan suns.

Joaqhuine Desdemondra was a common sight about the Ordo Xenos encampment, spending as much time on the sandy shooting ranges as in the Death Korps tent chapels. She was no less revered for this fervour, as was demonstrated in the way the Death Korps lieutenant and his platoon slapped their right knees into the wet sand and bowed their helmets. Tiny, sausage curls bounced with every step about her dark face, with full lips and big, brown eyes set in an expression of unforced calm.

She was known simply as Saint Joaqhuine or 'the Idolatress' among the Guardsmen. Originally Joaqhuine was part of the Path Incarnadine, a haemovore death cult that single handedly defended the Carfax Hive on the cardinal world of Aspiratyne from the predations of the dark eldar Fell Witch and her World-Scourgers. There Joaqhuine's death-dealing skills and supernatural abilities came to the attention of Inquisitor Furneaux – Czevak's Ordo Xenos mentor. Furneaux determined that although her capacity for taking life was admirable, her real gift lay in resisting the inexorable finality of death. Her reported immortality was mere rumour and myth on Aspiratyne but Inquisitor Furneaux himself witnessed several of her resurrections and despite disgust at her feeding habits, swiftly assigned her as his bodyguard and henchwoman.

Word of Desdemondra's immortality spread among the Ecclesiarchy, and Joaqhuine – Saint Joaqhuine the Renascent as she came to be known in the Ministorum Annals – was confirmed by Confessor-Militant Caradoq as a Living Saint of the Imperial Creed. When Furneaux died during the mysterious events surrounding the Second Klestry Forest War, Czevak engaged the haemovore saint's loyalties – as much to study her miraculous gift and its relationship to his researches as out of the need for an able bodyguard.

Joaqhuine padded through the shallows, her breastplate framed in the lines of the khaki Death Corps trenchcoat she habitually wore. She appeared indifferent to the collective reverence. Snatching up a Lucius-pattern lasgun and a meltagun from the shoulders of two kneeling Guardsmen, Joaqhuine tossed Klute the rifle and kept the meltagun for herself. The interrogator held the grit-encrusted weapon at arm's length for a moment before grunting and handing Czevak his spirit stone-pommelled cane. Shrugging his satchel higher up his shoulder, Klute went through the motions of priming the weapon. He knew how Joaqhuine felt about the protection offered by the brace of needle guns sitting criss-crossed on his belt – which was that they offered no protection at all.

'Praise be,' she told the High Inquisitor, flashing her implanted adamantium cuspids through her plas-mask, as she thumbed the sub-atomic primer on the meltagun.

'Praise be, indeed,' Czevak returned with a slack-mouthed smile. 'Lieutenant, proceed,' he ordered. The faceless Guardsman signalled to his platoon's demolitions man, who twisted his bulky detonator. The melta charge exploded with an eye-searing flash, leaving a gaping hole of dribbling wraithbone in place of the osseous archway. An ancient darkness beckoned, a darkness that did little to dissuade the Deathwatch Space Marines from darting inside, despite their armoured bulk. With less enthusiasm, Klute ventured through the ragged hole, flanking the High Inquisitor, who stabbed his ferrous-wood cane into the soft ground with Saint Joaqhuine bringing up the rear.

The lamps on the Space Marines' armour sliced up the blackness within, the beams pointing and pivoting in synchronised manoeuvres, as the Deathwatch advanced through the alien environment. The strike of the High Inquisitor's cane punctuated the kill team's progress. There was no way of telling how far the ruins extended out to sea and beneath the oily waves. When the Uthuriel craftworld crashed into Darcturus, it had shattered into an unknowable number of colossal fragments and derelict ship sections were spread across the surface of the planet. The runes on the exterior of the wraithbone were indicative of the section Czevak was looking for, but the dimensions of the section itself were unknown.

The Deathwatch kill team went about their deadly business, clearing one dark space after another in the curvilineal world of arciform chambers and conduits through which they advanced.

Klute snapped on the filthy spot lamp hanging under the barrel of his lasrifle and scanned the obscurity of their surroundings. The wraithbone walls and floor were smooth and glistened with coolness. The dark surface of everything soaked up the light and glimmered with an inner, emerald translucence. The air was cool and oxygen rich and both Klute and the Idolatress found that they could slip off their plas-masks.

'High Inquisitor,' Captain Quesada called.

Czevak limped forward on his cane, his suspension suit gurgling and chuffing with its cryogenic preoccupations.

'That's it,' Czevak said after a moment's pause.

'What's it?' Klute asked, picking up on the hesitation.

'Something about the orientation of the runes,' Czevak answered – a distracted murmur.

Klute's spot lamp showed the smooth curves of the passageway ending in a wide arch, the floor of which adjoined the ceiling. Czevak chuckled to himself in the blister-helmet.

'It's upside down,' the High Inquisitor informed everyone. 'The section must have landed on its back – the floor is the ceiling.'

In their alien surroundings Klute was taking little for granted; strange orientations were the least he expected from a ruined section of an eldar vessel. Something crawled across the interrogator's shoulder. He span in the darkness, only to find Joaqhuine's hand there. She pulled him to one side and presented the muzzle of her meltagun to the sealed archway.

'No need for such fireworks, my dear,' Czevak assured the Idolatress as he extracted the spirit stone from the fixture on his cane. The High Inquisitor hobbled up between the mountainous Astral Fist and his Death-watch captain and, with confidence, slipped the spirit stone into an imperceptible slot to one side of the arch.

The dark wraithbone of the archway fluttered with a phantasmal glow, feeling its way through the trans-lucence. Czevak waited. The Deathwatch remained still. Joaqhuine scanned the danger of the open dark-ness behind them while Klute watched, entranced, as what he could only imagine was the spirit of a former Uthuriel inhabitant coursed through the matrix of the wraithbone's soulstructure. The archway opened, not downwards as Klute might have expected for a doorway opening out onto the ceiling, but apart as a myriad of black-bone discs that rolled away and aside.

'Kaela Mensha,' Czevak announced to the revealing gloom beyond. 'The Shrine of the Bloody Hand'.

The Deathwatch shuttled in, one after the other, under the bolter sights of the previous Space Marine. Joaqhuine and Klute flanked Czevak, the interrogator sticking close to his master, lasgun raised and the feeble spot lamp beaming around the surroundings of the new chamber. With the meltagun supported in one arm, Joaqhuine fished around in the pockets of her Death Korps coat, producing a flare tube. Slam-igniting it against her knee, she fired the pyrotechnic and tossed it out into the inky open space.

The chamber flickered in the blinding flash of the flare. It was a sight to behold. Even the Deathwatch Space Marines slowed to an awe-inspired snaking of the eyes.

In the roof of the shrine was a gargantuan throne. Standing on the ceiling, the Imperials had to crane their necks skyward to take in the floor and the vision above them. Sitting in the throne, equally resisting the colossal force of gravity imposed on its unthinkable mass, was a giant figure. Its mighty metal claws clutched the arms of the throne in suspended rage and its armoured body, bloody and bronzed, supported the grandiose exaggerations of the vision's helmet. It had the proportions of a god, yet the nightmare appearance of something alien, unholy and warp-furious.

'Holy throne!' Klute blurted.

'Yes, I rather think it is,' Czevak agreed.

'Some grotesque parody,' Klute said, 'of our very own God-Emperor?'

'No,' Czevak told him. 'But this is a god, have no doubt of that. This is an incarnation of Khaine the Bloody Handed – the eldar god of war.'

The Deathwatch would have tensed, but their fat blood vessels were already torrents of adrenaline. Quesada nodded to his team, who moved in unison and with purpose. The Excoriator took the archway, bringing the heavy bolter up to cover the gaping corridor. The Scythes of the Emperor Space Marine jabbed two bionic fingers at his faceplate, then proceeded to do the same at his Crimson Consul brother and then up at the inverse helmet of the immense presence that was beaming a frozen mask of baleful wrath down upon them. The huge Astral Fist fell in behind the High Inquisitor like a guardian angel of death.

'This is a god?' Klute hissed.

'According to eldar mythology,' Czevak told him, 'Khaine fought the Chaos god Slaanesh and lost. The eldar believe that the essence of their god was smashed and disseminated, the divine fragments of its being now fuelling wraith artefacts at the heart of their craftworlds, like the one you see before you–'

'My lord,' Klute cut in.

'If we could retro-engineer the soul-transference technology–'

'Retro-engineer, my lord? This is ancient, alien technol–' Klute said, then caught himself, 'alien mythology.'

'If nothing else, it demonstrates that it can be done.'

'We don't know that. Also, I fear the Grand Master will not approve researches into this warp-sired thing,' Klute said.

'The hell with Specht and ghost-livered cowards like him,' Czevak growled. 'I will leave this galaxy a better place than the spiritual cesspool into which I was born, percolating in its own self-righteous stagnation.'

'Sir, would it not be wise–'

'You are going to tell me what would be wise are you, Raimus, with your forty standard?'

Klute felt Czevak's ancient eyes burn into him like two suns, magnified though the plastek lens of his blister-helmet.

The High Inquisitor's railings continued. 'Our triumphs are built upon the accomplishments of others. We stand on the Emperor's shoulders, Interrogator Klute, and our gaze is far. On such shoulders, is it not our very responsibility to reach further?'

'Praise be,' the Idolatress echoed.

Czevak thrust his ferrouswood cane at the dreadful

visage of the eldar war god. 'I understand your uncertainties – who wouldn't question themselves when faced with such an abominate prospect? But ask yourself this. Who would you rather listen to? The men who interpret the words of the divine – the Puritans with their selective hearing and the Amalathians who hear everything but do nothing – or divine words themselves? To hear such words from the living, breathing lips of our beloved Emperor, I would face a thousand abominate prospects.'

'I'm sorry, my lord,' Klute admitted. 'I just found the image of this alien barbarism unsettling.'

'That is undoubtedly the effect that it was attempting to project,' Czevak said, admiring the dimensions of the daemonic avatar. 'No matter, my acolyte. The right path is not always the easy path.'

'The path is less easy than you think, inquisitor,' Quesada thundered dangerously across the chamber.

The muzzle of the Astral Fist's bolter dropped from covering the alien effigy and came to rest on the shoulder of Czevak's Fenrisian mastodon-hair coat.

'Of course it is,' the High Inquisitor said with irritated resignation, 'haven't you been listening, captain?'

'Treachery!' Klute exploded but fell short of actually turning his weapon on the Adeptus Astartes warriors.

'Treachery indeed,' the Space Marine agreed. He put an armoured finger to his vox-bead. '*Anatoly Ascendant* this is Captain Quesada. You may begin your manoeuvres. I'm placing the marker now.' The Aurora Chapter battle-brother unclipped the targeting aid and activating its magnetic base, allowed the marker to fly horizontally across the chamber at the Bloody-Handed god and latch onto the side of its colossal helmet. 'Once my kill team, Inquisitor Czevak and Imperial forces are clear, you may commence orbital bombardment.'

'I didn't know the Deathwatch issued Inquisitorial Cartas,' Czevak said icily.

'We don't,' the Space Marine captain corrected him with

disinterest. 'That will be for someone else to decide. Grand Master Specht just wanted to make sure that you didn't bring the ordo into disrepute with your radical ways.'

'He thought I'd succeed,' Czevak nodded to himself. 'Well, that is something from a man who has the imagination of a mootch fly.'

'You haven't succeeded, inquisitor. We have orders to take you from here and place you under arrest for shipment back to Heigel Prime and then on to Our Lady of Sorrows. This archaeological find of yours will be erased from the face of the planet – almost as though it never existed – which it didn't, because this never happened and we were never here.'

'And yet we are,' Czevak challenged.

'Have I given you the impression that the Adeptus Astartes appreciate the common wit of less than ordinary men?' Quesada stung back. 'Jest not, good inquisitor. I take your unconditional compliance as a given, or my orders extend to destroying you and your people along with this damnable artefact you've discovered.'

Klute's head began to drop. Czevak had a perverted sense of humour and delighted in taunting those that held power over him. The interrogator had believed that this came from the High Inquisitor's age and the assumption that his heart would let out at any moment, regardless of threats issued to him by his enemies. Those who had known Czevak longer had told Klute that the inquisitor had just been born that way. The interrogator fully expected Czevak to drive Quesada to the point of killing him, probably on the erroneous assumption that a member of the Deathwatch – a simple, fighting Space Marine – would not really want to be embroiled in the death of an Ordo Xenos inquisitor – especially one that as the two men had identified, hadn't even officially been designated Carta Extremis. Czevak's response surprised the interrogator, however.

'I see your point,' the venerable inquisitor conceded.

He nodded to Klute and Joaqhuine. 'Your weapons.'

Without hesitation, the interrogator tossed the Lucius-pattern lasgun to the floor and unbuckled his belt, allowed his brace of needle guns to drop. Klute's hands drifted back skyward as he noticed the yawning barrels of the Scythes of the Emperor and Crimson Consul's bolters silently tracking his movements.

Joaqhuine was less inclined to part with her weapon. 'Over my dead body,' the haemovore announced darkly through her adamantium teeth.

The reaction was instantaneous. No perceivable communication had passed between the hulking Astral Fist and his Deathwatch captain, but there undoubtedly had been. The Space Marine simply pivoted, bringing his bolter off Czevak's shoulder and hammering a shaft of armour piercing shot through the Idolatress. With the Death Korps coat still flapping in the gust of the bolt-rounds that had passed straight through her, Joaqhuine Desdemondra tumbled.

Klute dashed towards the fallen figure, but the Space Marine fixed him in his unswerving sights, bringing the interrogator to a full stop. Stepping forward, the silent colossus forced both Klute and Czevak back towards the archway. Klute retreated but put himself squarely between the Astral Fist and his ancient master.

Quesada moved towards the archway and joined the Excoriator, leaving the Scythes of the Emperor and Crimson Consuls warriors to cover their armoured backs. The lightest scuff of the canvas coat on the wraithbone floor made itself known to the Astral Fist's super-sensitive hearing and he turned immediately.

The Idolatress had come unsteadily to her feet and was swaying in shock. The Deathwatch weaponry came up once again but their trigger fingers were given pause for thought by the way the gaping wound in her chest seemed to be knitting itself back to health.

Joaqhuine's lip wrinkled in silent agonies, flashing one of her adamantium fangs at the Space Marines. The primed meltagun rumbled its readiness, dangling loosely from two dazed fingertips.

The brothers from the Astral Fists and the Scythes of the Emperor were roaring at Joaqhuine to drop the weapon, while the Crimson Consul had thrust his bolter back in Czevak's face.

'Order her!' the Crimson Consul barked.

The chamber fell to uneasy silence.

Czevak extended one gloved hand. 'Sister,' he chided imploringly. 'Your weapon – let them have it…'

In a blur of motion the meltagun came up. The righteous fury of the Adeptus Astartes' bolters flew at Joaqhuine once again, but not before the sub-atomic inferno of the meltagun had vaporised the Astral Fist's helmet clean off his towering shoulders. As Joaqhuine's body was subject to further explosive-tip molestation – her arms and sausage curls thrown this way and that – the battle-brother's hulking body hovered and then crashed to its knees. Both Saint and Space Marine hit the floor simultaneously and lay still.

Captain Quesada wasn't taking any chances. He slid a frag grenade across the wraithbone, which slipped into the folds of her bolt-shredded coat before exploding.

'Joaqhuine!' the High Inquisitor called but by the time the smoke cleared, the Crimson Consul had both Czevak and Klute on their knees, with the kill team Space Marine pointing his bolter at their heads from above in an executioner's pose. Joaqhuine's body was a blood-soaked, ragged mess. The detonation had ripped up the wraithbone floor and dark shards of the alien structural material projected through the Idolatress's body.

The kill team held their positions, as still as the woman's impaled form as they waited for further surprises. That was until her chest did move, violently sucking in a gurgling breath. The Deathwatch wouldn't underestimate her again and watched as the Living Saint simultaneously demonstrated both immortality and futility. Her wounds were indeed closing, but a shaft of wraithbone, ripped up from the floor by the explosion, had erupted through her spine. Without her spine, the Idolatress could not extricate herself from the deathtrap; without extricating herself from the wraithbone stakes, her miraculous powers could not repair her spine.

The shrine chamber crashed with noise again as the Excoriator at the archway unleashed his heavy bolter into the darkness beyond.

'Targets!' he hollered over the clamour of the weapon, as he man-handled the bulk of the belt-fed monster around. The Deathwatch Space Marine's lamps and the flare of the explosive rounds gushing from the barrel did little to illuminate the corridor beyond and it was impossible to tell who or what the targets were.

'Is it the Death Korps?' Quesada bawled, assuming – not unreasonably – that the wily inquisitor had found a way to alert the platoon garrisoning the derelict or that they had simply entered at the sound of gunfire on their own initiative.

'Xenos!' the Excoriator called, struggling, even with the displacers and counterweights on his armour, to bring the heavy bolter round swiftly enough to defend against multiple targets.

Klute had been staring at the struggling Joaqhuine, wondering what he could do for her without getting himself killed. He turned to Czevak. He mouthed, 'Eurypterids?' at the inquisitor, thanking the Emperor that the alien organisms had chosen to nest in the wraithbone ruins. Czevak was lost in thought, however, his rheumy eyes glazed with a concentration that dissuaded the interrogator from disturbing him. Suddenly, the two of them were back on their feet and thrown towards the wall by the Crimson Consul Space Marine.

The Scythes of the Emperor battle brother and the captain fell to their knees, Quesada's arc of fire covering the Excoriator. Meanwhile, the Scythes of the Emperor Space Marine moved his bolter sights rapidly between the archway and the prone form of the crippled immortal.

The belt feed on the heavy bolter chugged to a sudden halt, empty shell casings rattling to the floor for a few moments longer. The kill team Space Marine darted the fat barrel of the weapon around the gloom of the corridor.

'Report!' Quesada snarled.

'I could have sworn by the primarchs, I saw–' the Excoriator began, but he got no further.

'Brother Loomis! Report!' Quesada shouted again, moving up on his position.

The chamber echoed with a sickening crunch, which the heavy weapons Space Marine seemed to feel as a physical sensation. The Excoriator's screams followed swiftly after, their reverberations bouncing around the open space. On a squealing note that Klute could hardly have imagined the deep, barrel chest of an Adeptus Astartes could achieve, the Excoriator dropped the heavy bolter and crumbled backwards onto his pack. By the time the view-obscuring bulk of the Space Marine fell, however, the enemy responsible for his felling had gone.

'Brother Loomis!' Quesada called once more, letting loose a horizontal stream of bolter fire down the corridor as he skidded to a stop at the collapsed Space Marine's side. 'Brother Aldwin. Door,' the captain called back at the Crimson Consul.

Dragging the High Inquisitor along the chamber wall, the Crimson Consul pinned Czevak's blister-helmet to the dark wraithbone with his bolter, giving him a privileged view of the inside of the weapon's barrel.

'Close it,' Brother Aldwin commanded. His battle-brothers were falling around him; he would not ask twice.

With the infinity circuit reactivated, the inquisitor didn't find it difficult to activate the rudimentary runes that controlled the archway door, despite its upside down orientation. Wraithbone discs rolled back into place, the doorway jigsawing its way back together. Dragging the Excoriator's body away from the sealed archway and across the smooth floor of the chamber, Captain Quesada deposited the Space Marine in front of Klute and pointed at the medicae symbol on his satchel.

'You're a medic?' Quesada demanded, as the Scythes of the Emperor Space Marine left the motionless Joaqhuine and came forwards to cover the archway.

'Chirurgeon,' Klute informed him.

'See to Brother Loomis,' the Aurora Chapter captain ordered.

Klute nodded reluctantly and came forward, squinting at the wound.

'Singular puncture wound to the chest,' he mumbled to himself. 'Went straight through the armour…'

'Speak up,' Quesada growled, but Klute motioned the captain to move his Deathwatch comrade.

'Get him on his side,' Klute asked the Space Marine. There was no way the young interrogator could move the still, power-armoured form.

Quesada grasped the ceramite plates of Loomis's polished, black armour and turned him over.

'Emperor's wounds!' Klute erupted as liquefied gore slushed from the puncture wound and slopped into a growing pool about Klute and the now apparently dead Space Marine. 'A single entry wound but his torso has been pulped from inside the armour. I've no idea what kind of weapon could do that,' Klute admitted.

'I have,' Czevak said grimly.

Klute, Quesada and the Crimson Consul turned on the High Inquisitor.

'And if it belongs to who I suspect it does, we're dead,'

the inquisitor told them, his eyes and mind elsewhere.

'Oh, now we're dead,' Klute muttered miserably.

'No,' Czevak corrected him. 'All of us.'

The inquisitor's fatalism clearly angered Captain Quesada, who left Brother Loomis and got back to his feet. He picked up the heavy bolter and tossed the deadweight of the object to the Scythes of the Emperor Space Marine, who began realigning the bolt-belt and checking the weapon for feed-jams.

A single impact sang off the wraithbone of the wide archway door. It had originated from the other side and was cold and daring in both its power and restraint. The Scythes of the Emperor battle-brother hunkered down on one knee, resting the heavy bolter and putting his eye squarely behind its sights and along the chunky barrel of the weapon. Quesada took the opposite angle, expertly exchanging ends of the twin-crescent magazine he had taped together and slammed the full clip into the breach of his bolter. Czevak nodded at Klute and the two of them began to step back, away from the archway and the pool of gore still pouring out of the Excoriator Space Marine. The Deathwatch captain dipped his hand in his thigh holster and withdrew a chunky bolt pistol. He pointed the sidearm at the two men without even looking at them.

'Stay where you are,' he ordered. 'Away from the wall. Now.'

The inquisitor and his interrogator sidestepped. Klute assumed that the Aurora Chapter Marine was afraid that Czevak would activate some rune-secreted doorway and slip out. He hoped for his own sake that the captain was correct to suspect his master of such invention.

Another single impact on the door echoed around the chamber. The Crimson Consul came forward, putting his gauntlet and the side of his helmet to the wraithbone entrance.

'Here they come,' Czevak whispered to Klute.

A shower of colour appeared in the chamber like a kind of spectral revenant and streamed at the Crimson Consul from behind. It appeared as though a stained-glass window had materialised behind the battle-brother and had then been blasted out with a shotgun. The spectrum of fragments flew and then reformed into a humanoid visage that stood behind the Deathwatch Space Marine.

The figure was tall and dressed in the eldritch fashions of the alien eldar, although Klute had never seen one of their kind garbed in such gaudy colours and outlandish patterns: kaleidoscopic chequers and stripes beside bold symbols and intense fabrics. Pipes protruded from a launcher pack on the eldar's back – presumably for grenades, the interrogator hypothesised – that formed a crown behind the hood and featureless mirror-mask that the interloper wore. He held out a gloved and delicate hand, into which the impossible length of a leaf-shaped witchblade appeared, smoking with runes and the psychic power of it wielder.

'Harlequins…' Klute heard his master murmur in fear and amazement; he could only imagine that the High Inquisitor was familiar with the alien warriors from his time spent on the Iyanden craftworld.

With the Crimson Consul still listening through the wraithbone door and his back to the Harlequin Shadowseer, he neither saw his attacker appear nor witnessed the elegant sword swipes that criss-crossed his pack and back armour. The blade cut through each of his calves – ceramite, muscle and bone, as though they were nothing.

The Crimson Consul stifled a wail and both Quesada and the Deathwatch heavy bolter answered the call. A storm of explosive death flew at the alien attacker, only for the creature to vanish in a spectral shower. The bolt-rounds blasted into the doorway and the mauled back of the Crimson Consul, one blowing the side of his helmet and its contents over the wraithbone wall.

It all happened so fast, there was little time for the inquisitor or Space Marine in the chamber to register the shock of disbelief. A dark, hulking shadow appeared above the kneeling Scythes of the Emperor warrior. Whereas the Shadowseer had been lithe and predatory, the second ghost was thicker set and radiated power and presence. Also, in contrast to its colourful Harlequin compatriot, the figure was broader, all black carapace and flowing folds of leather. It had a ribcage-style breastplate and a mask fashioned in the broad, beaming grin of a maniacal skull; a Death Jester.

The Scythes of the Emperor Space Marine tumbled to one side, rolling off his Chapter shoulder plate and onto his back, the bulk of the heavy bolter brought around to face his materialised attacker. The Death Jester's movements spoke of solidity instead of the dancer's grace of the Shadowseer – its murderous agility manifested in the way it swung the blade that decorated the end of his elongated shrieker cannon. The wicked attachment smashed through the heavy bolter, ripping both the weapon and the bionic arm clutching it from the body of the battle-brother.

The Scythes of the Emperor battle-brother's reaction was instantaneous. He kicked out at the Harlequin, but the figure was gone – a black mist dissipating to nothingness. The Space Marine got to his feet, slipping a little in the blood gushing from his empty shoulder socket. Bent double like a wounded animal, the Adeptus Astartes tore his bolt pistol from its holster. His enemy had reappeared some distance away – the cannon now aimed squarely at the blood-splattered Space Marine. The horrific whine of the weapon filled the shrine chamber as the cannon spat a single shot at the battle-brother from the Scythes of the Emperor. The round found its mark through the Space Marine's ruined shoulder. Another kind of screech echoed around the chamber; pressure was building, seals were giving and armour cracked. It did more than crack. It expanded, then exploded under the biological force of what the terrible weapon had done to the Space Marine's genetically-enhanced body. The power armour shattered and rained ceramite gore covered fragments in all directions, leaving a bloody haze where the Space Marine had been.

Behind Czevak and Klute appeared a third phantasmal presence. A spindly Harlequin warrior that wore a gargoylesque helmet-mask, sporting a furious, pink plume that not only made the eldar appear even taller but was also suggestive of some sort of rank. The leader materialised in mid-charge, trailed by a blur of past moments, holding a willowy pair of plasma pistols. Klute gasped as the Great Harlequin flicked his wrists, one after another, sending bright balls of fuchsia-coloured firepower at them. Like tiny suns, the plasma blasts banished the shadows from their path – a path that curved in a bending arc and sailed around Klute and the High Inquisitor. The balls slammed into Quesada beyond. The Deathwatch captain cried out in pain and frustration. His power armour sparked and smoked where the plasma had seared into him. With his face a mask of contortion and ugly vengeance, the Aurora Chapter Marine brought up his bolter. Czevak and Klute were still between Quesada and his attacker but the captain didn't register their existence.

Klute knew he had to act but in the milliseconds preceding could not come up with anything more inventive than roughly pushing the fragile Czevak out of the battle-brother's line of sight. A stream of fire passed between them. The captain found that the Great Harlequin was not only an expert at bending his plasma bolts but also his gangling body. Lifting his arm, the eldar allowed the Space Marine's barrage to pass beneath him, the bolt-rounds punching harmlessly through the material of his flowing coat. As the Space Marine's second clip ran dry he, threw the weapon at the charging Great Harlequin and snapped his bolt pistol into a firing position.

The Great Harlequin vanished into thin air but was simultaneously replaced by the appearance of another alien attacker. This one dropped into reality right next to the captain. A female of the race, the Harlequin trouper wore a half mask bearing a single, theatrical tear and a tail plume that reached down her back. She held up a tapered, tubular fist spike in one clenched gauntlet and a set of twin, razored riveblades in the other, assuming the appearance of a carnival-like scorpion. She was as fast as she was eye-catching, the riveblades coming straight down on the captain's elbow, severing the Space Marine's pistol, gauntlet and forearm. With a savage roar, Quesada went to reach for her, but the Harlequin moved with blinding speed and economy, sweeping underneath his expected animal lunge and smashing the captain in the face with a double-jointed, boot-heeled back-kick.

Out of his mind with pain, frustration and wrathful abandon, the Deathwatch Marine swung his elbow back at the dancing vision. By the time the battle-brother's comparatively sluggish manoeuvre played through, the Harlequin had vaulted and back-flipped immediately above Quesada's head and landed behind the captain. Then, with every muscle taut, driven and focused on the tip of her tubular fist spike, the slight creature drove the tapered end straight through the Space Marine's pack, ceramite and all.

The wide-eyed captain was facing Klute and Czevak as he was stabbed from behind and the two men were privy to the Deathwatch captain's spine-snapping end. Some kind of horrific monofilament wire-weapon had uncoiled inside the Space Marine's body and, just as with his Excoriator brother, it proceeded to whip and lash around, liquefying bone, carapace and internal organs. Klute watched, sickened and entranced by the way the wire's tip frantically needled out of the captain's ruptured eyeball and face, until finally, as the wire retracted and blood and brain matter emptied from the Space Marine's gaping mouth, the hulk toppled like a felled statue.

The Harlequin disappeared and Klute helped his master to his feet. Backing to the middle of the chamber the two men watched as the aliens played with their senses – shattering and re-materialising around the room in different configurations, closing on them slowly, the air empty and silent.

Saint Desdemondra – all but forgotten during the alien intrusion – started coughing up her lungs; still impaled in the wraithbone floor.

'Hang in there, Joaqhuine,' Klute called, clutching the arm of Czevak's suspension suit and gently dragging him over to the Idolatress. Klute knew that their only chance was to get the Living Saint back to her immortal self. As his boot scraped her meltagun he hesitated, every instinct imploring him to grab the weapon.

'Don't be foolish, boy,' Czevak told him. 'You've seen what our guests are capable of.'

'Somehow, I think we're the guests,' Klute replied shakily. 'Besides, I thought you said they'd kill us.'

'Events since then suggest otherwise,' the ancient inquisitor said. Czevak stared at the fallen Saint. 'Will she live?'

'Doesn't she always?' the interrogator said.

As Klute reached Joaqhuine's broken body, the eldar appeared in a group before them, each silently cradling their exotic weapons. Together they looked like a freakish circus: the gangly, plumed leader; the deadly dancer with her claws and helmet-tail; the grotesque skull-faced Death Jester and the eerie mirror-mask of the psyker-swordsman. They stood there for the longest time, simply studying the two men.

'What!' Klute erupted at the alien troupe. 'What do you want?'

'I don't think they speak,' Czevak interceded, before his interrogator's unnerved explosion provoked the eldar. 'Their medium is drama and dance, they speak through their performance.'

'What the hell are they?'

'They are so rarely seen, that I hardly dare guess,' Czevak revealed, his voice dropping to a whisper. 'But, by their dress and the way in which they dealt with humanity's finest here – I believe that they are indeed Harlequins, a sub-sect of the eldar, the keepers of their knowledge and history and tellers of their epic story.'

'You've seen them before?'

'Once. On Iyanden. Farseer Iqbraesil was kind enough to acquaint me with their names and ways.'

As the ancient inquisitor spoke he cradled his head left and right as though studying the aliens where they stood. 'As servants of a living deity they call the Laughing God, they are guardians of the Black Library of Chaos, an ancient, secret reliquary and repository of forbidden lore – containing everything that the eldar race has or will ever know about the Ruinous Powers.'

Czevak stopped as the mirror-masked Shadowseer slipped a precious crystal from his gaudy attire and holding it mime-like in his open palm, leaned in as though blowing on it. The stone leapt from his glove and shot across the chamber, embedding itself in an imperceptible slot in the wall. A ghostly sheen haunted its way across the wraithbone walls. The structure was cracked with age and impact damage but that didn't prevent each section of wall from becoming a living screen, each bearing a grim ornamental visage. The chamber was upside-down, and disconcertingly so were the projected figures that fixed Czevak with their deathless stares. Each was an eldar, impossibly old and hidden behind the long faceplate of the pointed helms favoured by their race. Runes danced across their robes. Precious stone and antique gilding decorated their armour and their eye-slits burned with jade. As they spoke, their voices had an elegance and grace, otherworldly and immediate. They all spoke together – but they spoke as one. As their alien tongue filled the chamber, Czevak mumbled a translation.

'Bronislaw Czevak of the Orders Holy; of the fledgling Imperium; of humanity young. You will not find the answers you seek in this... dead place.'

Klute looked from the alien ancients, to the still figures of the Harlequin troupe, to his master – unbound excitement beaming through the years of his aged features.

'What answers do I seek?' the High Inquisitor asked boldly.

'You test us, human?'

Czevak considered his response. 'I test myself,' he answered cryptically.

'Unnecessarily. You wish to know the means by which your corpse Emperor is resurrected.'

'Then it comes to pass,' Czevak said, his voice trembling with his feeble heart.

'Everything comes to pass, eventually, Resurrection Man. You trouble yourself with questions of the divine, like many of your short sighted kind, when you should be divining answers to your questions.'

'How can this be done?' Czevak demanded.

'By accepting what few among you have dared to long and longed to dare. An invitation to a place of dark answers, Bronislaw Czevak of the Holy Ordos. An old man of a young race, taking last breaths with questions heavy – take those last breaths with us, in the living Library of our ancestors. In the Black Library of Chaos you will think not on how your cadaverous god may help you through his resurrection, rather how you may help him through yours.'

'My lord,' Klute said softly. Czevak turned his blister-helmet and looked blankly on the young interrogator. Klute shook his head.

'If I refuse?'

'Such invitations are not refused, unworthy man. You will take your invitation and prevent another taking his, who exceeds even you in his human thirst for knowledge.'

Czevak allowed the cryptic references of the eldar to pass over him.

'But if I am unworthy…'

'You are, foolish human – have no doubt of that, but blind steps take you towards a worthy future. It is the word. It is written. The Library has spoken.'

An ancient vanished from a section of wraithbone only to be replaced by the other-dimensional radiance of what Klute could only assume was a warp portal.

'Vespasi-Hann will escort you through the webway to our dark and hallowed halls,' the eldar told Czevak and then stared, their jade eye-slits seeing straight through him. The mirror-masked Shadowseer came forward, theatrically indicating the portal and his intention that Czevak should move towards it.

As Klute felt his master pull away, he said urgently, 'My lord, this is no invitation. This is kidnapping by any other name.'

Czevak laid one suited hand on his interrogator's shoulder.

'Raimus, you have been my doctor, my good apprentice and an undeserved friend. You got me to this point – and death could wait for me beyond that portal. But I'd exchange however many moments I have left, for one glimpse of the hallowed halls of the Black Library of Chaos. You understand…'

'Then I'll come with you,' Klute said, coming forward himself, but the Shadowseer, Vespasi-Hann, brought up his hand in silent refutation.

'Stay with Joaqhuine; see to it she lives to see eternity,' the High Inquisitor soothed. Czevak patted his interrogator's shoulder in feeble reassurance and stabbing his cane into the wraithbone floor, began moving towards the warp portal, flanked by his motley escort of Harlequin carnival killers.

'Czevak,' Klute called to his master. The ancient turned. 'Wait.' Klute took off his medicae satchel and rifling through the pack, took out a series of syringes. Grasping a tiny tube clasped to the shoulder of Czevak's cryogenic suspension suit, Klute unclipped a valve and proceeded to inject the High Inquisitor with a swift succession of chemical cocktails.

'Something for the journey?' Czevak smiled.

'Inoculatia, my lord. These should protect you from a host of infectious diseases – the eldar are particularly susceptible to Paratyphis, Quyme's Disease and pneumonic fevers – all fatal to humans. The only vaccine I've given you for a non-lethal pathogen is the meme-virus, but I have to tell you that the cryonic cooling of your suspension suit will likely inhibit the immune system response.'

'So,' Czevak said low and slowly, 'you may have just infected me with a meme-virus?' Czevak was familiar with the pathogen and the way it was supposed to afflict the infected with a cognitive data addiction. Victims not only experienced a constant, unquenchable thirst for knowledge but also the memory capacity to store such a torrent of information – both significant and trivial. To the infected, there was little distinction between the two.

'I'm afraid so my lord. A particularly powerful one. I hope you can find it in yourself to forgive me.'

The High Inquisitor smiled acknowledgement. He was just about to enter the largest repository of forbidden lore in the galaxy, infected with a pathological agent that would trebly enhance his graphic memory and already voracious thirst for knowledge.

'Goodbye, Raimus.'

Bronislaw Czevak turned and disappeared through the warp gate into oblivion, leaving Klute alone with the dead and the undying.

Solus

ACT I, CANTO I

Archeodeck, Rogue trader Malescaythe, *The Eye of Terror*

Enter INQUISITOR RAIMUS KLUTE, alone

IT WAS THE Feast of the Forty Hierarchs – the last day of the Dantian Octave. Raimus Klute cast rheumy eyes across the archeodeck of the *Malescaythe*. He was tired and rubbed his temples between finger and thumb before running both through his greying moustache in a long-learned, unconscious action that could almost qualify as a nervous twitch. Heliotide was already upon them and Captain Torres was doing her level best to create some sense of a festive atmosphere, despite their dismal surroundings. She'd had sweetmeats and minced pastries distributed as well as authorising an extra ration of spiced gin for the crew. A number of off-watch petty officers and booming crewmen had taken to singing canticles in one corner of the hangar as they warmed themselves by the idling thrusters of a freight skiff. *Hark the Pyromartyr Cleanses* lifted Klute's spirits, as once it had on Gehenndra 4-17, until he realised that if the Pyromartyr had continued his good works unto this day then Klute and his compatriots would very much constitute the Pyromartyr's heretical prey.

Torqhuil certainly would. The Relictor Space Marine had joined the inquisitor for prayers that morning on the archeodeck, before their brief but horrific visit to Iblisyph. Down on one ceramite knee, the young Techmarine still towered over the inquisitor, the cybernetic rig of servo-arms and mechadendrites craning from the Adeptus Astartes' pack making him appear even larger, if that were possible. As they said their benedictions, earlier that day, with the deep onyx of Torqhuil's bowed, shaven head gleaming in the dreadlight of the Eye, Klute had given thanks to the Emperor. Without Torqhuil to share his credence and Torres's efforts to keep a tiny slice of the Imperium alive amongst their damned surroundings, the inquisitor was certain that he would have lost his mind.

Klute had chartered the *Malescaythe* under Inquisitorial decree and had brought Reinette Torres to the Eye of Terror. Torqhuil, he'd found there. On the nightworld of Alpha-Glau their paths and purposes had crossed over the cursed Casque of King Kuanscrall. The actual Casque turned out to be nothing more than an ancient myth and therefore useless to both of them.

Formerly known as the Fire Claws, the Relictors Space Marines and their shameful quest were well known to Klute's ordo, however. Before the inquisitor had left the true path himself he had briefly been part of a Privy Conclave advising the infamous Inquisitor Cyarro and the Grey Knights Chapter on a little known race called the lophiformes, for whom a small cell of Relictors were trading mercenary duties for Chaos artefacts and information.

Initially, the Relictors had been given the solemn duty of guarding the frontiers of the Eye of Terror – a task to which they were well suited, known as a particularly stoic Chapter and seemingly resilient to the corruption of the warp. Both of these assumptions turned out to be erroneous, however, as the Relictors' passion to destroy Chaos took them to that dark place – that realisation that perhaps the relics and weapons of evil were double-edged swords that could indeed be turned upon their depraved wielders, a dark path that some of Klute's brother inquisitors believed him to have taken.

'If my heresy was only that simple,' Klute mumbled between his benedictions.

Declared Excommunicate Traitoris and hunted mercilessly by Cyarro and his Grey Knights Purgation Squads, the Relictors disbanded as a Chapter and immersed themselves in personal quests to retrieve Chaos artefacts and take their battle to the Enemy – deep within the Eye. Torqhuil had worked largely alone, but his interests repetitively clashed with Klute as both of them scoured the primitive Peninsula worlds of the once damned Quoyah Empire for remnants. Klute was looking for Glyph sticks on the moon of Thromba, where the ancient Rapatang tribe people had succumbed to a bloodhunger, when he encountered the Techmarine first in the flesh. They fought amongst the giant stone hands of Throm – the tainted writings of the Rapatang already in the inquisitor's possession.

If it hadn't been for Phalanghast and his sacrobound monstrosity, the Techmarine would have rendered Klute limb from limb (as he had done Zedd, Keplar IV and Bhasker Singh). Phalanghast's daemonhost Hessian could be persuasive, however, and the resulting impasse allowed time for tempers to cool, words to be exchanged and a truce to be forged. Over time, that truce had become a valued partnership between inquisitor and Relictors Space Marine. Like Torqhuil, Klute believed his intentions to be pure, but the road to damnation is paved with such fancies and they had both sullied their souls in congress with the daemon and the renegade. Torres maintained the *Malescaythe*'s Geller field at full power, whether they were in the warp or simply traversing the damned space of the Eye and this had long kept the taint of Chaos at bay. This was one of the reasons Klute had engaged Torres and her rogue trader in the first place. Both were veterans of forays into the Eye of Terror and few onboard – thank the Throne – had succumbed to the unclean influence of dreadspace. Despite Klute's baptismal baths, blessings, purity injections and the myriad of wardings carved into the rust red of Torqhuil's sacred Mark-VIII Errant armour, it was hard to believe that the corruptive environment of unreality hadn't in some way breached their careful defences. The mere insanity of their voluntary presence in the Eye of Terror might already have been evidence of this.

Klute's jaundiced eyes took in the amethyst glow of rift space and the site of their last planetfall, the crone world of Iblisyph. Like a swirling ball of bloodied vomit, the planet hung there, an affront to itself. Gone was the verdant paradise of the original eldar home world. In its place sat a spherical hell of glass shard gales and murky storms within storms, dragging half of the planet's surface up into the atmosphere. Here, Hessian and Captain Torres's Savlar Chem-Dog soldiers kept flocks of pygmy furies at bay as they swooped and squealed as one, blacking out the light of a dismal sun and dive bombing Klute's party as they extricated their prize, the Lost Fornical of Urien-Myrdyss.

Somehow, Torqhuil and his small army of archeoxenologists had managed to excavate the colossal artefact intact and haul it to Torres's *Malescaythe*. Klute felt bad about inflicting the horrors of Iblisyph upon the Mechanicus archeoxenologists. Torres and her rogue trader crew were well paid for their services and between

them, Torqhuil and Epiphani Mallerstang had led them
there. What the rest of Klute's retinue called hell, the daemonhost Hessian called home – so the inquisitor wasted
little of his sympathy on the abomination. The archeoxenologists, on the other hand, had been hijacked by
the *Malescaythe* en route to the swarmworld of Vespula
on Klute's orders and so had taken no part in their heresy until Torres's ragged Chem-Dogs had turned their
weapons on them. That and the promise that the skiffs
would return and lift them out of the nightmare that was
the eldar crone world – only after they had helped Saul
Torqhuil to excavate the Lost Fornical.

Freshly unearthed, the mighty warp gate sat on the
deck, its osseous archways still rooted to the massive
block of wraithbone dais upon which it was set. In the
relative safety of the rogue trader hangar and feeling
more than a little committed after risking their lives and
souls for the haul, the Mechanicus were more enthusiastic about their new duties and had fallen to scrutinising
the ancient piece of alien technology with Torqhuil.

Around them a small cordon of Savlar Chem-Dog
penitents loitered, cradling filthy lascarbines and dripping with stolen equipment, mismatched armour and
scavenged archeotrinkets. Their faces were obscured by
dust goggles and the nitro-chem inhalers that lent the
criminal scum the narcotic courage that would have
ordinarily abandoned them when battling the fearful
denizens of the Eye. When Klute had learned that the
Malescaythe was outfitted with a contingent of Savlar
Chem-Dogs he was dismayed, but as the inquisitor's
search took him deeper into the Eye, he came to appreciate the mercenary, kleptomaniacal nature of the regiment
and the way in which it complemented his objectives.
They never questioned his sometimes ludicrous orders
or the motives that forced them to fight in the hellish
environs of daemon worlds, their narcotic fantasies and
the nightmares of rift-space indistinguishable. If the

penitents had a mind to escape their brutal existence, they never demonstrated it – besides, there was nowhere to escape to in the Eye. The vessel's Geller field provided the only safety for light-years around. As long as the deviants were allowed to scavenge and steal from the dark places the *Malescaythe* took them and take refuge in the mind-numbing haze of their chem-inhalers, they seemed content to take orders and provide security for the rogue trader and its guests. The inquisitor had only had to intervene once, when an ill-advised find had corrupted the light fingers of an unfortunate trooper and Klute had had to execute the Guardsman. Largely, the Savlar's had an almost feral instinct for salvage, however – long learned in the toxic environment of their prison home world – and stayed away from anything obviously tainted or possessed.

Captain Torres had insisted on manning the warp gate with a heavily armed, round-the-clock vigil, arguing that they had little or no idea of what the thing was capable. Klute did, of course, but informing the good captain of that would only have exacerbated her fears and, in any case, he didn't think that a guard post was such a bad idea. Wiring six barrels of promethium to the artefact was erring on overkill, Klute reasoned – not enough to breach the hull of the ship, but enough to blast the Lost Fornical to pieces if the circumstances demanded it. The inquisitor had made his feelings known, but ultimately the *Malescaythe* was Reinette Torres's vessel and she felt responsible for the safety of every soul on board – undoubtedly a throwback to her naval days.

It was not the only reminder of a past life in the service. As she approached, flanked by an ensign carrying a tray of flambéed amasec, Klute came to realise that apart from the regulation-breaking length of lustrous black hair and the curvaceous breasts and buttocks almost falling out of her attire, the rest of her garb was entirely her old dress uniform.

'Inquisitor,' the captain greeted him.

Klute took a glass out of courtesy and in recognition of her festive efforts – although as a rule he wasn't much of a drinker. As a rule, he wasn't given much in the way of excesses of any kind, which seemed strange given his circumstances.

'To the Forty Hierarchs,' Klute pledged with the glass, 'and how I wish they were with us now in this benighted place.'

The captain similarly raised her drink and then raised it again upon the approach of Brother Torqhuil. The hulking Space Marine had to suffice with a respectful bow of the head. Torqhuil never indulged in common liquor, but Torres always had an extra glass dressed for him. The Techmarine towered over them both, the great servo-arms of his cybernetic torso-harness extended almost protectively about the small gathering, hydraulic claws and bionic toolage at ease.

Klute acknowledged the Adeptus Astartes before snuffing out the flame and supping his drink. It was more pleasant than he had first expected, with a collection of tangy, festive berries floating in the amasec.

'So, inquisitor. You have your prize. What now?' Captain Torres asked.

Klute chuckled into his drink. 'What, that xenological abomination? The Lost Fornical is merely a means to an end. What I seek, this hellish gateway may deliver – but I leave that up to Brother Torqhuil and his Mechanicus kin.'

'We have spoken on this, inquisitor,' the Relictor cautioned, 'I don't want to indulge false hope. Locating and extricating the Fornical was blind fortune enough. This is an alien artefact, a piece of technology older than man himself; we could spend a lifetime in study and experimentation and still get nowhere close to unlocking its secrets.'

'That and the fact that it has been buried at the heart

of a daemonic world for innumerable centuries,' Torres added. 'Why the hell I let the thing on board, I still don't know.'

'Because,' the inquisitor informed her, 'to you this is just another of our warped relics, part of a dusty collection – something to take up space in your hold or... sell for profit.'

'I'll drink to that,' she smiled.

As a Relictors Space Marine, Torqhuil researched and sought out the weapons of Chaos, adding to the huge collection of Chaos weapons, artefacts and tomes that were stored in the Geller and stasis reliquaries leading off the archeodeck. With these, the Relictor Space Marine carried out his Chapter's controversial crusade against the Ruinous Powers. Klute's reasons were known only to himself and the warp-seer Epiphani Mallerstang, but Torres had only ever braved the terrors of the Eye to rebuild the fortunes of her mother's dilapidated estates on Zyracuse. Carrying excommunicates and heresiarchs like Torqhuil and Klute was testament to her desperation and calling; sadly the inquisitor had indulged the poor captain's fantasy that his rosette of office – all but limitless in its power to exonerate in almost all other circumstances – would protect her and her family's interests. Something else to weigh heavily on Klute's burdened soul.

Torres stared blankly out into the deep darkness of the void. The *Malescaythe* had banked, putting the sickening spectacle of Iblisyph behind it. It was the swirls and eddies of the Geller field that the captain was watching and the ghostly outlines of beasts and behemoths, sidling along the vessel and pressing their warp-ghastly forms up against the ship.

Klute had seen her warn her crew against such spiritual licentiousness, but occasionally, when something particularly vile took an interest in the vessel, it was difficult not to look back. Torres was no fool. She had her ship enveloped in the protection of its powerful Geller field at all times – whether the rogue trader was immersed in warp travel or simply trawling the dreadspace of the Eye, the reality shield ensured that the crew of the rogue trader enjoyed an immediate environment that was normal and natural in the most unnatural of places. The Eye of Terror was so confused about what it was that the real and the unreal often floated past each other in the terrible place and the daemonic entities that haunted the immaterium swam past the vessel like soul-hungry sharks, waiting for the opportunity to strike.

'But Raimus, really,' the captain said. 'You know I'd follow you to hell and back – and I have – which gives me, I feel, the right to comment.'

Klute smiled. A simple, knowing smile. Torres only dispensed with the formalities of his formal title when attempting to trick more details of his secretive mission from him. On some level – and this was not common territory for the inquisitor – he felt that she must be jealous of Epiphani, and the confidences he had with the young witch. Epiphani wouldn't have been his first choice of confidante, but it was difficult to hide anything from a prognostic.

And then it came. 'Think on the false prophets you have followed. Think on the dark, fruitless places they have led you. Phalanghast. Dancwart the Elder. Cardinal Killias. And now this girl.'

There it was.

'Epiphani found the Fornical, did she not? Was it not exactly where she predicted?'

'Yes, but…'

'And has she not plotted a course through the maelstroms, impossibilities and perverse expanses of the Eye safely and surely, where no ship's Navigator could?' Klute put to the good captain.

'One who can see what will come to pass, before its time, through whom the currents of the warp flow so freely; how can we trust such a freak? She has no neural inhibitors and hasn't even been soul-bound.'

'It would dull her skill,' the inquisitor countered with plain, dangerous logic.

'Don't worry.' Epiphani Mallerstang's sweet inflections bounced around the hangar. 'The inquisitor will dispose of me when he has no further use for my talents. That's what the Inquisition does.'

She had not heard a thing; she was too far away, but making good speed across the deck, despite the disability of her blindness. She'd known about the conversation, however, long before Torres had chosen to initiate it. Klute tried not to pry too deeply into the workings of her strange ability. He separated himself as much as he could from the temptations of the polluted and their gifts. To take only what he needed. To give only what he could afford. To that extent they were both correct. Epiphani had not been soul-bound and without doubt was a constant danger. The inquisitor would also not think twice about putting a bolt-round in the girl if she so much as sneezed against his interests and he made a point of surrounding himself with others who felt the same way. Torres's feelings, and therefore those of her crew, were obvious and he could always count on Torqhuil to act in accordance with his training and genetically engineered purpose.

The young warp-seer walked up behind them and took a small ornate snuff box from the neckline of her corset and opened it with a well practised snap of the thumb. Inside was a crystalline powder that shone with the lustre of crushed emeralds. Taking a pinch, the warp-seer snorted a generous dose, before rubbing her nose and fluttering her cloudy eyes. Klute knew this to be Spook – a dangerous and highly illegal psychoactive drug, known to enhance an addict's ability to channel the energies of the warp to enhance their psychic capabilities – and Epiphani *was* an addict.

For a moment she seemed to stare straight through the gathering, out into the dreadlight beyond. Klute couldn't begin to imagine what she was 'seeing' there. A vast sea? A stellar sky? Unnatural energies in constant flux and turmoil. A formless etherscape of indescribable forms; colour, emotion, currents, flows and floods; storm fronts of soulspace, crashing amongst nebulous cloud formations of immaterial somethingness. Perhaps nothing at all. Or perhaps it was these impossible arrangements that she saw and described in sing-song mumbles, 'In a ruined palace – of dust and bones – sits a fool on a burnished throne; from his finger hangs a spider, framed in a window of empty night, that twinkles with a thousand stars and echoes with a distant laughter…'

Tuning into such insights had been Epiphani's gift and this had become greatly useful to Klute in his search. She'd guided the *Malescaythe* through the dangers of the Eye and led him to the Lost Fornical of Urien-Myrdyss – which she'd insisted was essential to the inquisitor's quest – and even revealed the treachery of Klute's mystic, Phalanghast – her own father – in advance of his betrayal. And so Klute's reluctant reliance on the warpseer Epiphani Mallerstang became complete.

'Captain,' she greeted Torres as she returned to them. She had thrown together a baroque corset, finished with the brazen bones of some alien creature with which Klute was not familiar, and a Harakoni celestial gown. It shouldn't have worked yet somehow did. Epiphani always had an outfit ready for every occasion. Her wardrobe was reputably almost as large as Saul Torqhuil's collection of artefacts and forbidden relics.

She reached for Torqhuil's glass of flaming amasec, her other hand resting on the grotesque servo-skull that had glided in ahead of her, leading the way. The warp-seer's pet name for the familiar was 'Father', which made Klute feel uncomfortable enough. This degree of unease was enhanced further by the knowledge that the skull had indeed belonged to his old guide and her actual father, Phalanghast. Epiphani never spoke of her mother, but while he had lived, Phalanghast told Klute that she was the result of his brief union with Lady Casserndra Laestrygoni, a powerful member of the Great Laestrygoni Navigator Family and Heir Apparent Paternova. Such dishonour could not be tolerated if the Laestrygoni's fortunes were to remain intact and Phalanghast was paid handsomely to leave the segmentum with the infant, mere moments following her birth.

Epiphani fixed them all with her eyes – both the milky, useless orbs of her youthful face and the cold, blue bionic lenses burning out of the hang-dog visage of Father. The servo-skull was not only a guide for the blind warp-seer, it was her actual eyes. A mind-link between Epiphani and the drone helped to counter the witch's disability, that and her prognostic skill.

'Epiphani,' Klute said. 'What did you see? Was it the God-Emperor? Is it his throne? What does that mean?'

'Yes,' she smiled. Then a frown. 'No'. Then the addict's smile again. 'Something bad is going to happen.'

'This is the Eye of Terror,' Torqhuil announced sagely. 'That is a given.'

Floating out from behind the excesses of the Harakoni gown came Hessian. Pulling back the hood of his simple robes, the daemonhost revealed his smug, angelic face and horn buds. If the eyes were the windows to the soul, then Hessian's were dead, black, oily orbs – like those of some cold-blooded, deep sea predator.

Torres reacted immediately. 'How dare you, child! You have no permission to bring that creature on deck,' the captain seethed at the Spook-soothed Epiphani.

It was true. Blasphemous as it was, Klute kept the daemonhost imprisoned within the confines of the newly fortified ship's chapel, surrounded by the most powerful of Torqhuil's recovered holy relics. Epiphani had grown up with the daemon around, however, and as a result seemed less ill at ease than the rest of the rogue trader's company in its presence. Some part of her might have even felt some pity for the monster. Phalanghast had always taken precautions – many of which he had taught Klute – but the inquisitor was taking no chances. The Relictors Space Marine's instruments of faith bled the creature of its supremacy and energy – the Imperishable Cloves of Saint Cerene, that decorated the bulkhead, taking their particular, blessed toll on the warp-sired thing. Hessian mostly took to sleeping the days away – those when Klute did not need his dark services, at least – draped sacrilegiously across the chapel altar.

The daemonhost smiled derision at them.

'A Merry Feastday, to you all,' he hissed with upturned lips and downcast eyes.

When Klute had originally met Hessian, the entity had been bound in the body of the misshapen twist Phalanghast had used as an initial vessel. Where the beast had been before that, nobody knew. An inquisitor, Klute may have been – but inquisitive by nature he was not, particularly when it came to exchanging pleasantries with creatures of darkness. Some say that he was the tormentor of the Regulator Hvalken and saw that doomed family through forty generations of woe; some that he was responsible for the Mount Idas Massacre where thirty Sons of Horus lost their lives and the contents of their skulls to the monster's appetite; a few even that he was in fact Gallkor-Teth the Decimate in all his different incarnations and was worshipped as a demigod across a hundred different barbarian worlds.

Regardless of his horrific origins, Phalanghast had found him trapped in a solitary mutant by a common dirt shaman in the Ilk forests of Gorm. Years of service to the shaman and in turn to Phalanghast had taxed the poor mutant's body beyond endurance so that when he crossed the sealstone of the Fornax Adventist

Crusade, that day on Tancress Minor, the thing looked
like a vivisectionist's practice piece. The holy power of
the stone split the flesh vessel apart and would have
re-released the full horror of Hessian the Anathemic
on the Imperium, had it not been for the embarring
powers of the stone itself. Over three hours of maniacal
struggle – the powers of the warp blasting forth from
the daemonhost's ruined, flaccid flesh – the creature
managed to break the holy stone and its hold on it.
By then, Phalanghast had imprisoned the entity in a
fresh vessel, the body of one of his boyish vassals. It
had been a hasty but necessary choice for the dark mystic – since no one else among the rogue trader's crew or
company would have volunteered for the job.

It was the comely face of that youth – Klute had
appallingly never bothered to ask his name before that
point – that beamed at the inquisitor now, the only
blemish to his Adonis-like complexion being the slight
angularity of the letters under his skin. These occasionally caught the shadow and turned his fair features into
a face-page from the *Tabula Deletum*. This was a further
precaution Phalanghast had visited upon the poor
youth's tortured flesh, once he'd gotten Hessian back
to the *Malescaythe*'s surgical bay. He'd grafted under his
skin thousands of individual lawthorn characters from
Erasmus Beltaine's first printing press – the very same
machine Beltaine had used to print faith tracts from the
Biblia Incertitus during the Palatyne Sceptoclasm. The
procedure had taken days, and undoubtedly limited
the Anathemic's more devastating capabilities, but everyone on board the rogue trader – including Klute – felt
better knowing the daemonhost was secure.

'She's right,' Klute told Epiphani, ignoring Hessian's blasphemous greeting. 'Explain yourself,' he said
sternly, adding to Captain Torres's outrage, suspicion
growing with the inquisitor's every word.

The warp-seer pursed her lips with petulance, whilst

behind her the daemon smirked at Klute like some self-satisfied simpleton.

'Hessian's here,' she began, pausing only to down the contents of Torqhuil's flaming glass, 'because something bad is going to happen and we're going to need him.'

And as always, the warp-seer was right.

Flourish

I

ACT I, CANTO II

Archeodeck, Rogue trader Malescaythe, *The Eye of Terror*

The same

SOMETHING WAS WRONG. Klute had already begun to sense it.

Not a thought or a suspicion but an actual physical feeling of internal strangeness. Like surfacing too quickly, or the effect a loose airlock pressure seal has on the inner ear. Sound seemed to slow and become distorted and for a moment everything turned into its reverse negative. Black became white, faces became ghoulish contrasts. The inquisitor considered the possibility that it might be Hessian, but the daemonhost's expression matched his own – one of mixed confusion and mild discomfort.

As Klute's senses returned to normal he became aware of a building sense of apprehension in his gut – again something corporal rather than emotional, a deep, alien trembling that seemed to grow in him and everything about him. There was no sound, yet the booming resonance was everywhere.

Torqhuil's ceramite arm suddenly came up. He was shouting – despite the deck plunging into a silent calm.

'The Fornical!'

Klute span.

The Lost Fornical of Urien-Myrdyss… was alive.

'Inquisitor…' Torres began with growing trepidation.

'They activated it? So soon?' Klute gabbled at the Relictor, but the Space Marine was already striding past the inquisitor, towards the rumbling warp gate.

'Not possible – they've barely begun,' he snapped, ending speculation that the archeoxenologists had struck gold on their first examination of the ancient artefact.

Klute had agreed to all precautions: the hangar location, the Savlar presence, the wired promethium – but that had all been built on the premise that one day Torqhuil and the Mechanicus might make the impossible possible and gain access to the gate. The inquisitor never really thought that the gate might be opened from the other side; it might have been ridiculously foolish of him, but he'd been listening to the Relictor's long-odds estimations of success for so long in their search for the thing that he never really considered it feasible.

Torres began barking orders to the ensign before cutting him off and yelling across the hangar at the Savlar Chem-Dogs.

'Man the detonators!'

'Belay that!' Klute countered, his mind racing to catch up. He understood the captain's caution, but he didn't want the Fornical blasted to warp-dust. Not unless it was absolutely necessary. They'd risked so much to acquire it. 'Secure the perimeter,' Klute bellowed at the collection of shabby troopers, prompting the devout Steward-Sergeant Rourke to slip onto one knee and make the sign of the aquila before smacking skulls and pushing dozy Guardsmen into position.

The rogue trader captain's scowl softened slightly. The thought of the Chem-Dogs pointing their motley collection of scavenged lascarbines, autoguns and shotguns at the warp gate opening filled her with a little more confidence for the safety of her ship. Still, she was taking few chances and pushed the ensign away with orders to secure the hangar door and lock off the archeodeck from the rest of the rogue trader.

With the captain and Torqhuil bawling a judicious mix of questions and orders at the Mechanicus and Savlar penitents, Klute was left with Epiphani and the void-spawn, Hessian. The daemonhost looked at him blankly with his youthful face and ancient eyes. Epiphani simply shrugged her slender shoulders.

'Isn't this what you wanted?'

'What I want,' Klute stormed at her, 'is less in the way of riddles and more in the way of warning, Epiphani.' He flung his glass at the metal decking and proceeded to stumble towards the Fornical. Epiphani and the daemon did not follow – and perhaps Klute should have taken this as a sign, but he had come too far, sacrificed too much and had spent too many years of his life working towards this moment to hide from it. The inquisitor crossed the hangar and marched towards his destiny.

Slipping his fingers through his robes, Klute unconsciously grabbed for his sidearm. Klute believed that an inquisitor's weapon was a measure of him and his own clearly showed how much he'd changed. Before his unhealthy occupation in the Eye and his dealings with the darkness, Klute was very much a Glavian man. Glavia produced some of the finest needle weapons in the known universe and as a young interrogator he was the proud owner of a brace of Glavian 'Silver Tongue 770s'. This would be a fool's weapon in the Eye, however, as he soon discovered. A needle gun is an elegant taker of lives, but with so many of the foes there of abnormal invention and capability, Klute found that he needed something that packed a little more punch and that could actually harm the warped and ungodly. What good was even the most advanced of toxins against the soulless and often bloodless creatures that walked the fine line between the real and the unreal?

So the Glavia had to go. They didn't go, so much as were eaten by a catacomb angler-wyrm the inquisitor had found in the Flesh Mines of Marriar. Their replacement could not have been more different and belonged to a friend Klute had lost on Phibos IV. Obarbus Keene had been a Cadian Chastener whose cold, hard advice Klute had come very much to value but to whom he could never admit his real purpose in the Eye of Terror. Klute engaged his services under false pretences and sent a thoroughly good man to his death for a heretical lie. All the inquisitor had left of Keene's uncompromising ways was his uncompromising weapon, a lever action Cadian Kasr close combat shotgun. Originally meant as a close quarters street silencer, in the cramped zigs and zags of the garrison world metropols, Keene cut down the weapon further to its pistol grip and carried it as a bombastic sidearm – as Klute did now – in part to honour a good man.

The inquisitor began thumbing fat shells into the pistol. As a rule Klute didn't walk about the ship with a loaded weapon. It wasn't polite. Klute was old fashioned in that way – as in many others – and besides wasn't much of a killer. His aim was average and his interest in weaponry only ever extended as far as the antiquity and worksmanship of the Glavian. As a man long trained in the arts of medicine, however, he knew how to incapacitate and execute, as he knew how to patch and revive. But this was little in the way of a handicap in the Eye, where the quick and ignorant died in their droves and a little knowledge could carry trigger-virgins a long way.

Klute worked the slick lever action and sent the final cartridge home, thrice-blessed silver scatter shot embedded in a slug of Saint Vesta's salts. Nowhere near as effective as bolt, stalker or penetrator rounds, which the Cadian Kasr could easily accommodate. The salt and silver shot did, however, have the advantage of soul-scalding the infernal and etheriate. It was no more pleasant for those who didn't happen to be incorporeal or daemonic, which made the choice an ammunition for all seasons and situations and the deep pockets of Klute's robes had fast became receptacles for as many of the blessed slugs as he could carry. Old-fashioned he may have been, but prudence was an old-fashioned value.

No longer a dusty excavation piece, the Lost Fornical of Urien-Myrdyss blazed with bleach-bone brilliance. The grit and age that had once blemished its elegant arches now hung in the air about the relic in a cloud of warp static and excitement. A ghostly shimmer rippled through the wraithbone superstructure, rolling continuously from lancet to dais. Klute didn't have to be an alien to understand this meant something was about to happen.

Bolts of energy – of colours he'd never seen before, and had no words to describe – spewed forth from spines in the archways. The warp currents elegantly synchronised, finding each other across the central space of the arch, with tributary beams crackling across the air in between. As bolts connected they seemed to fuse the reality of the space inside their borders and piece by piece, like some diabolical puzzle, the inquisitor caught patchwork glimpses of the space beyond.

The entire hangar was stricken, at once with the desire to see what the Fornical would vomit forth and the simultaneous gut-wrenching need to be ready to destroy it. Under Steward-Sergeant Rourke's devotional drill, the Savlar Chem-Dogs were all goggles and barrels. Torqhuil stood like some great statue nearby, his hydraulic arms and servo limbs extended protectively in front of him; his actual arms supporting the weight of his rune-engraved power axe, which he gripped in his gauntlets, ready for battle. Torres hovered behind, her faith – as always – instilled in the simple, curved blade of her naval hanger.

As the warp gate completed its jigsaw assembly of the reality on the other side of the portal, Klute became witness to the bitter, alien tenebrosity of the transdimensional tunnel beyond. The fabled webway…

The inquisitor had little time to enjoy this mythical vision, however, as the Lost Fornical's first sojourner in a thousand years was thrust upon the *Malescaythe*. A silhouette of light burned through the shadow of the alien tunnel and a figure vaulted forth through the miasma of warp static. He stumbled and rolled – his footing fleet and uncertain, until he fell into an untidy crouch in front of the sizzling archway, head down, the tips of his boots and fingers holding onto the solid surface of the wraithbone dais like a ship's cat, unsure of its foothold.

It could have been the shock of this gracefully clumsy entrance or simply the fact that the fingers of penal colonists were itchy as well as light, but it was at that point that several Savlar troopers unleashed a brief blast of auto and heavy stubber fire. The bullets tore up the warp gate platform in a line that ripped into the floor about the figure and ended their journey plucking harmlessly at the unreality through the gate.

The figure was fast. It wasn't so much his movements – he clearly could not outrun gunfire – but within a blink of the weapons silencing he was a blur of colour and then was gone, his back to one of the Fornical's many runed totems and flourishes.

Klute went to berate the wired Chem-Dogs, but Steward-Sergeant Rourke, the Savlar Top-Dog, was already among them, expressing his displeasure with correctional catechisms, fists and snarls. With the cavernous muzzle of Klute's pistol leading the way, the inquisitor moved uncertainly up onto the dais. The wraithbone felt every bit as solid as the metal decking he'd just left, but Klute disliked the sensation and felt strangely vulnerable.

'Make yourself known, visitor,' he called to the figure beyond. Klute didn't really want to venture up into the obelisks and needles of the gateway's design and would much rather the interloper supplicate and walk out to him.

A harsh laugh echoed around the alien architecture.

'No thank you,' the reply shot back in Low Gothic, although the tone was clipped and cultured. 'I've already experienced enough of your particular brand of welcome today.'

'A malfunction, I assure you,' Klute returned with equal civility. There was a pause, but not much of one. Despite his diffidence the figure seemed hurried, perhaps even agitated.

'Where would I happen to be?' he asked casually.

Klute was moving around the exterior totems and already thought he'd had him twice, only for the inquisitor to have found himself stalking empty space.

'The *Malescaythe*,' Klute informed him. 'Registered rogue trader, under my jurisdiction. But she is in the Eye my friend, and here, there is no jurisdiction. Only force, which is what you will shortly experience if you do not present yourself.'

Another corner; another empty space. Klute was glad he'd packed the silver-and-salt shot now; the visitor might speak Imperial but he didn't move like any Earthly creature – that was for sure.

'When?'

A ridiculous question, but – Klute reasoned – was probably appropriate for someone who had just stepped out of a warp gate. The inquisitor obliged him with the information, but more just to keep the conversation going, so that he could get a lock on his position.

Torres's patience was up, however. 'Raimus, just shoot

him.' No doubt she wanted the gate secured while it
remained dangerously open – her men couldn't do that
while Klute played labyrinth with their guest.

'Raimus… Klute?'

Klute span. The question had drifted over his
shoulder.

Panic coursed through the inquisitor's limbs and he
instinctively brought the fat pistol up between the two
of them. The figure had been there the whole time.
Klute's brain had known it but his eyes had lied; something about the figure's attire rippled with chromatic
disorientation. Something in the timbre of the voice
was equally disorientating and familiar.

'My lord?' Klute blurted.

Down the barrel of the street silencer Klute was staring at a face he'd long known and for the longest time,
hoped to know again.

The figure's slender palm came to rest on the muzzle
and he gently pushed it deckward, giving Klute a better look at his face. Impossibly, he was younger than
he'd known him, his sharp eyes keener than ever and
the scornful lines that cut into his formerly ancient face
were now smooth and taut; virgin territory for fresh disdain. Klute struggled with this youthful appearance and
the bizarre logic of what he was seeing.

Klute, on the other hand, must have appeared quite
the reverse. Tried, tired and weather-beaten, with a
scalp and moustache shot through with the silver of
his years. The dark leather of his once gleaming armour
and mantle was now scuffed and bolt-plucked.

His opposite, on the other hand, was dressed in a
trench coat of an outlandish alien fashion. While Klute
stared directly at the material it seemed to be covered in
a garish pattern of interlocking diamonds, making up
a myriad of flamboyant colours. The garment sizzled
with a form of field technology that played with the
eye, trailing a diamond blaze as the inquisitor moved

while fading and mirror-mimicking its surroundings at moments of absolute stillness.

The two men stared at each other. Klute had looked forward to this moment for so long that now it was here – unexpected as it was – he could not help holding onto it.

'Raimus Klute,' the figure repeated, as though he could barely believe this meeting himself.

'Czevak…' Klute mumbled in wonder. 'My lord… I…'

Czevak's features had never been soft – not at study, not at ease – but the High Inquisitor's eyes did seem to flood with an uncharacteristic gladness. It was enough for Klute to assume that there might not be too many friendly faces to be found – even ones as haggard as his own – on the long, dark corridors of the alien webway.

As the portal was about to prove.

Klute went to speak again but Czevak's face suddenly changed – the way it used to as the elusive solution of some long fraught problem came to him in the middle of an unrelated conversation. His finger shot up as Klute's lips went to work on a greeting he'd long rehearsed in his head and dreams. 'Raimus, help me out here. Do you remember that frightful business on Tannit's World?'

Klute's face creased in recollection, then his eyes widened in realisation. No further words were necessary. The sprightly Czevak simply grabbed Klute with a strength and athleticism he could never have exhibited in his 'younger' days and flung the inquisitor around, towards the archway of the Lost Fornical. With their backs to the structure, they could see little of the bolt-swarming portal; they didn't have to. The *Malescaythe*'s second visitor of the evening had just arrived.

The wraithbone trembled and Klute fancied that he even heard a creak. Everywhere at once there was the effervescent gush of furious waters, like a dam had broken, which on some level it had. A gargantuan entity spilled from the Fornical and into the reality of the hangar.

A torrent of quicksilver suddenly streamed from the archway, exploding out across the ancient dais and flooding the archeodeck. The liquid metal seethed and spumed, blistering the hangar floor. It sloshed and spread perversely, flowing up and over obstacles and pooling towards anything with a soul.

The Savlar response was obvious and immediate. The Chem-Dogs – breathing deep in their nitro-chem inhalers – unleashed a hesitant hell, throwing up fountains of silver in the onrushing surge. Slugs and las-bolts lanced the entity in a fire-at-will firestorm but the barrage did little to halt the advance of the ichorous creature.

The front line of Chem-Dogs died quickly. This wouldn't have surprised many of them; it had become somewhat of an in-joke among the Savlar that those chosen and released from the stockade by Steward-Sergeant Rourke and assigned to duties with the inquisitor and his retinue were unlikely to return – such was the danger of the ordo's work to ordinary men. This was demonstrated in the way the Savlar Chem-Dog Guardsmen panicked in the face of the terrifying supernatural force and became intent on reloading their scavenged weaponry, allowing the sentient mercury to pool about their boots, before soaking up them like litmus paper. It oozed in through their ears, eyes and between their screaming lips, filleting them from the inside out as irregular blossoms of blades and spikes suddenly exploded from their backs and chests like an iron maiden in reverse.

Torqhuil was nearby also. He snatched his helmet from one of his mechanised appendages and donned it swiftly, effectively sealing him off from the predations of the possessed quicksilver. The silver deluge flooding the hangar seemed to flow around the Relictors Space Marine, however; almost repelled magnetically by the presence of the sacred oils, wards and purity seals emblazoned on his ornate armour.

Hessian had been caught in the sterling torrent as it blasted its animate way across the hangar and disappeared into its daemonic depths. Epiphani and Torres – sword drawn – had demonstrated the good sense to take to high ground, climbing up one of the mounted catwalks that adorned the hangar wall. Father followed them using his tiny anti-gravity drive and the three of them looked down upon the chaos and confusion of the archeodeck through two pairs of eyes.

The Mechanicus archeoxenologists who hadn't been cut to pieces and swamped by the warp creature were now hiding behind the huge shoulders of Saul Torqhuil. The Space Marine's servo-arms and mechadendrite tool bits snapped and whirred at anything warped and daemonic that in turn reached out for him. For extra insurance, the Techmarine swung his power axe experimentally about him in a provocative arc.

Like the decorator painting himself into the corner of a room, the Chem-Dogs were huddled together around their prayer-booming steward-sergeant, presenting a nest of barrels to the hangar and casting an improvised arc of crackling las-bolts and firepower around them. The silver waters seethed and sprayed as the supernatural tsunami rolled in and swallowed their ammunition whole.

Klute and their visitor remained on the bleached dais of the Lost Fornical, giving the dwindling stream of mercury a wide birth as the last of the entity spilled out of the warp gate from the webway beyond.

'What is it?' Klute yelled over the din and destruction.

The young Czevak's eyes were roving, his mouth moving but his mind elsewhere.

'An ichneuplasm,' Czevak explained, 'called the Milk of Malevolsia. It breached a derelict section of the webway and the damned thing has been trying to flay my soul across three sectors.'

'How can we stop it?' Klute bawled at this fresh-faced version of his master.

'Well, quite,' Czevak said, mistaking Klute's question for the kind of pessimist defeatism that he usually encountered in visitors to the Eye.

Klute took in the desolation of the hangar. The monster was everywhere, sloshing against the hangar walls and sucking souls into a swirling vortex that was burrowing into the centre of the archeodeck. A mirror-glazed breaker drove towards him, devolving as it did into a fang-faced, appendage-fiend. Klute stood there, staring at himself, reflected in the brazen jaws of his killer.

Like a chromatic comet, Czevak shot between them, the metallic effervescence following the movement and shattered afterimage of his coat. As the inquisitor skidded to a halt – the prismatic haze reforming around him – he waved his arms, keeping the monstrous appendage-fiend's attentions on him. Klute made the most of the opportunity by bringing up his shotgun sidearm from the folds of his robe and blasting the amorphous daemon with silver shot and consecrated salt. The blast buried itself in bubbling warpflesh before streaking pellets of blessed shrapnel exploded throughout the plasm. The shot left a ragged hole that Klute enlarged by working the lever action and repeatedly mauling the monster with a scatter shot exorcism.

The appendage-fiend turned back on Klute, hissing through its mirrored maw as he cranked and emptied the shotgun at it. The inquisitor blasted the impressive set of jaws into shattered fragments with one final shot before realising that the hissing wasn't coming from the creature at all. Imbedded grains of Saint Vesta's salt were doing their worst, burning through the warpflesh. The appendage steamed, dribbled and deteriorated back into the daemon flood.

Klute allowed his rigid arms to slacken and the weapon with them. He grunted; there wasn't enough Saint Vesta's salt in the sector to saint-seed the colossal entity with. Czevak was wandering across the wraithbone dais, taking in the carnage the beast was wreaking across the archeodeck: the armoured Adeptus Astartes fighting for his life, the huddled tech-adepts, the Guardsmen – barrels alight and low on ammunition – and the figures retreating up the catwalk.

'How do we destroy it?' Klute put to his friend and master once again.

'Where's the nearest logic engine?' Czevak snapped back.

'Why?'

Czevak was not used to consulting on impulsive plans of action. 'Codifier, runebank, anything with cabling and an impulse interface.'

Klute nodded with exaggeration at the large bulkhead Torres had ordered sealed from the outside.

Klute watched the High Inquisitor step across the dais towards the bulkhead. Between the Fornical and the bulkhead lay a small ocean of daemonic deluge and the inquisitor wasn't keen on losing his master to some suicide run mere moments after finding him.

'You can't make that,' Klute said with grim confidence. 'No one can make that.' Czevak knew that his former interrogator was right. The Domino field on his Harlequin coat gave the appearance of speed; it didn't make the wearer – especially a graceless human – any physically faster. And that was what Czevak would have to be to reach the far end of the hangar.

'We're going to need a distraction,' Czevak said.

'That's one hell of a distraction,' Klute replied, and then again to himself. 'One hell of a distraction.' Epiphani's prediction came back to haunt the inquisitor.

Klute died a little inside. He knew what was necessary, what had to be done. Action or inaction, damnation waited for them down either road and in the end, Klute was forced to pick what he thought was marginally the lesser of two evils. He'd damn himself before actually setting the abominate free, but Klute could live with loosening the daemonhost's bindings a little. Through gritted teeth he began reciting some of the incantations Phalanghast had taught him.

A horrible churning began at the centre of the daemonic lake. The silver waters suddenly thrashed with a molten glow. A gargled roar of exaltation built from the epicentre of the hellish brilliance, the climax of which blew apart the hangar lamps in a cascade of sparks. As the archeodeck descended into a furnace-like twilight, lit only by the molten metal at the heart of the ichneuplasm and the ghostly radiance of the Fornical, the air rang with a harsh sibilance signalling an alteration of states. Liquid to gas. The aqueous warpflesh glowed to whiteness before seething towards the ceiling in a cloud of mercurial vapour. At the centre of the evaporation knelt Hessian, like an obscene statue – a heretic's idol, pulled presently from the fire of the forge. His perfect skin was a blinding shell, scorching the air about him.

The ichneuplasm, which had tried to swallow the daemonhost whole, now found itself warp-scolded from the inside out. As Hessian cooled to nakedness, his eyes still aflame with terrible beauty and brilliance, the full extent of Phalanghast's handiwork became apparent, with every centimetre of the vassal's body covered with ornate lettering and High Gothic. The creature was a walking scripture. The daemonic deluge's response to the threat was immediate and devastating, sweeping in on the daemonhost in the form of a colossal, argent tidal wave. As Hessian's form became a vortex of flame once more, the daemonhost ran at the Milk of Malevolsia and left the deck, surging at the rogue wave on the stream of flame erupting from its body. Like a fireball, the abomination punched through the sea wall of warpflesh and out through the other side. The entity crashed back to the deck in infernal agony.

Klute turned to Czevak, but the High Inquisitor was already gone.

With the attention of the enormous entity dominated by Hessian's furious assault, the silver shores of the ichneuplasm had receded, gathering in the centre of the hangar. This reclaimed space was now an assault course of debris and twisted metal: archeocrates, forklift dozers and torn up decking. As the younger, agile Czevak shot along the wall, hurdling and rolling under obstacles, a ghostly spectrum of splintered colour trailed the inquisitor.

The horrific entity was more than able to deal with multiple threats or victims, despite the distraction of the daemonhost. This was evidenced in the fashion in which it still snatched archeoxenologists from under the sweeps of Torqhuil's axe and showered the Savlar Guardsmen with droplets of sentient evil that trickled for their eyes and ears – wherever the globules could do most agonising damage. Streams of silver jetted from the entity's nebulous form, the monster attempting to hose Czevak down with its living effluence. The inquisitor changed course, bounding several steps up the wall before leaping for an overturned Sentinel powerlifter. The fountain followed, dowsing the walker and stalking Czevak as he vaulted for a demolished stairwell, swinging like a gymnast from the smooth metal of a detached handrail. Landing awkwardly on top of a cargo-skiff, Czevak rolled – avoiding another converging stream of metallic discharge – before sliding across the roof on the sheen of his coat. Dropping off the edge and down behind the safety of the cargo-skiff, Czevak bent over to catch his breath.

The inquisitor found himself suddenly exposed as the shadow of the cargo-skiff shortened to nothing. Initially, the inquisitor expected to turn and find that the ichneuplasm had seized the craft in its tentacular grasp and removed it. Instead, he found that Klute's daemonhost was the root of the problem. The cargoskiff was ablaze with the same unnatural flame that enveloped the daemonhost. The creature's eyes flared with psychic intensity as he moved the heavy craft with the free-flowing telekinetic power of the warp. Flicking his horn-budded head at the entity, the daemonhost slammed the ichneuplasm with the tumbling dead-weight of the cargo-skiff. Flaming catwalks and platforms were mercilessly ripped from the wall of the hangar by the monster's unseen power and flew over Czevak's head at the spuming entity, cutting whirling columns of silver in half.

Czevak made his move, blasting up the final stretch, darting and weaving between the cables and bars that were falling from the supernatural carnage above. Slamming his shoulder into the bulkhead, the inquisitor came to a skidding halt under a walkway bearing a shapely patrician in naval garb and captain's epaulettes, flanked by a servo-skull and what at first he took to be an unusually modish astropath. They had been following his progress across the archeodeck and were now staring down at him through the walkway floor grille.

As their attention transferred back to the titanic battle, Czevak turned in time to see the daemonhost spear the aqueous body of the ichneuplasm with a mangled catwalk. The blazing abominate had missed a perverse channel of the silver sentience, however, which took his legs out from under him. As he tried to get up, wave upon towering wave of plasm crashed down on him, slamming the creature senseless into the deck.

Time was running out. Thrusting his fist into the air, Czevak unlocked a wrist-mounted stinger. Similar to the much larger Harlequin's Kiss used by the guardians of the Black Library to inject monofilament wires into their victims and slice them up from the inside, Czevak sported a small tubular attachment, culminating in a tapered point. This injector spike was effective enough as a weapon – although the inquisitor had never used it as such. With as much force as he could muster, Czevak punched the injector point of the alien object straight through the metal wall and into the codifier bank next to the bulkhead. Like the Harlequin's Kiss, the Stinger shot its spool of monofilament wires explosively into the wall. Tearing his wrist back, the wires and hooks retracted, dragging with them a bundled collection of aging power cables, vox-wires and hydraulic lines. Czevak tore the bundle out of the wall arm over arm with all of its associated ports, vents and consecrated unguent.

'What are you doing?' Captain Torres called down at him harshly.

'Saving your ship,' Czevak muttered imperiously to himself – the fact that his actions had introduced the ichneuplasm to the vessel was lost on him at that moment. His fingers slipped and slid over the bundle as he stripped back wires and lines in his search for one specific cable. The inquisitor risked a glance across the hangar. The Milk of Malevolsia was pressing its globular advantage. While the entity whipped itself up into a silver cyclone, whirling the archeodeck into a vortex of destruction, the daemonhost was down on its knees, struggling to re-ignite. As his perfect body writhed once more in lucent flame, he took several defiant steps and launched back into the darkness of the hangar. At that moment the hurricane swept forward, swallowing the daemonhost and throwing it around its circumference. As the fiery figure swiftly became a halo of flame plummeting uncontrollably through the whirling warpflesh, the ichneuplasm collapsed, its silver waters crashing in on themselves. The elemental energy had been spent on propelling the daemonhost, with as much centrifugal force as possible at the hangar wall.

With limbs flailing and its body spinning head over torso, like a knife tossed from some giant hand, the extinguished daemonhost flew through the air. It hit the

large archeodeck bulkhead with such excruciating force
that the heavy gauge door buckled and deformed around
the creature's rag doll body. Crumbling to the deck with
a sickly thud, the daemonhost created an untidy pile and
remained still.

The ichneuplasm wasted no time in reaffirming its
affection for Czevak and, like a redirected river, washed
off the far wall of the hangar and coursed across the
archeodeck at the bulkhead. As desperation built and
fingers slipped, Czevak shared his horror between the
oncoming entity and the oily bundle. Hidden in the
slimy nest he found what he was looking for: a mind-
impulse interface and port. Scooping the muck out of
the interface with his finger, the inquisitor screwed the
gritty threads into an interface socket in the back of his
skull.

The ichneuplasm raged on. The *Malescaythe* gave a visible shudder.

'What?' the captain exploded on the walkway above,
finger to her vox-bead. 'The Geller field is dropping!'
Then, to Czevak. 'What are you doing?'

As the silver torrent swept the deck, Klute emptied his
shotgun at the beast, frantically working the lever action
on the street silencer. Torqhuil sliced through the passing deluge with his crackling axe and the remaining
Savlar – driven to inspiration or insanity – peppered the
creature once more with their assorted firearms.

'Forty per cent… thirty per cent, still dropping,' the
captain repeated from her vox-bead. 'Madman! This is
the Eye – you'll kill us all!' she screamed at Czevak, but
the inquisitor was too busy interfacing with the ship and
preparing himself for the bone-crunching slam of the
ichneuplasm's unstoppable surge.

The *Malescaythe* rang with the cacophony of bells,
alarms and searing klaxons, heralding the impending
doom of the vessel. The amethyst dreadspace outside
the hanger turned sickly white. The dark, airbrushed

outlines of daemonic warp predators pushed the indescribable horror of their soul-ravenous faces up against
the weakening bubble of reality surrounding the rogue
trader. They snapped and leered at each other and the
ship as their combined warp-ethereal mass began to
overwhelm and seep through the collapsing Geller field.
Like frightened children, the *Malescaythe*'s crew and company covered their eyes to save polluting their minds and
took solace in rote-learned prayers and catechisms.

The silver entity flowed on, furiously building into the
wave with which it intended to pulverise Czevak and
then – in its perverse currents – feast upon his soul. The
Milk of Malevolsia was close enough for Czevak to see his
own face in its silver waters, when the daemonic creature
lurched. Ironically, it reminded the inquisitor of a swim-
mer seized from beneath by a monster of the deep. Every
drop of the damned creature seemed frozen in position,
unaffected by gravity or reality even. A shocking moment
later the silver flood rushed towards the hangar ceiling,
cascading the distance upwards; splashing and pooling
on the roof of the huge chamber as it had on the deck.
Then, once again it fell – the mercurial shower seemingly
thrashing in an internal torment and horror of its own.
When it hit the archeodeck once again, splashing and
settling to stillness it was devoid of the warped sentience
it had demonstrated up until that point. It was merely
a small lake of tranquil silver. All in the hangar stepped
forwards and stared into the sheen of its reflective waters.

'Get back!' Czevak called with authority across the
hush of the hangar.

At first there were swirls and eddies; reversed ripples
and then forms, drenched in the slick, silvery warpflesh
of the ichneuplasm. The immaterial monstrosities from
outside the ship were breaching the weakening integrity
of the Geller field and using as their anchor the warp
presence of the ichneuplasm to help heave their savage ethereal selves across the border into reality. As a

legion of daemonspawn drew themselves up out of the mirrored surface of the pool – from the creeping to the colossal, the horned and the horrific, both mockeries of nature and the formless natures of the unseen and unknowable – Czevak adjusted his mind-impulse interface. The inquisitor was fearful that he would lose his connection with the ship. He'd exchanged one hellish entity for a thousand and they had done their part in burying their proverbial and literal claws into the warp-flesh of the ichneuplasm. Czevak decided that it was now time to send them all back to the nightmare from which they had come.

'Reinstating Geller field; directing all power from the warp engines…' Czevak mouthed as he communicated the same to the *Malescaythe*'s machine spirit through the hard-wire interface.

As the Geller field built to full power, effectively cutting the link that the daemonic entities had forged between the unreality of the Eye and the inside of the rogue trader, the foothold that the creatures had established became progressively less stable. Like liquid in zero gravity, pulled droplet by droplet towards a crack in the spacecraft's outer hull, the daemon interlopers began to dissipate. They reached out with claw and pincer, tentacle and jaw, for the souls on the archeo-deck. The essence of their existence bled from them, drizzling their argent manifestations back to the dread-space from which they were spawned. One by one the daemons were forced back behind the prison walls of reality, re-erected by the *Malescaythe*'s powerful Geller field force generator. As the phantasmal miasma of the entities wept to nothingness, accompanied by the fading insanity of unearthly screams, Czevak unplugged himself from the mind-impulse interface and tossed the cable to the deck.

From the catwalks to the Fornical, mouths were agape and weapons trembled in adrenaline-addled grips. Klute strode across the decimated archeodeck towards his master, touching Torqhuil's armoured elbow as he went. The scene had a hint of the ridiculous about it, the all too human inquisitor checking that a superhuman member of the Adeptus Astartes was all right, after the trauma of the daemonic incursion. Torqhuil himself simply towered in Czevak's vicinity, helmet still on, power axe still humming away in his gauntlets – deciding which side of insane the newcomer really was.

Epiphani had Father lead her over to Hessian's broken body. No one else in the gathering would have cared if the daemonhost was alive or dead, but as Klute suspected, Epiphani had a soft spot for the monster, sharing years together trailing Phalanghast on his warped ventures across the segmentum.

'He's alive,' she called softly, remarkably softly for Epiphani, as she leant in to listen to his breathing. Klute shouldn't have been surprised; loosening the wards and spiritual impediments to the realisation of even a fraction of Hessian the Abominate's true power had allowed the beast certain invulnerabilities. These invulnerabilities had saved the creature's life as he in turn had helped save the lives of everyone in the hangar. It was not an experiment Klute intended on repeating often, and he was unashamedly glad that the daemonhost had been smashed senseless. It would make the process of inflicting fresh wards and circumscriptisms on the creature all the easier.

'It's alive, Epiphani. It's an "it",' Klute reminded her with an almost paternal authority. The inquisitor moved towards the spectacle of his rediscovered master, his chest bursting with a mixture of pride and relief. He had achieved the impossible; thank the God-Emperor, he'd found his long lost master – it was over. Before Klute could reach Czevak, Torres got to him first.

The captain opened with, 'Are you out of your mind?'

Czevak seemed to notice her for the first time: the full

figure, the Imperial Navy uniform, the lustrous hair and less attractive furrow of her brow and fury in her eyes.

'Well if I was – how would I know? You tell me. How do I look?'

The captain was caught off guard by the playful answer, but rallied swiftly.

'You almost got us killed. Twice.'

'I've always found the operative word in that sentence to be "almost".'

'Little surprise that you make a habit of such reckless-ness. Your flippancy disgusts me, sir. Men did die here today. Defending this ship: my ship, my men.'

Czevak's words grew colder. 'No man enters the Eye of Terror under the illusion that he will face anything other than a horrible death. Like sword swallowers and men who climb mountains for sport, I have little sympathy for them. They have it coming.'

'I hope you would include yourself in that category,' the rogue trader captain shot back.

Czevak turned, straightening the collar on his outland-ish coat and hanging his hands on his gaudy lapels.

'Doubly, madam.'

Exeunt

ACT I, CANTO III

Stellagraphium, Rogue trader Malescaythe, *The Eye of Terror*

Enter HIGH INQUISITOR BRONISLAW CZEVAK, attended by KLUTE, CAPTAIN REINETTE TORRES, EPIPHANI, FATHER and SAUL TORQHUIL

Torres had forgotten about Guidetti.

As the assembly swept into the stellagraphium, the rogue trader captain came to regard her former Navigator. Rasputus Guidetti had been a tall, proud, alabaster-skinned charmer whose family had charter ties with the Torres-Bouchier Mercantile Sovereignty on Zyracuse. During the *Malescaythe*'s extended stay in the Eye of Terror, Guidetti's singular talents had become all but redundant – the Astronomican failing to penetrate the deeper reaches of the maelstrom. Some of the ship's company claimed that the Navigator had caught a variety of ether-fever, others that without the Astronomican's

constant chorus of angelic light, Guidetti went insane.
When several crew members were discovered with their
throats torn out, initial suspicion had fallen on the monster Hessian or some daemon world stowaway. This was
until the body of the *Malescaythe*'s chief astropath was
found on the lower decks with Guidetti still feeding on
her.

Torres had been tempted to destroy him there and then
but reasoned that in his lucid moments, the Navigator
and his extensive knowledge of the segmentum might
still be useful to her. Instead she opted to imprison him
in a gibbet cage, restricting his movements and hang him
in the corner of the stellagraphium. She had placed him
there for two reasons: firstly, as the *Malescaythe*'s chart
room, it was a place that the insane Guidetti felt calm-
est – which was the way Torres preferred the psychopath;
secondly, since entering the Eye of Terror, where star
charts were all but useless, the stellagraphium was rarely
used.

Czevak barely acknowledged the scaly mutant, merely
ducking beneath the snatching grip of Guidetti's dirty,
webbed claws before walking on. Captain Torres placed
a threatening hand on the grip of her laspistol and
held it there, which was enough to prompt the Navigator to slink back into his cage. He blinked subservience
from where his head was secured in an iron bridle and
restricted himself to sibilant mutterings.

Turning, Torres went to take her traditional position
at the head of the stellagraphium's great table but found
that Czevak had already taken the ornate leather chair
for himself. Casually reclined, he propped his boots up
on the polished surface of the great table – as well as
the ancient vector charts, celestial cartograms and warp
dilation tabulata that had been the captain's inheritance
along with the *Malescaythe*. In silent disgust, the captain
took an alternative seat and began assembling the delicate collection of scrolls and maps. Epiphani took a seat

opposite, resplendent in a two-piece bedlah of bronzed silks, a chain circlet and a high collar gown of magnificent cyclopteryx feathers, and began shuffling a pack of psychoactive crystal wafers.

Despite Klute's own youthful forays into spire fashions, the inquisitor had initially thought it strange that the blind warp-seer took such an interest in clothes and her appearance. Her mother, Lady Casserndra Laestrygoni had been a spire-style sensation, but Epiphani was not privy to that information. She saw the future and not the past. The inquisitor slowly came to understand, however, that while most people saw others and consulted mirrors to see themselves, the warp-seer constantly saw herself through the eyes of another. Constantly viewing herself through her drone's bionic eyes had made her more self-conscious – and fashion conscious – than anyone Klute had ever met and this manifested itself in the spectacular arrangements the warp-seer was seen wearing about the rogue trader.

The servo-skull, Father, hovered over Epiphani's silk shoulder, watching the tarot unfold. Saul Torqhuil was forced to stand by the wall, the ornate furniture not hoping to accommodate his bulk, armour and servo-appendages. As Klute hurried in past the two goggled Savlar Guardsmen stationed on the entrance arch, he positioned himself at the other end of the table. He was followed in by a servitor carrying a tray of food and drink. Laying a dish of steaming ichthid eggs and black bread before Czevak with a decanter of amasec and a glass, the silent servant left the chamber.

Sitting up to the table, the young-looking inquisitor scooped up a pronged spoon before shovelling the food down. The assembly waited, fascinated by the spectacle of the clearly ravenous Czevak wolfing down such luxurious fare. Still chewing and with some of the tiny eggs running down his chin, the inquisitor addressed the room with an all encompassing gesture of his spoon.

'Don't wait for me,' he said through a mouthful, before pouring himself a generous glass of amasec.

Torres didn't wait, she launched into a series of questions directed at Klute, 'Raimus, please. What is going on? Who is this man?'

Klute nodded in acknowledgement that the captain was absolutely right to ask.

'May I introduce,' Klute began, 'High Inquisitor Bronislaw Czevak, of the Ordo Xenos.'

Apart from Guidetti's gibberings and the snap of crystal wafers on the smooth surface of the table, the chamber fell to a dumbstruck silence.

'This isn't Czevak,' Torres spat. 'Czevak's dead.'

'Well, that is a relief,' Czevak said between spoonfuls.

'She's correct,' Torqhuil weighed in. 'Even those that believe him alive say that the eldar have him. Others, that the dark sorcerers of the Thousand Sons Legion made him their plaything.'

'Besides, what would he be?' the rogue trader captain put to them. 'Four hundred years old?'

'Four hundred and thirty-three,' Czevak corrected her, his face hard.

'This *is* Bronislaw Czevak,' Klute told them as the two inquisitors regarded each other along the length of the table. Czevak went back to his eggs. 'I should know; before achieving rank in the ordo, I served as his acolyte and apprentice for twenty of those four hundred and thirty-three years. I then used that rank, influence and power to engage the three of you in locating him in this benighted place.'

'But…' Torres murmured, her mouth running before her mind.

'The eldar, to be sure, are a long-lived race,' Czevak said with authority. 'This longevity is only partially determined by their biology. I don't pretend to fully understand it, but the trans-dimensional travel that dominates their faster-than-light movements across the

galaxy seems to have a regressional effect on their cel-
lular senescence.'

Torres turned from Czevak to Klute. 'In simple
language?'

'Increasing time spent on the webway stalls and then
reverses the ageing process. And not just for the alien
eldar,' Torqhuil informed her with professional interest. Then, to the inquisitor, 'You visited the fabled Black
Library of Chaos, did you not?'

Czevak tossed his spoon on his plate and then went to
work on the amasec. 'As both guest and prisoner. I don't
intend to return as either.'

'And what of Ahzek Ahriman and his Thousand Sons?'
Epiphani put to the High Inquisitor, her voice excitable,
like a child trying to be noticed in an adult conversation.
Her eyes never left the wafers of the Imperial Tarot and
their Aquilique layout.

Klute seemed agitated at the mention of Ahriman in
Czevak's presence.

'Ahriman covets the Black Library and the arcane,
forbidden lore it contains,' Klute enlightened her with
gravity. 'His search for its secrets is galaxy-wide and never
ending, for surely if such a master of the dark arts ever
gained access to the shrine, the Imperium would witness
the birth of a Chaos god.'

'And you were slave to this accursed sorcerer for how
long?' Torqhuil pressed darkly.

'Brother Torqhuil, that's enough,' Klute interjected, but
the question remained.

'I am a member of the Holy Ordos. I have a title and
I'll remind you to use it, Brother Torqhuil,' Czevak testily
returned.

'Inquisitor,' the Space Marine addressed Klute – laying
special emphasis on the title. 'Ahriman of the Thousand
Sons is peerless in the arts of deception, and cunning.
How can you be sure that this is Czevak and not some
imposter – even worse, how do you know that this is not

some servant of the Ruinous Powers or even Ahriman himself?'

'He has a point,' Czevak agreed mordantly.

Losing patience with the hostile reception and Czevak's antagonism, Klute said, 'It's crossed my mind. Please, friends – enough of these inflammatory questions.'

Now it was Czevak's turn to lose what little patience he had. 'I am surprised, Brother Torqhuil to be lectured thus by a member of an Excommunicate Chapter. A Chapter whose glorious history ended in dishonour, a Penitent Crusade abandoned and vile acts committed in the name of the Emperor to cover searching out artefacts and using the forbidden weapons of Chaos…'

'… against Chaos!' Torqhuil rumbled with conviction.

'A fool's bargain,' Czevak said. 'Chaos cannot be turned against Chaos, proud Relictor. You are less a heretic than an imbecile if you believe that. The Dark Powers know your desire to use their sacrilegious tools; they exploit and manipulate it for their own ends – even in the loyal subjects of the Imperium.'

'As Ahriman's slave, I assume you would have learned much of those Dark Powers,' Torqhuil returned harshly.

'I learned not to put my trust in them.' Czevak then turned on the rogue trader captain. 'And you, captain. You trade in corrupt and destructive wares, pilfered from this damned place, to return their polluting filth to an unwitting Imperium – all to line the hold and pockets of your precious cartel. You talked of my recklessness in the hangar; consider your own, captain.'

Epiphani smiled at the High Inquisitor. She already knew she was next. 'Witches and daemonhosts?' Czevak spat incredulously. 'And you sit here and judge me. Klute?'

Klute held his master's gaze.

'We are in the Eye of Terror,' Klute informed him. 'Searching for you. Only now do these people learn of my objective. You might want to allow them a moment to adjust. God-Emperor knows, I instigated the endeavour and I'm still reeling. An Inquisitorial rosette does little to buy you allegiance in this lethal place – as I'm sure you know, my lord. These people work for me and for themselves. They all have their own reasons for being here – as they must. If anyone had agreed to travel with me without those reasons I would have dismissed them out of turn for being insane.'

Czevak nodded with a grim certitude.

'By that reasoning, you yourself must be insane,' Czevak accused, with returning lightness.

'Another thing that had crossed my mind, my lord.'

Czevak looked back at the daggered glares of Torqhuil and Torres and the simpleton's smile of the zoned-out warp-seer.

'One thing that you might come to learn about me – if you live that long – is that my words are often hasty and choice. Raimus will tell you this. Think not on what I have said. In turn, if my time in the Black Library taught me anything it was – rather controversially – that Chaos is already very much part of us. It deals in the currency of mortal souls and feeds off states and emotions that are in essence natural. Without us there would be no Chaos. Good and evil? Right and wrong? These are binary oppositions that the inhabitants of this galaxy use to comfort and define themselves. I'm afraid much of the God-Emperor's work is done in the grey area in between.'

There were nods, slow and unsure, from about the room.

'Let us put this to the test,' Czevak decided, suddenly animated. 'Enough of the past, warp-seer. Leave history to dusty books on lonely shelves. It's the future that interests me. Ask no more questions. Tell, instead.'

Klute gave a hesitant nod. Epiphani manipulated the wafers with light ease, all fingers, thumbs and edges. She had uncovered several already, providing context for the reading.

'Three, High Inquisitor,' she instructed.

Leaning over he walked his fingers across the tarot spread, touching three cards as he went. Using one card, she flipped the other two over. The gathering, including the caged Navigator, watched with interest.

Flicking the pack of wafers, Epiphani laid out Minor Arcana determiners aside their Major Arcana counterparts.

'"Knave of Wands",' Epiphani began, nudging the first card of the reading, 'and "The Wanderer".' The wafer to which she referred showed a colossal space hulk, vomited forth from the warp. 'A visitor, unannounced – bringer of opportunity and destruction.'

'That would be you,' Klute said. Czevak gave a small shake of his head.

'The warp-seer speaks of the future, not the past.'

Klute returned his attention dourly to the tarot spread.

'"Eight of Swords",' Epiphani whispered, drawing it alongside a wafer bearing a pale saint in ornate golden armour. The wafer was upside down, allowing Czevak to make out a bloody tear drop on his breast and the halo above his head. '"Sanguinius",' the prognostic announced. 'Inversed. Sacrifice and strife before its time.'

Between the two, Epiphani turned the wafer she had used to flip the previous two, laying it down with the final determiner. '"Maiden of Spheres" and the "Galactic Lens"; great distance and little time – the swift movement of events that are to come to pass.'

Epiphani let the reading hang in the silence, her audience wrangling with the possibilities the Imperial Tarot had touted.

'Interesting,' Klute said, breaking their thoughts. 'Could the High Inquisitor and I have the room?'

'Raimus, there's still much to discuss,' Captain Torres insisted. 'The warp gate cannot remain on the *Malescaythe*. It poses a constant danger to the ship and our lives.'

'The Lost Fornical of Urien-Myrdyss is an operational artefact of incalculable power and opportunity,' Brother Torqhuil reminded her. 'We have barely begun to understand its full potential.'

'I don't care about its xenoarcheological significance.'

'It's priceless.'

'So are my ship and my life.'

'The portal is sealed, for now. The gateway is dormant. Nothing more can pass through,' Czevak more informed than assured her.

'And what about Hessian?' The rogue trader captain was not asking after the daemonhost's wellbeing.

'Secured in the chapel,' Epiphani told her, standing and gathering up her wafers. From Father came a succession of clicks and scratches as the vellum spool suspended where the servo-skull's jaw should have been began to unscroll. Epiphani tore off the enscribed length and handed it to Klute. 'The wards and circumscriptions you asked for.'

As the Relictors Space Marine strode out of the stellagraphium, followed by the cyclopteryx-feathered warp-seer and her servo-skull, Torres stared hard at Klute.

'All this, for one man?'

'Yes.'

The rogue trader captain went to leave the chart chamber. Klute called after her. 'Reinette.'

'Inquisitor?'

'Plot a course for Cadia. You'll need Epiphani. Get us out of this hell hole.'

'With pleasure,' she answered coldly before closing the stellagraphium door.

A long silence passed between the two inquisitors.

'I was hoping for the Golden Throne,' Klute admitted. 'A wafer that signified safety, security or at least a return to normality.'

Czevak held his former interrogator's gaze, the glimmer of a smile appearing on his lips.

'The Golden Throne means none of those things, my friend.'

Klute couldn't find it in himself to match Czevak's smile with one of his own.

'I don't care what the cards say. Come back with me, my lord. Return to the Imperium. To the ordo. Leave this terrible place with its corrupting and alien influence.'

'I won't go back to Cadia. Or to Our Lady of Sorrows or Nemesis Tessera,' Czevak told Klute in syllables of stone. 'A cell, an eternity of questions and a heretic's death wait for me there, and it waits there for you too, my friend. And if it isn't the Puritans, it would be the cultists. Ahriman has eyes and ears everywhere. Your precious Imperium is rotting from the inside out. My freedom must be my own. I cannot put it in the hands of others – not again.'

'My lord,' Klute begged, his head bowed, recalling events from their past. 'Please forgive me. If I'd remained by your side, perhaps…'

'Raimus, you can't blame yourself for…'

'I do.'

'Then you're a fool. If you had been by my side, then you would be dead right now, instead of sitting opposite me debating the fact.'

'I have long tried to imagine the trials you endured at the dark hands of that abominate sorcerer,' Klute went on with feeling, but Czevak cut him dead.

'Don't,' the High Inquisitor said – his words once again laced with hard edges. 'You couldn't. But I don't blame you for the actions of a warp-souled heretic.'

Silence passed between them.

'He'll never stop, will he?' Klute admitted to the High Inquisitor and himself.

'And that, my friend, is why I must stop him – by any means at my disposal. He wants the Black Library and its secrets. He knows I am a key to those secrets. He must be stopped. I must stop him.'

'There must be another way,' Klute insisted. 'With the knowledge you carry we could unite the ordos behind a single cause and the Imperium behind them. Launch a White Crusade, if you would, and take the battle to this horrific place and its denizens.'

'Romantic.'

'Better than running and hiding from shadows,' Klute shot back cuttingly.

'Touché,' Czevak said. 'I may be running but I'm not hiding. I asked you not to imagine what I suffered at Ahriman's hands, but if you did, even for an agonising second, then you would know what I had to give him. A thousand facts from a thousand pages of the Black Library of Chaos – just to keep the location of its hallowed doors from the bastard. Every life Ahriman takes with those secrets burns my soul. The least I can do – the very least – is try to undo some of that damage. Get ahead of him, destroy the artefacts he seeks and turn his ambitions to dust.'

'You are but one man, my lord.'

Czevak bit at his lip before nodding slowly to himself. Reaching down into the seemingly bottomless depths of his outlandish coat, the inquisitor extracted a bulky tome and laid it on the table before him. Its gilded covers were crafted from a burnished, golden metal that had a sheen like nothing Klute had ever seen. A set of three robust clasps held the volume closed and the spine housed an intricate and ancient mechanism that sighed rhythmically, like the beating of a mechanical heart. Placing his fingertips on its aureate, ornamental surface, Czevak slid the tome down the table towards his former acolyte.

Klute stopped it and was immediately surprised at how light the object was – bearing in mind how much metal covered its surface. The crafting and gilded depictions on the cover looked both ancient and Imperial and its title was rendered in High Gothic.

'The *Atlas Infernal*,' Klute translated in a whisper. 'You stole this from the eldar?'

'Liberated it – from the Black Library of Chaos.'

Klute's face creased with disapproval. Czevak continued defensively. 'It's obviously Imperial. I stole back an artefact that was already stolen.'

Klute returned his attention to the magnificent tome. Carefully unclasping the covers, he opened the volume. Almost immediately Klute's face changed. A feeling of distaste and discomfort washed over the inquisitor. It was difficult to look directly at the Atlas and instead he looked up at Czevak.

'Is it corrupted?' Klute asked fearfully, wondering if Czevak was showing him some cursed or possessed object.

'Quite the opposite,' Czevak reassured him. 'My researches into this object are limited – I was too busy trying to steal it. I have theories though.'

As the High Inquisitor spoke, Klute forced himself to look inside the *Atlas Infernal*. He was surprised to find an absence of paper. In its stead were a stacked panel of lightweight golden frames, all built into the spine, that sat like pages between the *Atlas Infernal*'s covers. Each page contained a piece of ancient flesh, stretched to transparency across the frame so that its labyrinthine network of veins, arteries and capillaries were visible at its surface. Klute was amazed to see that actual blood circulated through the tiny system, fed oxygen by the clockwork pump in the spine.

'Before the Horus Heresy, ancient texts in the Black Library tell of the Emperor's efforts to create a human section of the webway, connecting Terra to the rest of the galaxy through the eldar's labyrinthine network of transdimensional tunnels. Through the webway and without the danger, uncertainty and inconvenience of warp travel, the Imperium's conquest of the galaxy would be complete. That was what we can assume the Emperor's intention to be, anyhow. Events leading up to the Heresy made this project impossible to pursue and the human section of the webway – sustained by the Emperor's divine power – collapsed.'

'This is a map of the eldar webway?' Klute marvelled. 'But created by whom?'

'That, I don't know,' Czevak admitted with not a little vexation on his young face. 'There is, however, some compelling evidence in the text itself.'

'It's amazing,' Klute managed as he thumbed through the flesh pages. Scribbled over each were annotations – light scars originally sliced into the flesh with a crystal-tip quill.

'The casket-covers of the tome are made of a light-weight metal that I have yet to identify. It is incredibly resilient – leading me to believe that it was originally armour. Amongst the filigree and detail I found markings remarkably like those honouring the Terran Unification Wars.'

'That doesn't answer my question. It just generates more questions.'

'The guardians of the Imperial Palace and personal bodyguards of the Emperor himself would have worn such markings on their armour previous to the Heresy. They would undoubtedly have provided security for a project as ambitious as building a human section of the webway. The Magos Ethericus and Artisans Empyr of the Adeptus Mechanicus are probably responsible for its construction – although I doubt the Priesthood of Mars has seen anything of this kind for thousands of years.'

'And the flesh?' Klute interrupted, clearly unsettled. 'What unfortunate sacrificed themselves to become part of such a treasure?'

'The Mechanicus and Adeptus Custodes would have required psychic protection on the human section of the webway and the militant arm of the Adeptus Astra Telepathica would have been the ideal choice to deliver it. The Sisters of Silence were exclusively recruited from Untouchable stock. This is the flesh of such a Sister, a Pariah, your reaction upon opening the Atlas testifies to that – and you and I aren't even psykers. The blacksoul blood that still flows through these vessels floods veins, arteries and capillaries in representation of the webway's labyrinthine pathways – as the nullified pathways of the webway weave through the immaterial plane.'

'Incredible,' Klute mumbled in wonder.

'I can only imagine that this text was a macabre, if inventive, attempt to catalogue the wanderings of the unfortunate army of Adeptus Custodes, Sisters of Silence and Adeptus Mechanicus working on and securing the human section of the webway after their gateway to Terra collapsed.'

'An incredible story,' Klute agreed.

'Yes,' Czevak nodded with regret. 'And that alone infuriates me. Who beyond the God-Emperor himself could corroborate even half of it?'

'But if the webway is as expansive as we are led to believe it to be, then how could one tome – even one as fabulous as this – map it all?'

'Look again,' Czevak prompted.

Klute looked back at the page he had been perusing.

'It's changed,' he murmured in wonder. The blood vessels were reconfigured; fresh ones flooded with blood were now at the surface, while others had faded to obscurity in the parchment flesh as the flow of blood dissipated. The skin tone of the flesh had changed slightly also, allowing different scars to appear in the forms of white scratch-writing, annotating the new pattern on the page. 'Mirador?'.

Czevak smiled. 'Cadia, presumably before any Imperial had set foot there. I haven't worked out how it does that, but it certainly seems to be sensitive to the eyes on its pages. You want to return to the Imperium. It shows you Cadia.'

'A wondrous artefact, truly,' Klute told his master before

carefully closing the golden casket-clasps and placing it carefully on the table before him. 'But, my lord – answer me this; what do you want?'

'What do I want?'

'It's a simple enough question.'

'I know what I don't want.'

'My lord,' Klute said, his words straining. 'I've spent decades of my life searching this horrific place for clues of your existence. I've kept company with renegades, heretics and daemonhosts and committed acts of faith-treachery that can never be forgiven, by my brother-inquisitors or by myself.' Klute paused – the weariness and exhaustion of his search seeming to take over. 'This place, it pollutes my very being. I can feel it, under my skin. I've taken every physical and spiritual precaution but still, I fear for my soul. I want to leave. I want to go home – to persecution, if that is the price of a ticket.'

'What you want is an absolution,' Czevak said sharply. 'Which no Puritan or bonfire can offer you. What do I want? Well, I never wanted this. I'm deeply honoured that you would do this for me. If there was a soul in the galaxy upon whom I would rely, it would be yours. You have been an excellent apprentice and as I've said before, more of a friend than I deserve. But I never asked this of you. You asked this of yourself – your guilt asked this of you. The same guilt that would have you return to an Imperium that would rack you for your loyalty and good intentions. As you have discovered, my friend, the road to the Eye of Terror is paved with such intentions.'

'Then you won't come back? All of this has been in vain,' Klute settled, getting older and greyer by the moment in his stellagraphium seat.

'Raimus – you have achieved the impossible. I'm terrified that you actually found me. If my enemies had half your instincts then I would already be a dead man. Take some of that fire in your belly and continue what you really started, the Emperor's work – here, with me, in a place where few have the courage to carry it out. I've been alone for a long time and you of all people know I have my ways, but I've always valued your counsel and would value it again, should you decide to stay the course.'

Klute's expression remained unreadable.

'"The Wanderer",' he repeated from Epiphani's reading. 'A visitor, unannounced – bringer of opportunity…'

'…and destruction,' Czevak added, completing Epiphani's description. 'Your young warp-seer may have the gift, but her reading leaves a great deal to be desired. You worry about "Sanguinius". You fear his sacrifice is yours and that you will share his fate.'

Klute raised an eyebrow. 'The wafer was inversed,' Czevak continued. 'It represents not sacrifice – especially combined with a Sword wafer – but an enemy exposed, a chink in the armour – as the strike of Sanguinius exposed Horus to destruction.'

Klute nodded and a long silence passed between the two men.

'Do you want to hear something ironic?' Klute finally asked his master.

'Always.'

Klute gestured at their surroundings. 'Because of the controversial nature of its destination, I chartered the rogue trader under the Inquisitorial authority of your rosette. The *Malescaythe* is chartered in your name.'

The two men risked a smile. 'I'm not authorised to order this vessel back to Cadia.' Their smiles turned to laughter and pouring a dram of amasec for Klute and taking the decanter for himself, Czevak toasted their spiritual health.

The peel of the *Malescaythe*'s alarm bell cut across the decks and through their laughter, although hilarity was still dying in both men's throats when Captain Torres came over the vox-hailer.

'Code Crimson: we are under attack. Inquisitor Klute to the bridge, immediately.'

Grabbing the *Atlas Infernal* and stuffing it into the folds of his Harlequin coat, Czevak followed Klute out of the stellagraphium, leaving the quietly insane Guidetti to rock gently in his gibbet cage.

Alarum

ACT I, CANTO IV

Command deck, Rogue trader Malescaythe, *The Eye of Terror*

Enter KLUTE and CZEVAK

THE BRIDGE WAS in an uproar.

Captain Torres was everywhere, bawling orders above the sound of the alarm bell at several deck officers. Numerous servitors hardwired into the Gothic splendour of the bridge chattered runecode at one another through drawn lips and yellowing teeth as the logic banks on the command deck exploded with data.

Epiphani and Father were present, the warp-seer's arms draped around the back of the captain's throne and Torqhuil was down in the transept with the logi and bank servitors, his servo-arms and mechadendrites moving across ancient dials and plungers. The lancet screens towering around them were flooded with the heliotropical haze of the Eye and the baleful glint of distant stars.

'Get me a pict-feed,' Torres barked past Klute as the inquisitor arrived on the bridge. 'And kill that damned bell.' Czevak ghosted around the rear of the command deck, hands in the pockets of his breeches, occasionally reaching across an oblivious lexomat to twiddle a switch or toggle. 'Where's that feed?' the rogue trader captain called with menacing insistence.

A lancet screen above the transept blinked and crackled before the dismal vision it presented immediately outside the ship was replaced with a rear-angle view. As the *Malescaythe* blasted away from the distant memory that was the stomach-churning disc of Iblisyph, another vessel hove into view. Her engines blazed and her hull was a sickly white. 'Magnification!' Torres ordered.

As the lancet screen brought the full horror of their attacker into focus, Torqhuil interpreted the data chugging through the logic banks.

'Iconoclast-class destroyer – closing at sub-light speed. She's running with no shields and her batteries are cold – no power signature.'

'What's happening?' Klute demanded.

'Ask the High Inquisitor,' Torres said. 'When he collapsed the Geller field the ship launched an automatic distress beacon. Our predatory friend here couldn't have been cruising more than a system away and was drawn down on us like a shark to a distressed fish.'

'Can't we outdistance it?' Klute enquired.

'The nearest opportunity for a safe jump point is hours away,' Torres informed him, and then to a nearby lieutenant, 'Get me specifications. I want to know that vessel's reach. We need to stay out of range for as long as possible.'

'This whole area is a confluence,' Epiphani threw casually into the conversation 'If we were to enter the warp here the fast-flowing currents alone would tear us apart.'

'I have a partial registration,' Torqhuil announced. 'She's very old – looks like the Strigoi Shipyards – her designation at launch, at least, was the *Hellebore*.'

'Why run without shields?' Klute put to the captain.

'Why run without charging your batteries?' she said, answering a question with a question. 'You can sure as hell bet that we're running with both of ours.'

'She needs all power for her engines,' Czevak called from the rear of the command deck. Klute and Torres turned. 'Shields and batteries would considerably hamper her ability to catch us. Besides, she won't be using either.'

'And how would you happen to know that?' Torres asked with sarcasm.

Czevak came forward, hands still in his pockets.

'Magnify!' he ordered across the deck. The lancet window displayed an even closer rendering of the fast-closing vessel. The reason for the *Hellebore*'s colouring became obvious now. Every square metre of her hull was decorated with skulls – both human and alien. Something else demanded the attention of the bridge and the exchange of orders and information across the chamber died. The *Hellebore*'s hold was open and trailing zero-gravity gore into the dreadspace of the Eye, marking its bloody path and progress towards the *Malescaythe*.

'She's a Khornate renegade destroyer,' the High Inquisitor told the bridge with confidence. 'That form of decoration is particular to pilgrim raiders out of the Blood Moons of Koryban. They're berserkers who jump around the Eye of Terror attacking anything and everything in their path. No prey is too large. Besides, she probably carries thousands of pilgrim warriors, ready to overwhelm enemy vessels. The trail is undoubtedly the celebratory carnage and butchery of the last crew they captured.'

'They'll run down under our guns with no shields and try to board?' Torres said incredulously.

'Even if they didn't need the extra power to catch us,

shields would be a coward's precaution. Long range gunfire is also frowned upon by the Korybanians. The Blood God does not reward such tactics and the Blood Moon pilgrims want to meet their Master. They pray that one of their sporadic, warmongering jumps around the Eye will take them to the Blood God's realm where they will be rewarded by their god. Their vessel, adorned with the skulls of their fallen enemies, will be added to his throne.'

'Well, they won't get their chance,' she assured him and then barked, 'Ordnance – charge and run out the starboard battery.'

'That's a mistake,' Czevak told Torres.

The captain was aware that the bridge had heard the inquisitor make the claim. She couldn't risk not hearing him out.

'Proceed.'

'They're berserkers – they know no fear. Your broadsides will not daunt them. Besides – look at that graceless prow, it's obviously been adapted and reinforced for such an eventuality. The *Hellebore* will soak up everything you throw at it and then draw alongside, throwing every bloodstained soul they have back across at your exhausted gun crews. They're Khornate berserkers – they'll be insane with rage and will not wait to suit up. They'll come straight across, armed to the teeth.'

Torres couldn't believe what she was hearing. 'They'll board, unsuited, across the void?'

'That is the Korybanian's typical strategy, yes,' Czevak assured her. The captain shook her head. In all of her years as a rogue trader and frigate captain in the Imperial Navy she'd never heard of such insanity.

'Are you suggesting that we make a warp jump?' Klute asked his master.

'Highly unadvisable,' Epiphani piped up.

'Well?' Torres said. It was clear that she little liked or trusted their new guest, but neither was she ready to give up her precious *Malescaythe* to a blood-crazed cultship and become part of the horrific gore-splattering celebrations down in the enemy vessel's hold.

'I can give you the victory your professional pride demands, Captain Torres,' Czevak announced, soaking up the attention of the command deck. 'And secure our escape, but only if you follow my instructions to the letter – no matter how disagreeable you find them.'

Torres choked back an involuntary objection – the kind that seemed to sail from her lips whenever she was in the High Inquisitor's presence. 'I mean it,' Czevak insisted, turning to Klute for authority and support. 'Once committed, any deviance from the strategy would spell doom for everyone on board this vessel.'

Torres looked from Czevak to Klute to the Iconoclast destroyer growing in their sights. The captain recalled Czevak's previous 'strategy' on the archeodeck.

'I know I'm going to hate this,' she admitted to the bridge and herself, before collapsing into her throne.

Czevak stepped forward. 'Brother Torqhuil, a word.'

Alarum

I

ACT I, CANTO V

Starboard gun deck, Rogue trader Malescaythe, *The Eye of Terror*

Enter BROTHER TORQHUIL

THE WORD CZEVAK had for the Relictors Techmarine was 'cogitator'. The inquisitor put to the Space Marine the very real benefit that might be reaped by laying their hands on the *Hellebore*'s bridge mnemonic cogitator. If the suggestion hadn't seemed so ludicrous to Torqhuil then he might have readily agreed. As a Khornate raider, the *Hellebore* would enter the squalls and storm fronts of the warp at a whim, only to have the haphazard immateriology of the Eye spit them out on the other side of the warp rift. There they would hunt for prey, spill blood and take skulls in the name of their god before returning to the insane, unreality of the warp again and its perverse serendipitude. This would mean that the

Hellebore's mnemonic cogitator would have recorded the raider's encounters in the Eye, across thousands of years and hundreds of different cultist captains. A wealth of information, obediently logged by the cogitator's logic engine from its original inception as a loyalist Imperial escort ship to the heretical, piratical and wide ranging practises of its present, lay in the equipment. Information, that might very well further the aims of both the inquisitor and the Relictors Space Marine.

When Torqhuil had raised the possibility of corruption, Czevak assured him that the Korybanian heretics were simple in their barbarism and tended not to go to the lengths of incorporating daemonic entities into their machinery or possessing their vessels. To the Khornate cultists blood was the object, that and the slaughter required to spill it. A vessel – no matter how grotesquely decorated – was simply a means to achieving that end across as large an expanse as possible. Since the *Malescaythe* had little choice but to endure an attack by the Iconoclast, Czevak reasoned that they might as well attempt to achieve something into the bargain beyond a simple escape. Besides, the last thing that an attacking Khornate raider would expect was a simultaneous attack on themselves.

The idea appealed to Torqhuil, despite little knowing the inquisitor. Czevak seemed an inherently dangerous person to be around and the Relictor should have put as much space between himself and the inquisitor as possible. He was likely to have the most powerful of enemies, alien, Chaotic and Imperial, and seemed recklessly adept at getting other people killed. On top of that, Torqhuil simply didn't like him and still harboured suspicions that the real Czevak was dead and that the *Malescaythe* now harboured an imposter. In opposition to the myriad of reasons not to entertain the inquisitor and his outlandish plans was the simple reason that no other human in the galaxy could boast his knowledge of Chaos, its tools and machinations and that, above all else, made the High Inquisitor's presence and leadership an unavoidable necessity for the Relictor.

The Techmarine had been simultaneously appalled and secretly impressed with Czevak's solution to the *Malescaythe*'s daemonic intrusion and expected nothing less in respect to the inquisitor's plan to recover the *Hellebore*'s bridge cogitator. The Adeptus Astartes was not disappointed.

Standing behind a gunnery deck bulkhead, the Techmarine waited. Bringing his servo-arms in tight behind him, he held his power axe in one rust-red gauntlet. The deck was silent and still. On Czevak's suggestion, Torres had evacuated and sealed off the starboard side deck compartments and then presented the *Hellebore* the *Malescaythe*'s starboard side. The inquisitor reasoned that even if the *Malescaythe* fired first, the gun crews would be swiftly hacked to pieces by degenerate cultists and the vessel stormed. Whatever damage Torres could inflict upon the cultship would be nothing compared to what the roaring deluge of Khornites would do to her crew. Czevak had instructed her to give the Iconoclast a run but ultimately to allow it to steadily overhaul the rogue trader and assume a boarding position. Torqhuil, on the other hand, was to wait on the empty gundeck, lined as it was with the lonely colossi of ancient, megabore laser cannons. They looked odd without crews and power coursing through their accelerators – odder still, sitting in their mighty carriages, unpresented to an enemy aggressor whose hull Torqhuil could see passing a short span from the lifeless gunports.

The *Hellebore*'s gunports were anything but lifeless. Like the *Malescaythe*, there were no cannons presented at the field-phased openings, but there were armies of feral, blood-drenched cultists howling their rabid intention to tear the rogue trader and everyone inside it apart. Some wore crude rebreathers and goggles; others sported

improvised ponchos of foil and had wound insulation
tape around extremities. They wielded hammers, axes
and chainswords – as well as their own warped limbs –
anything that would make a god-pleasing, bloody mess of
their victims. They blinked a simple, uncomprehending
rage at their target. The Relictors Space Marine watched
as they swarmed the gundecks, tearing and thrashing at
each other to get a place near the exterior airlocks. As
the bulkheads fired, streams of blood-crazed, corrupted
cultists poured from the port side of the raider, propelling themselves out of the airlocks like skydivers and
sailing across the black, frozen distance between the two
vessels with faces frost-glazed in masks of wrathful determination. Torqhuil couldn't see anything daemonic or
monstrous coming across, which would have reassured
Captain Torres – Czevak had assured her that the Gellar
field would keep anything possessed or immaterial from
breaching the vessel again.

The deck fell to darkness as the lamps cut out along
the silent row of cannons. Positioning himself at the
airlock, Torqhuil felt the *Malescaythe's* artificial gravity
die about him and his power-armoured form began to
drift up weightlessly from the deck. That had been the
second part of Czevak's plan. Cut the power – the light
and heating – then the artificial gravity of the starboard
deck compartments. Then, the final life support system
still operating in the noiseless, rapidly cooling darkness,
the atmosphere. The airlocks fired, rolling aside in unison, explosively expelling the gunnery deck's oxygen in a
howling maelstrom that blasted Torqhuil at high speed
across the deep cold of space.

Unlike the Khornate cultists, who had only scraps of
foil and their mindless fury to sustain them, Torqhuil
had an enclosed suit of ceramite plates and a helmet
feeding him oxygen. As a relatively young Techmarine, who had returned to his Chapter from Mars just
months before the Relictors' excommunication, he had

been blessed with a Mark-VIII suit of Errant armour, the most advanced suit of power armour available to Adeptus Astartes forces. While a silent agony preoccupied the cultists – no doubt charging their demented hearts with further rage, Torqhuil could afford the luxury of concentration. As he bolted across the inky blackness towards the side of the Khornate vessel, the empty sockets of a thousand skulls stared back at him.

Smashing across the bone-encrusted hull, Torqhuil spread his servo-arms and mechadendrite limbs, locking onto the architecture of the moving vessel. After a brief tumble along the *Hellebore's* side, the Techmarine anchored himself and went to work priming the lock mechanism on a maintenance airlock that hadn't been used in millennia. Artificial atmosphere screamed from the destroyer's side, dragging several unfortunate pilgrims along the adjoining corridor and braining them against the hatch. Allowing the bodies to spin off into the void, Torqhuil crawled spider-like inside, his servo-arms and the magnetic soles of his boots providing constant stability against the gale of evacuating atmosphere.

Two bulkheads into the cultship's interior, Torqhuil re-established atmospheric integrity. At a viewport, the Techmarine saw cultists, frothing at the mouth, complete their crossing. Without the force of escaping atmosphere propelling them they didn't have to worry about shattering their bodies against the rogue trader's side. They had other things to worry about, however. Ordinarily, the army of maniacs, fuelled by a raving thirst for carnage, would recover swiftly from the brief flash-freeze of open space and go about their business of wanton murder. What they found were sections devoid of victims, warmth, gravity, light and oxygen. Swiftly, the Blood God's pilgrims began to fall to an enemy they couldn't bring to battle – the empty void.

Fortunately for Torqhuil, the *Hellebore* was almost as deserted as the rogue trader's starboard sections. Very few cultists had remained to garrison the Iconoclast. This had been key to the raider's tactical success in the past, throwing every gore-mental degenerate the vessel had in one barbaric storm at craft sometimes much larger than itself. This time the strategy had resulted in decimation and a clear path to the *Hellebore*'s bridge.

Like the corridors leading to it, the raider's command deck was a homicidal nightmare. Torqhuil led the way with his unholstered bolt pistol. The deck was partially flooded with a bloody gruel, a mixture of freshly splattered gore and old, blackening blood, percolating with disease and danger. The walls and ceiling sections were red and dripping with recent death although it was difficult for Torqhuil to tell if the dribbling mess came from fluids that had fountained upwards out of mutilated bodies or down through the grating of higher decks. The Relictor found more of the same as he made a cautious entrance to the *Hellebore*'s bridge.

The flood was deeper there and the port screens splashed with jets of smeared gore, making the Techmarine wonder how the power supply to the bridge's logic engines, codifiers and runebanks hadn't already shorted out. Piles of entrails, fingers and fragments of shattered bone sat in the stinking sludge. Corpulent rats the size of hounds fought and squealed over shrivelled limbs, while other assorted organs – hearts, livers, kidneys – sat like ghoulish trophies, arranged on consoles and instrumentation in different stages of decomposition.

Brass automatrons sat hardwired into their filth encrusted stations, motionlessly monitoring the *Hellebore*'s systems. Above, the vaulted roof of the command deck jangled with heavy chains, suspending a forest of corpses. The bodies dangled upside down with arms trailing; all sporting ragged neck stumps where their heads used to be. Torqhuil assumed that the skulls could be found decorating the exterior of the vessel.

Moving along the command deck wall, it didn't take

Torqhuil long to find the bridge mnemonic cogitator. It was a thoroughly neglected piece of equipment – the cultists taking more interest in where they were going rather than where they had been – but it was operational and actively logging the present ship to ship engagement in its remembrance banks.

Rubbing a clotted handprint from the bottom of the nearest port screen, the Relictor saw that the *Hellebore* had slowed and drawn parallel to the *Malescaythe*, careful not to overshoot and completely overhaul the rogue trader. The frozen bodies of Khornate pilgrims were now drifting from the *Malescaythe*'s starboard sections and bouncing down the side of the vessel, smashing and shattering about the rogue trader's architecture. Something bothered Torqhuil about the vessels and their relative positions. Drawing alongside a fleeing vessel – in a pursuit – to mount a close boarding action was much too sophisticated a manoeuvre for a mechanical automatron or automated ship's system. Despite the seeming distance, the two vessels were almost touching.

Holstering his bolt pistol and bringing his power axe back to life with a sizzle, Torqhuil turned and cast his eyes around the gloom of the command deck. Moving up the slippery steps to the pulpit, the Techmarine found he had to push through the thicket of dangling bodies as the fingers of their suspended forms touched the elevated mezzanine deck. Torqhuil found the captain's throne in the nest of leaking cadavers, turned eerily away from him. Reaching out with his servo-arm and bringing his power axe up in readiness for the kill, Torqhuil slowly turned the throne.

It was empty, but for a single power armour helmet – red, like the Techmarine's own, but studded, squalid and ancient. It bore an ugly Mark-V type faceplate grille and the frontispiece was crafted into the semblance of a bovine skull, brown with age and armed with wicked horns.

Something thunked its way to the pulpit decking.

Torqhuil turned, servo-arms split between the ominous helmet and the noise. Then – everywhere at once, echoing across the confines of the command deck – the horrific *chug-chug* thrashing of a chain weapon. Torqhuil fell to a crouch on the filth-puddled floor. He caught a glimpse of the weapon, a chunky flail made up of an untidy pile of interlinked saw blades, all ripping and sparking against the deck and each other.

A gore-glistened shadow reared to full height amongst the swarm of swaying corpses. As its arms came up, the stinking rags that had disguised it cascaded from the shoulders of the giant. They revealed burnished, blood-drenched Heresy-pattern power armour – at once both magnificent and foetid to behold. The hulk dripped with gruesome trinkets and markings dedicated to Khorne, Butcher of Souls, Lord of Hate and Deep Drinker of Mindless Rage. His studded shoulder plate was splattered with fresh carnage and the gaping jaw markings of his Traitor Legion – the infamous World Eaters. From the Chaos Space Marine exploded a thunderous roar of demented fury.

It was the screech of the brutal chainflail that demanded Torqhuil's attention, however, as the beast brought it up off the deck and around his head in one dreadful, practiced motion. Remains span and limbs flew as the devastating weapon sang through torsos and burst through bodies, circling the monster in a continuous circumference of unremitting mutilation and carnage. The Chaos Space Marine bawled through the bloodshed in some kind of dark tongue, slicing up the instrumentation and floor of the mezzanine pulpit deck and clouding the area with a haze of cadaver gorespittle.

Torqhuil allowed the angry flail to pass over his helmet before storming through the fleshstorm and raining bodies at the World Eater. The adrenaline-flooded berserker was much swifter than the Relictor had anticipated, however, and managed to make a sudden half-turn. With mindless skill he brought the flail singing back at the Space Marine in an arc that Torqhuil found almost impossible to avoid and the appendage of one of his servo-arms came clean away from its mechadendrite limb.

Torqhuil instinctively dropped backwards, his power axe smashed out of his armoured grip by a sudden and unexpected encounter with the floor. The Relictor slid onto his pack and skidded under the blur of sawblades, the blood and gore swamping the command deck providing him with an excellent surface to toboggan the World Eater's armoured legs from under him.

Ceramite plates clashed as the two Space Marines toppled messily. They were still gliding through the bloody mire when their bodies fell from the mezzanine pulpit deck. The warriors hit the bridge stairwell and both smashed and crashed their way brutally down the steps. The berserker landed on his back, slapping the deck for the chainflail that had fallen and died dangerously nearby. Unfortunately, Torqhuil's power axe was still sitting in the macabre filth of the pulpit deck, but he did have his bolt pistol. As he drew the weapon the World Eater got his hand on the stalled chainflail. Swinging it around with one hand the Chaos Marine smashed the Relictor across the faceplate with the barbed thing before backslashing the bolt pistol from his grasp.

The Techmarine landed helmet first in the blood and slime, reaching through the muck for the pistol. Failing he rolled back across, burying the elbow of one armour-enhanced arm into his enemy's contorted face. Up close, the Relictor realised that the World Eater had a pair of upturned, tusk-like sabres. These cracked with the rest of the monster's face, imbedding fang fragments in the Khornate warrior's already brute-ugly features. Spitting blood and smashed teeth at the vaulted ceiling the

World Eater snarled and hammered Torqhuil in the face with a knuckle-spiked gauntlet before backhanding the Relictor once again with a clump of lifeless chainflail, gathered up in the other fist.

This graceless brawling continued until two of Torqhuil's mechadendrite limbs reared and hovered above the prone Chaos Marine before plunging forward with the sharp tips of their servo-claws. The pincers opened as they pierced the corroded deck either side of the World Eater's wrists, effectively pinning the Khornate to the floor. The monstrous demigod went wild, thrashing limbs, snapping his hideous blood-stained maw at Torqhuil and howling his hatred and frustration at the Relictor.

Crawling up through the World Eater's bloody work and over his ancient, armoured form, the Techmarine was calm and deliberate by comparison. Slipping his armoured palms around the Chaos Marine's straining neck, Torqhuil began to squeeze. The maniac warrior bucked and strained, desperate to get its arms free but the armoured limbs were bound to the deck. The grotesque features of the Space Marine suddenly lurched for Torqhuil as the thing arched its back and threw its head forward, butting the Relictor's armoured chest time and again with warped, skull-smashing determination. Torqhuil's grip tightened further as he felt the digits pulverise the knots of muscle and sinew around the Chaos Marine's brawny neck and begin to go to work on the robust vertebrae.

Like some wounded beast of the plains, brought down by a fleet-footed predator, the World Eater's chest heaved and his thrashings ceased for a moment, before the skull-taker began writhing around within the foetid plates of his own armour. What the Techmarine took for more mindless thrashing was something else entirely and as the bones in the heretic's bullish neck began to crack and splinter, the World Eater punched clean through the bloody and rusted space between his chest plate and the shoulder section of his own hate-hallowed armour. How he did this Torqhuil could barely imagine; perhaps inside the shell the monster was an emaciated mess with atrophied limbs and a warped body. It was more likely that the beast was simply so out of its mind with blood hunger and violence that it didn't think twice about dislocating its own arm and shattering its fist. The strategy had worked, however, and the Relictor now found himself with the danger of an unaccounted limb.

The ruined hand clutched at a collection of blood-drenched hides and furs tied about the monster's waist. The World Eater found what he was searching for and Torqhuil suddenly found himself looking down the barrel of a chubby bolt pistol, the muzzle of the weapon crafted to resemble one of the Blood God's single-horned daemonic steeds. Dodging his head to one side, the Techmarine allowed the first few bolts to crash past his ear before releasing his throttling grasp on the World Eater's throat and grabbing for the pistol.

As the two Space Marines fought for control of the sidearm the pistol barked its explosive fury around the command deck, ripping up the walls and runebanks further before doing its worst and slamming a staccato of wild bolts into the reinforced plate glass of one of the bridge port screens. The bolts had failed to penetrate but the impact was enough to initiate a bloom of spidery cracks, sheering through the glass in all directions.

The World Eater gave a bestial roar and threw the muzzle of the bolt pistol point blank back into Torqhuil's face. The Relictor knew he had to end this fast and although not usually given to bouts of furious frustration like his counterpart, batted the unarmoured wrist of the creature aside with one arm before sending his ceramite fist like a jackhammer, straight through the sinew and pulp of the Chaos Marine's bull neck. Armoured knuckles snapped the brute's spine, collapsing the warrior's windpipe and grinding up ruptured arteries. Hanging over the monster with another retracted blow, Torqhuil watched and waited as the last of the World Eater's insensible life left him in a series of grotesque, gulping attempts to fill his lungs with air instead of blood clots and shredded flesh. For the first time in a long time, the abomination stopped fighting and allowed the inevitability of death to take him.

Getting to his feet, the Relictor rescued his axe and reholstered his blood-drenched pistol and went to work on the runebank, literally carving the mnemonic cogitator out of the console section adorning the far wall.

A slurping scrape between his hacking alerted Torqhuil to the danger he was in. Turning slowly, with the power axe held high, the Techmarine came to regard the sickening spectacle of the World Eater, dragging himself and his armour out of the crimson slush. The World Eater's head hung horribly to one side, spine shattered and bloody bubbles frothing from the punchhole in the monster's ruined neck. With one bale eye and the will to kill supplementing the will to live, the Chaos Marine fixed the Relictor with the bolt pistol in one feeble-wristed grasp. The muzzle trembled with the creature's exertions but was steady enough to cut the Techmarine in half if the superhuman degenerate had the oxygen left to pull the trigger.

Torqhuil turned his helmet. He had punched his servo-arms deep into the runebank and was held there motionless under the World Eater's explosive-tip threat. Moments passed. Torqhuil decided.

With the cogitator in his hydraulic grip, the Techmarine tore the mnemonic engine out of the wall and spinning, sling-hurled the hefty mem-bank at the World Eater. Insanely – there still being a little adrenaline left in the warrior's blood – the armoured figure lurched its shoulder to one side, allowing the tumbling mem-bank to pass by. With daemonic determination, the Chaos Marine again brought up its weapon and prepared to fire. It would have, but the mnemonic cogitator sailed straight through the bolt-weakened window behind.

The *Hellebore*'s bridge became a bloodstorm of bodies and howling gales. Snatching at anything that might prove a handhold in the blinding maelstrom, Torquhil secured his footing and held against the shrieking vacuum. As the swirling muck cleared, the Relictor found he was alone – his helmetless adversary taken with the gore he'd undoubtedly helped to spill. Releasing his servo-grip, Torquhil took several magnetic steps across the now cleared deck, before diving at the gaping hole smashed through the bridge port screen.

The venting gale, drawn from the length of the Iconoclast, shot the Space Marine like a bolt-round across the freezing void. It didn't take the Techmarine long to catch up with the mnemonic cogitator – the power of his awkward throw and the inconvenience of the plate glass no match for the explosive force of the depressurising vessel. As the starboard side of the *Malescaythe* grew in size and decreased in distance, Torquhil could see the magnificence of the rogue trader's laser cannons running out in unison. With the cannibal cultists now frost-shattered, Torres had re-established life support in the starboard sections and flooded the gundeck with eager, suited crewmen who set about priming and rolling their gargantuan weapons to bear. The captain, in accordance with her Navy training, wasn't about to leave her enemy combat-capable.

The spectacle wasn't enough to distract Torquhil from the certainty that at present speed he was going to hit the rogue trader. The mnemonic cogitator would be smashed to pieces and its potentially precious data lost. Grabbing at a trailing power cable, the Techmarine pulled the bulky piece of equipment protectively to his armoured chest. Bending his servo-arms around like an improvised cage, the Relictor aimed his hurtling form at one of the vessel's hangar bays. Washing through the pressure phase field, Torqhuil succeeded in avoiding the rogue trader's armoured flank and thunderbolted into the bay. The Space Marine braced for impact. Like a meteorite, he struck the deck with a ceramite-pulverising crunch and then rolled between a pair of Arvus lighters like a whirling firework, showering sparks and smashed servo-harness components.

Hitting the hangar wall with much less force that he would have experienced colliding with the *Malescaythe*'s side, the Relictors Space Marine came to an ugly stop. Still clutching the battered mnemonic cogitator and with patches of his power armour glowing with friction, Torqhuil watched several hangar crew members sprint across the deck with fire extinguishers. As they gathered around the fallen giant, he held up a gauntlet to prevent them from dousing him with carbon dioxide and foam. Several Mercantile Sovereignty serfs were on vox-casters, reporting the incident to the bridge, while others – intent on helping the Space Marine to his feet – were forced back by the heat coming off his armour.

As the serfs confirmed the Relictor's presence on board, Torres gave the order to fire. The broadside rippled down the rogue trader's starboard side, mega-bore laser cannons disgorging raw power and shaking the ship on their slamming carriages. The *Hellebore* took the firestorm at almost point blank range and without shields. The Iconoclast staggered immediately away from the force of the blast, her port side a mess of blazing wreckage and her decks racked with the vengeance of internal fires and explosions.

The Techmarine watched the Chaos vessel fall away. The vox-bead in the Relictor's helmet chirped. It was the bridge. It was Czevak.

'Do we have it?' the High Inquisitor asked, direct and to the point.

'Yes, inquisitor,' Torqhuil informed him. 'We have it.'

Exit

ACT I, CANTO VI

Ship's chapel, Rogue trader Malescaythe, *The Eye of Terror*

Enter CAPTAIN REINETTE TORRES

TORRES HAD INSISTED that the secrets of the *Hellebore*'s mnemonic cogitator be explored in the ship's chapel. The captain reasoned that if the large adamantium aquila, the images and representations of the God-Emperor and the recovered holy artefacts that Torqhuil had installed were enough to restrict Hessian's powers, then it would be safe to store the damned mnemonic runebank there.

Czevak had insisted that it wouldn't be possessed or afflicted and the Relictors Space Marine confirmed that beyond appearing gore-spattered and long in need of blessed oils and maintenance devotions, that the cogitator was simply a piece of ancient Navy technology.

As a door guard of bruiser Savlar Guardsmen admitted her to the chapel, Torres caught the eye of Klute, who was kneeling and offering prayers. He was separate from the group gathered around the cogitator and looked almost apologetic for the lengths of runecable and power lines draped across the chapel pews and altar. It was just another thing to upset the captain, who had barely calmed down after their close run-in with the Khornate destroyer.

The cogitator was a ragged, buckled and filthy piece of equipment that looked like it had been unceremoniously ripped from the bridge of the *Hellebore* by pure force. Wires sparked and components smouldered as they hung out of both sides of the thing, like entrails from a dissected cadaver. The Relictor Techmarine and the High Inquisitor were deeply invested in the workings of the piece, committed to bringing it back to operational life. Following some speedy repairs on his servo-harness and appendages, as well as an Omnissiah-honouring coat of red paint on his deck-grazed power armour, Torqhuil had the cogitator attached to a variety of other pieces of non-standard template equipment, the workings of which the rogue trader captain would rather not be privy to.

Epiphani paced around the gathering in an outfit worthy of the Hive Baptiste Carnivale-Cardinale. A lacework neckpiece ran up into her hair – that in turn cascaded with metallic ribbons; her eyes were a dark spectrum of colour and wire-framed long-gloves and stockings wound up the warp-seer's pale limbs; a bustle completed the piece, supporting the extravagant frills of a pseudo-skirt hanging above the tops of her rivet-picker boots. She was taking an interest in Czevak and the Space Marine's efforts and was completely oblivious to the sacrosanct nature of her surroundings. The servo-skull, Father, hovered above the cogitator, lines running between the smashed bank and grotesque familiar.

Hessian rested, draped across several pews, his head hanging off one of the harsh ferrouswood seats in smug slovenliness, staring upside down at the cogitator and its workings.

'Well, for anyone who's interested – we're clear,' Torres informed them, as if delivering a report. 'If Epiphani's calculations are correct–'

'They are,' the warp-seer inserted with self-satisfaction.

'–then we should reach a safe jump point within the hour.'

'Excellent work, captain,' Klute said, hastily completing his prayers and getting to his feet, when the report drew little in the way of interest from the rest of the room.

'Got it,' Torqhuil complimented himself as one of his intricate tamperings brought new life into the ancient piece of technology. The cogitator hummed and rattled like an old refrigerator unit, tiny wisps of smoke trailing from its controls and cracked runescreen. Data flashed across the display in inanimate panic and a profusion of glyphs and symbols began pouring out of the mnemonic crate on dry, blood-stained vellum. Tearing off a section, the Techmarine admitted, 'Not a dialect I've seen before.'

Czevak took one of the crisp sheets.

'The cultist crew were from Koryban,' Czevak said with confidence, 'but the vessel's point of origin was…'

'The Strigoi Shipyards,' Captain Torres completed for him.

'Would make sense,' Czevak agreed pointing out several patterns on the vellum. 'The long vowels, the harsh roots. Father?'

A short vellum scroll of the servo-skull's own unravelled with some short scratchings inked onto it. Epiphani tore it off.

'Hessian will know.'

Czevak turned on the warp creature, 'Abominate, make yourself useful.'

Czevak handed the paper to the languid daemonhost. Hessian took a disinterested glance at the runes and glyphs and nodded.

'The technacular is Lesser Skattawaul,' Hessian hissed.

'Strigoi,' Czevak nodded.

Torqhuil was already rooting around in a nearby crate. He tossed the High Inquisitor a fresh vellum roll and extracted a tubular interface, made up of a revolving key of signs and symbols.

'I don't have anything that specific,' the Techmarine acknowledged, separating a nearby runecable and connecting the disassociated ends to the chunky conduit. 'But this dia-log should get us most of the way there.' Spinning the symbols on the shaft of tubular keys, he swiftly settled on a sequence. The cogitator runescreen blanked before flashing uncertainly and then gushing forth information in bastardised Gothi-lex.

'I want the *Hellebore*'s mnemonic log,' Czevak told the Techmarine as he went to work on the main bank controls.

'Order?'

'Reverse chronological – starting with the attack on the *Malescaythe*.'

As the cogitator began vomiting forth fresh vellum and its secrets, Torres leaned in, watching the High Inquisitor scrabble through the pages, his eyeballs almost to the ink.

'What piece of information is so important, that you would risk the lives of everyone on this ship to attain it?' the captain asked.

Czevak hesitated. Then, 'This, for one.'

'What is it?' Klute said.

'Two weeks ago the *Hellebore* ran down on an Imperial heavy freighter called the *Pluton* in the Gehennabyss Reaches, much in the same way it ran down on us.'

'So? So what? Imperial vessels lose their way near the Eye all the time,' Torres shot back.

'As the *Hellebore* closed the appearance of the vessel changed. It had been disguised using some sorcerous illusion,' Czevak explained. 'The ship maintained a high-speed pursuit for so long that the *Hellebore*'s runebanks record the vessel sustaining significant damage to its sub-light engines, which must have driven the cultists onboard the raider wild.'

'Why would they do that?' the captain asked.

'Well, firstly – as you've witnessed for yourself, they are insane.'

'And secondly,' Klute added, 'the Blood God reserves a special kind of hatred for illusions, witches and psykers.'

'They're considered unsportsmanlike on the battle-field,' the High Inquisitor said, building further on his former-interrogator's point. 'The *Pluton* actually turned out to be a Gladius-class frigate called the *Rubrician*.'

'The Thousand Sons…' Klute mouthed.

Czevak nodded. For thousands of years, Ahzek Ahriman had had his Thousand Sons Space Marines scour the galaxy for artefacts, arcane knowledge and psychic talent, relentlessly raiding the librariums and reclusia of the Imperium, as well as stealing the secrets of sorcerous power from brother Chaotics and the xenos alike. His thirst for power was insatiable and his ambitions led him to believe that the collective knowledge of the eldar's Black Library of Chaos could elevate him to godhood. It was the Chaos lord's search for those alien halls of arcana and enlightenment that had led Ahzek Ahriman and his lieutenants to Czevak.

'The *Rubrician* is commanded by the Thousand Sons Chaos Sorcerer Korban Xarchos,' Czevak explained, clearly ill at ease with his subject matter. 'What were you doing in the Gehennabyss Reaches, Xarchos?' Czevak thought aloud, fading into concentration. Then to the chapel. 'Ideas? Anything? What would a Thousand Sons frigate be doing in the Reaches?'

'There's not much there,' Torres admitted.

'A few gas giants,' Klute offered. 'A few dead moons.'

'Perhaps they were conducting repairs?' Torqhuil put to the High Inquisitor.

'And yet could maintain a distance far beyond our own and outrun the *Hellebore*.'

'The Reaches are Galactic South of Phanagoria Prime. We had to give Phanagoria a wide berth a few months ago because of some heretic fleet action there,' Captain Torres described.

Klute nodded, remembering the incident. 'Perhaps they were en route to Phanagoria and just passing through the Reaches.'

'At sub-light speed?' Czevak questioned.

'Bad weather?' Torqhuil said.

Czevak turned to the roaming Epiphani, 'Warp-seer?'

'The immateriology of the region is fairly stable. Nothing a Chaos Marine frigate couldn't handle.'

'Come on,' Czevak prompted them all, clearly agitated. 'Think. What interest would the Thousand Sons have in the Gehennabyss Reaches?'

Klute watched Czevak pace the chapel, his face screwed up in a kind of subtle agony, like an addict suffering withdrawal symptoms. Czevak's need for the information – for at least an answer that made sense, to tide him over – was almost physical. Klute remembered the powerful meme-virus with which he had intentionally infected his master just previous to his entry to the Black Library of Chaos. As he paced by, Klute leant in, keeping his voice low.

'My lord, I have drugs in the infirmary that can relieve your symptoms, or perhaps even cure them.'

Czevak shook his head with a scowl before continuing his restless movements. Klute had expected little else from an addict. In that way he was like Epiphani and her Spook addiction. Klute felt ashamed, especially in the shadow of the mighty aquila, that he indulged the compulsions of both.

'Anything?' Czevak insisted.

'What does it matter?' Torres finally said with no little irritation of her own. 'I thought we were heading back to the Cadian Gate.'

'There might be a change of plan,' Klute said, clearly uncomfortable under the captain's glare of betrayal. Settling her backside against the back of a pew, Torres sagged, defeated.

Torqhuil's jaundiced eyes flashed with data he was extracting from the cogitator screen. 'Gehennabyss Reaches,' he began reading off. 'Kerch 161, Sybaris, the Nardanelles, Cravenia Minoris, Vanderdecken's Star, Iskellion XI, Iskellion XII, Arach-Cyn...'

'Arach-Cyn? That's in the Reaches?' Czevak said suddenly.

'On the spinward border. Galactic East.'

'I've never heard of it,' Torres said.

'Eldar crone world,' Czevak clarified.

'You've been there?' Klute asked.

'Many times – there's a warp gate on the surface and a huge archeomarket.'

'You think Korban Xarchos was there to make a purchase?' Klute said.

'An intriguing possibility.'

'Why are we looking for this... Xarchos?' Torres tried one last time. 'What is our business with him?'

Czevak was on his feet, settled. He came face to face with the captain – his eyes dark and sure.

'The Inquisition's business, Captain Torres. Need I remind you that your precious vessel is under charter to the Holy Ordos. Chasing down arch-recalcitrants like Korban Xarchos is what we do. That should be enough for you. That voidspawn sorcerer is responsible for Imperial deaths on a thousand worlds and if not stopped will be responsible for millions more. But that wouldn't matter because his foul legion has long been declared Excommunicate Traitoris.'

'So has Brother Torqhuil's Chapter,' Torres challenged.

Czevak's lip wrinkled and then he gave both the Techmarine and the captain a disarming smile, 'One heretic at a time.' He moved for the chapel door. 'I want to know what business that witch-bastard and the Thousand Sons have at Arach-Cyn.'

'The Gehennabyss Reaches are on the other side of the Eye,' Torres told him coldly. 'It would take weeks to plot and execute a safe route there.'

Czevak pulled an ornate, golden tome from the bottomless folds of his Harlequin coat and shook it at the room. 'And yet my boots will be dusted with crone world dirt within the hour.'

'You're going back through the Lost Fornical?' Klute said with some tension.

Czevak was thoughtful for a moment and then rattled the reflective surface of the ancient text at the gathering.

'Anyone who wishes to stretch their legs is welcome to join me,' he told them and then disappeared through the chapel door.

'Raimus...' Torres began.

Klute looked around the chapel. The Relictors Space Marine, warp-seer and daemonhost stared back in expectation of an order. Even the servo-skull hovered, waiting for something. There was a dread anticipation in their eyes. The inquisitor snorted. He would probably have difficulty preventing Torquhil from visiting the archeomarket, regardless. Epiphani would go just to upset Torres and the daemonhost would simply welcome time away from the draining influence of the chapel and its holy relics. As far as the inquisitor himself was concerned, after decades hunting for his long lost master, Klute didn't really want to let Czevak out of his sight. And that meant only one thing.

'Archeodeck. Five minutes. Go with him,' Klute finally ordered, prompting the henchmen to hurry from the chapel and ready themselves for the excursion. Klute held back and then drifted over to Captain Torres. 'You have Epiphani's course data.'

Torres looked at him moodily. 'It's convoluted and by no means direct, but it's the safest route to the Gate.'

'Get us to the jump point,' Klute said with heavy heart. 'Have the *Malescaythe* start making its way to the Cadian Gate.'

The rogue trader captain frowned. 'You're sure?'

Klute nodded. Torres left, leaving the inquisitor in the chapel wondering if he had time enough for one more prayer before heading for the insanity that was waiting for him on the archeodeck and through the Lost Fornical of Urien-Myrdyss.

Solus

ACT I, CANTO VII

Tyrakesh archeomarket, Arach-Cyn crone world, The Eye of Terror

Enter CZEVAK with KLUTE, BROTHER TORQHUIL, EPIPHANI with FATHER and HESSIAN

INQUISITOR CZEVAK STEPPED out of the warp gate. As Klute and his henchmen filed out after him, the static of inter-dimensional transference still clinging to their armour and clothing, the portal became dormant. Klute turned, quietly disturbed by the fact that the opening he'd just stepped through was now solid stone – ancient and flak-ing. Czevak completed a sequence of subtle hand signals in front of the flowing glyphs and runes etched into the wraithbone that encircled the stone, sealing off the link with the labyrinthine dimension.

Looking beyond the solidified gateway, Klute found that the webway portal was part of the surrounding architecture. He joined the others on a ruined balcony that commanded a view of the structure and the daemon world upon which they had arrived.

The ruins that surrounded them were all that remained of a third storey building. Crumbling artifice and the derelict shells of adjoining chambers and corridors clung to a central column – a grand and ornate spiral staircase that was now little more than fine structural design and stubborn rubble. The derelict column leaned a little like a tower but after some initial vertiginous flutters of the heart, Klute found the ruin to be completely stable. As he rested on the splintered stone of the balustrade, Klute surveyed a world at odds with itself.

As part of his search for Czevak, Klute had had the misfortune to visit several daemon worlds in the Eye of Terror, each more twisted and terrible than the last. Each was warped and corrupted by perpetual exposure to the rawness of Chaos. The unreality of the warp saturated the tenuous reality of their existence and the powerful desires of the daemonic entities that lived upon them crafted their actualities into sub-realities of hellish experience.

Klute had found the Lost Fornical on the nightmarish world that was Iblisyph. Before that he had visited Nardonis, a world devoted to the daemon prince of the same name. The inhabitants of the daemon world had slowly changed to resemble the horrific mutations and gifts that the daemon prince himself had received from his Chaotic sponsor, Slaanesh. Nardonis was the only name used on its surface, for inhabitants and locations alike and the natural geography of the planet had even come to resemble parts of his disturbing and unnatural physicality.

Arach-Cyn was different but no less horrific. The skies of the eldar crone world were an angry mirror of cloud, blocking out the dreadlight of the Eye and reflecting the chaos below. The surface was a swirling maelstrom of blood-blackened sand and earth, constantly boiling and churning. Fragments of ancient architecture and the polished bones of the eldar that once existed on Arach-Cyn were brought to the surface of an earthen ocean of regurgitated history. At the foot of the column there extended a peninsula of stable land, which did not seem to suffer the same constant churning as the rest. It resembled a sandbar breaking the surface of a blood-muddy lagoon. From there Klute saw that a thriving shanty archeomarket had sprung up, with the daemon world's denizens selling the ancient finds that churned up on their shores to the highest off-world bidders.

'Tyrakesh,' Czevak told them with a sweep of his arms. He led them down the spiral steps and out into the twisted sandbar community.

'So often, the physical representations of Chaos frustrate our efforts and become the obstacle to the prize,' he said as they passed through the degenerate shanties and market booths. 'Here, Chaos in all its perversity, has worked the opposite. Treasures both indigenous and imported at some time in Arach-Cyn's considerable history are expulsed from the planet's depths and purchased with ease.'

'Incredible,' Torqhuil mumbled as he cast a professional eye over the myriad of antique wares on offer from vendors in all directions.

The vendors, like the pickets and minders that hung off the stalls, were all gibbering, misshapen savages, a community of eldar monstrosities warped by the planet's malign influence. The fat, antique weaponry pieces clutched by the denizens were largely reclaimed shuriken casters – single shot accelerators primed with grape storms of monomolecular frag. Slipping through the wretches and stalls were other visitors to the archeomarket. Klute could see groups of all but naked eldar, jangling with blades and decorated in revealing scraps of spiked, chitinous armour. Off-world mutants, twisted mercenaries and warp-blessed human cultists went about their business, bawling and bartering with the vendors. Czevak almost walked into a posse of Fra'al pirates, who seemed hungry for confrontation until Torqhuil's hulking form hove into view in his power armour and servo-harness.

The only true currency in the Eye was power and it was this that drew a myriad of its denizens down to the crone world surface. In the supernatural arms race that perpetually existed in dreadspace, advantage was everything. Cursed artefacts and warped technology of ancient and often alien design were routinely unearthed and sold on the bustling archeomarket to bidders of dark purpose. Daemon worlds were as different as they were damned. Arach-Cyn was no Iblisyph, but still harboured dangers of a more subtle kind. The corruptive powers of the warp flowed freely through Epiphani and Hessian but, between the *Atlas Infernal*'s Pariah pages, Torqhuil's purity seals and Klute's baptismal baths, the group experienced some protection from the constancy of the planet's malign influence.

Czevak took in the scene, clearly looking for something. Klute and his team waited by a flaming metal barrel which was warming a huddle of eldar aberrations. The creatures slunk off into the market throng, leaving Torqhuil to admire the vendibles on a nearby stall and Epiphani to pluck her hands from her gloves and warm them by the fire. The blind warp-seer had been resting her hand on the grisly crown of her servo-skull, who had been leading the way; but now, keeping one palm to the fire, Epiphani reached inside her brassiere and produced her snuff box. Taking a lengthy snort of the green crystals, she flared her nostrils before massaging the bridge of her nose. Klute watched, simultaneously fascinated and sickened. Father's blue, bionic orbs feasted on the fire – and Epiphani with him – taking in the lick of the flame and the darkness that danced between the orange tongues.

'Do you see something, Epiphani?' Klute asked quietly among the crowds.

She turned and with no little drama said, 'I see… light in the darkness.'

Hessian cackled in his horrible, infernal fashion and Klute turned away.

'Is that the best you have, child?' Czevak put to the warp-seer but didn't wait for an answer. 'This way.'

'Even if Korban Xarchos was here, he's surely going to be long gone now,' Klute confided in his master as he followed. 'What good can come of this?'

'If he was here, he was buying. If we can find out what he was buying then that might give us some indication of his future intentions. Those intentions might lead us to the bastard sorcerer and he might lead us to Ahriman himself.'

'Thin.'

'Skeletal. But where the Thousand Sons are concerned I'll take what I can get.'

Klute shook his head.

'What?' Czevak asked.

'You. Ahriman. Using the galaxy like your own private Regicide set. He's hunting you; you're hunting him, with the eldar's repository of forbidden lore and the Imperium thrown in for good measure.'

'It does focus the faculties,' Czevak said dismissively.

Klute gave up. 'What are we looking for?'

'Not what. Who. Una Belphoebe. She runs a reclamation operation out here. I've traded with her before.'

Klute didn't want to ask but felt that Czevak was referring to something more than just common bartering.

'Xenos?' Klute asked with rising bile.

'She's a ranger. A Pathfinder. She buys spirit stones and ancient eldar relics from the daemon markets to take back to the waning Iyanden craftworld.'

Klute nodded slowly, knowing that Czevak knew the Iyanden well.

'Here we are,' the High Inquisitor said as they passed

out into a sandy square. At a stall loaded with relics and artefacts and swamped by gabbling degenerates Klute saw a striking figure, tall and commanding – even in the depths of a hood and the camouflage swathes of an eldar cloak-coat. She put up three fingers to the mutant vendor, attempting to make herself understood. An exchange was made in which the degenerate handed her three brightly coloured spirit stones that the figure deposited in a soft belt-bag.

'Belphoebe!' Czevak called but couldn't make himself heard over the din of the archeomarket. She made off into a nest of tents and stalls and Czevak had to dodge between misshapen arach-cynites and the spoiling Fra'al pirates to catch up. With Klute and his henchmen in tow, the High Inquisitor strode through the pathways, rapidly losing the figure in the maze of barter-tents. Stopping to gain his bearings, Czevak found the group hovering behind expectantly.

'Don't you live in a labyrinth?' Epiphani put to him dreamily, pulling one of her boots on tighter. She was still bug-eyed from her hit of Spook.

The retort on Czevak's lips died as he caught sight of the cloak-coat and hood pass across an adjacent junction. 'Belphoebe!' he called again. As she walked on he said, 'How can she not hear me with ears like that?'

Trotting up the pathway, eager not to lose her a second time, the inquisitor rounded the corner only to find himself at the entrance of a large, filthy tabernacle. Tearing the canvas aside, Czevak plunged into the darkness of the tent, increasingly annoyed. As the team followed and the darkness of the space enveloped them the High Inquisitor slowed to a more cautious, 'Belphoebe?'

The gloom suddenly came alive as a network of crisscrossing beams appeared, lighting up the tabernacle interior. The beams were intensities of different tint and hue, each invading the tentspace from the ragged tears and holes in the dirty canvas. The rainbow of targeter dots they projected moved with predatory grace across the armour, garb and bare skin of the group.

'Don't move,' Czevak hissed harshly. Several of the laser sights were moving, converging and building in brightness as they crossed the inquisitor's vulnerabilities, like his heart and temples.

'Good advice,' a voice sailed through the darkness from behind them. Una Belphoebe had been standing by the entrance and had watched the humans blunder in past her. Single beams in succession blinked off as the Pathfinder passed before them, walking up through the middle of the group. 'My rangers have orders to cut you to ribbons with their long rifles if you attempt to do anything else.'

As she brushed past Czevak, she whispered, 'Nice coat.'

'Belphoebe, what is going on?' the inquisitor demanded as the eldar ranger pulled back her hood. 'I'm here to do business.'

The ranger's face was plain for an eldar, enhanced a little by the precious stones embedded in her teeth and the rune-inks swirling off her cheeks and up around her eyes. Eyes that blazed with a rage, the depths of which emotionally stunted humans would never know.

'Business,' she repeated, savouring the word. 'It was foolish of you to return, Czevak – yet knowing you as I do – I suppose it was inevitable.'

'Again, please,' the inquisitor put to her, bemused.

'You're back for those damned pages. I had my men extract the middle sections from each of your heretical tomes – a little insurance if you will – just in case you crossed me.'

Czevak looked to Klute, who was returning a stabbing glare – clearly upset that the High Inquisitor had walked them into unannounced hostilities. Czevak gave his former interrogator a gentle shrug of the shoulders to indicate that he had no idea what the eldar ranger was talking about.

'Belphoebe…'

'Don't,' the eldar warned. 'My ears still drip with the poison of your last set of lies.'

'What lies? I was here–'

The ranger erupted, a stream of sibilance pouring forth from her mouth in passionate mother tongue. She finally calmed and glared accusingly at Czevak. 'You were here one week ago. You took those texts without payment and now you're back for the missing pages – as the extra muscle you've brought testifies. Well, the price has gone up since you've been away, inquisitor. This time it could cost you your life. Now, give me what you owe me, you double dealing mon-keigh.'

'I'm going to reach into my coat now,' Czevak informed the Pathfinder, loudly enough to reach the ears of the hidden rangers. 'As I do, let me tell you that one week ago I was in the Arx Gap with Morton Klortho.'

'And how is Morton?'

'Morton's dead.'

'Convenient.'

'I swear, by Iyanden's mighty fallen, I wasn't here and I have no knowledge of the books or pages you talk of.'

When his hand cautiously reappeared it was holding a clutch of chains, attached to a jangling collection a rune-inscribed spirit stones. Belphoebe froze. These were not the tears of crystallised warp essence that she collected for the Iyanden, to fix to their armour and secure their souls. These spirit stones contained souls already.

'These – among other things – are what Morton gave his life for,' Czevak informed her solemnly. He tossed her the collection of precious stones. 'Consider whatever debt you believe I owe you repaid in full – and then some.'

'Prince Evaelor…' the Pathfinder marvelled.

'And friends,' Czevak added, but the jest was lost on the eldar. 'My researches revealed that Evaelor and his Spectre Companies lost their struggle against Umbragg of the Brazen Flesh and the Rage Lords of Taurm. Morton and I found these around the neck of a daemonette on Oligula Tertius. I recognised the markings immediately. She didn't want to give them up.'

'Prince Evaelor – Iyanden's Lost Autarch.'

Czevak nodded.

'Well, what was lost is now found. You can take him home. Now, if you would be so good as to stand down your rangers then we might be able to get to the bottom of this misunderstanding.' Czevak's voice softened, 'Una, I tell you, I was not here a week ago.'

Belphoebe could barely tear her eyes from the priceless artefacts hanging from her gloved hand. When she did, they were full of thought and conflict. Finally she whispered something into a commmunications device in her native language and the beams cutting their way across the darkness of the tabernacle died in unison. A sag of relief swept through Czevak and his retinue.

'Against the better judgement of my ancestors, I believe you. But somehow you were here. You forfeited payment, posed threat to my blood and stole from me and mine. Explain that to me, good inquisitor,' Belphoebe challenged.

'It might help if you told me specifically what "I" did. What of these pages?'

Rangers – solemn and silent – slipped into the back of the tent behind their Pathfinder. Their camouflaged coat-cloaks were works of art, abstract and entrancing; their smooth helmets were scope-adorned and the silky lengths of their long rifles slung. Long rifles which moments before had been pointed at Czevak and his people at impossible angles through the tattered canvas of the tabernacle.

'You were alone, as usual. You demanded the Vycharis sarcophocrate for reduced payment in sterling adamantium ingots.'

'Vycharis? So the *Skeptoclast* is here?' Czevak said.

'Pieces of it have been surfacing for the past couple of

months, including cargo,' Belphoebe confirmed.

'Excuse me,' Klute interrupted. 'The *Skeptoclast*?'

'A Reliquary vessel fleeing Imperial forces during the failed Vycharis Skeptoclasm.' Czevak informed him. 'It carried the Dark Cardinal's arch-archivist and the palace's extensive collection of heretical tomes and forbidden documents – Cardinal Vycharis undoubtedly hoped to bribe his unholy allies into coming to his aid in the final stages of the failed six-system heresy. The *Skeptoclast* disappeared, however, in the violent warp storms that had plagued the subsector. The Black Library places the craft in the Eye of Terror after that and Henslowe's *Astra Incogna* suggests that it crash landed on Arach-Cyn.'

Czevak returned his gaze to Belphoebe. 'And he – I – looked just like me?'

'Different clothes; your manner though. Insistent. Aggressive. I doubted you would even pay the ingots you promised for the sarcophocrate and so I had my rangers tear out the middle section of each text as insurance. To force you to return and settle accounts. When I saw you'd brought a member of the Adeptus Astartes, I assumed you had come for more than the pages.'

'Your life,' Czevak said, echoing the Pathfinder's words from earlier. 'But Una – this doesn't sound like me. Weren't you suspicious?'

'Very – but you were standing as far from me as you are now. Bronislaw Czevak, as I live and as I breathe,' Belphoebe said.

Czevak and Klute's eyes met.

'The Thousand Sons,' the inquisitors said together, nodding.

'Sorcery and illusions are their way,' Czevak continued. 'It was probably that fiend Xarchos. He would have had plenty of time to perfect his chimeric representations.'

'That was someone pretending to be you?' the eldar Pathfinder said.

'Looks that way,' Czevak agreed, 'if you'll excuse the pun.'

'So, this imposter took the sarcophocrate?' Klute put to Belphoebe.

'No,' the ranger said. 'He rifled it, took two of the texts, resealed it and left – as I suspected – without payment.'

'You still have the crate?' Czevak said with some surprise.

Belphoebe smiled and lifted the jangling spirit stones, 'Czevak, it's yours.'

The Pathfinder led Czevak and his retinue out of the tabernacle, followed by her rangers, and into the maze of archeostalls and tents. Her path led them along the bank, where the bloody earth churned up against the shoreline of more stable land. Klute watched, entranced, as bones, coins and shattered masonry bubbled to the surface as well as several larger items: half an arch, a wraithbone stabiliser fin, a smeared firing prism.

Here Belphoebe greeted another of her rangers, who was sitting at the entrance to a marquee that was sheltering Belphoebe's reclamation purchases. The tent was packed to the canvas roof with crates and bundles, wraithbone technology and chests of spirit stones. The Pathfinder led Czevak and his people in. While Epiphani and Hessian looked decidedly bored, Brother Torqhuil examined the exotic pieces around the marquee with interest. The ranger on the door kept a careful eye on the armoured hulk to make sure he didn't steal anything. Belphoebe went straight to a filth-encrusted sarcophocrate in the centre of the tent that stood upright and was taller than the Pathfinder. The markings were Imperial, the seals ancient and the casing rusty and pitted.

Czevak looked to Klute and then rubbed his palms together.

'So this thing's full of heretical tomes?' Klute asked.

'The Dark Cardinal had an extensive library,' Czevak

answered with enthusiasm. 'Let's get this sarcophocrate open.'

He was about to proceed to the seals when something strange happened. A deep glow built from within the sarcophocrate, blazing an azure radiance that bled from every rust hole and warped seal. Light in the darkness.

'Belphoebe?' Czevak managed, suspecting a double-cross.

'Not mine,' the eldar ranger confirmed fearfully.

The metal door of the crate blossomed with frag as bursts of bolt-rounds exploded from inside. An explosive volley caught Czevak in the side, tearing up the exotic material of his Harlequin coat and punching the inquisitor through a stack of Belphoebe's crates and bundles.

'Czevak!' Klute bawled as his master was brutally felled.

The door of the sarcophocrate was slammed to the floor as the goliath inside stepped out. Its Iron-pattern power armour was pure, cerulean beauty and its helmet a nest of Coptic ornament. The suit shoulder plate bore the mark of the Thousand Sons – the eternal image of a serpent eating its own tail, and in its gauntlets it clutched a smoking bolter.

'Rubric Marine,' Brother Torqhuil spat through clenched teeth. The Rubric Marines were victims of the most powerful of the sorcerer Ahriman's spells and enchantments. The bodies of his Space Marines had been turned to ash and dust, their obedient souls sealed inside their armour for all eternity. Unquestioning, unbreakable, unstoppable.

'Destroy it!' Klute commanded, running to his master's aid.

The Techmarine's servo-arms and mechadendrites flicked out with sharp and sudden hostility. The Rubric Marine began an indefatigable march from the sarcophocrate, moving like a mindless automaton. Torqhuil stormed at the Chaos Marine but found that despite its monotonous movements the thing had searing reactions and laid down a withering arc of fire. This forced the Relictor to sidestep and take cover behind a recovered wraithbone pillar.

A rainbow of sights beamed through the smoke pouring from the barrel of the Rubric Marine's relentless weapon. The Chaos Space Marine halted momentarily to look at the colourful dots as they moved frantically across its armour. All remained weak, however, displaying none of the intensity they displayed while zeroing in on the vulnerabilities of Czevak and his henchmen. It seemed that the walking suit of armour had no such vulnerabilities. The marquee became a lightshow of blasts and sparks as Belphoebe's rangers lanced the monstrous thing with sniper fire. Las-bolts slashed off the Rubric Marine's chest and helmet with futile precision and coordination. It half stumbled for a moment under the barrage but recovered and stomped on through the las storm, returning deadly fire.

As the blasts lessened, the blue colossus went through the perfunctory motions of a reload. Torqhuil came out from behind the pillar with both gauntlets wrapped around the grip of his bolt pistol. He hammered several rounds at the Rubric Marine, each flashing off the curvature of the ancient armour. Hessian suddenly appeared beside the Chaos Marine from behind a stack of crates and latched himself onto the Thousand Sons Space Marine's weapon. The two fought for ownership of the bulky, archaic bolter, the strength of both monstrosities coming from some unearthly place. Both attempted to shift the weapon but came up against the immovable hold of the other. The Rubric Marine's helmet angled slightly in what might have been confusion. Hessian's lip curled, ruining the comely lines of his face and the letters under his skin seared the flesh from beneath, sizzling and

smoking. The daemonhost head-butted the Chaos
Space Marine in the grille plate with his horn buds,
knocking the monster's head back. The Rubric Marine
held onto the bolter with one determined fist, however, and with the other gauntlet – still wrapped
around a replacement magazine – smashed the daemonhost to the floor with one pneumatic strike.

By the time Torqhuil came at him from the other side the
Traitor Marine had slammed the clip home and blasted
the bolter – close range – at the Relictor. Torqhuil battered
the weapon aside with a swing of his servo-arm, sending
the bolter wide and blazing into Belphoebe's rangers as
they attempted to enter the marquee and snatch their
leader to safety. The Rubric Marine held onto the weapon,
despite the force of the blow and it took a backslash from
the Techmarine's clawed servo-arm to knock the bolter
from the Chaotic's grasp. One of Torqhuil's other bionic
attachments found its way into his enemy's grip, however, and the Rubric Marine span around its considerable
centre of gravity and propelled an off-balance Torqhuil
through a forest of crates and cargo containers.

As the Chaos Marine bent down to retrieve its bolter,
Epiphani walked for the marquee entrance. The Spook-
induced smirk had been wiped from her face by the
dramatic turn of events and the young woman found
herself at the mercy of timing. With her palm on Father,
the warp-seer allowed the servo-skull to lead her from the
fray, casually plucking a stiletto blade from her boot – an
outfit accessory – and slicing through a collection of marquee support lines.

As the tent collapsed over the Rubric Marine and its
search, Klute crawled through the exposed path of destruction that Czevak had carved as the Chaos Marine's bolter
fire had in turn carved through him. Heart in his mouth,
the inquisitor reached his unconscious master, Czevak's
body limp and akimbo across Belphoebe's destroyed
collection.

Mercifully, Klute found a carotid pulse and moved swiftly on to exploring the site of the wound. Czevak was suddenly back with him, the High Inquisitor sucking in a gulp of air. He spasmed and grabbed out at Klute.

'Son of a–'

'Sir! Thank the God-Emperor. Czevak!' Klute screamed at the inquisitor, desperate to keep him still. 'Don't move. I need to find the point of entry.'

Breathless, Czevak continued to squirm, feeling inside the plucked material of his Harlequin coat and extracting the burnished, unblemished cover of the *Atlas Infernal*. The armoured surface of the text had absorbed the wrath of the barrage. Klute slumped into thankfulness and shook his head. Finally getting air to his lungs, the High Inquisitor seemed more concerned about potential damage to the Atlas than his own well-being. That was until inhalation brought a dull agony from his side.

'Hurts like hell,' Czevak hissed through his teeth.

'When you were shot, the force of the impact drove the tome into your ribs – probably broke a couple.'

A stream of bolter shot screamed skyward, cutting a slit through the collapsed canvas. The Rubric Marine was suddenly out of the tent and striding with inevitability towards the two inquisitors.

'Klute!' Epiphani called.

'Get back!' Klute called, slipping the Cadian street silencer from the folds of his robes and working the pistol's lever action.

'No,' Czevak grimaced through his pain and grasped the inside of Klute's elbow. The inquisitor shrugged him off and turned.

'Go,' Klute said softly before unleashing the roar of silver and Saint Vesta's salts on the Rubric Marine. With blessed scatter shot hailing at the impassive force advancing towards him, Klute watched as the repeated blasts sparked, sizzled and spat off the surface of the Rubric

Marine's unholy armour. 'Go!' Klute howled at his master who lay transfixed by the approaching Rubric Marine.

Czevak narrowed his eyes, searching both his mind and his surroundings for possibilities. Belphoebe had been snatched away by her rangers and his retinue were smashed. Snarling through the stabbing throb of broken ribs, Czevak slipped the *Atlas Infernal* into his coat and rolled over. Crawling arm over arm across the collapsed canvas of the marquee, away from the Thousand Sons Space Marine, away from certain death, the High Inquisitor heard Klute's shotgun run dry. Craning his neck, Czevak saw the Rubric Marine batter the inquisitor mindlessly aside with the sweep of one ceramite arm. Czevak knew what was coming next. He willed it on.

'Come on, you abomination,' he called, daring the Rubric Marine to follow him. Czevak felt the extra weight on the canvas as it shifted slightly under him, the power-armoured figure's heavy steps coming up behind. Arm over arm he clambered, with pain cutting through his broken side. He turned over, kicking away from his assassin across the undulating material.

'Come on!' Czevak roared at the Chaos Marine.

The Space Marine trudged on across the material, grasping the grip of its weapon and turning it on the inquisitor.

'Come on!'

Two more steps.

Czevak felt a sudden tug on the canvas. As the Rubric Marine stepped off the tent-covered shore, it sank. The heft of its bulky armour went well beyond the weight distributing effect of the material and the Chaos Marine plunged into the churning ocean of regurgitating blood and earth below. Czevak would have whooped in triumphant delight but the sinking Space Marine was still bagged in canvas; the further it sank, the closer the inquisitor was dragged towards the monstrosity on the gathering material. The traitor had dropped its weapon in favour of spreading its arms and slowing its descent. As Czevak slid ever closer the thing reached out for him. The inquisitor was sure that the Rubric Marine intended to drag him down to the daemon world depths with it.

Twisting and squirming in hot agony, with broken ribs grating in his chest, Czevak crawled across the moving canvas and bubbling ground beneath, out of the Rubric Marine's grasp and up onto the stable bank. The material slipped out from under him, rolling the inquisitor once more onto his back. He watched the Rubric Marine's snatching gauntlet disappear beneath the blood-black, earthen waves, followed by a torn length of marquee canvas.

As the excruciating pain in his ribs pushed him towards unconsciousness again, like the advancing tide of a sea of darkness, he saw Epiphani and Father at Klute's motionless side. Torqhuil was making his way out of the wreckage of reclaimed artefacts, followed by a dazed Hessian. The blasted bodies of bolt-felled rangers littered the ground and a crowd of degenerates and visitors to the archeomarket had gathered in the gaps between the tents and stalls to witness the spectacle.

Among the filthy rags of the daemon worlders, Czevak fancied that he saw a coat he recognised. Pushing through their hunched, deformed ranks was a figure from his past. The gaudy patterns and the sting of colour; the hood and the mirror mask. Vespasi-Hann was here. The Shadowseer was here. The Harlequins were here – to take him back.

Belphoebe was suddenly at his side, her words and face choppy and unfocussed in the gathering gloom.

'Rest,' she whispered gently. Czevak's head fell back with his eyes pitched at the ghoulish crowds. He searched for the Shadowseer and the silver doom of his mask, but the Harlequin was gone. And with that, Czevak went also.

Exit

I

INTERREGNA

Grand cabin, Battle cruiser Indomitable, *Above Cadia*

CHORUS

'THIS DOESN'T MAKE sense.'

High Inquisitor Bronislaw Czevak looked at his new interrogator with ancient and irritable eyes across the scriptorium desk. The cabin was no longer filled with the static of the inquisitor's scratching stylus – only the accusation of Czevak's sour gaze.

'Is it not enough that I have to work with the infernal noise outside? For Throne's sake child, could we at least not have silence in here?' Czevak asked Kieras.

'The positions in these transcripts are diametrically opposed,' Kieras went on, unperturbed.

Through the blast doors that covered the great cabin's rear viewport, the thunder of battle intruded. The vessel trembled as *Indomitable*'s rear void shields soaked up the cannon fire of an enemy vessel crossing its wake.

'The God-Emperor did not thrust you upon his blessed Imperium to make sense of some grand design,' the ancient told him. The acolyte knotted his slender brow further, drawing the rings and piercings that decorated his Harakoni features together with a slight jangle. This, among many things, annoyed Czevak about his new apprentice. He had been Klute's choice, since during the High Inquisitor's sabbatical in the Black Library, Raimus Klute had attained rank as an inquisitor of the Ordo Xenos in his own right. Although Klute had been charged with Czevak's security, following Czevak's return to the Holy Ordos, it had made sense to the former interrogator to give Czevak his own interrogator, Ferdan Kieras.

'You are but one shard in a shattered mirror,' Czevak told him, grasping his ferrouswood cane and limping across the cabin unaided. His time in the Black Library had been highly restorative, and although the High Inquisitor still felt his four hundred and eight years on his sagging face and racking his ancient bones, he no longer had need of his suspension suit with its body frame and artificial atmosphere. His smock and waist-coat still draped off his sharp bones like sacking and the ornamental fringe of his hanging cummerbund caressed the deck bearing the sinister emblazonry of the Ordo Xenos.

'One shard in a shattered mirror reflecting a thousand truths, off a thousand other shards. And you ask for the mirror whole.' Czevak grunted his disdain. 'The search for a divine truth is a fool's errand and even if you found it, it would be beyond your comprehension to understand it.'

As though Czevak had said nothing, the interrogator continued.

He read off one transcroll, 'Address to the Council of Ryanti, "Only a galaxy pure, purged and free of the filth xenos will be fit for the Emperor's return. You who have enjoyed freedom, who have done nothing to earn it, your time has come. This time you will stand alone and fight for yourselves. Now you will pay for your freedom in the currency of honest toil and human blood."'

'What a pleasure to hear back what I wrote only minutes ago,' Czevak said acerbically, above the rising din of the naval battle.

'Then,' Kieras continued, 'the Conclave of Har. "There is a terrible darkness descending upon the galaxy, and we shall not see it ended in our lifetimes. A time of inconceivable horror is about to begin. A time that mankind with all the might of the Imperium cannot endure, when the strength of the xenos eldar fails. Even now, our doom stalks us across the stars. The light of that ancient civilisation has run its course. It is humanity's turn to take up the torch and become an elder race. It is the time of the God-Emperor's return, time to continue what he started and unite the galaxy under one beneficent cause."'

'So?' Czevak barked as he re-took his throne. 'So what?'

'These messages contradict one another.'

'You think I've lost my mind, interrogator?' Czevak asked him with slow menace. 'Old and confused? Perhaps polluted?'

'No, High Inquisitor. I meant no offence,' Kieras assured him with submissive syllables.

'Offence?' Czevak said as more impacts rumbled through the battle cruiser's superstructure. 'That is all you are capable of giving with your incessant, needless questions, you foolish child.'

In the months since his return from the Black Library, Czevak had come to miss the silence. Ask the eldar a question and you would receive three answers – all terrifying and all true. The xenos had long outgrown the need to ask successions of stupid questions, a trait that Czevak had come to greatly appreciate. Back among humankind he was constantly bombarded with simple inquiries from the mouths of simpletons. The grand cabin doors parted to admit an alabaster-faced astropath, who had arrived to take and telepathically transmit the High Inquisitor's many transcripts. His many unfinished transcripts. The psyker stumbled and a collection of scrolls tumbled from the scriptorium desk as the *Indomitable* rocked again.

'How goes the battle?' Czevak charged the hooded figure.

'I know nothing of the battle, sire. Only your will,' the astropath replied solemnly.

Czevak grunted. He despised the questions of others but was and always had been a man of questions himself. More so since Klute had infected him with the voracious meme-virus, just prior to his entry to the Black Library. An inquisitive nature was not a poor attribute in an Imperial inquisitor and he could certainly stomach Kieras's questions better than uninvolved, blind obedience. He routinely questioned the authority and motives of others and expected no less from his compatriots.

'Wait outside,' Czevak told the astropath, to which he received immediate compliance. The High Inquisitor turned to the interrogator.

'Since my return from the Black Library of Chaos, my name has become... somewhat celebritised,' Czevak admitted to him. 'Not at my instigation – I assure you. It was inevitable I suppose. I carry the burden of many secrets and there are many who would like to alleviate me of that burden. To every crooked Radical I am a figurehead – a fount of knowledge. To the Puritans I am more dangerous and contaminated than ever – but they too would have those secrets before burning me atop a heretic hive. And the Chaotics and cultists, they covet my knowledge endlessly.' Czevak's face softened in grim contemplation.

'Only yesterday a report came across this very desk detailing a living autopsy chamber, discovered by Klute's agents investigating a Tzeentchian cult called the

Cryptoclidii on Ingolstadt. It seems their plan was to capture me and extract my brain, in the hope of psycho-slicing the secrets out of it. Madness. This is what the galaxy has come to.'

As the High Inquisitor paused, Kieras went to ask a question, but stopped himself.

'There is little I can do about the predations of crazed cultists,' Czevak admitted. 'Even Imperial ones. My own misguided Cardinal Carodoq heads a citizen crusade in the Spurcia subsector to have me declared a Living Saint of the Creed Imperial. Meanwhile the Witch Hunter, Pavlac razes worlds that would host my conclaves and executes inquisitors that would meet and hear my words on the charge that we are all pawns of the xenos or the Ruinous Powers. The only way to end this insanity is to be all things to all people.'

'So we're not going to Har?'

'Or to Ryanti. Or to the hundred other places I have sent dictats. They are all deadrocks, places to which cultists, witch hunters and false friends will be drawn but cause little harm. Well, apart from to each other. And I will lose little sleep over that.'

'A campaign of misinformation,' Kieras nodded.

'Also a little something to keep the more moderate Radicals and Puritans appeased. And the resulting equipoise...'

'...will abate the Amalathians like Lord Goredon and Grand Master Specht,' the Harakoni interrogator completed. 'So where are we going?'

'If we can break this blockade,' the High Inquisitor confided, 'Hydra Cordatus. Klute has organised an actual conclave in the Sentinel Worlds. I am but one man. There I can make my position known to others and put a little of the knowledge I have gained on my travels to good use.'

'But which of the many positions you have advocated, is actually your own,' Kieras asked.

'Get me to Hydra Cordatus and you'll find out,' Czevak told the Harakoni.

Czevak's stylus bounced off the scriptorium desk as the cabin suffered a sudden judder and the excruciating whine of forced metal quaked through the floor, walls and ceiling.

'What the hell was that?' Kieras blurted.

'That was no cannon blast,' Czevak said. Bells and klaxons started to echo up the battle cruiser's corridors. 'Something hit the ship. And close.'

Keiras was on his feet with the elongated barrel of his autopistol clear of its holster. The two men waited. Listening. Praying. From inside the vessel there was the discharge of weaponry and shouting. From outside, the growing intensity of enemy laser batteries tested the integrity of the void shields.

'Put that away,' the High Inquisitor told the interrogator. 'Naval security can—'

The cabin entrance slid open. The aperture was door to door Naval security. The chamber was suddenly full of cobalt carapace, dark-visored helmets and tactical lascarbines. They were all around Czevak within moments like a shield of bodies, lifting him from his feet.

'Lieutenant Van Saar, sir,' the security officer identified himself curtly. 'High Inquisitor – the ship has been breached and Inquisitor Klute has ordered me to escort you to the aft shuttle bay. Please excuse the informality.'

With that, the security detail hustled the High Inquisitor from the grand cabin and out into the corridor, knocking the alabaster-skinned astropath to the ground as they passed.

'Are you the High Inquisitor's pilot?' Van Saar put to Kieras directly.

'I'm his interrogator,' the Harakoni replied, 'and his pilot.'

Grabbing Kieras by the arm the lieutenant jogged up behind his detail dragging the acolyte beside him. As

Kieras passed the downed astropath he called, 'The High Inquisitor's messages on the scriptorium desk, send them, now!'

'As you wish,' the astropath droned as the two men were bundled out of sight.

The corridors and passageways flashed by Czevak, jostled as he was and taking only one step in ten himself. Between the carapaced bodies the High Inquisitor got the impression of wailing klaxons, scrambled troops and little else. Several times the security detail had to be re-routed by their lieutenant because of blazing firefights or life support failures in battle damaged sections and compartments.

As the detail exploded from the corridor and out into the open space of the small shuttle bay, they fanned out with their lascarbines thrust forward. They assumed a cover formation around the lone Arvus-class lighter, two of the visored detail running the High Inquisitor to the shuttle. Kieras arrived moments later with Lieutenant Van Saar. From another entrance, Inquisitor Raimus Klute strode across the hangar floor, his neatly trimmed moustache and robes at odds with the gore-splattered medicae apron and gloves he was wearing.

As Czevak's limbs once again became his own he caught sight of his former interrogator, flanked by one of his henchmen, a turbaned Imperial Guard veteran, wearing the colours of the Gurdeshi Colonial Rifles and carrying a grenade launcher.

'Raimus, what's happening? Are you all right?'

Klute looked down at the blood.

'None of it's mine. The sickbay was hit. Most of the medicae staff incapacitated. I'm just helping out. We've been boarded in engineering, starboard. Naval security will hold them off but it's only a matter of time until our blockade run grinds to a halt. We've sustained damage and the *Indomitable* is already slowing.'

'Options, inquisitor?' Czevak put to him.

'None for the *Indomitable*, my lord,' Klute said honestly. 'Chaos cruisers, escorts and just about everything else is running down on us as we speak. Captain Landau has contacted the *Ramilles* and the *Anatoly Ascendant*. They should be able to provide fire support and evacuation within a few hours.'

'A few hours!' Czevak burst.

'No options for the *Indomitable*, but one for you, my lord,' Klute said gravely. 'There is a closer vessel. Landau informs me that we're passing the moon of Bast. An Inquisitorial Black Ship corvette on a purgation sweep answered our call. The *Divine Thunder*. She doesn't have the sort of firepower to aid us in the battle ahead but she's sleek, fast and more than able to continue the blockade run. I have used Grand Master Specht's authority to commandeer the vessel for the journey to Hydra Cordatus. Saint Joaqhuine and your security detail await your orders there.'

Czevak nodded, impressed with his former interrogator's strategy and coordination – all the while up to his elbows in the blood and guts of Navy grunts. Klute might have become an Imperial inquisitor but he would always be a member of the Officio Medicae Imperialis.

'Gather your people,' Czevak said.

'No sir, there's no time for that,' Klute insisted. 'In a few minutes I'll give Captain Landau the order to change our course. You will be off the *Indomitable* by then and the battle cruiser will slow further to draw the enemy's fire and continue the chase. That will give you time to get to the *Divine Thunder* and then time for the *Divine Thunder* to get away.'

'Don't be an idiot, Raimus. Get on the shuttle.'

'Can't do that, sir. I'm going to finish what I started here. I've asked these people to give their lives for you to have a fighting chance to get to the conclave. I choose to share their risk. With the Emperor's blessing, we shouldn't be far behind you on the *Ascendant*.' Czevak shook his head with a mixture of vague guilt and admiration. Klute put a bloodied glove on Kieras's shoulder. 'You're in good hands here; Ferdan is an excellent pilot.'

Kieras nodded and started climbing the cockpit ladder, up past the shuttle's nameplate: *Bucephalus*.

'Say hello to Joaqhuine for me,' Klute added, walking backwards across the deck, then, 'Lieutenant Van Saar, take four of your men and escort the High Inquisitor to the safety of the *Divine Thunder*.'

'Yes, inquisitor.'

'If you'll step aboard, my lord,' Van Saar said to Czevak, 'we appear to be a little pushed for time.'

As Czevak stepped inside the lowered passenger compartment with his Navy security detail he put a hand up to Klute.

'I'll see you at Hydra Cordatus.'

'God-Emperor willing,' Klute called back as Kieras fired the engines of the Arvus lighter and the belly compartment began to rise into the main body of the shuttle. Czevak watched Klute and his Gurdeshi henchman return to their improvised sickbay before the door on the passenger compartment slammed shut.

By the time the compartment lamps came on, the Navy grunts were already strapped into their seats. The lieutenant directed Czevak to a small throne under an observation window set in the shuttle roof.

Kieras's Harokoni lilt filled the compartment.

'Buckle in High Inquisitor, if you will…'

Van Saar swept on – seemingly everywhere – checking the harnesses on his men and then helping the aged inquisitor with his throne. The lieutenant snatched a vox headset and gave it to Czevak, before taking his own seat.

'…something tells me this won't be a smooth passage.'

'They rarely are, child,' Czevak voxed back. 'So just to put the good lieutenant and his men at ease, you have done this before young Kieras?'

'Before I was your interrogator, I was Inquisitor Klute's

acolyte; before I was the inquisitor's acolyte, I was his personal pilot.'

'Good, good,' Czevak mused sardonically. 'Just didn't want to raise any pulses.'

'The Chaotics will see to that, my lord.'

Through the observation window, Czevak watched the hangar vault rotate as the shuttle completed a manoeuvre that the inquisitor only fully appreciated in the pit of his stomach. Kieras was very comfortable at the controls of the shuttle, Czevak soon came to understand as the Harakoni pilot blasted the Arvus craft out of the hangar, around and along the length of the *Indomitable*.

The damage to the battle cruiser was considerable, the grandeur of gargoyle-encrusted architecture replaced by mangled wreckage and the inferno of internal fires sweeping through the decks. The *Indomitable*'s void shields were still operating, deflecting the long range sporadic energy blasts of enemy cannon fire. This led Czevak to believe that the battle cruiser had been rammed or at least broadswiped by another colossal vessel.

From out of the *Indomitable*'s colossal wake, Czevak saw their attacker emerge. It had undoubtedly been a vessel once, but now it was something else, a daemonic fusion of craft and creature. The vessel's mid-section was a metallic mass of writhing bodies, crude and gargantuan. Obscene orifices and protrusions served as horrific weapon batteries and the Chaos vessel's bulbous aft trailed a profusion of whip-like tails that gave the daemonically possessed vessel an unnatural manoeuvrability. Breast clusters bled an ichorous substance down the vessel's length and the prow came apart like a thick, muscular claw, eager to reach out for the *Indomitable*'s fleeing form.

Behind the possessed cruiser blasted a flotilla of other vessels, Chaos escorts and freighters – twisted and heretically altered – eager to descend upon the daemonship's leftovers. Beyond the length of the trailing column, Czevak could see the permafrost and deep ocean splendour of the Cadian fortress-world. Since the Despoiler Warmaster's 13th Black Crusade had begun, the skies of Cadia had been dark with vessels, fleets Imperial and Traitor alike, swarming above the gateway world and contesting its future in blood and broadsides. Czevak had met with Admiral Quarren, the Imperial Navy's ranking officer in the sector and found him to be a surprisingly imaginative and competent officer, giving the High Inquisitor hope for Cadia's future. Daily, however, Warmaster Abaddon's united legions poured from the Eye, through the Cadian Gate and straight at the sitting fortress-world. Czevak had read plenty about Ezekyle Abaddon and his threat to the galaxy in the Black Library of Chaos and could feel little but pity for the billions of Cadians upon which the Warmaster's disciples were descending.

As the *Bucephalus* surged past the length of the *Indomitable*'s laser batteries, Czevak could make out the dreadful damage they had done to the daemonship's unnatural structure. This had no doubt allowed the battle cruiser to pull away, but that tactic would end with the sabotage carried out on the Imperial vessel's engineering decks. Czevak couldn't bear to think about the *Indomitable* in the clutches of the monstrous thing.

The daemonship's revolting claw-prow yawned open once again, this time revealing a sphincter bay within the pincer's recess. The possessed vessel spasmed and a throng of Swiftdeath fighter craft shot from the prow.

'Kieras!' Czevak called down the vox.

'I see them, inquisitor. Stand by for evasive manoeuvres,' the Harakoni returned. Czevak nodded silently to himself as the twisted fighters razored their way up the Imperial battle cruiser's colossal starboard side.

Laser banks on the Swiftdeath's narrow wings danced fire off the *Indomitable*'s ornate hull as Kieras tried his best to make use of the cover fast flying by. The light-storm intensified as the swarm of fighters closed the gap. Like the Navy grunts in the passenger bay, Czevak's fingertips cut into his harness as the Swiftdeath fighters rocketed up behind the stately pace of the Arvus lighter.

At the last moment, Kieras threw the craft to starboard, away from the protective influence of the battle cruiser's side and out into the exposed blackness of empty space. Czevak lurched as the Chaos fighters flashed past on their original, unswerving course. The High Inquisitor watched in sickening disbelief as the Swiftdeaths drifted wide themselves and then gracefully cornered. The *Bucephalus* made its own less graceful turn as Kieras threw the Arvus immediately back at the battle cruiser's superstructure, surging up rather than along the *Indomitable*'s flank.

Czevak followed the response of the Swiftdeaths as they careered around and shot up after the shuttle. It was difficult enough for Czevak to keep track of the lightning bolt movements of the Traitor fighters but the inquisitor thought that his ancient eyes were playing tricks on him as he saw the dozen craft suddenly melt into a miasma of smaller, even faster moving objects. Then it hit him.

'Missiles!' Czevak yelled.

'Preparing countermeasures,' Kieras said, amazing Czevak with his composure.

The cloud of missiles streamed along the *Bucephalus*'s wake.

'Firing countermeasures!' the young Harakoni pilot called and the shuttle bucked as it launched its one and only chaff cloud into space. 'Hold on!' the interrogator bawled as he intentionally threw the Arvus shuttle into a tight spin – a manoeuvre that the craft was clearly not designed for.

As the missiles detonated in the cloud of counter-measure chaff, the Chaos pilots sliced through the blaze. Kieras must have predicted such a move, Czevak reasoned, as the *Bucephalus* indulged a vomit-inducing continuous roll. The slashing fire from Swiftdeath wing banks cut through the open space between and around the Arvus's spinning wings.

For heart-stopping moments, the shuttle felt out of control. Kieras attempted to maintain their life-saving rotation yet simultaneously rolling with the curvature of the *Indomitable*, as both the Arvus lighter and the Swiftdeath swarm blasted across the topside of the battle cruiser. Despite the interrogator's brave manoeuvre, several las-blasts clipped the rear of the *Bucephalus*, blasting out the passenger compartment lamps and rocking the shuttle.

Suddenly, the need for the Harakoni to regain control became even more acute as the hull of another vessel surged up from the port side of the *Indomitable*. Czevak recognised the lines of an Inquisitorial Black Ship immediately. The corvette was passing dangerously over the battle cruiser in a desperate attempt to reach them.

This time it was the sluggish top velocity of the Arvus that saved their lives. Slamming the protesting craft into a gut-renching reverse thrust, Kieras awkwardly took them out of the spin, using the remaining centrifugal force still aching within the structure of the shuttle to turn them away from the corvette's armoured side. Several of the Swiftdeaths were not so fortunate, Czevak noted from the dizzying view of the observation window. The Traitor pilots' speed freak ways taking them into the brief blaze of thunderbolt impacts fired from the vessel's hull. Two more attempted a suicidal wrench on the stick and tried to ride out an attempt to fly over the Inquisitorial ship only to mangle themselves in the purity seals and high wrought decoration of the vessel's side. The remainder made their turn and rocketed away – clearly outclassed, but as the corvette heaved itself over the battle cruiser its turrets lit the darkness of space with thick beams that cut a path of oblivion through the half-swarm and scattered the rest.

As Kieras forced the *Bucephalus* into a blunt course correction, aiming for the hangar bay of the moving Inquisition corvette, he began to struggle.

'We have a problem,' he reported, his calm slipping. 'I'm losing control.'

'We have a fire!' Lieutenant Van Saar called, unbuckling himself in the tight confines of the bay and reaching for a compartment extinguisher. Czevak watched from the observation window throne as acrid smoke filled the tight space. The Swiftdeath firepower had found its way to something essential and the *Bucephalus* was fading fast.

Then Czevak heard the words he had been dreading.

'Impact positions!' Kieras screamed.

'There's a fire!' Van Saar called back, somewhere in the maelstrom of smoke, foam and limbs.

The High Inquisitor found himself fading as the poisonous fumes seeped through the lungs in his aged chest. He began to cough and wheeze. The observation window suddenly flashed with hangar bay lighting. The Arvus lighter hit the deck and then hit the wall. It all happened so swiftly that there was little time to think. Although the throne, its belts and its buckles kept the High Inquisitor's frail body in place, the compartment itself was smashed this way and that. Czevak couldn't tell which way because the passenger bay and observation window were thick with smoke and the flash of flame. His ancient body wouldn't tolerate such treatment however, and the High Inquisitor felt his hip jar and fracture. Czevak howled in agony.

As everything ground to a nauseous halt, panic and a base survival instinct began to set it. Navy grunts were burning and screaming. There was shouting, some of it relating to the fact that the lieutenant was badly injured. Someone was shouting that the hydraulics that lowered the passenger compartment and opened the door were not working. Czevak couldn't be sure but he suspected

that the *Bucephalus* was at an odd angle. It had probably lost one of its landing gears in the crash and had
a wingtip to the deck. That probably explained why the
compartment couldn't lower. The vox simply bled static
and in the confusion and alarm it was all Czevak could
do to pathetically claw at his throne straps and gulp for
air.

Searing light was suddenly everywhere. The unbearable sound of torched metal accompanied the blinding
brilliance. Specks of molten hull sizzled into Czevak's
robes and skin, then suddenly the gush of fresh air.
There were hands on the High Inquisitor and knives
to his throne straps. Czevak was roughly hoisted from
the choking chamber and passed through a succession
of arms, until he was unceremoniously deposited on a
stretcher carried by two burly Ordo Hereticus serfs. He
roared in pain as his broken hip was twisted from side
to side. The serfs buckled thick belts across the stretcher,
ensuring that the inquisitor was firmly strapped down.

Czevak could see black smoke gushing from the hole
where the observation window had been. The Naval
security detail were screaming for their lives inside and
the rear of the Aquila lander was las-smashed and in furious flames. The cockpit was even worse, having crunched
into the side of the hangar. Much of the *Bucephalus*'s
nosecone, weaponry and port side was mangled into
the wall and with miserable dismay, Czevak saw Kieras's
head and body resting against the shattered armaplas of
the blood-splattered canopy.

'Seal it,' a voice sailed over the gurney.

'What!' Czevak finally managed through a fit of coughing and lung wrenching convulsions. 'What are you
doing?'

The Inquisitorial serfs who had cut him out of the
shuttle wreckage proceeded to replace the observation
window and plasma torch it back into place, with the
Navy grunts still trapped inside.

Czevak yanked himself from left to right, wriggling in his restraints, shouting incredulously at the figures atop the smashed lighter and then at the figure who'd come to stand over him.

She was a member of the Adepta Sororitas, Czevak was certain of that, although the absence of power armour and weaponry marked her out as a member of one of the Orders Minoris. She wore a ribbed, leather body glove and a carnodon fur cloak; the only armour she did wear was decorative plates of ceramite on her shoulders and crafted around her bust. Her gloves, boots and decorative loincloth were all intricately flame lined in gold thread. She looked down on Czevak through a wire spectacle assembly, building in a multitude of different lenses – presumably for close work. Her long, grey hair was wound into buns on either side of a youthful face that had clearly benefitted from rejuvenation work but had failed to remove the sly droop of one side of her rouged lips.

As the Ordo Hereticus serfs completed their welding the screams inside the downed shuttle reached a crescendo. Czevak wrestled against his restraints as the shrieking and pleading died away. As it finally went silent, the Sister nodded for the hangar extinguishers to be brought in to handle the exterior flames.

'Why?' Czevak demanded in a wheeze.

The Sister didn't answer, then into a handheld vox-link she said, 'Captain, inform the *Indomitable* that we have received the High Inquisitor. Wish them good luck and the God-Emperor's speed. Once you're clear of the Bast moon and the battle you may make your warp jump. Voightdecker, out.'

'Voightdecker…' Czevak repeated. He was sure that he'd heard that name before.

'Sister Archangela Voightdecker, Order of the Eternal Candle. Pleased to meet you at last, High Inquisitor Czevak,' she said with no little pedantry.

The Order of the Eternal Candle, Czevak did know. The

Sister's Order specialised in the reclamation of ancient Imperial relics and artefacts for the Ecclesiarchy.

'I want to see the ranking ordo representative on this vessel, right now,' Czevak seethed.

'Inquisitor Malchankov is indisposed as we speak, but he has set aside some time for the both of you later.'

Malchankov. Something died inside Czevak.

The Sister directed the Ordo Hereticus serf bearing Czevak's weight to lift him again. 'Take the High Inquisitor to his quarters. Ensure that he is comfortable.'

Half the ship away, through a maze of dread, dark decks and long corridors, the serfs walked the restrained Czevak into a lightless chamber in the bowels of the Inquisitorial Black Ship. Dropping the stretcher on the harsh, filthy floor of the cell, the serfs left Czevak, howling in his restraints, in hip-fractured agony. As they closed and locked the door, the deep cold of space began seeping up through the frozen floor and into the High Inquisitor's defeated body.

Solus

I

ACT II, CANTO I

Infirmatory, Rogue trader Malescaythe, *The Eye of Terror*

Enter KLUTE

AFTER THE CLAMOUR on the bridge, the infirmatory was a haven of peace and silence. Once again, Klute had been asked to arbitrate in a disagreement between Captain Torres and Epiphani. As a warp-seer, Epiphani could read the currents, movements and dangers of the Eye in a way that a Navigator never could. Klute had trusted her to take the *Malescaythe* safely to the destinations he had given her in the most perilous of places and the inquisitor felt that the girl required some genuine credit for this. Epiphani could be childish and erratic, however, and liked nothing more than upsetting Reinette Torres. The captain had her ship, crew and future as a rogue trader to worry about and it couldn't have been easy entrusting all of those to an infantile warp addict. When

Epiphani directed the vessel through the Heigel Rapidity instead of the safer but more circuitous San Korvus Cascades, Torres had been furious. This had resulted in the captain bawling at Epiphani on the bridge regarding her hazardous fancies, while the warp-seer gave her provocation in the form of a glazed, Spook-addled grin. Again, Klute had been forced into the unenviable position of acting as adjudicator and parent. This, on top of the guilt with which Klute was already racked, as a result of ordering the vessel back to Nemesis Tessera at all. It was Czevak discovering that the *Malescaythe* was en route to Imperial space that Klute dreaded. That was when the sparks would truly fly.

The only sparks flying in the infirmatory presently were those from Klute's pipe flint. The inquisitor was only an occasional pipe smoker, usually indulged in moments of relaxation or contemplation. The tobacco blend was his own – mostly a mixture of medicinal and nectared – that was sometimes effective at taking away the pounding headaches with which the inquisitor was occasionally afflicted.

Drawing on the pipe and ensconced in a cushioned chair, Klute put the heels of his boots up on Czevak's cot. The High Inquisitor had been unconscious ever since they had returned to the *Malescaythe.* Klute closed his eyes – alone with the throb in his head – but his peace did not last long.

Czevak was awake. With a sharp intake of breath, the High Inquisitor sat upright – eyes alert, mouth unsmiling.

'Where is it?' were the first words escaping his downturned lips.

'Welcome back,' Klute said, fluttering his eyes back to wakefulness and chomping down on his pipe.

'I'm serious,' Czevak insisted coldly.

'You never were a good patient,' Klute said before taking Czevak's Harlequin coat and throwing it to the

High Inquisitor. Czevak thrust his hand into the inside pocket, tensed and then relaxed. The *Atlas Infernal* was safe.

'I took good care of it for you,' Klute insisted. 'The damn thing saved your life.'

'Wouldn't have been the first time,' Czevak mused. The High Inquisitor twisted his torso from side to side with a face full of expectation.

'I braced the ribs and gave you a morphia shot straight into the marrow. You won't feel them for a week.'

Somehow, Czevak found his way hesitantly to unfamiliar words. 'Thank you.'

'What I should have done is broken a few more to restrict you to a bed,' Klute told him. 'That – on Arach-Cyn – that was close.'

'If that thing had wanted us dead, very little would have stopped it,' Czevak informed the inquisitor regarding their encounter with the Rubric Marine.

'Very little did stop it,' Klute reminded his friend. 'And you were shot. Looked like it definitely wanted you dead.'

'Thousand Sons Marines are excellent marksmen. That was just an unlucky shot. Xarchos wants me alive – as a prize – to take back to his unholy master.'

'Ahriman,' Klute nodded.

Czevak raised his eyebrows and slipped out of the blankets on his infirmatory cot.

'Talking of Arach-Cyn,' the High Inquisitor began, rubbing his chest and probing his ribs with fingertips. He slipped his Harlequin coat on over his bare back and drawstring infirmatory slacks. 'How did we get back to the ship?'

'Your ranger friend,' Klute informed him. Una Belphoebe and the remainder of her rangers had escorted Klute and his beaten retinue through the myriad tunnels and junctions of the webway, back to the Lost Fornical. What was a labyrinthine nightmare of similarities and

inter-dimensional perplexity seemed a fairly straightfor-
ward journey for the eldar rangers. Torqhuil carried the
High Inquisitor's unconscious form over one shoulder
and two of the Pathfinder's rangers carried the precious
sarcophocrate that Czevak had purchased.

'She was returning to Iyanden, but she had a message for you,' Klute said.

'Would it be something like, turn myself into the
Harlequinade – for my own protection,' Czevak
hazarded.

'Something like that.'

'And the sarcophocrate.'

'On the archeodeck.'

Czevak immediately started barefoot for the infirmatory bulkhead. Klute shook his head as the High
Inquisitor left.

'I'm fine, by the way,' Klute said to himself. He took
a long draw on his pipe. 'Just a few cuts and bruises.
Nothing serious, thank the Emperor – but thank you
for your concern.'

'Gather your people,' Czevak called back up the corridor, his voice growing more distant with every step.
'And I'm going to need some more clothes.'

Taking a further couple of puffs on his pipe, Klute
rubbed his temples. The thunder in his head was getting worse. He flicked the deck vox-switch on the wall
nearby.

'Klute to bridge. Captain Torres, would you be so
kind as to meet me on the archeodeck in five minutes.
Please have Epiphani bring Hessian down from the
chapel. I trust Brother Torqhuil is already there. Klute
out.'

By the time Klute had found his way to the archeodeck, Czevak already had the derelict sarcophocrate
open and was rifling its contents. The inquisitor
wasn't happy with the way his people were similarly
gathered about the crate, taking the vacuum-sealed

texts and small artefacts that Czevak was handing them. Torqhuil was re-stacking them on an itinerant table for ease of transportation to the archeodeck reliquaries. The Space Marine checked them against the sarcophocrate's inventory while Father hovered nearby and catalogued the items. Torres was standing on the other side of the table, perusing the texts and relics for worth while Epiphani and Hessian knelt by the box in front of Czevak, flicking through the damned, priceless tomes before handing them to the Relictor Space Marine like bored students in a library. Epiphani had changed – yet again – prompting Klute to consider where they might be going, the prognostic opting for a rubber jump suit – verdigris and copper coloured and ribbed throughout. It made the warpseer look like some forge-world menial but Klute was sure that the outfit was the height of fashion somewhere. She completed the outfit with shiny hip boots and a poncho of layered plas.

'So this belonged to Cardinal Vycharis?' Klute asked.

'Part of the Dark Cardinal's extensive library,' Czevak replied as he continued digging through the contents.

'Heretical tomes and Chaos codicia, buried at the heart of a daemon world,' Klute said cautiously. 'Should we really be rummaging through it like that – without... precautions?'

Czevak barely noticed him.

'And without clothes?' Klute added irritably, throwing Czevak the garments he'd gathered for him. Czevak grabbed them, stood up and proceeded to dress himself right there before them.

Klute shook his head. 'God-Emperor protect us.'

The Guard issue briefs and socks Klute had gathered from the Savlar stockade – Klute appreciating no little irony in stealing from members of a kleptomaniacal penal regiment. The Navy tailcoat, braces and breeches were all from Captain Torres's ensign; the Cretacian hunting boots and a white, full-dress shirt with copious ruffles of fine lace were his own. He'd never had occasion to wear the boots and he positively hated the shirt.

'You're too kind,' Czevak remarked before slipping the thing on over a defined, athletic chest that bore a lifetime's worth of marks and scars.

'Hive Baptiste; very fashionable, I'm told,' Klute assured him.

'Epiphani?' Czevak asked buttoning the shirt.

The warp-seer nodded, 'Hive Baptiste? Fashionable? Yes. Before the Heresy.'

Czevak grunted. 'Where are the pages Belphoebe removed from these texts?'

Klute took them from his robes. They were ragged and torn but had been tied in a neat bundle with dirty string. He tossed them to the High Inquisitor who began fingering through them feverishly. The meme-virus flowing through his veins and infecting his brain was never more evident. His eyes blazed across the pages, soaking up the heretical detail.

'Father, what's missing?' Czevak asked without taking his eyes from the parchment.

Vellum unspooled under the hovering servo-skull. Torqhuil took the trailing scroll.

'*Kronochet's Anatomae* and the *Corpus Vivexorsectio*,' the battle-brother read.

'That's what Korban Xarchos was doing on Arach-Cyn,' Czevak concluded with confidence. 'He used his illusory powers to impersonate me at Tyrakesh and secure the contents of the *Skeptoclast*'s sarcophocrate.'

'And the assassin?' Torqhuil asked.

'It wasn't an assassin,' Czevak corrected the Techmarine. 'It was an opportunity, an ambush or abduction. Xarchos was simply betting that I would return to Tyrakesh at some point. The Rubric Marine was primed with some opportunistic enchantment and would have waited for a thousand years if it had to.'

The High Inquisitor continued to thumb through the clutch of extracted pages.

'What would he want with those particular texts?' Klute asked. 'He left the rest.'

Czevak kicked the rusted sarcophocrate.

'There's undoubtedly some interesting material here,' Czevak said. 'Would have thrilled arch-recusants like the Dark Cardinal and his depraved followers but only one or two of them have any real power or use to sorcerous witch-fiends like the Thousand Sons. *Kronochet's Anatomae* I know of; it is a diabolist manual detailing both the material and immaterial features of daemonic physiology. The eldar held a copy in the Black Library of Chaos. It is well known but exceedingly rare and very few have actually been privy to its contents.'

'What of the other?' Klute pressed as Czevak extracted pages from his collection.

It was the Relictors Techmarine who answered with solemn importance.

'The *Corpus Vivexorsectio* is a technical tract drawn from the collected Malifica writings and experiments of a Dark Mechanicus sect called the Daecropsicum.'

'You know of this sect?' Klute asked.

'Their shame is secret but still haunts the infotombs of the Cult Mechanicus on Mars,' Torqhuil told them dourly. 'The Daecropsicum had perfected the art of summoning daemonic entities into corporeal form while using arcane and experimental Geller technologies to perform daemonic vivisections. Their belief was that warp creatures were solely the sum of their parts – in fact it was their parts that interested the Daecropsicum the most. They created obscene fusions of harvested infernal organs and Mechanicus technologies from their tortured daemonic subjects and bound exorcised essences to artefacts and weaponry.'

'So Xarchos intends to use this tract to summon daemons...' Klute said.

'...and perform "living", if that's the word, autopsies on them, harvesting their parts and associated power,' Czevak said.

'Like the Daecropsicum, he intends to bind these parts and powers to objects and relics,' Torqhuil added. 'A factory – if you will – for creating daemon weapons and cursed artefacts.'

'I take it that such a tract would be of great use to you, Brother Torqhuil,' Klute asked fearfully.

'It would be a powerful weapon.'

'A weapon to create other weapons in an existing daemonic arms race – not exactly what the galaxy needs,' Czevak said. The High Inquisitor felt the rumble of an objection build in the hulking chest of the Space Marine and added, 'On the other hand, it might be fun to take Hessian apart and bind him to different objects about the ship.'

'Try it,' the daemonhost dared playfully.

Czevak ignored the abominate creature.

Torqhuil came up behind Czevak, dwarfing the inquisitor. Czevak held a fistful of pages above his head and the Relictors Space Marine took them.

'If you want the text then you have to find the man,' the High Inquisitor said.

'So Xarchos took the tome but there's no way of telling where the *Rubrician* went next,' Klute said.

'We're still interpreting the *Hellebore*'s mnemonic log,' Torqhuil informed them, looking through the pages. 'There's a good thousand years of data on there – but no other encounters with the Thousand Sons frigate have come up so far.'

'We don't need to know where Xarchos has been, we need to know where he's headed,' Czevak corrected them. 'Epiphani?'

The warp-seer got up off her knees and straightened her transparent poncho, drawing attention to the rubber underneath.

'All I know is that "we" are heading somewhere wet,' Epiphani admitted.

'Well, that narrows it down,' Klute said with more of an edge than he intended. He probed the balls of his eyes with finger and thumb, hoping to rub the pain away.

'Brother Torqhuil, what do the pages we have actually detail?' Czevak asked. He wasn't familiar with the Dark Mechanicus codilect.

'These pages describe the design and orientation of the Geller technologies required to vivisect a captured daemonic entity,' the Space Marine said with obvious fascination. 'Truly remarkable psychosurgical tools and procedures.'

'Yes, well, before we run off and join the Daecropsicum,' Czevak cut in, 'is it fair to assume that Xarchos will not be able to complete the rituals described in the *Corpus Vivexorsectio* without those pages?'

'The Thousand Sons wield great sorcerous power,' the Techmarine acknowledged. 'They can certainly raise daemons and bind them to weapons and objects using a myriad of different ceremonial rites and costly rituals. Very little could match the procedures outlined in the *Corpus Vivexorsectio* for economy and power, however. The Daecropsicum perfected the craft. Using their procedures, the enormous effort and energies required to bring a warp entity into the real world could be used to create a thousand damned objects and weapons – each with different capabilities and powers – rather than a single weapon possessed by a single entity. Without knowledge of the complexities of psychosurgical dissection, however, the *Corpus Vivexorsectio* is just another diabolist manual for summoning the dark creatures of Chaos.'

This seemed to please Czevak.

'Do the Daecropsicum still exist?' Klute asked fearfully.

'Like my own Chapter, they were annihilated by the Ordo Malleus,' Torqhuil continued. 'That pig, Cyarro, and

a half company of Grey Knights put not only the Daecropsicum but every man, woman and menial construct
on the surface of the fabricator moon of Feldspar to the
sword. Feldspar was then purified from orbit to prevent
salvage hunters scavenging from the Adeptus Mechanicus world. Politics between the Mechanicus and the Holy
Ordos are strained to this day. None of the Daecropsicum
adepts remain however, only their collected works.'

'Looks like the trail has gone cold,' Klute decided. 'At
least we've frustrated Korban Xarchos and his like.'

'Let's not be too hasty,' Czevak said. 'Amongst the Dark
Mechanicus codilect, I saw the true names of daemonic
entities.'

'The subject entities of failed warpthereal vivisections,'
Torqhuil told him.

'And what of the successful ones? You said they perfected the procedure.'

'The *Corpus Vivexorsectio* in the main follows the successful execution of one ritual procedure from beginning to
end. The subject entity's true name is Mammoshad.'

'Mammoshad…'

'You know of it?' Klute asked his master.

Czevak nodded. 'Mammoshad is a daemon with a long
and illustrious history – even before this Dark Mechanicus cult got their scalpels into it.'

'Powerful?'

'Yes,' Czevak nodded absent mindedly. 'Well, at least
before the Daecropsicum cut it up into tiny pieces. Its
name comes up in texts both xenos and Imperial all over
the Black Library. A very old and powerful Tzeentchian
daemon. Its full title is Mammoshad – King of Kings,
Enslaver of the Craven Worlds and Keeper of the Vault
Abyssal.'

'I don't understand,' Torres threw in from the table, disturbing the High Inquisitor's train of thought. 'Is this a
problem for us or a solution?'

'Both,' Czevak answered her. 'As with most solutions, it

comes hand in hand with its own set of problems. Mammoshad's name will have been used throughout the rest of the tome. Korban Xarchos may not have the pages detailing the heretical Geller technologies and the procedures but he might be able to lay his hands on someone who witnessed the procedures first hand.'

'But Brother Torqhuil said that the Daecropsicum was annihilated,' Torres said.

'Mammoshad was there,' Klute declared.

'Who better to detail the procedures and technologies than the daemonic entity that suffered them?' Czevak explained. 'If Xarchos finds Mammoshad then he won't need the pages. If we find Mammoshad then perhaps we can lay our own trap for Xarchos.'

'Where's Mammoshad?' the Relictor Techmarine asked.

'Well, the Black Library places it – or at least a bound piece of the daemon–' Czevak told him, 'on the hive-world of Ablutraphur.'

Klute watched Captain Torres's eyes flick across at his own. Klute had asked her to engage in a series of relatively safe warp jumps and sub-light crossings to take them towards the Cadian Gate and out of the Eye.

'But the *Hellebore*'s log already places the *Rubrician* some way into such a journey,' the rogue trader captain warned.

'Don't worry about that,' Czevak assured them with new-found enthusiasm. 'The webway will get us to Ablutraphur far in advance of Xarchos, even with a head start.'

He started for the Lost Fornical, sitting inactive as it was on the other side of the archeodeck. 'Epiphani's right. Pack for an equatorial Ablutraphurn summer, hot and wet.'

Exeunt

I

ACT II, CANTO II

Archeotech hoard 3°4'33"S 37°21'12"E, Ablutraphur, The Eye of Terror

Enter CZEVAK with KLUTE, BROTHER TORQHUIL, EPIPHANI with FATHER and HESSIAN

'HOW MUCH FURTHER?' Epiphani whined.

'You tell me,' Czevak said. The inquisitor was enjoying making fun of her gift.

Torqhuil led the way up through the haphazard collection of chambers, grottos and stairwells – the logic being that if their crumbling surroundings could sustain the weight of an Adeptus Astartes, it could bear the weight of anyone else in the party. The Techmarine's suit lamps lit a path through jumbled architecture that was distinctly Imperial but ancient, fractured and claustrophobic. Crevices led to landings, archways to steps, crawlspaces to ladder-hatches. Sometimes the collapsed kingdom of caves and undercrofts opened up through a shattered ceiling, revealing the colossal chasm of which their benighted realm formed the floor. The space above them was black and empty, the beams of the lamps disturbing flocks of flittersnappers, but occasionally a circle of daylight was visible many thousands of metres above them – giving the impression that they were inside the bottom of some dormant, man-made volcano.

The warp-seer puffed out her cheeks. 'I think I'm going to be sick.'

'Incredible,' Czevak shook his head as he climbed past her doubled form. 'I bring you across light-years of space in mere hours and you retch at a few steps?'

The group had left the webway through a toppled wraith portal, now a gateway in the floor. The retinue had some difficulty at first re-orientating themselves to their surroundings. It wasn't just moving from one dimensional state to another or from the horizontal to the vertical; the small cavern into which they climbed was ink-thick with darkness and drowning in rubble, ancient detritus and a ramshackle hoard of priceless archeotech.

As the High Inquisitor kicked up dust on the derelict stairwell, bounding three steps at a time, he came to an abrupt stop – staring at the wall.

'What is it?' Klute called through the gloom from behind.

'Abominate,' Czevak said. 'Get over here.'

'You have need of me, High Inquisitor?' Hessian hissed with spiteful servility.

'I need you to shut up and get over here,' Czevak insisted.

The evil behind the daemonhost's eyes lit up the darkness with a sickly hue and illuminated the age-splintered wall. Robust vines had punched their way through the masonry, twisted, bunching and constricting their fat way through the rockcrete. The vines, creeper shoots and root anchors snaked their way skyward up the inner wall, aggressively twisting about and throbbing their way through tiny gaps and fissures.

As Klute came up behind, their Space Marine point man paused on the steps above. The warp-seer remained but Father drifted in for a better view, seeing for both of them.

'See this,' Czevak said, indicating the vines.

'Great, now we're stopping to admire the flora,' Epiphani complained.

'You will want to admire this. This means we've reached ground level. Brother Torqhuil,' Czevak called prompting the Techmarine to descend and join them.

Czevak went to touch the bulky servo-harness from which Torqhuil's mechadendrite limbs and servo-arms sprouted. Gears whirred, lines stiffened and counterweights shifted as the Relictors Space Marine retracted suspiciously.

'I mean your armour no disrespect,' Czevak assured the Techmarine, the High Inquisitor understanding that the Mark-VIII Errant armour's machine spirit would not tolerate desecration. 'What have you got there? Give me one of the pneumatic lines to your servo-arm.'

The Space Marine was still wary, but had been with the High Inquisitor long enough now to appreciate method in his madness. With a hiss of equalising air pressure, Torqhuil unclasped the pneumatic line to one of his claw-like appendages and handed the rigid hose to Czevak. Taking the tapered pin-point end of the line attachment, the High Inquisitor selected a knotted nest of vines that had bundled near the base of the fractured wall where the destructive vegetation had originally breached the ancient stonework. Stabbing the sharp point of the line through the waxy surface of the vine, Czevak nodded to Torqhuil, who twisted a small valve on his harness, allowing pressurised air to pump down the line and into the body of the plant.

'It's a vapour fig,' Czevak informed the retinue. 'See, these amazing organisms work by growing shoots up through holes in the rock and then slowly releasing gases through tiny tubes and cavities that run through the vine, hydraulically expanding and shattering the host surface.'

'Fascinating,' Epiphani lied. 'What are you doing?'

'Just speeding the process up a little, doing in seconds what would ordinarily take years,' the High Inquisitor told her.

As the pneumatic line pumped air into the vines strangling the wall masonry, expanding the fat creepers and tendrils, rents and splits began to splinter their way across the ancient rockcrete. The group backed both up and down the steps as stone began to crumble and shatter into dust about them. As the exploratory vines of the vapour fig ballooned, chunks of masonry began to fall away. The wall emitted an excruciating gasp as it fought and lost its battle with the invasive plant and in a cloud-shower of pulverised dust and grit, disintegrated.

Coughing through the nebulous rockcrete and shafts of swirling sunlight, Czevak ventured forth. As an Ablutraphurn dawn blazed its way through the ragged opening, spooking swarms of flittersnappers beyond, the group was struck by the sub-tropical mug that rolled in from outside like an elemental force. They were bathed in a foetid heat and haze and began to drip with beads of humidity that formed like a second surface over their cool skin and armour.

As Czevak strode through the stone mist and the pumped network of vapour fig vines, the others followed, stepping out onto a tangled incline of rubble and twisted foliage. The High Inquisitor picked his footholds carefully as he skipped from felled pillars to ruined chunks of rockcrete and corroded struts and girders, all of which were ensnared in a carpet of dank shrubbery and crawling with rust mites that took to the languid air in lazy clouds.

They were standing on the rubble-strewn side of a man-made mountain that rose thousands of metres above their heads. Similar structures dotted the landscape beyond, islands of architectural collapse rising out of a carcinogen swamp that oozed and percolated with both pollution and ablution. Carbonic sedge and fern palms dominated a mangrove wetland of acidic peat, cancerous fungi and petrochemical floodwater. The vegetation was a sickly sulphur in colour, which clashed horribly with the stagnant expanse of the floodplain, reflecting as is did the puce dreadlight of the Eye from the sky above. In the distance a colossal structure dominated – a swollen hive city, like a ripe pustule, reaching out of the filth in the hydrocarbon haze. This was the Ablutra Hive, the planet's reeking capital. The urban nightmare sat in a shallow sea of its own waste, perpetually fed by the torrents of sewage and industrial contaminant spewing from its broken drains and terminus pipes. This environment created new opportunities for the hardy and adaptive flora and fauna of the burgeoning hive-world and soon Ablutra and its sister hives came to crown the carcinogen swampland that rapidly colonised the toxic flood.

The hive and its surrounding spire remnants had formed a network of powerhouse manufacturing metropoli, the plasfibre sweatshops of which had supplied Cadia with cheap, durable flak armour for the fortress-world's vast regiments.

Between the 12th and 13th Black Crusades, the Eye of Terror expanded, bursting its borders and rolling its thunderhead of warp storms and dreadspace out into new territories. Ablutraphur had been one of the planetary causalities and now, cut off from the Imperium and under the influence of Ruinous Powers, the stinking plasmills of Ablutra were more likely to be manufacturing armour plating for the False Castellan's Unbound, the

Blightlanders and various other cult armies of the Great
Lord of Decay.

Picking his way carefully down through the scree and
mangrove tangle, Czevak made his way to the shoreline, the retinue in dumbstruck tow. As an ancient and
abandoned satellite hive, the derelict highland formed a
mountainous island upon which the bubbling, methanogenic fenwater of the wetlands lapped.

'Is that where we're going?' Epiphani called down the
slope, the warp-seer now intent on complaining about
their descent rather than the climb.

'What we seek is in Ablutra – yes,' Czevak confirmed,
standing at the water's edge. He mouthed, 'How are we
going to get across there?' as the same words fell out
of the psyker, for once able to predict the prognostic's
actions.

Czevak allowed the question to hang in the rank
humidity as Klute and the team joined him. He fully
expected to have an answer for them by the time they
arrived and was as surprised as they were at his continued silence.

In the end, all he could manage was, 'It can't be that
deep,' as the group stared out across the muckscape
of sluggish channels, fermenting pools and peat bog
islands that were held together by nothing more than
the decaying root architecture of carbonic sedge and
palm anchors.

Objections died in the throats of almost everyone
present as the oily waters beyond the shore suddenly
began to churn and vortex. A wide, flattened jaw of huge
dimensions was opening beneath the surface, allowing
a small lake to flow in down its huge, inflating gullet.
Czevak and his team stared down its gaping, toothless
and seemingly bottomless throat as the beast feasted
on the filtered methanogenic organisms swarming in
the captured sluice. The gulping giant was repulsive to
behold. Although not equipped with the daggered maw

of a man-eater, the sudden appearance of the umbrella-jawed behemoth from the mire shallows had given the band a taste of what dangers the carcinogen swamp had to offer.

'Depth doesn't seem to be the problem,' Klute said and the five of them backed away from the swelling shore.

An unexpected coolness drew Czevak's eyes skyward as the sunrise was momentarily blocked from sight. Sensing danger from above, rather than below, the High Inquisitor crouched. Klute and the others followed suit. With dawnlight once again burning their faces, the retinue followed the progress of a vehicle that had passed overhead. It was all but silent, accounting for the fact that nobody – even Torqhuil with his superhuman hearing – had detected anything out of the ordinary above the gurgle and slosh of the swamp. A balloon, made of patchwork plasfibre and rigging, reinforced and filthy. A rough methane burner on gimbals rotated between heating the air inside the balloon and providing steerage. Beneath the airship was suspended an open plasteel frame from which dripped chains, tackle and a large torsion engine, resembling a giant ballista or crossbow hanging from the airship and pointing towards the ground. Swale gypsies swarmed both the rig and rigging in their filthy rags, desperate to crank the windlass and prepare their jumbo harpoon for launch.

Hiding in the long sedge, Czevak and the team watched as the balloon swung in from above and fell towards their position. The wicked grapnel tip of the harpoon passed over their heads before gaining a little altitude off the shore. Here the balloon hovered, waiting for the moment to strike. The hideous monster surfaced again, gulping half the channel in one impossible mouthful. The ballista fired explosively and the gypsies buried their uncompromising weapon in the wide head of the beast. The harpoon speared the monster through the mouth – the grapnel releasing on the tip. As the gypsies cheered and locked off their line the filter feeder spasmed, rolling this way and that, desperate to free itself. With the lightweight frame bucking and chains jangling back and forth, the swale gypsies secured themselves by hooking the plasteel bars with the inside of elbows and knees. The gypsy in charge of the blast valve hit the burner and took the airship up into the sky, dragging its monstrous catch out of the shallows. While still huge, the creature was mostly mouth, the rest of its body a trailing, serpentine tail with primitive gills and pectoral sails running down the considerable length of the beast.

'High Inquisitor,' Torqhuil warned Czevak. 'Multiple targets closing on our position.'

'Oh no,' Czevak said flippantly to himself. He had been hoping for such an intervention ever since they had spotted the balloon. Czevak nodded to the Relictor, thankful for the Space Marine's enhanced senses. Both Klute and Torqhuil went for their weapons but the High Inquisitor waved them down. Czevak had no doubt that his henchmen could handle a group of gypsies. As patient prisoners, however, they might all be treated to free passage to Ablutra and avoid the worst of the swamp.

'Follow my lead,' Czevak told them.

The mangrove was suddenly alive with bodies crashing through the ferns. Swale gypsies were everywhere in their filthy, plasfibre rags and headdresses, jabbering at them in a guttural mixture of bastardised Low Gothic and shanty-speak. The gypsies were unkempt and hairy with faces full of hoops and cheap trinkets. They thrust the barrels of blaze-dribbling flamers at them, the battered methane tanks of which they carried like satchel bags on their hip. What appeared to be the swale gypsy leader came forward, a stubgun and holster on his belt and a pair of scavenged magnocular goggles in his headdress. His face creased with fury and demands.

Czevak raised his hands. 'Follow my lead,' he said with hushed insistence.

Torqhuil looked down with infuriation on the angry little men with their primitive weapons.

'I don't know if I can do that,' the Space Marine told the High Inquisitor.

'You're sure?' Klute said as gypsies darted in, slapping his robes aside for his sidearm.

'We surrender,' Czevak told the gypsies confidently in Low Gothic.

Klute and Epiphani raised their arms, while Hessian settled for the grin of an imbecile. The Relictors Space Marine brought his servo-arms in close to his harness so that they appeared a little less threatening. He couldn't bring himself to do anything with his actual arms. The gypsies instinctively gave the Space Marine and daemonhost a wide berth but were very hands on in their prompting of the inquisitors and the warp-seer.

The retinue were marched through the mangrove and along the putrid shoreline. The gypsies walked about them with their chugging incinerators at the ready, led by the be-goggled leader, who every few steps stabbed his stubgun into Czevak's back in insistence. The High Inquisitor took this with good grace at first, but on the seventh or eighth jab started to get the feeling that the be-goggled leader was enjoying it. 'We surrender,' Czevak told him in slow syllables that even the jabbering gypsy should have been able to understand.

For his trouble he got the gaping muzzle of the stubgun in his face.

Rounding the overgrown spire of the island, the group saw the sickly sky fill with balloons both large and small: one man gyro-blimps, harpoon-trailing sky hunters and largest of all, a hovering shanty settlement of canvas and corrugated plasteel – all held in place using a ramshackle collection of plasfibre balloons of different shapes and sizes, draped in chains and rigging. The be-goggled leader took them to a chain-ladder hanging from the underside of the floating community and prompted them to climb, which Czevak did with enthusiasm and aplomb and his companions less so.

Climbing up through a hatch in the shantytown deck, Czevak stood up only to find himself doubled back over when almost immediately the stock of a flame thrower slammed him in the stomach. The High Inquisitor gasped and went down on his knees, gagging on his incredulity.

'We surrender!' he wheezed. 'Do you understand?' he asked an approaching gypsy with a greasy beard. 'We offer no resistance. We are happy to go with you.'

The bearded escort ignored the High Inquisitor's insistence and two gypsies grabbed and half-dragged his winded form across the rusty surface of the deck. His flame-prompted team followed, requiring considerably less instruction.

'You should have let me tear them limb from limb on the ground,' Torqhuil rumbled from behind.

'I still might,' Czevak croaked, turning his head in acknowledgement but his custodians shook him back around roughly. Gypsies screamed at them in shanty-speak to remain silent.

As the group was escorted across the scrap-welded decking, between corrugated shacks and canvas extensions, the ragged community of men, women and children stopped on the rigging and rope-bridge walk-ways, showing the newcomers their hostile eyes and browned teeth in a universal expression of dislike and distrust. Around and above them the raggedy caval-cade of balloons and airships soared, while about their legs, narrow-jawed dwarf archosaurs sidled with hissing requests for food scraps.

Pushed through canvas drapes and into the darkness of shelter, Czevak came to find himself in some kind of meeting place. Inside, the ragged beards of the gyp-sies were longer and the headdresses more lice-ridden.

Shanty hags hobbled about the gathering, looking over the new arrivals while both the be-goggled gypsy and his bearded compatriot came forward to deliver proud testimony of the capture to the gathered elders. The chieftain council dissolved into a cacophony of chatter and squawking shanty-speak, giving Czevak opportunity to reach inside his Harlequin coat.

The be-goggled escort grabbed his wrist but by then the High Inquisitor had tossed a collection of finger-sized adamantium ingots onto the deck in front of the gathering. The bars clattered on the deck and glittered in the pilot flames of their escorts' weapons, silencing the crowd of elders and drawing the crones down on them with greedy glances.

Czevak snatched his wrist back and tore back the canvas drape to reveal the menacing shape of the Ablutra Hive looming in the hazy distance. He pointed at the ingots on the deck and then at the distant metropolis.

'We require transportation to the hive,' Czevak told them with deliberate syllables, looking from one liver-spotted face to another for some form of recognition, 'in exchange for payment.'

The aged throng parted and a sag-skinned elder came forward, his wrinkled visage stretched to grotesque youthfulness by the sheer weight of rings, hoops and decorations hooked through and dangling from his face. A muscular frame of yester-years was visible through his open rags but like his face, the chieftain's chest was a sorry remnant of wasted muscle, white wisps of hair and the cheap jangle of torso jewellery.

'You not go there,' the chieftain told him, 'there is no welcome for you there.'

Czevak and Klute exchanged glances.

'Of course,' the High Inquisitor said under his breath. 'They speak Low Gothic.'

'We're not getting much of a welcome here,' Klute sighed back.

'We know of the dangers,' Czevak told the chieftain.

'We do?' Klute asked.

'We only require transportation,' Czevak continued, 'to the Spire.' The High Inquisitor gestured at the floor where the hags were recovering the adamantium ingots. 'Take these as half payment, the same again when the job's done.'

The gathering descended upon the gypsy and the gabbling recommenced, the adamantium ingots snatched from the crooked fingers of the hags and passed to a toothless adviser beside the hook-faced chieftain. As his scrawny hand came up the chamber fell to a hush. The chieftain chattered in gumspittle shanty-speak at both the gypsy in the goggles and the escort with the greasy beard before hawking horribly and spitting into his hand. Offering the palm of his hand to Czevak the High Inquisitor bridled slightly before doing the same and engaging in the squelchy agreement.

As it transpired, the monstrous catch Czevak and the team had witnessed being harpooned and landed was also a trade. The airship they had seen earlier now had orders to transport the colossal gulper up to the hive spire for the palace kitchens. As the balloon drifted across the carcinogen swamps, the loathsome behemoth still swinging from the harpoon line below, Czevak and his team clung to the rusty plasteel frame and rigging. Swale gypsies leapt from rig to cage and cage to line with an agility, if not a grace, learned almost from birth in their sky shanty.

Klute demonstrated some surprise that the palace kitchens would entertain such a horrific dish in the form of the giant swamp feeder. Czevak, who had been up at the burner with his goggled friend, informed them all that Ablutra Hive was in open rebellion. Starvation had wracked the obscene metropolis as it had done with Hive Katharse, Hive Squalus and other megapolis sprawling across Ablutraphur's stinking surface. The capital had descended into a financial meltdown with what little control the Houses and the Spire commanded in the city swallowed in full scale civil war between various ganglords and cultists. The war was tumultuous and bloody, with new victors emerging weekly and occupying the hive city's Spire palace in mock-governorship. As ammunition and food supplies ran dry, gang loyalties dissolved and starvation riots tore the hive apart. The hivers themselves began to degenerate into cannibalistic armies with untold billions of emaciated Ablutrans dying in gutters or rampaging murderously through the mills, habs and underhive, feeding in ghoulish masses on the dead and unfortunate. The goggled balloon captain told Czevak that they only traded with the changing denizens of the Spire and scavvies from the Deeps, who not unlike the nomadic swale gypsies, had found security in environments where even rabid, cannibal hordes would not roam.

Klute shook his head in saddened disbelief.

'Hive worlds…' Klute said. 'Rat nests of vice and villainy. This world is being punished for turning away from the light of the God-Emperor.'

'To be fair,' Torqhuil returned, 'the petty denizens of this planet can hardly be held responsible for the freak immateriology of the Eye. Warp storms swallowed it whole.'

'Agreed,' Klute said, 'but why Ablutraphur? Perhaps the manifold wickedness of this world had already attracted the attention of some dark power – and that's why they were taken?'

'Some say Lord Variccus and the Unbound have a presence here and that the False Castellan's cult armies benefit from Ablutran body armour,' the Relictor informed the inquisitor. 'Variccus's master, the Great Lord of Decay holds sway here now.'

'The Ablutrans had to deal with somebody,' Czevak said.

'You would excuse this hive scum their embrace of the Ruinous Powers?'

'No,' Czevak returned with conviction. 'The Imperium abandoned this system. Nobody sent assistance. No military support. No supplies. An embargo on trade. What did you think they were going to do? Wait forever? The denizens of the Eye have to eat also.'

'Well, if our guide is right, they've taken to eating each other,' Klute said.

'That we can't blame on the False Castellan,' Czevak insisted.

'The daemon Mammoshad?' It was more of a statement than a question, but the High Inquisitor nodded in confirmation.

'King of Kings, Enslaver of the Craven Worlds and Keeper of the Vault Abyssal. When the Daecropsicum visited their Gellersection on the unfortunate entity, Torqhuil tells us that they bound individual parts of the creature to different artefacts and Chaotic weapons,' Czevak added. 'The daemon's definitive essence – its greed and ambition – was bound in a single artefact, a coin. The Black Library detailed the existence of this accursed object and the incalculable damage it has caused over the centuries.'

'What damage can a coin actually do?' Klute enquired.

'It is called by many names,' Czevak revealed, 'since it is rumoured to change its appearance, but its most common incarnation is the Black Sovereign of Sierra Sangraal. As the Black Sovereign changes hands, passing from person to person, hive to hive, across planets and even sectors, it brings poverty and riches to those it touches. Through this indiscriminate good and bad fortune, economies are destabilised, value is debased, plutocracies are created and everything in between crumbles. Mammoshad makes kings and he breaks them.'

'The Black Library places the coin here?' Klute asked.

'The thirteenth book of the *Ulthanash Rhapsode* – an

eldar epic poem detailing the tragedies of lesser races, tracked its movements from Belial VII to Pfennig's World to Ablutraphur.'

'A hive-world is a big place,' Brother Torqhuil said, 'and the Black Sovereign is but one coin. How do you know it will be at the Spire?'

Czevak considered the Relictor's question before smiling the answer back at the Space Marine, 'Because Mammoshad makes kings – and kings live in palaces. The Ablutra Hive houses the largest, most obscenely opulent palace on the planet's surface.'

As the balloon crossed the rancid wetlands in the shimmering heat of the burgeoning day, the haze that had masked the hive city began to fade. The Ablutra Hive was no longer a bloated and ominous shape looming on the tropical horizon. As the balloon closed on the megapolis the nightmare detail of the place ached into focus. The hive city was on fire and bleeding trails of acrid smoke into the sickly sky like smudged charcoal under an artist's thumb. Pocket fires raged unchallenged from deep within the city, weaving through the hab and factory levels, fed by sink shafts and at the mercy of the perverse air currents moving across the uneven architecture of the vertical sprawl.

As the methane burner roared, the swale gypsy airship made its daunting climb up the urban accretion that was the conical majesty of the hive. From the twisted nest of pipes and drains oozing centuries of effluent toxicity into the floodplain of filth, the balloon passed over the industrial foundation of the towering hive. Below them was the throne of chimneys and vents in which the hive sat. They belched a noxious miasma across the urban lowlands and the surrounding stilt-berg shanties. Flak mills and sweatshops grew out of the industrial night-marescape – the manufactory thorax of the city – now silent and abandoned. Above, the smashed and blazing condominia, hab-slums and the precarious domiciles scaffolded to the sides of various structures seemed to have suffered some of the worst damage.

As the balloon climbed, the silent stillness of these quarters gave way to the roars and screams of human beings in corporal and spiritual torment. Like the poisonous fumes rising out of the rusted smokestacks below, the starving city multitudes had risen up through the hive in growing numbers and desperation. They had stormed the upper plazas, gates and boulevards, with their estate housing and villas. Underhive scum had feasted upon the menial hordes; the cannibal proletariat had conquered the urban highlands of their betters. Here howling mobs of flesh-fuelled degenerates seeped out of the architecture, hunting each other like crazed packs of wild animals, splattered in each other's gore and the shame of necessity. As the balloon tantalisingly trailed the stinking carcass of its gargantuan catch over the roofs and towers, Czevak and his retinue fell to dread silence. They eavesdropped on the gut-hungry bellows of savage swarms clashing with and feeding upon one another, their minds struggling to soak up the magnitude of death and destruction.

They found the Gothic splendour of the Spire to be similarly afflicted. This was where the barbarism reached its zenith with the tapering architecture bottle-necking the cannibalistic throng as it tore its frenzied way ever higher. Some semblance of order remained in the Spire as evidenced in the flashes of firepower holding back the raging hordes in the lower levels of the Planetary Governor's palace. Czevak pointed out a shuttle platform attached to the tallest of the palace's manse towers and the balloon captain, lowering his magnocular goggles, directed the balloon in above the landing pad.

A small tractor with a bulbous engine column waited on the platform attached to a tracked flatbed. The rear of the trailer was dominated by a hydraulic claw used for loading and unloading shuttled cargo and palace supplies. As gypsies scampered through the rigging and manned the chains and windlass, the be-goggled captain brought his monstrous catch in expertly over the flatbed. Unlocking the grapnel, the beast fell the short distance to the trailer with a heavy slap, a sickening shudder rolling through the gargantuan swamp-feeder's rank flesh.

When Czevak had initially put his plan to get inside the palace to the retinue, the group had been deeply unimpressed. Klute had suggested using his rosette and the authority of his Beneficent Majesty's Inquisition to breach the fortifications. Czevak had to remind his friend that the hive was in the thrall of the Chaos Powers and that the authority of the Holy Ordos in all likelihood meant little there. If anything it would probably result in their summary execution and devouring. The High Inquisitor insisted that their search for the Black Sovereign of Sierra Sangraal was best conducted covertly – at least in the first instance – and if they didn't want to be met with a hail of las-bolts, with some stealth. Czevak's solution to this problem was inelegantly repugnant.

As the plasteel balloon frame housing the ballista and its jumbo harpoon hovered above the flatbed, Czevak and his team disembarked, the retinue swiftly making their way down the broken-backed behemoth's slimy length. At the monster's great umbrella mouth, Torqhuil used the pneumatic power in his servo-arms to part the colossal, lifeless lips and allow the group to pick their way tentatively inside.

The stench inside the beast was like a physical force that they had to push through. This would have been bad enough in the swamp-coated cavernous mouth but Czevak insisted on pushing deeper into the beast, just in case the creature was inspected and had the Techmarine cut through the gill-rakers and baleen plates at the back of the monster's foetid throat with his plasma torch appendage. Their progress through the beast was mercifully impeded beyond this point by the ruptured stomach of the thing. Disgorged entrails and intestinal innards had exploded their way through the lining and into the gullet cavity, preventing further progress.

With the bale light behind Hessian's eyes and the suit lamps on Torqhuil's power armour ghoulishly lighting the inside of the creature, the retinue had little to do but suppress their gag reflex and wait. When the small but powerful tractor roared to life, the judder of the power plant quaked through the carcass, signalling the initiation of Czevak's plan.

'God-Emperor, the stink!' the warp-seer hissed.

'Epiphani?' the High Inquisitor asked.

With Father hovering inconspicuously by the platform blast doors, the blind warp-seer had a view of the tractor and the beast on the trailer from the outside, although it was difficult for her to concentrate on the servo-skull's mind link with the assault on her other senses by the monster's unctuous, stinking innards.

'The blast doors are open,' the warp-seer described down a wrinkled nose. 'The gypsies are being paid by the palace proctors. The proctors look weak and thin.'

'What about security?' Torqhuil put to her.

'Six or seven Guardsmen.'

'How can you just stand there and breathe this muck,' Epiphani said, half-retching.

'PDF?' Klute pushed.

'How should I know? Yes. No. Too well equipped', Epiphani decided, snorting. 'They look like shock troops.'

'Cadians?'

The warp-seer suddenly grimaced as one of the armoured figures turned. Its face flesh was rotten white and gelatinous, like it had been slowly putrefying at the bottom of the ocean.

'Their faces…' the warp-seer shuddered.

'Markings?'

'Three skulls in an inverse pyramid,' Epiphani told them.

Czevak nodded. 'They're the Unbound.'

The five of them stumbled, putting palms and gauntlets into the gloop of the cavernous mouthflesh as their surroundings jolted into movement.

'The proctors are bringing the carcass in on the flatbed,' Epiphani said. The warp-seer hocked and spat. 'I can taste it,' she said in revulsion.

'What are the Unbound doing here?' Klute asked nervously.

'They were originally the Cadian 969th. They were deployed to Cetus Tertia during the Gothic War. Their colonel, Abner Varicuss, was favourite at the time for Lord Castellan but he and his men were struck down by some horrific water-borne plague that corrupted the regiment, preventing their return to Cadia and crushing Varicuss's political ambitions. To this day Varicuss goes by the title of the False Castellan, and his Unbound, as the regiment came to be called, threw in their lot with followers of the Great Lord of Decay. Ablutraphur is one of the worlds that still supply them. It makes sense that they garrison it.'

'This might have been useful information before we arrived on the planet,' Klute complained.

'Don't worry about the Unbound. Mammoshad will be giving them problems enough,' Czevak tried to assure him.

'Blast doors closing,' Epiphani said, as Father drifted into the palace, sticking to the shadows of the vaulted ceilings. Through the servo-skull's bionic orbs she watched the doors closing and the be-goggled gypsy captain walk away with his fee.

'I need to get out of here,' the warp-seer said with sudden determination, moving for the mouth of the creature. Klute intercepted her, slipping his arms around her from behind.

'What you need is a distraction,' Klute told her, slipping his fingers into her brassiere with no little squeamishness of his own and extracting her snuff box. He placed it in the blind girl's fingertips. In a fluid motion, Epiphani took a pinch of crystal Spook and snorted the viridian powder up one nostril, then the next. With his arms still around her Klute asked, 'Better?'

The warp-seer's face had completely slackened, assuming a dreamy softness.

'Better,' she mumbled. As she stumbled away, Klute found Torqhuil and Czevak looking at him.

'When you lose one of your senses, the others compensate,' Klute told them with a doctor's authority. 'However bad it is for us in here, it'll be ten times worse for her.'

'I don't doubt it,' Czevak said. 'But now the girl's blazed. How can we use her when she's out of her mind on Spook?'

'It's my experience,' Klute advised him, 'that regrettably, that is when she is at her most useful.'

As the trailer rocked to a halt, the warp-seer staggered backward, falling into the ruptured back wall of soft entrails and lengths of jumbo intestine. Sitting there in a throne of guts and slime, Klute fully expected Epiphani to scream and lurched for her. The warp-seer didn't, however, and moments later Klute found the girl quaking with suppressed hilarity, occasionally catching a wheezing breath between chest-contracting bouts of stifled laughter. Hessian joined in, depraved, indulgent chuckles passing his lips.

As Epiphani brought up her arms, Klute found her finely manicured hands clutching lengths of gut and entrail. The glee on her face fell and the hilarity shaking her body died as swiftly as it had started. As she stared sleepily through the funk of the cavity she passed the grotesque coils of the dead creature's intestine through her hands. She would squeeze the muscular tract before snatching its length from one hand to another frenetically, before tugging for more slack and sampling another section with her fingertips. Her head nodded as though she were counting something.

Hessian sniffed at the immaterial energies coursing through the warp-seer's veins.

'Epiphani?' Klute put gently to her.

'Bye… laugh… seen… inflecting… true,' the warp-seer said, each word in swift succession as through her fingers were reading it in the entrails. 'Bye… laugh… seen… inflecting… true… bye… laugh… seen… inflecting… true… bye… laugh… seen… inflecting… true…'

'Enough, Epiphani,' Klute said, snatching the slimy length of intestine from her grasp. The warp-seer looked right through the inquisitor before becoming presently aware of her surroundings. Her face contorted with disgust and Klute pulled her out of the bed of entrails. She seemed upset and after brushing off the worst of the stringy ooze and picking gut fragments from her plastek poncho, she held herself like a frightened child.

'It's a message,' Czevak said grimly.

'She's a prognostic, not some possessee or telepath,' Klute disagreed.

'I've seen feral world shamans examine the entrails of small animals,' Torqhuil volunteered, 'to divine deific approval for a tribal course of action.'

'It's a message – just not one we were meant to get – yet,' Czevak insisted, 'or possibly we were, the Ruinous Powers are perverse in such dealings.'

'That doesn't make any sense,' Klute told his friend.

'And neither did what she said,' said Czevak who began to fade away himself into thought. As he became suddenly aware of the eyes on him he said, 'I told you she was a poor prognostic. She has the gift – but she's like a wide-angle antenna picking up any and all signals. This explains her seeming ability to achieve empyreal congress across the different disciplines of divination – many she probably isn't even trained to interpret: haruspexia, pyromancy, cartomancy.'

'Now I haven't the faintest idea what you are saying,' Klute said.

'That's it,' Czevak smiled at him. 'Garbled transmission. This is the warp we are talking about here. She's receiving but not understanding – like, I don't know, prognostic paraphasia.'

'Paraphasia,' Klute said with relief. Finally, a word he understood.

'Paraphasia?' Torqhuil asked.

'It's a medical condition – associated with head trauma,' Klute informed him. 'Patients can speak but the content of their language is incorrect – they substitute words for others in terms of association or sound.'

'Or both,' Czevak said, already at work on the meaningless stream of words Epiphani had shot at them. 'Bye, laugh, seen, inflecting, true,' the High Inquisitor said to himself. He repeated it several times before smiling in triumph. 'It's phonetic. Bye... laugh... seen... inflecting... true – I... have... been... expecting... you.'

A chill passed through the group.

A moment later the trembling carcass became still and the five of them heard the tractor's engine die.

'What's happening?' Klute asked the warp-seer in a hushed whisper.

Epiphani seemed to be waiting; her face tensed a little before relaxing once more.

'They're gone,' she finally said.

'I... have... been... expecting... you,' Czevak repeated. 'We've got to move fast. This is a daemonic entity of Tzeentch we're dealing with, expect anything.'

Torqhuil was swift to barge his way through the baleen plates of the filter feeder and use his servo-arms to prize open the jaws of the behemoth from the inside. The others stumbled out of the beast, sucking in fresh air and flicking slime from their armour and clothing. Father descended from the ceiling to become the unsteady warp-seer's guide once more.

The party found themselves in a tiled scullery leading into the vast, empty palace kitchens. The kitchens had traditionally needed to be large to supply the equally large halls and ornate dining rooms of the Spire. There the Governor would hold court with influential families and individuals from the city and surrounding hives as well as entertain powerful off-world dignitaries and representatives with their own considerable entourages.

The expanse of worktops, sinks and pots were splattered with old blood and splinters of cracked bone. Epiphani washed her hands, while Klute picked up a femur for closer examination, revealing teeth mark indentations and the marrow sucked clean.

'Doesn't look good, does it?' the inquisitor said to no one in particular. He took out his shotgun pistol and clutched it down by his side. There was a sudden hiss before the great ovens of the kitchen fired. The palace proctors had gone to fetch their remaining kitchen staff – those that hadn't cooked and prepared each other. They would return any moment.

'Let's just find the Black Sovereign and get the hell out of here,' Czevak said to steady nerves.

'And how do we do that?'

'Simple,' Czevak returned. 'Find the richest, most powerful person in the building. The coin will be with them.'

As the group moved through the cavernous corridors and vaulted chambers of the Spire palace, the distant echo of suppression fire bounced around them. Not even Spire nobility were safe from the hunger of the cannibal hordes and the flesh-desperate millions had reached the palace defences. Howls and shrieks rose up through the elaborate palace balconies and windows. The air sang with the constant percussion of fists on faltering barricades and the chatter of autoguns ripping explosively into droves of emaciated madmen.

At a security bulkhead, set in the ornate finery of a gallery archway, Czevak gestured for Torqhuil and Father to approach.

'Find the vault, it will probably be attached to the royal apartments,' Czevak told them. 'Hurry.'

The Techmarine worked fast, using the delicate array of instruments adorning two of his flexible mechadendrite limbs to breach the palace security. Interfacing the servo-skull with spiriflex lines and plug wires from the bulkhead, Torqhuil directed Father to extract the information they needed. The familiar's vellum scroll unspooled, which the Space Marine read rather than tore away, leaving the servo-skull trailing parchment.

'Above the royal apartments and personal chambers,' the Relictor nodded before adding, 'this way.'

Hessian and the inquisitors followed the Space Marine, leaving Epiphani to disconnect Father from the wall and pursue at a more measured pace. Through a set of state rooms, Epiphani arrived in a dusty cloister, set aside for private devotions with velvet curtains covering chapel-booths.

Hands suddenly leapt out from one curtain and dragged the servo-skull and the warp-seer inside by the plas of her poncho. Czevak was behind, already with a finger to his lips. The velvet parted slightly in the slipstream of armoured troops stomping up the cloister in heavy boots. Their armour was a faded Cadian green and the circles of the regimental digits adorning their shoulder flak pads were daubed with white paint. Instead of the 969th the plates now bore three skulls in an inverse pyramid, the badge of the False Castellan's Unbound and a tribute to the Great Lord of Decay's own runic emblem. As the traitor regiment soldiers thundered past, Czevak and Epiphani were witness to their elephantine limbs and bloated bodies, lending the corrupted Guardsmen solidity and sturdy resilience. Their dead, pale skin barely held together the gelatinous flesh of their faces

and a sickly paste formed a membrane that covered their
diseased forms, in turn creating a sticky trap for the bugs
and flies attempting to feed on their passing putrescence.

After the Nurgle troopers had passed, Czevak watched
Torqhuil check the cloister. Trusting in the Space
Marine's superior senses, the High Inquisitor followed
with Epiphani after. The smashed and trampled furniture of state rooms decorated their route and it was
another landing and staircase before the retinue reached
the royal apartments.

'Lord Emperor,' Klute mouthed.

A reception hall formed the nexus of the apartments
and private chambers with a myriad of doorways and
arches leading anywhere and everywhere. The lofty
ceiling of the great hall was dominated by the decorative cogs and clockwork mechanics that moved the
considerable weight of a thick, circular adamantium
door. The door had been cranked aside and numerous ladders extended from the marble floor of the hall
up into the huge vault above. As Czevak and his team
wandered cautiously inside the reception chamber,
they were mesmerised by the collection of riches contained there.

The palace vault was clearly full, gleaming with precious metal and valuables that were stacked to its own
ceiling. The reception hall and adjoining apartments had
become an unceremonious overspill for the incalculable
wealth that had been jealously hoarded there. Priceless
antiquities of xenos and ancient Imperial design leant
against rolls of exotic silk and holy relics. Every tiny
scrap of wall space was decorated with layer upon layer
of rare paintings and works of art, early Farranbourgs,
Disrallileo's and banned pagan representations. The
chamber was awash with mountains of coin, while the
marble of the floor was carpeted in plastek credits and
papered money, the currency of a thousand worlds.
Mounds of chests, caskets and even common crates and

baskets spilled over with precious stones and entangled
jewellery while small forts had been constructed from
ingots of rare metals.

At the centre of this finery was the reception table,
at which sat the polar opposite of the surrounding
opulence. Skeletal Spire nobility in stained and ragged
splendour rocked back and forth in their chairs. They
plucked hairs from threadbare scalps and nibbled the
marrow from old bones, the shattered remains of which
were the only food items decorating the platinum and
porcelain of the table. These were scraps tossed down
the length of the table by the corpulent mass sitting at
the head of the gathering. The figure could not truly
be described as sitting at all, since her spine could no
longer support the mountain of blubbery fat that hung
from her bowed bones. She was strapped into a reinforced ferrouswood throne. The huge chair was braced
with titanium struts and housed a puppet show harness
arrangement of robust leather straps, suspension cables
and counterweights, allowing the monstrous woman
to move her arms. These she had been using to bring
bones and slabs of dripping flesh to her maw from a
body that lay butchered and prepared on a platinum
platter in front of her. From the empty chairs at the
top end of the table it seemed as though the ravenous
nobles had started to satisfy their cannibal appetites on
each other.

For moments Klute was speechless, the enormity of
the task before them overwhelming the inquisitor. He
gestured around the huge hall and its gathered riches.

'How are we going to find one coin in amongst all
this?' he hissed.

'With me,' Czevak told Klute. To the others he said,
'Find it.'

Epiphani drifted towards a heap of bejewelled ball
gowns in the corner, while Torquhil took a chunky visor
and lens arrangement from his belt and pulled it down

over his face, scanning the treasure hoard with alternating aura-scrye and psyoccula filters. Hessian sniffed through the stagnation of the chamber like some daemonic bloodhound, peeling off into a precarious coin stack.

'Lady Sabine Krulda,' Czevak announced as he skipped up an empty chair and onto the table. As he walked up its length, crashing through the porcelain and crystal, dead-eyed courtiers jealously snatched their scraps to their chests. 'Your hive – in fact, your world – has become the victim of a daemonic intrusion. We are the high officers of his Beneficent Majesty's Holy Inquisition. Cooperate and we will remove and destroy this scourge.'

Klute strode up the side of the table but stopped as Czevak had done before the cannibal queen.

Lady Krulda awoke from a doze. She was even larger close up, her rolls of corpulence hanging off both her and the throne. Her skin was pallid but threaded through with a web of ruptures and bruising where the gluttonous devouring of human flesh had caused her own to stretch and distend.

She was naked in the chair – for no clothes would fit the Spireborn – her quadruple chin and gargantuan bosom speckled with old blood and fragments of flesh, hair and bone. What little modesty she had was preserved amongst the rolls of her amorphous form, with fat cascading down her sticky, unwashed body. Greying lengths of blood-matted hair – that ordinarily would be arranged in some extravagant style – meandered across her filthy body like lava down the side of a volcano. The tiny, doll-like eyes set in her ridiculous head blinked incomprehension at Czevak before the brute monarch grinned, showing the flesh-chunks that were stuck amongst her bloodied teeth and black gums. She licked her crusted lips at the prospect of fresh meat.

Czevak looked down at Klute. 'It was worth a try, in

the hope that we might avoid what we are now going to have to do.'

'Which is?' Klute said, feeling his lip wrinkle.

'Search her,' the High Inquisitor said.

The two men hovered for a moment in hesitation but with the howls of cannibalistic fury and accompanying suppression fire from the Unbound's outdated auto-guns drawing ever closer, there was little time for such scruples.

'Where do we start?' Klute said as he closed on the woman's grotesque carcass.

'Where?' Czevak repeated as the cannibal reached out for him with weak, pudgy arms. 'Any bloody where – just find that coin, it won't have gone far.'

As the two men went to work searching through the tyres of flab and the pools of congealed blood they found in between, the tower belfry began to boom. This was accompanied by a dissonance of tinny klaxons firing across the palace.

'Work fast,' Czevak grimaced.

'What is it?' Klute barked with increasing repugnance.

'The palace security has been breached,' the High Inquisitor said. 'The cannibal hordes are on their way.'

Czevak had realised how bad the situation was when they had reached the royal apartments. He'd expected to find members of the Unbound or at least their Ruinous officers there. That every single traitor Guardsman was required down on the palace perimeter was evidence of insatiable millions battering down barricades and soaking up the Unbound's not inconsiderable firepower. Even the cult army commander had been required to take arms to prevent the flesh-hungry mobs taking the city into degenerate barbarism. The Ablutra Hive was now useless to the Unbound; the manufacturing powerhouse that had been the metropolis was now a flaming wreck populated by savages. Like everyone else, the Unbound were now fighting for their canker-extended lives.

With renewed enthusiasm, Klute thrust himself arm deep into the layers of Lady Krulda's fat.

'Are you sure it's here?' the inquisitor asked, his eye catching the ribcage of cannibalistic delicacies still on her plate. 'Despite her riches, the Lady Krulda doesn't seem to be presently enjoying much in the way of good fortune.'

Czevak came out from behind the groaning, insensible mass of the great monarch. He stood there, thoughtful for a moment.

'Bye, laugh, seen, inflecting, true – I, have, been, expecting… you,' the High Inquisitor said to himself. Czevak pursed his lips and knocked a fist against his forehead, 'It's so obvious.'

'What's obvious?'

'So stupid.'

The ante-chamber outside of the royal apartments was suddenly full of ear-searing gunfire. Green flak and rotten faces flashed past the doorway. Traitor Guardsmen fell back through the chamber under blazing streams of high-velocity fire reaching out from the muzzles of their autorifles. The flash of grenades down the staircase accompanied the bombastic entrance of the Unbound, the putrid bloat of their ghastly flesh doing little to impede the precise battle manoeuvres of their Cadian origins. Traitor Guardsmen filed in through the great hall's mighty open doors, while the rearguard sprayed the unseen hordes with explosive fire from their rifles. Everyone in the apartment, cannibal and visitor alike could hear the unstoppable mob, their groaning hunger for flesh drowning out the traitor Guard firepower.

Suddenly they were in view, a sea of emaciated forms, degenerate savages crawling over each other's sharp bones and smeared bodies to get a taste of flesh. Within moments it was wall to wall, cannibal howling filling the rest of the space. Czevak and Klute watched in horror as Nurgle soldiers were swamped by the riotous mob, their own swollen bulk crawling with the light frames of ghoulish hivers. The inquisitors could suddenly appreciate how the might of the Unbound – a deadly, diseased and undying cult force in their own right – could be sundered so. Traitor Guardsmen were becoming gradually overrun – despite their withering arc of fire – and dragged into the throng. The cannibals were not waiting on ceremony and satisfied their voracious desires right there in the tumult – the foetid cult soldiers eaten alive.

An Unbound officer rasped orders at its remaining men, prompting the squad through the apartment doorway where two pus-engorged sergeants shouldered the great hall's doors closed. Almost immediately the thick metal rang with famished fists and the thunder of wasted bodies throwing themselves at the ornamental fretwork.

The officer turned, its head a glutinous sack of wan pestilence sitting in the fur collar of a Cadian greatcoat. It seemed shocked to find Czevak and his retinue there. As it opened its mouth to speak, a cockroach scuttled out from its froth-corrupted lungs.

'Off-worlders,' it hissed, flashing its swollen, cancerous tongue. 'Seize them!'

'Wait!' Czevak called, bringing the room to a halt. 'We can help each other. I'm looking for a coin – a sovereign, about this big,' Czevak explained making the shape with his fingers.

'The Lord of All cares nought for your coins and riches, his inheritance is eternity,' the Unbound officer cackled. 'Now, where's your ship.'

'At least we know he doesn't have it,' Czevak said.

'Some consolation,' Klute added.

As the doors of the great hall boomed and creaked, the officer pointed a pallid finger at Czevak.

'Tell me now off-worlder or you're dead.'

'I'm dead?' Czevak said. 'You should look in the mirror.'

The Unbound officer snatched a rusted bolt pistol from its belt and shot in explosive exasperation at the

High Inquisitor. Czevak became a chromatic blaze of light and colour, slipping out of the bolt-rounds' deadly path and up the side of a mountain of coin beside the table. The bolts tore into Lady Krulda's monstrous form, one taking her in the temple and putting a swift end to a life of cannibalistic debauchery.

The traitor Guard officer gurgled its rage, which the Unbound interpreted as an order to fire. Their tarnished weaponry blazed fire across the royal apartments, cutting through the precious silks, paintings and furniture stored there. Coins and jewellery became priceless frag storms that cut through the air, threatening to shred anything in their path to pieces.

As Czevak surged up the coin bank, his boots losing traction and sinking, the moundside began to roll and tumble, breaking away like a sand dune. Towers of stacked coin wavered and toppled under this molestation and the Nurgle frontline was buried in a downpour of silver and gold.

Torqhuil's axe, servo-arms and mechadendrite limbs were suddenly everywhere, shearing the barrels from autoguns, batting corrupted Guardsmen across the hall and plasma-torching Cadian cultists in two. With the Unbound's caseless ammunition creating nothing more than a light show of ricochets off the Relictor's power armour, some of the rotten soldiers turned their grungy weapons on the blind warp-seer. The Space Marine was there seconds later, forming a protective shell around the warp-seer and soaking up the high-velocity punishment as he walked her out of the maelstrom.

One of the pus-faced sergeants was stomping up towards Klute, a sluggish chainsword outstretched in one putrid fist. The blood-rusty weapon took heads off the still-seated Spireborns at the table, while four ghastly Guardsmen brought up the rear.

Klute brought up his shotgun pistol, blasting salt and silver shot at the Unbound and working his lever action as he side-stepped behind Lady Krulda and her throne. The traitor Guardsmen bubbled and smoked where the blessed ammunition found its mark but the street silencer had done little to stop their thunderous advance. Their gelatinous flesh had simply absorbed the blasts like an insensitive paste.

Klute screwed up his face as more auto fire ripped into Lady Krulda's colossal girth and the ferrouswood throne around her. The inquisitor saw the daemonhost Hessian watching from behind a pallet of adamantium ingots. As the Unbound closed and their bullets drew ever closer, Klute found himself back in desperate moral territory. Spitting the first few lines of the emancipations Phalanghast had taught him, Klute allowed the daemon a fraction of its abominate power.

Hessian sensed the change immediately, its eyes burning with a golden light, its outline a flicker with the lick of ethereal flame. As the Unbound stormed along the table, the daemonhost launched a torrent of hellfire from its palms, roasting the traitor Guardsmen where they stood. As Hessian brought down his hands and the inferno died, Klute finished thumbing shells into his shotgun pistol and risked a glimpse around the edge of the throne.

The suppurating sergeant and his Nurgle soldiers stood there unharmed. The daps and stipples of their paste-soggy flesh were browned and burned but the viscous bloat of their limbs and rotten features were unscathed by the supernatural firestorm. Even their Ablutraphurn flak armour had fared well beyond a few flash burns. Klute sighed. Hessian's face creased with confusion and otherwordly anger.

The Unbound turned their antique weaponry on the creature, the sergeant bringing its chainsword around to meet the daemonhost. Hessian took unnecessary cover behind the pallet of adamantium before giving the traitor Guardsmen his palms again, this time using the rage of his hellfire blast on the ingots. Bricks of solid adamantium flew at the Unbound, breaking and braining the parody Guardsmen, smashing though their armour and rotten bodies.

The wall surrounding the hinges of the great hall doors gave and the large metal doors fell inwards, two more of the Nurgle Guardsmen crushed underneath. Behind the doors was a deluge of madness, a seeming single creature made up of sunken eyes, gnashing teeth and bloodied fingernails. Cannibals poured into the apartments and set upon anything with a pulse. Traitor Guardsmen near the entrance and courtiers both dead and alive became the fascination of the first wave, giving Klute and Hessian the time they needed to reach Epiphani, Torquil and the High Inquisitor on the other side of the hall.

The group ran blindly through the rooms and chambers of the royal apartments, with the Unbound officer and a few remaining members of his platoon stomping up behind. Their weapons were occupied with cutting down a second wave of cannibals that had dived through the side doorway after them.

Stumbling through the doors of the master bedroom, Czevak and his retinue clambered over Lady Krulda's reinforced bed and discovered to their dismay that they had run out of palace. The five of them found themselves on a large balcony, commanding the best view in the city of the flame-ravaged hive and the stinking carcinogen swamps beyond. Czevak looked down over the crafted balustrade, his stomach flipping as he discovered that the fearful distance down to the base of the tower was only the beginning of the vertiginous drop. The palace and Spire descended, and below that the villas and habscrapers reached for kilometres up out of the nest of factory chimneys and gaping smoke stacks upon which the city sat. The High Inquisitor looked up at the suicidal climb which separated Lady Krulda's balcony from the landing platform for her personal shuttle. As Planetary Governor as well as Lady of the Ablutra Hive she was expected to visit the leaders of the Ablutraphur's sister hives.

'Climb for your lives,' Czevak told the others before stepping up onto the balcony and launching himself at a gargoyle carved into the Gothic stone of the Spire. If there had been time there almost certainly would have been opposition to the plan. Faced with the gun-toting Unbound and the flesh-hungry hordes rampaging through the apartments after them, there seemed little else for them to do but climb.

Fortunately for the group, the Spire architecture was fussy and crowded, incorporating all manner of flourishes and design structures as well as statues, representations and gargoyles to help the uninitiated climber. Czevak had the benefit of youth and Hessian to all intents and purposes scrambled up through the architecture like a gargoyle. Klute found it difficult to keep visions of his flailing form falling down the side of the hive out of his mind, finding that only visions of cannibal hive city dwellers feasting on his innards kept him ascending. Epiphani didn't have to worry about vertigo at all, the climb up the Spire side feeling no different to the blind girl than climbing a deck ladder on the *Malescaythe*. Father rose gently behind her on his small anti-gravity drive, using his enhanced optics to give the warp-seer a clear view of the handholds to come. The Relictors Techmarine found the climb the easiest, despite weighing the most, ascending like some bionic spider up the Spireface, grabbing features with mechadendrite attachments and gauntlets and punching through the stone with his servo-arms when no suitable feature presented itself.

Czevak hauled himself over the lip of the landing pad, grateful for the grip on Klute's Cretacian hunting boots. Thrusting his arm down to his friend, he helped Klute up the last segment of the climb, lugging the inquisitor up onto the platform. As the two men lay on the deck, chests heaving, it became painfully apparent that Lady

Krulda's personal shuttle was not there. The inquisitors shouldn't have been surprised. As the food crisis had gotten progressively worse and the starvation riots had taken over, anything with wings and an engine would have been procured, hijacked or stolen to escape the hive city's woes.

Torqhuil and Hessian joined them moments later. Czevak got to his feet and looked down the unforgiving path of their climb. The balcony was swarming with frenzied degenerates who were taking it upon themselves to duplicate their ascent. Slipping his bolt pistol from its holster, the Techmarine sprayed the climbing cannibals, knocking bolt-blasted skeletals from their purchase. Looking up, the High Inquisitor found only the sculptured belfry and the sickly clouds that its tower pinnacle almost reached. This time they really had run out of palace.

'Where's Epiphani?' Klute said – up on his feet and wandering the shuttle pad. The four of them span around, searching for signs of the warp-seer. Father appeared behind Czevak, rising up the Spire wall and above the platform. Epiphani's head appeared also and Klute's shoulders sagged in relief. Moments later they tightened again as the Unbound officer's putrescent features came up behind the warp-seer. It had in fact been the Nurgle officer who had been pulling her up through the final stages of the exhausting climb. Clambering over the edge of the platform the Guard officer had the daemonhost, the Space Marine and the two inquisitors storming towards him. The Unbound officer stood on the lip of the pad, its Cadian greatcoat flapping in the wind with Epiphani clasped in one rotting hand and the rusty bolt pistol in the other. Bringing the weapon to her temple, the Guardsman brought its enemies to a halt.

Moving forward with confidence it rasped, 'Lose it.'

Holding his bolt pistol out, Torqhuil ejected his all but spent magazine.

'I am asking for the final time,' the thing promised. 'Where is your ship?'

Without replying, Czevak began walking towards the Unbound officer. The aberration held the bolt pistol at arm's length, the muzzle buried in the tresses of the warp-seer's hair. The High Inquisitor said nothing but kept walking at the putrid soldier.

'Czevak!' Klute called in alarm, but the inquisitor continued marching. The pale, bloated arm of the creature brought the bolt pistol around to meet the oncoming antagonist. With the weapon off Epiphani, Czevak flashed his eyes at the sky.

'Up there,' he indicated.

The corrupted Guardsman looked up just in time to see the thick shaft of the harpoon fall towards him like a thunderbolt. The weapon impaled the gelatinous carcass of the putrefying soldier, falling through its ruined face and down through the soft tissue of its ruptured torso. With the Unbound officer brought to its knees and skewered to the platform, the bolt pistol fell to the deck. Above, the swale gypsy balloon silently hovered, drifting out of the clouds. A wire ladder followed the harpoon down and Czevak directed his grateful retinue up its metal rungs. With cannibal hivers clawing their way over the edge of the landing platform, Czevak stepped onto the ladder, the others quickly following. Cutting the harpoon and line away, the be-goggled gypsy captain fired his methane burner and took the balloon, the ladder and the High Inquisitor to safety.

Once up in the plasteel frame, with knees and elbows locked around the cage bars and rigging, Klute bemoaned their wasted efforts.

'All for nothing,' he cursed, after a stream of less charitable mumblings. 'Is this always the way with you?' the inquisitor said with sudden accusation.

'Had you forgotten?' Czevak replied simply, drawing a slow nod from his former acolyte.

Below them the toxic lethality of the carcinogen swamp passed. The gypsy captain climbed down between them, showing Czevak five fingers, each representing a minute remaining of their journey. From his vantage point the High Inquisitor could see the vine-choked mound of the satellite hive from which they had emerged. He could even make out the opening he had created in the rockface with the assistance of one of Torqhuil's pneumatic lines.

'Lucky that the gypsies waited,' Klute put to the High Inquisitor.

Czevak smiled. 'Luck had very little to do with it.' He took the finger ingots he owed the gypsies and offered them to the be-goggled captain. 'The same again when the job was done,' Czevak said to the gypsy, echoing their earlier agreement.

The captain grinned like an idiot and unbuttoned a satchel pouch he carried slung across his chest and shoulder, inviting the High Inquisitor to deposit them inside.

'And there you are,' Czevak said, dropping the ingots in the money pouch and extracted a single coin from the inside, a large sovereign.

'May I?' Czevak asked the gypsy captain, who simply laughed and slapped the inquisitor's shoulder before making his way back up to the burner to execute the balloon's landing.

Klute sat astride the plasteel bar amazed. Both Epiphani and the Relictors Space Marine stared from the other side of the frame. Hessian remained asleep in the rigging.

'Is that it?' Torqhuil called across the open space.

'The Black Sovereign of Sierra Sangraal,' Czevak confirmed, admiring the grotesque imagery on the raised surface of the obverse side of the coin. He rolled the round, corrugated edges of the fat coin between his finger and thumb. 'I have you now you artful, insidious bastard,' the High Inquisitor told it.

'How did it… How did you… How?' Klute stammered at him.

'Epiphani told us,' Czevak explained. 'Bye, laugh, seen, inflecting, true.'

'But you said she was confused – you said the reading was, "I have been expecting you"'.

'When we give this thing a voice,' Czevak said, 'I have a feeling that those will be among the first words we will hear out of its mouth. This devious, daemonic scum couldn't resist leaving us clues of its true intention.'

Klute waited and then prompted. 'Like?'

'"I have been expecting you". The key words are "have been", as in – no longer. It was gone by the time Epiphani received her reading. It knew the hive was lost and Lady Krulda's time was up. Time to move on; it could hardly continue to do damage in the possession of a starving cannibal hiver. So, it had itself used as payment for the gypsies' delivery.'

'It left as we entered?' Klute asked, not quite believing the daemon coin's cunning and guile.

'There was a clue in the mistranslation also,' Czevak revealed.

Klute shrugged his shoulders.

'"Bye, laugh, seen, inflecting, true." The daemon Mammoshad leaves and is amused at our inability to see his reverse truths.'

'I don't believe it,' Klute admitted, astounded, as the balloon came in to land.

'Believe it,' Czevak said. 'I told you before, expect anything.'

Klute nodded, watching Czevak roll the accursed Black Sovereign across the knuckles of one hand.

'I think it's fair to say that that advice still applies.'

Exeunt

ACT II, CANTO III

Archeodeck, Rogue trader Malescaythe, *The Eye of Terror*

Enter KLUTE

IT HAD BEEN three days.

Three days for Klute to cleanse himself of Ablutraphur's stink and for the recurring images of the hive city's horrific demise to fade from his mind. The inquisitor had spent a good deal of this time either at prayer or submerged in plunge basins of scorching water, anointed oils and Saint Vesta's salt in the rogue trader's baptisterium. Unlike Czevak, who purged himself of the Eye's corruptive influence every time he opened his precious *Atlas Infernal* and bathed in the spiritual sterility of the tome's nullflesh, Klute had to go to great efforts to resist the contamination of dreadspace.

While Klute had been purifying both body and spirit, Czevak had immersed himself in matters less holy. As the inquisitor crossed the deck he saw Czevak and Torqhuil camped out amongst a nest of tables and the Relictors Techmarine's extensive collection of tomes, artefacts and recovered archeotech. The Space Marine safely stored the bulk of his Chaos relics and arcana in the large Geller and stasis chambers that adjoined the archeodeck, but the Relictor and High Inquisitor's joint project of communing with the daemon Mammoshad had demanded extensive experimentation and research. Czevak had the pages of *Kronochet's Anatomae* and the *Corpus Vivexorsectio* spread out amongst various other dark grimoires, banned xenos translations and daemonologist tracts while the Relictor moved back and forth between the deck and the stasis chambers with tools, ancient remnants and bastardised equipment, heretically configured without consideration for STC tech-designations.

Czevak didn't acknowledge Klute's approach, but the Relictors Space Marine looked up from his sacrilegious tinkering and nodded gravely. Czevak looked like hell. Despite his youthful complexion, his eyes were dark and his expression distant and empty. His mouth was tensed in a line of vexation and his fingers stiff and irritable as he flicked through the pages of his damned tomes.

The Black Sovereign of Sierra Sangraal was sitting in amongst a jury-rigged apparatus, constructed from a hotchpotch myriad of different instruments. The machine was all turntables, wires and finger glyphs. The contraption was crowned with a pair of speaking trumpets that twisted around one another, lending it the appearance of a twin phonograph. In the centre spun the Black Sovereign on an anti-gravity field with a psychoactive crystal stylus running along the grooved edge of the large coin.

Klute had been present as Torqhuil had completed

the sacrilegious project and the daemon's first words escaped the blooming funnel of the left hand trumpet. The inquisitor didn't understand the words, although it was clear that the daemonic entity was in full flow. Its voice excited the air around them and was an unholy mixture of raptorial screech and reptilian sibilance.

Torqhuil had to rescue his dia-log interface and rune-cable from the *Hellebore*'s mnemonic bank, adjusting the shaft of tubular keys and attempting likely combinations before settling on a configuration that turned the hissing cacophony of squawks erupting from the trumpet into words that the Techmarine and the two inquisitors had instantly recognised.

'I have been expecting you...'

Along one nearby table were an intimidating line of objects, arranged like instruments of torture – all selected from Torqhuil's collection of relics and artefacts. Many Klute did not know but among them he did recognise the sinister shapes of a grimoire-diabolicus of True Names, a hexagrammic stamphammer, a stasis-casked astramoebic warp infestation, blessed unguents of different grades and consecrations and the hymnals of the Confederation of Light – vox-captured on Dimmamar millennia ago. Torqhuil's prize was the Geller wave-tuned vibro-scalpel that he had improvised himself from the recovered pages of the *Corpus Vivexorsectio*.

Czevak drew his stool up to the second speaking trumpet.

'Tell me again,' he said with words of cold steel. 'Where can I find Ahzek Ahriman of the Thousand Sons?'

'Where can't you find him?'

Czevak dipped his fingers into a bowl of blessed unguent and flicked oil at the spinning Black Sovereign. The liquid sizzled and soaked into the unearthly metal of the coin, drawing an avian shriek from the trumpet.

'I told you,' Czevak said darkly. 'Stop answering questions with questions.'

Mammoshad's wounded screeching devolved into an insane laughter.

'Ahriman is everywhere. He is part of everything and everyone. His cult is legion. He is where you've been and where you're going. His influence is felt in the halls and palaces of the Terran corpseworld, in damnation's cradle and aboard this ship. No one knows where.'

'No one?' the inquisitor repeated. 'Except Ahriman, himself. Are you Ahzek Ahriman?' Czevak put to the beast.

'I am many things,' the daemon told him, provoking Czevak to reach for another of Torqhuil's instruments of infernal torture. '…but Ahriman I am not.'

The High Inquisitor rested an elbow on the nearby table.

'Where can I find Korban Xarchos, bastard sorcerer of the Thousand Sons?'

'You seek the student to find the master?'

'Test me void-spawn…'

'I pass through the hands of many. Those hands belong to bodies to which ears also belong. Those ears heard that Korban Xarchos was dead.'

'Impossible.'

'Seemingly, since he didn't die.'

'I tire of your games, daemon. Speak plainly.'

'Of course, High Inquisitor, but of which one? There are so many planes of existence – as you well know. Follow the screams. '

Czevak screwed up his face at the disappearing darkness of the speaking trumpet.

'Brother Torqhuil, some music please,' the High Inquisitor instructed, at which the Techmarine mounted a vox-disc of hymnals on the nearest turntable and allowed the ghostly choral music of the Confederation of Light to afflict the cavernous hangar. The Confederation's devotions had been driving the darkness from Imperial ears hundreds of years before the Ecclesiarchy established its stranglehold of faith on humanity.

Mammoshad began to moan and whimper in the background of the castrato choir. 'It hurts, yes?' Czevak seethed. 'You're going to talk to me, daemon. I promise that you are going to talk to me. Tell me what you have heard through your many ears. Tell me what you have heard of the whereabouts of that warpspawn sorcerer. Brother Torqhuil, the volume; I want our guest to experience the full power and piousness of the Confederation's heretical devotion.'

Klute felt the vibration of the booming hymnals on the air and in the metal decking below his feet. Mammoshad's agonies fragmented into different squawkish voices, each addressing Czevak's demand with a different answer.

'Delta Myrias.'

'Pyrrus.'

'The Triggonaut Sphere.'

'The Minerva Reach.'

'UV6-26.'

'Alpha Myrias.'

'Shenghis, Mizar Blue or Brannigan's Hope in the Archive Worlds.'

'Hive Havoque.'

'Eaten by Wombwort giant.'

'Vegatra.'

'Beta Myrias.'

'Beaten by the Counter-Clock Heart on Tituba Prime.'

The insanity went on.

'Enough!' Czevak commanded.

'But there's more,' the entity cackled, 'there's so much more…'

'What does Korban Xarchos want with the Daecropsicum's dark technologies?' Czevak put to the monster.

Mammoshad did not answer.

'Sensitive subject, eh?' Czevak said with self-satisfied scorn. 'Well, you'd better speak up daemon or the tortures you suffered at the hands of the Dark Mechanicus will seem like a pleasant memory.'

'I think that you just enjoy hearing stories of pain and torment, mortal weakling, to ease the memory of your own suffering. I have and continue to live the miserable agony of a living autopsy; it amuses me that you consider your feeble imagination capable of scaring me with worse than that.'

As Czevak continued barking at the polluted thing, gesticulating wildly and contorting his face in anger and desperation, Klute pulled the Relictors Techmarine to one side.

'He's been like this for days,' Torqhuil told him. 'Mammoshad just plays with him, twisting his words, feeding him hope, denying him satisfaction.'

A scream-tangled screech filled the hangar, cutting through the Confederation hymns. Klute turned around to find his master had dashed a pot of holy unguent at Torqhuil's contraption – which was now dripping with oil and purity – and was spitting blessings from the open grimoire down the speaking trumpet.

'It's the meme-virus,' Klute said, offering the Techmarine his medical opinion.

Czevak writhed with hatred. His face glistening red. He was clearly running a fever and the virus was running rampant through his system and out of balance with his body's usual ability to keep it in moderate check. The High Inquisitor had a corporal need for the information – like a hunger or whimpering desire for a pain or affliction to end.

'He asks the thing the same questions, over and over. I know your kind are trained in the arts of interrogation,' Torqhuil confided solemnly, 'but it is as if he expects the creature to lie to him.'

'Of course it is going to lie to him,' Klute said harshly. He didn't welcome the Space Marine's criticism. 'It's a creation of darkness.'

'Then why continue to ask it the same questions?' the Adeptus Astartes put to Klute with troubling logic. 'It has no corporal form. It won't tire. Like the Daecropsicum before him, he visits eternal agonies on the beast. He knows the daemon will deny him and this gives him justification to torture it further.'

'I told you,' Klute said, looking up and narrowing his eyes at Torqhuil. 'It's the virus. It flares up from time to time – especially during moments of great stress.' Behind the words, however, was a fear that the Space Marine was correct and that Czevak was simply acting out the agonies of his own past tortures and interrogations.

'But what you have to ask yourself, inquisitor,' the Relictor said, 'is why should this be a moment of great stress for him?'

Klute watched Czevak sweep up the stasis-casked astramoebic warp infestation and smash it on the antigravity turntable. More howling screams burst from the speaking trumpet as the infestation ate away at the entity's immaterial presence.

'Are you lying?' Czevak bawled at the contraption.

As the monstrous creature fought through the pain of this fresh torture, its squealing levelled out to a daemonic hiss, 'Even to myself…'

'This is getting out of hand,' Klute concluded. 'What would you do?'

'I wouldn't pointlessly torture the thing or engage with it unless I had to.'

'Your Chapter is not known for such squeamishness,' Klute said.

'We believe in using the tools of Chaos against Chaos, daemon against daemon. We don't enter into needless congress with the damned or inflict fruitless tortures upon the polluted. And it has become obvious that this enterprise is now both needless and fruitless.'

'Enough of what you wouldn't do, what would you do?'

'Honestly?' the Relictors Space Marine considered. 'I'd casually lose the damned thing on Medrengard or Sicarus. Let this monster crush the daemon worlds of its enemies in the best way it knows how and make our job all the easier.'

Klute shook his head, looking between the assured eyes of the Space Marine and the rage-enflamed orbs of his old master.

'I really have no idea what I am doing here,' the inquisitor said. 'You all seem as insane as each other.'

'And what would you do?' the Relictor asked.

'I would destroy it, of course,' Klute maintained with exasperation. 'I wouldn't communicate with it; I wouldn't attempt to use or manipulate it. I would banish the thing back to the infernal womb of immaterial damnation from which it was born–'

Klute was forced to break off. Mammoshad had provoked the High Inquisitor to frenzied apoplexy with some lie, twisted truth or daemonic silence and Czevak had seized the hexagrammic stamphammer and was smashing indiscriminate purity runes into both the bouncing coin and Torqhuil's heretical construct. Czevak was roaring at the coin and the daemon was bawling back through the speaking trumpet.

'Bastard thing!'

'Grow to enjoy it I think you did, Bronislaw!' Mammoshad squawked. 'Got a taste for victimhood and the lash. Enjoyed Ahriman inside you, I think, violating your mind and polluting your spirit.'

Klute grabbed his friend from behind, a hand digging into each thrashing shoulder. Torqhuil pulled his device of daemonic congress away from the swing of the hammer and the High Inquisitor's flailing boots.

Czevak shrugged off his friend and stormed across the archeodeck. Klute and Torqhuil gave each other a dark look before the inquisitor set off after his master. He had seen Czevak exit the hangar via an access bulkhead but now out on the corridor he found himself alone. Klute had assumed that the High Inquisitor had desired the privacy of his quarters but the passageway leading up to them was long, dark and empty.

'My lord?' Klute called. He advanced – intent on finding Czevak, barging his way into his private rooms if need be and talking sense into his master. Klute's march soon turned into a jog that half way up the corridor slowed to a suspicious halt. He looked both ways up the access way, eyes probing the shadows, the hairs on the back of his neck standing to a prickle. Something was wrong. The deck lamps were out. He didn't know why but the inquisitor felt as though he was being watched and unconsciously slipped his Cadian street silencer from its thick holster. He span, jabbing the twin barrels of the pistol at the thick shadow opposite, only to have a pair of hands grab him from behind, one over his mouth, the other around his neck. Klute struggled but the figure pulled him back into a devotional maintenance alcove and held him in a feverish embrace. He heard a gentle hush in his ear. It was Czevak.

Klute calmed and lowered his pistol. He tried to turn his head and if he had would have seen his master's eyes darting about the darkness of the corridor and little else. Held still in the deep shadow of the alcove, the Domino field on Czevak's Harlequin coat had immersed itself in reflected gloom and made the High Inquisitor all but indistinguishable from his surroundings.

'Up there,' Czevak hissed, motioning his former acolyte to peer up the corridor at the benighted section beyond. 'By the entrance to my quarters.' Klute squinted up the passageway. 'The masks. They wait for me.'

'Who?' Klute said. 'Who are they? Who waits for you?'

'The servants of the Laughing God – come for their prize. Keepers of the Black Library, come for its secrets and its secrets' keeper.'

Klute shuddered, remembering visions from his youth.

'The Harlequinade?'

'Raimus – I'll not exist a prisoner.'

Klute reached in his pocket and produced a vox-bead, inserting it into his ear.

'Captain Torres, meet me in archeodeck access way east, the High Inquisitor's quarters. Bring a security detail and my satchel. Klute out.'

The two men held there, Klute monitoring his master's shallow breaths, feeling the heat radiating from his meme-virus ravaged body, until the corridor rang with the boots of Savlar Chem-Dogs. Torres was leading them with weapon drawn, Steward-Sergeant Rourke beside her, cradling an assault autorifle. His men stomped up behind, faces obscured by inhalers, in an assortment of scavenged armour. They hugged their own motley collection of weaponry.

'Inquisitor?' Torres called, prompting Klute to step out into the corridor where she tossed him his satchel.

'Inquisitor Czevak believes that the *Malescaythe* has been compromised by an enemy force.'

Klute could see the rogue trader captain's mind racing; no breach alarms or proximity warnings.

'That damned gate!' she spat.

'The warp portal is a distinct possibility,' Klute said.

'Fan out!' Rourke shouted at his men before bringing a helmet vox receiver down, 'Dog-Two, secure warp gate and archeodeck. Dog-Three, take station on the bridge.'

'High Inquisitor?' Torres put to a fazed Czevak. When he didn't answer, she crossed the corridor and reached for a robust handpull set in the wall opposite.

'No klaxons,' Klute warned.

'The hell with that, we've been boarded – I'm sounding the general alarm.'

'Eldar,' Czevak murmured.

'What?' Torres said, swiftly losing patience.

'Eldar Harlequins.'

Torres stumbled on her own words and then took a moment to digest the very bad news that the inquisitor had just given her.

'F-for you?' she finally managed, provoking in the

young inquisitor a violent step forward and a frenzied dashing of palm to temple.

'Of course for me, you inbred void-whore! Who doesn't want the contents of this mind? Who wouldn't slit the throats of everyone on board to claim them?'

Torres had clearly been taken off guard by the inquisitor's uncharacteristic viciousness. She stared into Czevak's doom-filled eyes, which were all the more disturbing, situated as they were, in the High Inquisitor's flushed and feverish face. Czevak leant in further. 'Or reclaim them?'

The furious tension in the High Inquisitor's features suddenly slackened and fell as his knees gave out under him. Between them Klute and Torres caught him – at which the rogue trader captain realised that in Klute's other hand was a syringe. A sedative, freshly selected from the medicae satchel he had asked her to bring.

Steward-Sergeant Rourke stared at the scene in confusion.

Torres shared the sentiment. 'Raimus, what the hell is going on? A straight answer, for the God-Emperor's sake, please.'

'Paranoia,' Klute told her, securing the syringe and hoisting Czevak's arm across his shoulder, 'is not caused by too little information, it's caused by too much. The High Inquisitor suffers from a relapsing meme-virus. Now, help me get him to his quarters.'

'We're not under attack then?' Torres was above all else concerned for the safety and security of her ship.

'No.'

The two of them began to drag the deadweight of the High Inquisitor up the corridor between them. A Savlar Guardsman brought the blown deck lamps back on, bathing the crowded corridor in light.

'You're sure... just paranoia?' Captain Torres asked.

Klute bit at his lower lip as they manipulated Czevak's body through the bulkhead.

'Ma'am?' Rourke pressed.

'Yes, yes,' Klute said with irritation. 'Meme-virus, stress, high temperature, hallucinations.'

'Sergeant, false alarm,' Torres shot with irritation of her own. 'Stand your men down.'

'Wait,' Klute said as he held the High Inquisitor awkwardly. The inquisitor thought on the deck lamps. He'd assumed that Czevak had blown them to aid his concealment. But if he hadn't? If someone else had?

'Let's be sure,' Klute said to the Savlar sergeant. 'Secure the Fornical. Then have your men carry out a sweep of the ship.'

'Right you are, sir,' the Guardsman affirmed, still confused – or at least unconvinced.

As Klute turned back to Torres he found the captain's attractive features knotted with anger and suspicion.

'Help me get him on the bed.'

As the two of them manhandled the High Inquisitor into his cabin cot, Klute's vox-bead chirped.

'Inquisitor.'

'Brother Torqhuil?'

'Inquisitor, the Black Sovereign of Sierra Sangraal has gone. Mammoshad is missing.'

'You're absolutely sure?'

'The daemon is loose on the ship.'

Klute narrowed his eyes.

'What?' Torres demanded, not hearing Torqhuil's warnings over the vox-bead.

Klute turned to Czevak's lank body on the cot; the High Inquisitor's face was still flushed but was free of the torment and tension that had cut into it during his interrogation of the daemon Mammoshad. Bending, Klute rifled through the many pockets of Czevak's Harlequin coat, his fingers finally coming to rest on a circular object that was cool and hard to the touch. Withdrawing the Black Sovereign of Sierra Sangraal, Klute held it up to the light. The metal surface of the coin was gently morphing, almost as though it had melted in the High Inquisitor's pocket, assuming a new shape and features. It was already a different metallic hue and upon its surface a raised representation was bubbling and forming, a blasphemous mockery of the Imperial aquila as a snaggle-toothed avian monstrosity. Czevak could have taken the polluted object but Klute thought it more likely that the thing had found its way into his pocket during the High Inquisitor's attack on Torqhuil's machine – just as it had found its way into the swale gypsy's purse.

'Inquisitor!' Torres called, drawing Klute back to the moment and from the cursed spectacle of the Chaos artefact.

'Where are we?' he asked the rogue trader captain, suddenly himself again.

'On the Kroulx Circumpolar Drift. In a few weeks we might be able to make Nemesis Tessera.'

'Drop out of warp.'

'Is that wise?'

'It's not wise but it is necessary.'

Klute looked down at his master sleeping peacefully. The meme-virus could explain Czevak's hallucinations but so could the malign influence of Mammoshad playing with his expectations and infecting his mind.

'Then what?' Torres asked.

'Pick a star, captain.'

'And then?'

'Then?' Klute echoed, flicking the possessed coin with his thumb and snatching it savagely out of the air. 'Then meet me down in the torpedo bay. This damned coin is going to find a new home in the heart of a raging star.'

'You're going to destroy it?'

'Yes.'

'I don't think Brother Torqhuil or the High Inquisitor are going to like that.'

'Then I guess we'd best not tell them.'

Exit

I

INTERREGNA

Catechorium, Black Ship Divine Thunder, *Above Etiamnum III*

CHORUS

AGONY. LIKE NOTHING Czevak had ever felt.

It was impossible to tell how long he had been aboard the *Divine Thunder*. Stretchered between a filthy cell in the bowels of the Inquisitorial Black Ship and Inquisitor Malchankov's specially prepared catechorium, minutes became hours, hours days and for all Czevak knew, days possibly weeks. Pain seemed to make everything feel longer. During the inquisitor's four hundred and eight years, even in the Emperor's service, he had known many pleasures – almost all fleeting. In Czevak's experience, however, pain always lingered and the torture inflicting that pain invariably reached out beyond the limits of the mind and body to withstand its attentions. Czevak's calling had trained him in the art of such resistance, but it had also taught of its futility. He thanked the God-Emperor that he was not quite there yet.

'Lower him.'

Czevak felt the chains around his broken wrists judder as his smashed body began to descend from where it hung above the bloodied catechorium floor. He was routinely suspended there between beatings and interrogations, his ancient body pulled apart and off the deck by a retracting chain on each arm. Bones had cracked, flesh had torn and organs had ruptured. Routinely, devotional physicians of the Order Hospitaller swept in to perform emergency procedures, bent on keeping the aged inquisitor alive before returning him to further torment. Czevak's mind was a pain-addled fog in which the myriad agonies of his broken body competed for attention.

Czevak's legs could not support him as he reached the deck and his feet slipped and slid in a mucky pool of his own blood. The slack on the chains increased and the inquisitor was allowed to collapse to his knees. As the chains locked off, his shattered arms were stretched taut in place. Czevak moaned incoherently to himself, an interior monologue shot through with internal agonies, mumbled from his swollen, cracked lips. A single spotlight illuminated the dismal scene, blazing at the inquisitor, forcing his bloodshot eyes to retreat further into their bruised sockets.

Sister Archangela Voightdecker stepped out of the gloom, arms folded inside the length of her carnodon fur cloak and her eyes peering imperiously down on the broken body of the inquisitor through her wire spectacle assembly. As a member of the Order of the Eternal Candle she carried no weapon, but she didn't need to. Confessor Graefe was behind her. The confessor was built like a barrel and his shaved head and the brute girth of his forearms lent him more the appearance of a scud wrestler than a defender of the Creed. His hairy arms and fists were covered in hive-world tattoos and his robes wore the filth of a butcher's apron.

'Wake up!' he bawled at Czevak.

Through the crusty slits of his eyes Czevak saw the confessor approach.

Within moments the thug ecclesiarch was upon him, smashing the inquisitor's aged and emaciated body this way and that.

When the assault ended, Czevak was given a moment to think and experience the fresh tortures visited upon his body by the brute priest. The confessor waited to one side, his barrel chest expanding and contracting with exertion. What worried Czevak more was that Voightdecker was holding her ground. She was smirking nastily. Usually, after Graefe had sated his barbaric tendencies on the inquisitor, Voightdecker would advance with a barrage of her own, a barrage of questions and demands. All, Czevak had ensured, had gone unanswered. Why did you betray your race? How many others among your brother inquisitors are xenos lovers like yourself? What poisonous propaganda did you intend to spread at the Conclave at Hydra Cordatus? What impure alien technologies and Chaos artefacts have you exposed yourself to? What did you learn of alien intentions and threats mounted against the Imperium? What heresies did you commit with the xenos eldar? How do Imperial personnel gain entrance to the webway? Where is the Black Library of Chaos? Unending demands designed to incriminate himself and others. Unending threats and accusations of heresy. Until now.

Four armoured figures stepped forward, cardinal world crusaders garbed in simple plate upon which was inscribed runes and ancient Imperial glyphs of purity. Each bore a thunder hammer and shield carrying the sinister insignia of the Ordo Hereticus. They were Valentin Malchankov's Hexenguard and were his personal escort.

The inquisitor himself trundled forth between the honour guard of feudal henchmen. Valentin Malchankov was a Mondominant maniac and narrow interpreter of the Imperial Creed. He had fought every kind of heresy with a simple, unswerving devotion and murdered many whose loyalty to the Emperor had been seemingly less. He had little time for academics and politicians – even amongst his own ordo – and had committed himself to engaging the enemies of the Emperor face to face.

This strategy had unfortunately meant that the thing that presented itself to Czevak was much more machine than man. A set of counterweighted tracks supported a small derrick arrangement, upon which, what was left of Valentin Malchankov was suspended. He had long since lost his legs in his many battles with the alien and unclean and his torso was a tube-infested basket of dead flesh and cybernetic improvements. Like his legs, the Monodominant's arms had also been replaced with bionic attachments. These supported a set of heavy, wicked power claws, the digit quad of each snapped and crackled continually with the savage energy coursing through them. Malchankov's head was that of a man long dead. His flesh was an unhealthy grey and his nose a ragged hole. His ears and hair had all been burnt off and had been replaced with rumpled scarring across the top of his scalp and his face was a patchwork of old stitching and thin, stapled skin. The only things that blazed with youth, vitality and crazed determination were the vat-grown eyeballs that now sat in his skull.

The tracks came to a rest before Czevak, allowing Malchankov's wasted body to tower on its crane over the kneeling inquisitor. The Monodominant grasped one taut chain in his power clawed hand and leant his head down at the prisoner.

'I told you I'd claim your blood,' Malchankov slurped through reconstructed lungs and voice box. 'And now it's mine, every last drop.'

Czevak just gave the Ordo Hereticus monstrosity a bloody gaze. His lips remained sealed.

'You have been enjoying the hospitality of my compatriots,' Malchankov said. 'They tell me they have whipped and beaten you, stretched your body to breaking, cut, burned and choked you. Such barbarism. And yet you say nothing. Answer a few simple questions and this can be all over, old man.'

The same defiant glare from the broken inquisitor.

'I'm beginning to understand their frustration,' Malchankov hissed. Czevak's body suddenly came off its knees to spasmodic life as the Monodominant allowed energy to burn up the chain from his power claw and through his prisoner. Czevak screamed as power arced through his being.

At last the torture came to a close with Czevak slumping back to his knees, his neck slack and head rolling back, his pleading eyes staring at the ceiling.

'I would just kill you, heretic, but there is the small matter of your celebrity. You are one of the most celebrated xenophiles in the Imperium. Your experiences must be catalogued and your transgressions analysed so that I, and those that follow me, may better combat your kind within the ranks of the Holy Inquisition. I will not let you die old man – not even of old age – until you give me the secret heresies to which you have been exposed. I want to know where you have been, with whom you have consorted and what deviant wonders you have seen. Only then will I allow you the peace of death. Do you hear me, Bronislaw Czevak?'

Czevak went to say something, his voice a battered croak. The lines, weights and pulleys on Malchankov's derrick hummed as the Ordo Hereticus inquisitor leant in closer.

'Going deaf,' Czevak told him with a slack-jawed smile. 'Can you repeat that? Everything from "I would just kill you"? Didn't catch the rest.'

Malchankov's cadaverous features contorted before the Monodominant blasted him again, coursing agonising energy from his power claw down through the chain. Czevak spasmed and then trembled as the power burned through his veins.

'My lord,' Sister Archangela Voightdecker finally and fearfully ventured. If Malchankov killed the aged inquisitor then they would never discover the secrets he harboured.

After a few moments more of affliction Malchankov released the chain and allowed Czevak agonising control of his body and mind once more. Malchankov manoeuvred himself closer so that the two inquisitors' faces were almost touching.

'It hurts, yes?' Malchankov beamed. 'You're going to talk to me, heretic. I promise that you are going to talk to me.'

Czevak mumbled something, forcing Malchankov to turn the scarred and ragged hole in the side of his head where his ear had been to the High Inquisitor.

'The Inquisition won't...' Czevak managed feebly.

'Won't tolerate your kidnap and torture?' Malchankov grinned maniacally. 'Well that is where you are wrong, my learned friend. And you have been wrong about a great many things. As I said before, your celebrity poses some problems, but that isn't one of them. Your celebrity is in fact the solution. Everybody wants Bronislaw Czevak – famed High Inquisitor of the Ordo Xenos and visitor to the Black Library of Chaos. The Inquisition wants you. The High Lords of Terra want you. Every apocalyptic crazy in the galaxy wants you. Most of all, the followers of the Dark Gods want you. Renegades, Chaotics, daemons, sorcerers; all would pay in blood for the Black Library's secrets. Your vessel, lost over Cadia in the opening days of the Thirteenth Black Crusade. Let's just blame it on one of them, shall we?'

An Ordo Hereticus serf entered the catechorium and

passed a note to Sister Archangela Voightdecker.

'What?' Czevak croaked at the inquisitor, angling an ear and feigning deafness once more.

Malchankov reached for the chain.

'My lord,' Archangela interrupted again. 'Mordant Hex reports from the surface that he has located the gate.'

Malchankov threw the Sister an irritated glance before peering back into Czevak's rebellious eyes.

'You're right, of course. This has run its course. Time to step it up. Tell Mordant to begin the ritual.'

'But without the…'

'Let me worry about that.' Malchankov leant back in on Czevak. 'Inquisitor Czevak is about to give me that information now.'

'What information?' Czevak said.

'Why, the rune designations for the eldar warp gate on Etiamnum III,' Malchankov told him with maniacal certainty.

'And why would I do that, Witch Hunter?' Czevak asked weakly.

Czevak's vision faded for a moment, which didn't unduly worry the inquisitor. Under the barrage of Confessor Graefe's mighty fists he was often knocked unconscious. This felt different, however. It was almost like having his head held under water and then being allowed to resurface. Blinking the light back to his eyes, Czevak found that impossibly his surroundings were changing. Both the walls of his prison and the faces of his gaolers were melting. His stomach had long been empty but if there had been anything in it then Czevak was sure that he would have brought it up on the deck. His centre of gravity seemed to flip and his surroundings assumed a fresh terror.

He was no longer in the dank catechorium of an Ordo Hereticus Black Ship. The unsmiling Inquisitorial serfs were gone and in their place were droves of misshapen cultists, dressed in gaudy robes and afflicted with warped limbs and horrific mutations. They manned consoles and stations on a colossal, labyrinthine bridge, waiting in attendance on larger figures on the huge command deck who were all finished in cobalt and gold. The vessel interior had a flowing architecture with features and equipment rolling fluidly into one another, as though dissolved by some unnatural force that seemed to hang in the crackling air. Even the gigantic view ports appeared melted into irregularity and revealed the dusty, red surface of Etiamnum III gently spinning below them.

The Hexenguard were no longer hulking figures in blessed plate but Traitor Space Marines in ancient power armour, helmeted Thousand Sons in blistering azure, clutching bolters and waiting obediently for orders. The only armoured figures without helmets were the cloaked sorcerers who acted like lieutenants on the bridge, their unhealthy features glowing with dark power and minds in constant congress with the warp. Chief among these was an androgynous tyrant standing where Sister Archangela Voightdecker had been. With the traitor Space Marines and sorcerers standing about him, Czevak could only reason that he had never been an Ordo Hereticus prisoner aboard the *Divine Thunder* at all. His present predicament was far worse than that. His prison was in fact a Chaos Marine battle-barge belonging to the Thousand Sons traitor legion, masked through the duration of his confinement using Tzeentchian illusory magic.

'Welcome to the *Impossible Fortress*,' the sorcerer leered. Gone was the androgynous monster. His face had changed and seemed in constant motion: a Cadian grimace, a courtesan's smile, a nightworld barbarian, the alien eyes of an eldar, the rictus grin of a servitor, Voightdecker, Czevak himself. The transformations continued, less a morphing of the flesh than an elusive trick of the eye.

Turning, Czevak found himself face to face not with Valentin Malchankov but with the extravagantly horned

Crusader-pattern helm of the sorcerer's hulking master.
The ornate power armour gleamed blue brilliance and
was draped in robes covered in arcane runes and symbols. Polished skulls and ancient artefacts dripped from
the psyker and his entire being shimmered with otherworldly power. Where Malchankov's power claws had
been there were now the spindly gauntlets of the Chaos
sorcerer. Using them, he unclipped his helmet to the
twin, equalising sighs of the armour's pressure seals and
removed the horned helm. Czevak flinched as the raw
power of the Space Marine sorcerer was revealed to him.

Czevak felt as though he were in the presence of a
god – or at least one that aspired to such exaltation.
The air was bleached of all else but the being's will. A
cold desire – devoid of the fever of human passion –
saturated Czevak. A purity of purpose so powerful as to
scorch lesser evils and the taint of corruption from its
unswerving path. The inquisitor looked on Ahriman. It
was as though his flesh was on fire with a sapphire radiance. His eyes were hungry orbs of intensity but his face
a visage of godly calm. Ahriman seemed everywhere at
once – a being out of time – like a busy deity, simultaneously answering the prayers of his worshippers and
speaking through the mouths of distant prophets.

'Inquisitor,' Ahriman said. His voice hurt to be heard,
everywhere as it was, but the words were composed and
tranquil. 'Let us talk as men who have seen some of the
galaxy's wonder. Little should surprise us. If the frailty
of the flesh were not the key to the soul then believe
me, inquisitor, I would not waste time searching for the
secrets of others, in yours.'

With that Czevak's heart stopped and crippling cramps
began to reach out through his chest. The inquisitor's eyes
widened in panic and once again he began to convulse
against the restriction of his bonds. Ahriman's blazing
eyes narrowed before the sorcerer laid his gauntlet upon
the aged inquisitor's chest. The spasms subsided and the

cramps faded to terrifying memories.

'Like all others – of the flesh, of the other, of the ether – I am driven by need. I would no less allow your heart to stop beating than I would allow my own, inquisitor – for both now beat beyond their natural inclination. They beat that I might learn the rune designations for the eldar warp gate on Etiamnum III. They beat that I might breach the eldar webway without invitation. That I might enter, as you have, the hallowed halls of the Black Library of Chaos and further learn my fate, the fate of this galaxy and the relationship between.'

Czevak threw forward his face and spat a stringy gruel of blood and saliva into Ahriman's blazing eyes. Blinking, the Thousand Sons sorcerer unclipped one of his gauntlets and brought a glowing hand to his god-like face. With delicate fingertips he wiped the blood and spit from his eyes before rubbing the spittle between fingers and thumb with interest.

'For all this talk of hearts beating,' Ahriman told him with a cool, celestial certainty, 'blood is not my medium. But I have seen what you may do and what you will do. Please forgive me the horror we both know you will make me put you through.'

Flourish

I

ACT III, CANTO I

Executive quarters, Rogue trader Malescaythe, *The Eye of Terror*

Enter TORRES

'I'M GLAD TO see you are feeling better, High Inquisitor,' Reinette Torres lied.

'Groxcrap,' Klute heard Czevak reply between mouthfuls of restorative thistlebean soup and black bread. 'But thanks anyway.'

The High Inquisitor was sitting amongst the blankets of his cot, with one wrapped around his bare shoulders, while he balanced the bowl and tray across his breaches and crossed knees. Klute passed him a steaming cup of quince tea. Czevak continued to feast with Klute and his gathered retinue looking on, his hair a mess but the feverish madness gone from his face. Klute had forbidden contact with the High Inquisitor for the past two weeks, allowing Czevak time – away from the excitation of the

Eye and the retinue's findings – to beat this latest flare
up of the meme-virus and recover his former composure.
The final week Klute had left the recovering inquisitor
pretty much to himself, leaving day to day basics of care
to infirmatory servitors. Meanwhile, Klute had had his
hands full with Torres and Epiphani. The pair had taken
to screaming at each other once again across the rogue
trader's bridge. With them, Klute had been attempting
to navigate the *Malescaythe* through the nightmares and
perversities of the Eye, bound for the relative safety of
Nemesis Tessera. Epiphani's reckless gambling with the
captain's vessel had been a constant source of conflict on
the journey, however, leaving Klute with a migraine and
an unenviable reliance on both of them.

Klute had brought the High Inquisitor the tray of
food and the rest of the retinue – at Czevak's insistence.
Torqhuil stood hulking sentry on the cabin door, while
Hessian and Epiphani luxuriated playfully on the fine
furniture of the executive cabin. The warp-seer was disconcertingly dressed for battle, despite the fact that she
had not left the vessel for weeks. Her hair was up in a
plaited band that was wrapped around her head and
her chest was bound in tubular plates of mirrored flak.
Cargo pants and strider boots completed the relatively
simple outfit with urban camouflage silks coiling limbs,
plaits and plates to lend the outfit a martial unity. Father
hummed above them and Klute sat on the edge of the
cot, fussing with his satchel of medicae apparatus, taking Czevak's vital signs while the High Inquisitor ate and
drank.

Klute watched Torres close the bulkhead and make
her way inside the High Inquisitor's quarters. It looked
nothing like the cabin into which Klute and the captain
had deposited the ailing Czevak weeks before. The walls
and even the ceiling and floor were covered with chalked
diagrams, notations and numbers. Parchment and pages
were tacked to every available surface and lengths of

twine stretched across the room in a miasmic pattern, each carrying its own clothesline of pegged scraps of vellum, scribbled charts and graphs, torn from the sacred texts of the captain's own stellagraphium. Stacks of diabolical tomes, freshly requested from Torqhuil's stasis chambers, decorated the room and from the ceiling of one dark corner, Torres found the cage of her insane Navigator, Rasputus Guidetti. The mutant had been released from his skull-bridle but was still incarcerated in his gibbet cage. Webbed feet dangled through the bars and brushed the floor while his webbed digits thumbed through a portfolio of ancient star charts. The Navigator was surrounded by acres of crumpled vellum that was still spewing out of the *Hellebore*'s bridge mnemonic cogitator – the data bank having found a new home in Czevak's cabin.

'What the…' Torres began, but almost immediately came to a pause of her own. The fury that had danced across her face faded to exhaustion and the rogue trader captain rubbed one tired cheek with a weary hand.

'You done?' Czevak put to Torres.

She pursed her lips then nodded, allowing herself to fall back into a chaise longue. Czevak handed Klute the bowl and tray, as well as the wired pads the inquisitor had affixed to his chest. He took a quaff of the quince tea.

'Then I'll begin. Firstly, I'd like to apologise to you all. It seems that my ailments were responsible for some panic aboard the ship. Inquisitor Klute assures me that my delirious insistence that the *Malescaythe* had been compromised by an alien force was unfounded and that the ship has been searched from prow to keel. Even I get it wrong sometimes.'

'You think that the eldar are hunting you?' Torqhuil asked from the bulkhead.

'I know they're hunting me,' Czevak said.

'Because of what you saw and learned in the Black Library of Chaos?'

'Because of what others might do with that information,' Czevak corrected the Relictors Space Marine, 'should my knowledge lead them to its hallowed doors. But I was wrong. It was the virus, it was the fever. The Harlequins are not here.' Czevak got to his feet, drawing the blanket around him like a cloak. 'Bed rest has afforded me many hours to think on our present predicament: Mammoshad, Xarchos, Ahriman and the Thousand Sons.'

At mention of the daemon Mammoshad, Klute and Torres exchanged guilty glances that were lost on the High Inquisitor, who was taking position in the centre of the vandalised cabin. He uncoiled a cable from the *Hellebore*'s mnemonic cogitator and screwed it into the mind-impulse link situated in the back of his head. As he walked, the cable trailed after him about the cabin.

'As my fever broke and I began to dwell once more on Mammoshad's words – this time with my faculties intact – I came to realise that the warp-spawn thing had in fact given us the location of Ahzek Ahriman, as I had demanded.'

'I was there,' Torqhuil said. 'The daemon did nothing but twist us with its lies and insanity.'

'And I started to think on exactly that,' Czevak told him with growing excitement. 'The twists and turns of its lies and the warped logic of its utterances. Mammoshad is a daemonic entity, a Tzeentchian essence. There was truth in its lies on Ablutraphur. And there has been truth in its tortured lies since.'

'Did not dwelling on such things drive you to fevered madness?' Klute warned. He was eager that his former master not tempt a relapse of his ailments. More than that, he hoped that Czevak wasn't suggesting further conference with the daemon. A conference he could no longer demand.

'When following the dread logic of the damned and daemonic, a little insanity can take you a long way,' Czevak admitted. 'I demanded the location of Ahriman and when the monster denied me that I demanded the location of his apprentice. "You seek the student to find the master?" it said – which at the time I took to be a question. It was not.'

'What was it?' Torres asked.

'An instruction. Look for Xarchos and we will find Ahriman.'

'But we knew that,' Torquil said. 'And Mammoshad never told you where you could find Korban Xarchos.'

'But it did,' Czevak told them. 'In its own sick, perverted way. It could not resist giving us the first clue.'

'Which was?' Klute asked.

'Follow the screams.'

Klute nodded slowly. 'I heard that myself, but what does it mean?'

'I spent many hours in that cot considering possible answers to exactly that question.'

'And?' Klute had never enjoyed Czevak's penchant for suspense.

'Daemon tracts like the *Corpus Vivexorsectio* hold part of the answer. They detail the ways in which daemonic entities can be summoned – usually as part of arcane rituals that open rifts in the fabric of reality, interdimensional tears through which daemons can pass from the warp into the real world. These rituals are as bizarre and varied as the cultists that conduct them but many share a common practice. Would anyone like to guess what?'

'Human sacrifice,' Torquil rumbled from the bulkhead.

'Precisely,' Czevak said in mock congratulation. 'A general rule in these perverse proceedings seems to be that the more powerful the entity crossing over…'

'The larger the sacrifice?' Klute said.

'The larger the sacrifice,' Czevak repeated.

'You think that Korban Xarchos is involved with human sacrifice and daemonic summoning? That should hardly surprise us,' Torquil said.

'Right.'

'And "Follow the screams",' Klute added. 'The screams of the sacrificed? Follow them where? I would imagine the depraved sorcerers of the Thousand Sons – Xarchos among them – are sacrificing and summoning all over the galaxy.'

'Right again,' Czevak beamed, raising his mug of tea to the inquisitor. 'It's that brand of logic that led me to consider where.'

Moving towards the opposite wall Czevak directed the gathering's attention to what seemed to be a convoluted scrawl of a chalk diagram. The dramatic dimension of the schematic madness ran the length of the executive chamber and was annotated with scribblings and sweeping lines indicating some kind of pattern or relationship.

'What is it?' Klute put to his friend, who seemed fired and increasingly enthused.

'It's a star chart,' Captain Torres answered. In his cage, Rasputus the maniac Navigator gibbered. Standing and with outstretched finger, Torres identified, 'Coreward and Rimward declinations; sectors by three dimensions and system clusters. I don't know what these are,' Torres admitted sweeping her delicate fingers across a sequence of chalk circles – all of different sizes – that seemed to overlap. She leant in closer to examine one of Czevak's notations, 'But that looks like Tituba Prime and that is Ablutraphur.'

'Ablutraphur?' Klute shivered, having barely lived down the nightmare of their recent visit.

'These sectors are thousands of light-years away, on the far edge of the Eye,' Torres said.

'As we suspected, the *Hellebore* has travelled far and wide, from one side of this damned region of hellspace to the other. The further back we trawl through her mnemonic log the more we learn,' Czevak said. 'For instance, we now learn that the *Hellebore*'s encounter with the *Pluton*, or rather Korban Xarchos's *Rubrician* in Gehennabyss Reaches was not its first. The *Hellebore* had run down on the *Rubrician* at least nine times before, each time with the Thousand Sons' vessel using sorcery and illusion to evade attack. It seems that the captains of the two vessels were engaged in an ongoing rivalry. A game of cat and mouse.'

'Yes, but which was which?' Klute mused.

Czevak snatched a trailing fistful of vellum from Rasputus's webbed hands and walked over to the star chart chalked into the opposite wall.

'Sightings of the *Rubrician* as *Pluton* include Pyrrus,' he began, reading off the parchment and smacking his fist against a sketched planetoid down by his waist. 'Cardinal world, a beacon of pious civilisation on the edge of an otherwise dark corner of the galaxy. Pyrrus suffered an outbreak of mass corruption twelve years ago.' Czevak briefly consulted a scrap of paper pegged to one of the lengths of twine that were strung across the cabin like a spider's web. 'Six million devout Imperial citizens and members of the Ecclesiarchy died during a planet-wide service to Saint Stephano. Inquisitorial records show that victims perished over a four hour period. Observations made by medicae personnel suggest that an ingested mutative substance corrupted internal organs that then assumed a life of their own. They evacuated their owners' bodies, slowly killing them from the inside out. Nice.'

'And you think Korban Xarchos was responsible for this atrocity?' Klute asked, but Czevak held up a finger to request a pause.

'I traced cargo shipments of wheat cane to Pyrrus from the agri-worlds of Alpha, Beta and Delta Myrias. Wheat cane used to make the devotional wafers taken during the service. An Administratum audit from thirteen years ago indicates record crop yields for the Myrias agri-worlds – an increase so large that Administratum clerks were sent out to investigate.'

'Is this what you've been doing in here?' Captain Torres put to the High Inquisitor. Czevak ignored the rogue trader captain and continued, tapping his chalk against a trio of worlds not far from Pyrrus.

'Guess what they found?' the High Inquisitor smiled. He didn't wait for an answer. 'Expansive fields of wheat cane that should have been – even with optimum weather conditions – about a metre high, stretching for the skies. The Administratum auditors found it growing thick, fat and strong like forests. Alpha, Beta, Delta Myrias were all overrun with the rampant crop. Workers were shipping it out as fast as they could, to destinations like Pyrrus, but couldn't keep up with the growth. The crops were so vast they even started to change the balance of oxygen in the atmosphere and the agri-worlders were forced to wear masks for fear of atmospheric poisoning. Finally, just like Pyrrus, the Inquisition was summoned to investigate but by the time a team arrived, all they found were three raging planetoids each bathed in its own swirling firestorm. Oxygen levels had grown to such an extent that their very atmospheres had ignited and burned. Between all three agri-worlds, casualties were estimated at two million souls.'

'Where did you get this information from?' Torres asked. 'Astropathic communion across long distances is impossible in the Eye. And that kind of detail is not available on the *Malescaythe*.'

'But it is,' Czevak assured her with confidence and tapped his temple with the chalk. 'Many of these details are already in here, the trick is putting them together. The genius is in seeing the pattern.'

'The virus,' Klute explained. 'The afflicted soak up data – significant or otherwise – like a sponge.' The inquisitor turned back to Czevak. 'So the unnatural crop led to both the deaths on Pyrrus and the Myrias agri-worlds,' Klute connected.

'The question is what caused the unnatural crop growth?' Torqhuil said.

'And for that we take what detail we have from the *Corpus Vivexorsectio* and cross reference it with activities of the Dark Mechanicus Daecropsicum sect,' said Czevak.

'The group that dissected the daemon and bound its parts in objects like that damned coin?' Torres asked.

'Yes.' Czevak jabbed the chalk at her like a professor.

The captain and Klute exchanged another wide-eyed glance. Czevak fell straight back into his thesis.

'The Daecropsicum used many parts of the daemon Mammoshad's warp-corporal form and bound them individually to artefacts and dark technologies. We'll come to those in a moment. What interests us right now are the parts that were not used. My researches have revealed, for instance, that bones from the colossal beast's carcass were sold and traded between various cults and heretic groups on the Knubla Frontier before disappearing from record. A kilotonne of unregistered bonemeal, however, did arrive in the Myrias system as part of a consignment of fertiliser. In this way, Mammoshad's bones are responsible for the deaths on Pyrrus and the Myrias agri-worlds.'

'Emperor's wounds!' Klute said. 'All those people.'

'I still don't see how this tells us where Korban Xarchos is – or at least where you claim that Mammoshad claims he is,' Torqhuil called from the bulkhead.

'One line of inquiry at a time, Brother Relictor. The relics lead us to the screams and the screams will lead us to that bastard sorcerer. Trust me.' Czevak gave the Space Marine a piercing gaze. 'These initial findings led me into a pattern, a strange correlation between recorded sightings of the *Rubrician* in the *Hellebore*'s mnemonic log and the bound daemonic artefacts of the Daecropsicum.'

Czevak moved along the wall, trailing vellum and ducking between lines of string, consulting the pegged notes and scraps of parchment that dangled from them.

'*Rubrician* was sighted en route to Tituba Prime, where the Cadian Forty-fourth and a Slaaneshi warhost called the *Raptur* disappeared just months before in their entirety. According to lost Medrang transcripts, Tituba Prime was the last known resting place of the infamous Counter-Clock Heart.'

'Counter-Clock Heart?'

'A Daecropsicum creation,' Czevak explained with no little awe. 'A blend of Dark Mechanicus technology and a daemonic heart, a heart I have good reason to believe belonged to Mammoshad.'

'But what happened to the Cadian Forty-fourth?' Torres asked.

'Legend has it,' Torqhuil informed her solemnly, 'that the heart beats backwards. With every backward beat those around it, for hundreds of kilometres around, regress in age as though time is flowing in reverse for their own bodies, man to child, child to infant, until…'

'Until they die by never being born,' Klute concluded. Torqhuil nodded.

'The Cadian Forty-fourth, estimated number of *Raptur* cultists and the remaining population of Tituba Prime post-hostilities means that we're looking at about a million casualties,' Czevak calculated, his giddiness at odds with the loss of life he was weighing up. He drained his cup of cooling tea and deposited it on a side cabinet.

'Why the preoccupation with casualties?' Torres said, uncomfortable with the High Inquisitor's building excitement.

'Not yet,' he simply told her before moving from his chalk sketch of Tituba Prime to a large planetoid just out of his reach near the ceiling. 'UV6-26; in the Eye of Terror but originally designated a death world by Imperial expeditionaries. The Eye is always in flux. A huge population of warped ferals were found to have survived the horrific dangers of the planetary fauna. The only recorded survivors of UV6-26 – that is those who returned from its surface alive – claim that it wasn't the death world environment that did for them. A contingent of Doom Eagles Space Marines lost three-quarters of their number to savages armed simply with horn bows and arrows whose long, blue shafts had been crafted from the feathers of some huge, daemonic bird.

The Doom Eagles never sighted the creature itself on the surface but the arrows flew with an ethereal fire and effortlessly punched through power armour and the hides of the colossal reptiles that stalked the death world forests. The owners of such armour – both Adeptus Astartes and mega fauna – instantly spasmed and contorted into Chaotic spawn. An arrow recovered by the Space Marines and returned for analysis was found to bear markings I now find in the pages of the *Corpus Vivexorsectio*. The most recent visitor to UV6-26 was the rogue trader *Dark Frontier*, that found only a tiny tribe of abhumans remained – still armed with their daemonic weapons – the perpetrators of tribal genocide. Estimated casualties, four million.'

'Czevak–'

'*Rubrician* sighted, in the Archive Worlds. Here three heretic populations – the worlds of Shenghis, Mizar Blue and Brannigan's Hope – fought over an artefact called the Obsidoculus. Heretical accounts claim different things of its appearance but most identify it as a large, irregular shard of warpsidium on a heavy iron chain. Those that looked closely enough through the dark glass claimed that that jewel contained an actual eye, through the rotten lens of which the future was revealed. These heretic civilisations each fought for possession of the powerful gem and through possessing it, each was shown the survival of their race at the expense of the other two worlds. This set in motion a war of the worlds, initiated by the coordinated manipulations of the Obsidoculus, a war that ended with the destruction of all three heretic races in atomic fires of their enemies' making. Total casualties, two billion lives.'

'Czevak–'

'Vegatra IV – again, the *Rubrician* sighted. The Tzeentchian sorcerer Elba Draghan unlocks the potential of a grotesque staff, created by the Daecropsicum from Mammoshad's withered forearm and left claw. No name recorded but what is known is that it had the power to wrack the planet with tectonic quakes and all manner of seismic doom. Casualties, three and a half million.'

'High Inquisitor, please–'

'Wait!' Czevak ordered sharply. 'Daemon weapons in the hands of warped marauders, madmen and Chaos Space Marines; the screaming blades, spawncannon, inferno blasters and kris knives capable of cutting through the fabric of time and space. All engineered by the Daecropsicum using parts of Mammoshad's vivisected form. Casualties – Wombwort, Hive Havoque, Minerva Reach, the Triggonaut Sphere. Estimates of between one and two million souls.'

'Czevak!' Klute called at his friend. 'You could not have stopped all of these atrocities, even with the *Atlas Infernal*.'

The two inquisitors stared at one another.

'Stop them?' Czevak said.

'Ahriman and his foul followers are everywhere…'

'Ahriman did not commit these acts,' Czevak told him. Klute frowned. The High Inquisitor stepped forward. 'I have been so foolish. All our time on Arach-Cyn I thought that the Thousand Sons were gathering artefacts – the terrible tomes and works of the Daecropsicum in order to enhance their sorcerous power. The *Rubrician* has been sighted near the resting places of many of these artefacts.'

'Ahriman's hunger for knowledge and power is without comparison. His followers and cultists compete in their acquirement of such ancient artefacts,' the Relictor Techmarine put to Czevak.

'Korban Xarchos is trying to impress his master,' Czevak agreed. 'But not by acquiring these relics. He's destroying them.'

'That doesn't make any sense,' Torqhuil disagreed. 'Ahriman would have Xarchos flayed for such sacrilege.'

'Their power would be lost to Ahriman,' Klute agreed.

'You're not thinking big enough. The artefacts are not the prize. Xarchos must already have a copy of the *Corpus Vivexorsectio*; that's how he has traced these artefacts. He has collected the assorted work of the Daecropsicum – Mammoshad's fragmented evil harnessed in the work of the Dark Mechanicum. He has placed these items in the hands of lunatics in specific locations in this region of the Eye.' Czevak thrust his finger at the chalk-scrawled star chart. 'Many of the sightings occur after, rather than before the inevitable tragedies these planets suffered. Xarchos must have come back.'

'To destroy the artefacts?' Torres asked.

'He murdered countless millions using the artefacts and then destroyed them? Why would he do that?' Klute said. 'They would almost certainly have proved their worth.'

'You say countless millions,' Czevak said, moving back to the wall. 'But I believe that their actual number was important. Mammoshad said follow the screams, so that's what I did. Death is a corporal event in reality but has a spiritual equivalent in the warp. The Ruinous Powers themselves are said to be sustained by these energies – the actions and emotions of the living and the souls of the dead. That is why the eldar wear the spirit stones we saw collected on Arach-Cyn, for if their souls were not trapped by such technologies then they would be claimed by She-Who-Thirsts – the Chaos Power of Slaanesh. Using the faster than light average speed of astropathic communication through the warp as a baseline, I calculated the relative distance reached by these energies – released at the moment of death – given the time and location of these tragedies.'

'But there were many deaths in numerous events,' Klute said.

'Imagine the psychic essence of millions of deaths rippling out through the warp like raindrops hitting the still surface of a pond,' Czevak pictured for him. 'Each radiating out, ripple crossing ripple. Where multiple ripples overlap you would have pockets of intense spiritual energy.'

Czevak moved back and forth along the wall, drawing attention to the chalk circles around each massacre site that Torres had failed to identify and where they overlapped like a Venn diagram. He slammed the chalk into the only planet situated in an area of dreadspace covered by every circle.

'Melmoth's World,' Torres recognised.

'Which is where – by following the screams – we will find Xarchos and, therefore, Ahriman,' Czevak told the gathering, a self-satisfied smile sitting across his face.

'But why there? Why this collection of energy on that one world?' Klute asked.

'And why destroy the Dark Mechanicus artefacts? That still seems unnecessary,' Torqhuil said. Such waste bothered him as both a Relictor and a Techmarine. Czevak's smile cracked into an equally self-satisfied chuckle.

'Xarchos was never interested in the artefacts,' Czevak insisted. 'Only in what they could achieve. He wanted a much greater gift for his master. A colossal daemonic entity to do his bidding with the power of all of the artefacts combined. Xarchos believes that the Daecropsicum were wrong – a daemon is not more than the sum of its parts. As one whole powerful being it could demolish fleets, sunder worlds and possibly breach the barriers of interdimensional reality, gaining Ahriman access to the webway once more.'

'You're talking about…' Klute began fearfully.

'Mammoshad – King of Kings, Enslaver of the Craven Worlds and Keeper of the Vault Abyssal. Ahriman needs it. And Xarchos wants to bring it back. Raising such a daemon would take the energy created by so many coordinated tragedies and would entail the destruction of Mammoshad's individual parts – experimentally bound as they were to artefacts by the Daecropsicum. Then, with it released back into the warp, the Thousand Sons could repeat the rituals detailed in the *Corpus Vivexorsectio* and bring the daemon back, whole, powerful and bound. As ally or slave, Ahriman would use Mammoshad to wreak havoc across the galaxy with astronomical loss of life. Much greater than his apprentice achieved in the Eye.'

'If Korban Xarchos already had a copy of the *Corpus Vivexorsectio* – why return to Arach-Cyn for another uncovered copy?' Torqhuil asked.

Czevak's face creased with annoyance.

'Perhaps his copy was degraded, damaged or incomplete,' Czevak answered, swiftly piecing together a hypothesis. 'Either way, it was a trap. Xarchos left one of his mindless brethren waiting for me in the sarcophocrate, remember?'

'But what if the whole damn thing is a trap?' Klute demanded. 'God-Emperor knows, these Tzeentchian bastards seem perfectly adept at such a convolution. If anything, it's their specialty.'

Klute's question gave Czevak pause for thought, but with the cloud of irritation clearing from his face, the High Inquisitor shrugged.

'If it was, it failed. To bring that monstrous daemon back to existence on Melmoth's World, Korban Xarchos would have to succeed in destroying all of the Daecropsicum's artefacts. We have the Black Sovereign. We have the essence of Mammoshad's greed and ambition and without it the Thousand Sons simply cannot draw the entity back to existence.' Czevak put a savage, triumphant cross through the chalk representation of Melmoth's World on his map. Then he turned on Klute. 'But you were wise to keep the Black Sovereign away from me. Sooner or later the damned thing would have forced me to destroy it. And then where would we be?'

Czevak snatched Klute's ruffled dress shirt from the back of a chair where it had been cleaned and starched and threw it on.

'Where are you going?' Klute enquired with caution.

'Where do you think I'm going?'

'Well, I think you think you're going to Melmoth's World.'

'Korban Xarchos is there. Ahriman is there. Of course I'm going to Melmoth's World. I'm ahead of the curve now – and have the element of surprise. This might be my only chance to destroy him.' A little of the fever seemed to return to the High Inquisitor's eyes.

'Tell him,' Torres insisted, now on her feet.

'Silence woman,' Klute growled back.

'Tell him.'

'Tell me what? What do you have to tell me, Raimus?'

'You are so close to it; so involved in the intricacies of events that surround you that you fail to see the larger canvas, my friend,' Klute told his mentor with jaw-tightened honesty.

'What have you done, Raimus?' Czevak said.

'As I said before, it's all a horribly predictable trap. We are being played by an evil hundreds of light-years away – all of us. And you, my lord are the most predictable of all.'

Czevak turned on Torres with grim, uncompromising eyes.

'Speak now, captain.'

'I destroyed the Black Sovereign,' Klute admitted.

'We destroyed it,' the rogue trader captain corrected. Czevak's face fell and his shoulders sagged.

'You had no right,' Torquhil growled from the other side of the High Inquisitor's quarters, the Space Marine's own fury building. 'That artefact could have done unfathomable damage to the Ruinous Powers and their minions...'

'Do you have any idea what you have done?' Czevak roared at them.

'It was my decision,' Klute said.

'What? To condemn billions to death at the claws of a colossal, daemonic entity?'

'You were half out of your mind, my lord and could not be consulted,' Klute snarled back.

'But if you had – I don't think even I would have done something so insanely foolish.'

'I beg to differ, High Inquisitor,' Klute informed him, 'but I think you just might have. You said as much yourself.'

Czevak seethed for a moment.

'How?' he said to Torres. 'How did you destroy it?'

'We shot it into a star.'

'Which star?'

'Lupratrix.'

'Lupratrix? Lupratrix is on the Kroulx Circumpolar Drift,' Czevak said dangerously. He burrowed into Klute with unforgiving eyes. 'Are you taking me back to Nemesis Tessera, old friend?'

'Listen to me, my lord,' Klute pleaded but his words were cold like iron. 'You have a once in a ten generation mind, a brilliant mind – brilliantly predictable. These daemons and monsters have hooked you and now are drawing you in. Can't you see? You think you're hunting Ahriman but in reality he is hunting you and this trap – this elaborate trap, elaborate enough to fox even you – is the game trail upon which you will be caught. He cannot acquire you on the labyrinthine webway so he has drawn you out. Out to Melmoth's World, where he will finish what he started and take every last secret hidden in that brilliant mind. The Black Library will be his and the Imperium doomed.'

'You wish to save me from a trap by walking me into another?' Czevak said to his former student. 'You think the Inquisition will do any less to me than Ahriman? They'll kill us all, you fool.'

'After transporting us to Nemesis Tessera, Captain Torres intends to sell her cargo of recovered artefacts, including the Lost Fornical of Urien-Myrdyss, on the black markets of the Rubicon Straits. There she will undoubtedly recover her family's fortune. On the way she has agreed to take Brother Torqhuil, Epiphani and Hessian to any location they choose. They will live and so will we.'

'You are deluded.'

'You're wrong, my lord. The Thirteenth Black Crusade has changed priorities in the Eye. Abaddon has his claws in Cadia's sacred earth and the dark forces of the Despoiler are spread across the region, gaining ground every day. Necessity is our greatest ally at this desperate time. The Imperium needs you. I am confident that our ordo brothers will put aside their petty prejudice and see that our best hope to defeat Abaddon's warhost, and finally put an end to these murderous Crusades, lies in your experience, your knowledge of the Black Library and your links to the eldar.'

'Which they will extract on a rack!' Czevak bawled.

The two men regarded each other, eyes aflame. Hessian beamed at the men, feeding on the hatred flowing between them. Epiphani looked bored and flicked open her snuff box. She took a lazy snort of Spook and her eyes began to flutter with psychoactive ecstasy. Czevak unscrewed the cogitator cable from the mind-impulse link in his skull and allowed the line to drop to the cluttered cabin floor.

'We need to choose a side, sir,' Klute argued back. 'And there will never be a better time. For too long we have both been in the hinterlands of heresy, living a renegade existence. Remain and we will become what we swore to hunt down and destroy. It is inevitable. It is part of the essence of this damned place. It's time to go home. It's time to rejoin the ranks of our Holy Ordo and once again carry out the Emperor's work, actually under his banner and in his name. It's time, sir.'

For the longest time, Czevak stood still, staring at the floor and saying nothing. His face was a shattered mirror of emotions: anger, betrayal, exhaustion and fear. All eyes remained on him but no one spoke. When he did move, the gathering jumped slightly – not knowing what the High Inquisitor would do. Opening a nalwood wardrobe the High Inquisitor extracted his Harlequin coat and slipped it on. Pulling on Klute's Cretacian hunting boots he extracted the gleaming bulk of the *Atlas Infernal*. He pointed the ancient tome's gilded spine at Klute.

'You really want to visit Nemesis Tessera?' Czevak asked his former student with no little gravity.

'Yes, my lord.'

'And you would accept responsibility for the consequences of such a visit?' Czevak put to him.

Klute hesitated. 'Yes, High Inquisitor.'

Czevak nodded slowly.

'Then I'll go with you. But not through the front door. We aren't going to just walk up to a secret, sub-planetary Inquisition fortress, hold out our wrists and give ourselves up – you understand me? This will be done on my terms.'

'Fair enough,' Klute replied with obvious relief. He would take what he could get from the High Inquisitor.

'You,' Czevak said, indicating Captain Torres. 'Close on Nemesis Tessera and take station. Do not reveal yourself to the garrison vessels in orbit, as soon as they know what you are and where you've been they will blow you out of existence. May I suggest, Heinus Regula. It's a barren moon, with a dense iron core, which should be sufficient enough to mask the *Malescaythe*'s signature from scans and patrols.'

'Anything else?'

'A squad of your most light-footed and light-fingered Guardsmen.'

'As you wish,' Torres replied coolly, looking to Klute for confirmation, which the inquisitor gave with a nod.

'The rest of you with me. I want to show you something.'

With that, Czevak pushed past Torqhuil's armoured form and exited the cabin for the archeodeck.

'Inquisitor?' the Relictors Space Marine asked. Epiphani and Hessian hovered, with Father humming overhead. Epiphani was holding Czevak's empty cup.

'Well?' Klute asked her.

The warp-seer peered into the mug, her eyes still glossy with the future. She then angled it towards the inquisitor. Inside the bottom was speckled with tea leaves. 'What do you see?'

'A dagger. Unsheathed. I see a betrayal.'

Klute and Torqhuil exchanged grim, urgent glances.

'Watch him,' Klute told them as he went to follow the High Inquisitor. 'And be ready for anything.'

Exeunt

I

ACT III, CANTO II

Reliquary chamber XIII.3, Dungeon archive, Nemesis Tessera Fortress

Enter CZEVAK with KLUTE, BROTHER TORQHUIL, EPIPHANI with FATHER, and HESSIAN, flanked by STEWARD-SERGEANT ROURKE and a SAVLAR CHEM-DOG SQUAD

'TORCHES.'

'Where the hell are we?'

With the Savlar penal legionnaires still fiddling with their barrel-slung lamps and torches, the only light in the chamber came from Father's haunting, blue, bionic orbs and the faint, sickly glow of the daemonhost Hessian. The Guardsmen would have been faster but for the fact that without exception it had been their first experience of the webway and its inter-dimensional peculiarities. After the alien experience of the webway's labyrinthine

passages, getting used to solid ground, plain darkness
and their scavenged equipment was quite a challenge.

At Steward-Sergeant Rourke's sibilant insistence,
beams snapped on and sliced through the blackness.
The squad's torches lanced about the chamber giving
the gathering the fragmented impression of a large but
cluttered subterranean chamber. As Brother Torqhuil
brought his harness lamps to life their exit became illuminated. The Relictors Space Marine was still standing
in the aperture of a wraithbone warp gate. The artefact
was smaller than the Lost Fornical of Urien-Myrdyss
and the craftsmanship culturally removed. It had been
less fortunate in resisting the ravages of time and many
of the osseous flourishes were smashed and stunted.
The portal was halfway between an oval and a diamond in shape, sporting elegant bulb-bearing barbs
and spurs from each elliptical corner. A large crack
spiralled through one quarter of the structure like a torsion fracture and the dais it sat upon was little more
than a mosaic tessellation of crumbling fragments. The
gateway's crackling energies and glowing wraithbone
bulbs had faded to emptiness and Czevak and his team
had found themselves in the cavernous gloom of a dungeon archive.

'Where are we?' Torqhuil echoed.

'You said you had something to show us,' Klute said to
his master.

Czevak strode forward with confidence through
the murky environs of the cavern, walking around, in
between and ducking under the clutter that filled the
colossal archive. He examined objects and precarious piles as he went, clearly looking for something in
particular.

'When I find it I'll show it to you,' the young Czevak
insisted.

Klute bridled and then gestured to Steward-Sergeant
Rourke. 'Fan out and establish a perimeter.'

'Right you are, sir,' the burly Guardsman confirmed, slipping an aquila on a chain out from his flak vest and kissing the sacred image. 'Pattern Citadel!' he snarled at the Savlar Chem-Dogs idling about the chamber. The penitent Guardsmen began moving into a protective formation.

'No,' Czevak turned on them. 'There hasn't been anyone down here in at least two hundred years. But do fan out. You're looking for a bell jar stasis casket, about so big, bearing a symbol in gold, an inverse horse shoe struck through with a horizontal line. Call me as soon as you find it.'

Klute watched the Savlar Chem-Dogs nod and wander off, their eyes glinting in the torchlight and with the prospect of scavenging valuables from the chamber. Czevak's reason for summoning them became abundantly clear.

With Czevak and the Guardsmen lost to the darkness Klute felt strangely vulnerable and remained by the silent warp gate with Epiphani. The warp-seer had her hand on Father's crown, using the servo-skull as both her eyes and a guide. As she turned slowly, taking in the chamber, Hessian approached nearby objects and sniffed at them like a predator on a scent. Torqhuil had taken long strides towards the nearby wall, his harness lamps throwing long shadows across the polished rock of the walls.

'Inquisitor,' he said, drawing Klute to him.

'Anything?' Czevak called distantly through the gloom only to have a succession of mumbled negatives return.

'What have you found?' Klute put to the Relictor. The Techmarine gestured at the wall with a meaty gauntlet.

'We are far underground, I can tell you that,' Torqhuil said. He let a ceramite fingertip drift high up the wall to a metal brace running across the chamber. It disappeared into the murk at the limit of the Space Marine's illumination. 'Reliquary Chamber XIII.3,' the Adeptus Astartes read off the brace. Then both men's eyes settled on the insignia of the Holy Inquisition.

'Czevak!' Klute hissed.

But the High Inquisitor was already standing there with them.

'Where are we?'

'Nemesis Tessera,' Czevak answered plainly.

Fury and frustration erupted on Klute's face. 'Nemesis Tessera!'

'Several kilometres below it actually,' Czevak corrected him. 'But we're home. That's what you wanted. To be among the cold stone walls of the Holy Ordos – in one of the safest places in the Eye of Terror, no less. Nemesis Tessera – built at the behest of the Emperor himself, so it is said, following Abaddon's First Black Crusade.'

'But,' Klute stumbled, trying to find the words. 'The *Malescaythe*… You said you needed to show us something.'

'And I do,' the High Inquisitor admitted with distraction, peering once again about the darkness of the cavern. 'But now I think I left it in the other chamber.'

'You've been here before?' the Relictors Space Marine asked.

'Many times,' Czevak confessed with a cocky smirk.

'The last place they would look for you,' Klute said, slowly shaking his head. The urgency of the situation continued to dawn on the inquisitor. 'Czevak, we can't be here.'

'I said I'd come,' Czevak told his former acolyte, himself losing patience. 'I came. I kept my word. As I said, one does not walk up to a top secret Inquisitorial fortress and knock on the front door.'

Klute snarled. 'The Relictors have been declared Excommunicate Traitoris; Epiphani has an Ordo Hereticus kill-order across twelve sectors and Hessian – well, Hessian is the body of my mystic's boy lover, host to the filth-evil incarnate of a daemonic force. Not exactly who

I wanted to introduce to my brother inquisitors!'

'Well, we'll let them worry about that,' Czevak said and began walking away.

Suddenly there was light and sound. Excruciating klaxons filled the air with murderous urgency while the chamber was bathed in bloody, rapid, red light from the reliquary roof. It crashed on and off in time with the alarm.

The inquisitors and henchmen stared at one another, searching for evidence of the alarm's activation.

They found Hessian, sniffing his way amongst the damned and daemonic artefacts, standing astride an emblem carved into the floor, made up of concentric lines of High Gothic script. The crimson darklight revealed similar markings distributed evenly across the chamber floor space.

Torqhuil bound over to the daemonhost and grabbed it under one arm.

'Purity seal,' the Relictor confirmed. 'Incursion alarmed.'

Klute regarded his former master savagely across the gathered artefacts and relics. 'When they find us, they'll declare us all heretics and rack us for eternity!'

'They'll do that anyway, my friend,' Czevak told him grimly, 'that is what you have failed to appreciate all along.'

'Activate the warp gate,' Torqhuil said.

'Too late for that,' Czevak shouted back as he strode up through the reliquary collection of arcana and warped objects. 'But worry not. For when one door closes another door opens.'

Some distance across the cavern, in the direction the High Inquisitor was marching, the bloodshot sirens illuminated a colossal bronze bulkhead that was both a metal end-wall to the chamber and doorway separating one giant reliquary dungeon from another. The heart-stopping thunk of monstrous chains and gears thundered through the stone walls and handspan by handspan, the bulkhead began to judder for the ceiling.

A huge dust cloud erupted from the cavern floor, disturbed by the shifting air as the bulkhead shuddered skyward. One moment Czevak was there, the next he was a ghost – a shape swallowed by the rolling obscurity. Klute watched the silhouette duck beneath the rising metal partition and disappear completely.

'Czevak!' the inquisitor yelled.

The encroaching cloud, shot through with the flashing urgency of the sirens, billowed at them. 'Sergeant,' Klute directed, prompting Rourke to pull back and raise the scuffed barrel of his stubby lascarbine.

'Pattern Citadel, you scrotes,' he roared at the Savlar Chem-Dogs, but the penal legionnaires had already started backing away from the rising bulkhead and priming their own collection of scavenged weaponry.

The colossal bulkhead continued to rise as the dust cloud began to thin. Beyond, new shapes were forming. Six hulking silhouettes that stomped forward through the swirl and shade like a small mountain range of ceramite, plasteel and adamantium. Their armour glinted silver brilliance through the dusty murk and pitted age of ancient plating. The relentless approach left the white skirts of their surcoats trailing. Their small helmets sat squat in a chest plate nest of power cables and life support lines. These, in turn, were dwarfed by huge globed shoulder plates that dominated the suit outline and lent the armoured figures an almost vehicular bulk.

Klute felt cold dread wash through him. With each ponderous step the markings on the globed shoulder plates hove into view, an ancient tome impaled on a crusader sword – the slashed pages of the volume bearing the ominous digits 666. About their chests swung the insignia of the Ordo Malleus on heavy metal chains, advertising their role as Chamber Militant to the Holy Emperor's Daemonhunters.

'Grey Knights...' Torqhuil hissed upon sighting them.

Klute nodded stunned agreement. In Mark-I Tactical Dreadnought Armour no less – undoubtedly stationed on Nemesis Tessera thousands of years before. Torqhuil stepped forward, his servo-arms and mechadendrites immediately assuming an aggressive posture, like a cornered arachnid. The Grey Knights carried the long, thick shafts of halberds in their right gauntlets. They balanced hammer-like weights on one end and a broad flensing blade on the other, giving the weapon both the functionally and death-dealing capabilities of both axe and spear. This was not the worst, however – as Klute well knew. The Grey Knights were all powerful psykers and their weapons were psi-matrix interfaced so as to channel their immaterial energies, as well as their existing superhuman combat prowess. Klute could imagine few enemies he would rather face less.

'Epiphani!' Klute barked. The inquisitor had seen the warp-seer hitting the Spook hard from the snuff tin she secreted in her brassiere.

'I've got nothing,' the prognostic told him with a little uncertainty and a good deal of fear. Gone was the girl's cockiness and attitude. The uncertainty Klute had heard before. Never the fear.

'What do you mean?' he said.

'I see nothing of our future, inquisitor,' she replied. He turned to see her face white and stricken. She hardly ever used his title. Klute swallowed. This was bad. If Epiphani could not see their future then perhaps they did not have one.

'Daemonic incursion located – Reliquary Chamber XIII.3,' the Grey Knight justicar stormed with sober certainty over his vox-link. 'Inquisitor Cyarro – permission to commence purgation of threat?'

Both Brother Torqhuil and the daemonhost Hessian had heard the Space Marine. Hessian glowed with unnatural power and unearthly hate. The monster sensed the danger and its vulnerability to such thrice-blessed enemies.

'Unleash me,' it said, although it was difficult for Klute to tell whether or not the thing was begging him or commanding him to do the horrific deed.

'Cyarro,' the Relictor seethed beside them, barely containing himself. Klute knew that Gamal Cyarro operated out of Nemesis Tessera. Cyarro had made a life's work of hunting Relictors Space Marines as heretics and deviants and it had been from one of Cyarro's associate inquisitors that Klute himself had learned of the Relictors and the details of their shameful quest in the Eye of Terror. He would never have intentionally led Saul Torqhuil into the reach of such enemies. The Relictors Space Marine's reaction was both terrible and predictable.

The cavernous chamber was a reliquary for objects both damned and daemonic, claimed and catalogued by the Ordo Malleus. Many were inert or erroneously categorised – the Inquisition impounding objects that they simply did not understand or had no time to research. Those that had been identified as having observed, destructive capabilities were cradled in psi-inhibitors, stored in stasis caskets or Geller phase-field protected.

Torqhuil reached out and with little difficulty the Techmarine's gauntlet found the grotesque hilt of a daemonically-possessed weapon. The Relictor was an expert in the field of exotic, otherwordly weapons and knew exactly what he was looking for. Snatching it from an ancient rack of similar items, the Techmarine clipped through a thick security chain with the claw on his servo-arm. He swung the sword into the cavern floor, smashing apart the fractured crystal case and cradle psi-inhibitor in which it had been safely stored. The hideous sword hilt rattled in his grip in excitement.

The seals and blessed ointments within and adorning the Techmarine's power armour prevented the force flooding him with its corruption but the daemon weapon still managed to feed off the Space Marine's hate and desire for vengeance. The blade's wicked form changed, seemingly shaping itself to represent the dark thoughts of its wielder. From a relatively straight, short and thin blade the sword bled aged metal and rust into reality, morphing into a devastating weapon – as tall as the Space Marine himself, with a curved, flat, single-edged blade, more like a scimitar or falchion. Its dull edge grew twisted and knobbly like a contorted spine. From it sprouted thorny spikes and spines running down its length and onto a rusted, daemonic skull that performed the function of a pommel and counterweight. Snatching his power axe in the other gauntlet from where it rested in his servo-harness, the Relictor presented himself to his sworn enemies.

Ignoring Hessian and seizing his Inquisitorial rosette, Klute ran out in front of the Relictors Space Marine. He had to act quickly. It would take a few moments for the Adeptus Astartes to clash. The Chem-Dogs' trigger fingers wouldn't wait that long and the game would be up as soon as the bolt-rounds and lasblasts started flying.

'Hold your fire,' Klute commanded, flashing his rosette at the Grey Knights but nodding at Steward-Sergeant Rourke. 'By order of the Ordo Xenos.' Klute felt he had little to lose by invoking the authority of his entire Holy Ordo.

'An illusion, to draw us from our sacred purpose,' the justicar called with conviction. The rosette had not even given him a second's pause for thought. 'Minions of the Great Enemy will do aught to survive on this corporal plane. Purge this Inquisition fortress of the unholy and abominate in the God-Emperor's name. Destroy the interlopers. Suffer not the immaterial to exist.'

In unison the Grey Knights halted, extending their left gauntlets. On each sat a wrist-mounted storm bolter that let loose a stream of raw, yet disciplined firepower. The motley barrels of the Savlars came instinctively up and replied. Bolt-rounds tore through the bodies of the penitent Guardsmen, blowing off heads and limbs with brutal precision. The Chem-Dog firepower was pathetic in comparison and danced off the antique armour of the Space Marines. During the exchange the remaining Guardsmen swiftly scrambled for cover along with Epiphani and her servo-skull guide.

Klute was roughly pushed to the ground by Torqhuil. The inquisitor hit the rocky floor behind a robust security storage crate. It looked very much like a large coffin and undoubtedly contained something hideous. Brother Torqhuil dauntlessly strode at the Grey Knights, daemon blade and power axe stretched out in front of him. Bolts seemed to blast artefacts and Guardsmen to pieces about him but the shells rocketing directly at the Relictor Space Marine seemed to fall away to dust, disintegrating before the infernal power of the daemon sword. Hessian's flesh was aflame from within and the letters embedded in that flesh were clear to see against a background of dark light. The daemonhost was resisting his wards and litanies and from its contorted features Klute concluded that this constituted both physical and spiritual agonies.

Hessian's feet left the floor and the creature began to rise above the chaos and gunfire. Klute thought about unleashing the daemon as it had requested but despised the thought of it becoming a habit. Perhaps, the inquisitor considered with bolt-rounds chewing up the damned relics and curiosities about him, the problem was not Hessian and his appetite for freedom and destruction, it was the fact that since Czevak had returned they were increasingly in the kind of peril that necessitated Hessian's hellish powers.

Klute felt the security storage coffin move. It drifted off the ground wreathed in a faint, spiritual fire along with the daemonhost and several other heavy objects. Hessian screamed horribly. He wanted to launch the levitating barrage at their enemies but bound as he was simply could not draw on the telekinetic power it needed from the warp to accomplish such a feat. The coffin crashed back to the ground where its reinforced surface absorbed a staccato of storm bolt abuse from the Grey Knight justicar. Hessian hung in the air, barely drawing on the power to deflect oncoming bolt blasts from ripping its host's body up. Instead the ammunition deviated the hair's breadth needed to clip the daemonhost's arms and shoulders instead of punching a ragged hole through the centre of its chest.

'Free me…' Hessian hissed. This time Klute knew it was begging. The inquisitor's lips began to form around Phalanghast's incantations – incantations designed to give the monster its wish.

The air about them suddenly blazed. An arc of searing power roasted reality above Klute's head and buried itself in the daemonhost's floating form. The creature was flung back into the cavern wall, thrashing under the torment of the soul lightning. Klute realised that one of the Grey Knight's had unleashed his own warp-borne powers on the daemonhost. This was joined by a second arc that lanced its way across the chamber and savaged the daemon. Crucified against the cold rock with an arc streaming at each of the creature's arms the daemonhost was helpless.

Risking a glance above the coffin, Klute found that the arcs were raging from the tips of two Nemesis force halberds, each held by Grey Knights who sat immobile like tanks in their Tactical Dreadnought armour. Torqhuil was amongst his enemies now, moving with insane speed and precision. The Relictors Space Marine was drawing on every second of his Adeptus Astartes combat training but was also working in unison with the damned blade he was wielding and its dark will. Three Grey Knight Terminators were attempting to cleave the Techmarine in two with the crackling blades of their force halberds but time after time the Relictor managed to get a mechadendrite, servo-arm, gauntlet or weapon between him and his foe. It was awe inspiring to watch the Space Marine cross blades with his battle-brothers.

At one point Torqhuil managed to seize one of the Terminators with his servo-arm and throw his heavy weight opponent across his shoulder like a wrestler. The Grey Knight slid across the reliquary chamber floor, smashing a path through the gathered artefacts and damned arcanum, losing his helmet. The surprise and frustration were clear to see, etched into the ancient Space Marine's face. The Techmarine brought up his power axe only to have his weapon smashed to pieces as the pulsing Nemesis blade of a Grey Knight halberd passed through it. Despite his mindless bravery, the Relictor had little hope of besting three Grey Knights and gradually the force weapons were finding their way through the Techmarine's furious assault and opening his sacred armour up like a tin can.

With blood and oils leaking from Torqhuil's suit and the thrown Terminator back on his feet, the Techmarine was forced to redouble his already impossible efforts. His fury fed the dark weapon in his creaking gauntlet, swinging the curved blade about him in savage, superhuman sweeps that not only smashed aside the Grey Knights' blades and the aim of their storm bolters but occasionally managed to slice through the thick ceramite of the Grey Knights' vambrace and cuirass plates.

Klute knew that he had to do something but could not conceive of what. The odds were so staggeringly stacked against them that it was inconceivable to imagine the following minutes ending in anything other than a certain, merciless death. Slipping his Cadian street silencer out of his robes, Klute feverishly ejected silver and salt shot cartridges from the sawn-off shotgun and began replacing them with modified single bolt-rounds. Something moved to his left and the inquisitor yanked on the lever action to prime the weapon but found that it was only Father. The servo-skull was fleeing a scene of nearby destruction. The Grey Knight justicar had worked his bloody way through most of Rourke's Chem-Dogs and having now found Epiphani was swinging the length of his force halberd at the witch. The girl was down on her knees and blind without Father. The justicar batted crates, relics and heathen archaeology aside in an effort to cut the warp-seer in half. Moment by moment, the blind prognostic managed to read the second before her last and evade the path of the sizzling blade.

Torqhuil. Hessian. Epiphani. Klute had brought them all to this with his misguided manipulation of Czevak. The inquisitor was terrified but it was the guilt and responsibility he could not bear. Standing, Klute turned on the two Grey Knights from whose weapons soul lightning leapt at Hessian. He aimed the shotgun uselessly at the Adeptus Astartes warriors encased safely in their Terminator armour. Klute's lip curled. A thought crossed his mind. A desperate thought. The inquisitor's aim altered slightly and the shotgun pistol bucked as he hammered the broad Nemesis blade of the nearest Grey Knight aside with his bolt-round. As the Space Marine's arc of blistering warp power went wide Klute worked the lever action and repeated the action with the blade of the second force halberd.

Suddenly the daemonhost was free and dropped the considerable distance to the ground. The Grey Knights corrected their aim almost immediately, bringing their weapons back on target. Klute threw himself back down beside the coffin as the lightning streams passed overhead and blasted apart the contents of the chamber. From his vantage point Klute could see the smouldering heap of daemonhost, crumbled against the bottom of the wall.

The inquisitor could only hope that he had taken the right action. The justicar had Epiphani now, the hulking

Terminator knelt over the frail form of the young warp-seer. The blind prognostic was pinned to the dusty floor and the Grey Knight had his force halberd where he intended to slice the witch's head from her shoulders. Klute had been counting on the warp-seer's childhood pet not allowing that to happen. With scorched flesh still alight in places the daemonhost suddenly scrambled to its senses, bounding across the floor almost like some kind of infernal hound.

Launching itself at the justicar, Hessian landed on the thick armour of the Grey Knight's barrel chest. Seizing his force halberd the monster – eyes ablaze – tore the shaft of the weapon in two, allowing each half to fall away. The daemonhost needed its fists to pummel the armoured figure to the ground, which it incredibly managed despite the fact that it could pull upon only a fraction of its talents and had just been savaged by the formidable psychic powers of two Grey Knight Space Marines. With hands swathed in ethereal warp fire the daemonhost smashed at the Grey Knight justicar.

Again, Hessian was testing the limits of his bounding, drawing on what immaterial power he could. Ceramite plates and plasteel buckled with every impact. The Terminator attempted to get his wrist-mounted storm bolter between himself and the hell-sired thing but Hessian slammed the armoured limb to the floor with a foot. It then grabbed the justicar's helmet and brutally tore it, head and all, from the unfortunate daemon hunter.

As the daemonhost tossed the gore-streaming helmet aside the twin streams of soul lightning found him again, throwing his scorched body over Epiphani The warp seer was blindly attempting to crawl away. Hessian was blasted back into the wall where the streams of psychic energy held him and bled away his hold on the material universe. The thing roared in anguish and agony.

'Epiphani!' Klute shouted across the bedlam in an attempt to help the blind prognostic find her bearings.

On some deep, unconscious level the girl seemed to know something that he didn't and instead of crawling towards his voice she crawled away.

As Klute worked the lever action on his shotgun pistol another of his compatriots crashed by. Torqhuil was a mess. His armour was rent and smashed and his servo-harness was a tangled cage of broken appendages and severed limbs. His chest plate was a black, smouldering crater where one of the Grey Knights had blown him from his feet with a close range burst of soul lightning. The daemon blade in his gauntlet had changed both shape and size, further reflecting the now dying spirit inside the Adeptus Astartes warrior. The Space Marine's wrath – which had fed the weapon's dark needs – was bleeding away with his life.

Klute went to move to the hulking Techmarine's side but the Space Marine's enemies were suddenly upon him. In credit to the Relictor, each Grey Knight Termi-nator looked as though they had just walked out of a daemonic warzone. Where the possessed blade had found its mark it had not only cut through adamantium and Tactical Dreadnought plating, it had aged the armour on contact. The slashes and slices that Torqhuil had visited upon the Grey Knights were now yawning, rusted and ragged holes revealing the Adeptus Astartes within. Surrounded and floored, Torqhuil suffered a storm of blades as each of the Grey Knights fought for the honour of despatching the renegade Relictors Space Marine. Crouched and powerless, all Klute could do was will on the Relictor's survival. The Techmarine gave the inquisitor reason to believe this was possible with his feverish, prone defence. Somehow the Space Marine managed to get the daemon blade between himself and the Nemesis force halberds sailing at him. The helmet-less Adeptus Astartes, whom Torqhuil had thrown across the chamber, snarled superhuman desire to end the Rel-ictor, smashing the blazing blade of his halberd into the rocky floor upon which the Techmarine thrashed, squirmed and dodged.

Risking everything, Torqhuil moved from a defensive posture to one of attack, arching his broken body in order to give the daemon blade enough momentum to sweep his foe. The blade found the helmetless Grey Knight just below the knee and cut through both of the Space Marine's legs.

Without legs to support it, the bulk of the Terminator crashed to the floor. Gore streamed from the severed limbs and the Grey Knight's face became a nest of shock and confusion. Even in the face of such grievous wounds, Space Marines were trained to fight on. Klute knew that Adeptus Astartes warriors had walked and crawled off battlefields with much worse. With composure swiftly returning the Grey Knight went to swing his force halberd from his position on the floor. Then Klute saw something else happen to the Grey Knight's face. Creases of confusion rapidly became the deep lines of old, old age as the power of the supernatural blade took effect. From genetically enhanced human to dusty skeleton took less than a few seconds and was horrific to behold.

The daemon blade spasmed with new power and once again grew in length and death-dealing shape. Torqhuil clearly dared to hope and tried to get the weapon back between himself and his enemies but he had left himself wide open for other attacks. The first Grey Knight batted the daemon blade aside with the flat of his force halberd and then, blade crackling with warp-drawn energies, sliced the Relictor's power armour gauntlet off at the wrist.

Gauntlet, hand and sword fell to the floor where the Grey Knight Space Marine kicked it away. The second reared and tossed his own halberd like a psychically guided spear, the blade easily cleaving through the crater that was now the Techmarine's chest plate and impaling the Relictor through his primary heart.

Torqhuil roared but the suffering was drowned in a gush of bloody gruel that erupted from the Relictor Space Marine's lips. The Grey Knight put his boot on the Techmarine's belly and attempted to withdraw the force halberd from the twisted adamantium of Torqhuil's ruined armour. His intention was clear, to stab him again and finish the job.

Klute was not usually given to wildly stupid and heroic gestures, but they were all he had. Standing, the inquisitor blasted bolt-rounds at the Grey Knights, working the lever action and hoping that one of his wild, furious rounds could find one of the aged, rusting rents that Torqhuil's daemon blade had opened in the Grey Knights' Terminator armour. Both Grey Knights took their attention off the smashed Relictor and lifting their left gauntlets sent Klute explosive bursts of their own firepower from their wrist-mounted storm bolters.

To the Space Marines, Klute was but an inconvenience, a fly to be effortlessly swatted, and he would have been if it hadn't have been for the chromatic stream of fragmented colour and shape that passed before him and the Adeptus Astartes' aim. Tearing the inquisitor out of harm's way and behind an obscene Slaaneshi obelisk, Czevak's Harlequin coat and Domino field gave them the milliseconds of uncertainty they needed to escape an explosive mauling. Further gunfire crumbled the stone of the phallic, Slaaneshi monument.

Readjusting to a reality in which he hadn't just been blown apart by bolt-fire, Klute slapped the clutching hands away that Czevak had just used to save him.

'Where the hell have you been?' Klute said. A cold fury seized him. He'd engaged a retinue of henchmen to find the infamous Bronislaw Czevak. Now that they had, the same Bronislaw Czevak was sealing their fate. 'Answer me, damn it!'

Czevak looked back into Klute's hard eyes.

'Oh, we're serious now aren't we? Had enough of

Nemesis Tessera already, Raimus?' Czevak accused. 'You thought the Holy Inquisition would welcome us back with open arms? It's time for a dose of reality, my friend. We're on our own.'

'This is not a game!' Klute bawled. To prove his point, fragments of profane masonry rained down about them as the Grey Knights blasted at the Slaaneshi obelisk. 'People are dying. People who have risked their lives for you. Your people. I have told you this before; renegades and heretics they may be, but if we cast them aside like cannon fodder without thought of consequence or human compassion then we are no better than the warp scum and true evil we hunt.'

Czevak looked about him as the Grey Knights shredded the monument to dust. The reliquary chamber was a demolished mess that offered little in the way of nearby cover. Making a run for it – even with the Domino field – the High Inquisitor suspected that the Grey Knights' expert fire would find them.

'If you feel that way,' Czevak told his former acolyte, 'then you are really going to hate what I'm going to propose next.'

'Answer my question,' Klute snarled. 'Where have you been while the Imperium's finest have been taking us apart?'

Czevak extracted a bell jar stasis casket from inside the bottomless pockets of his Harlequin coat. It swung on a handle, like an oil lantern and bore a symbol in gold, an inverse horse shoe struck through with a horizontal line.

Klute's anger flared once more but Czevak held up a finger. The gunfire had stopped. He stuck his head out from behind the obelisk.

'Over here!' he yelled. The Grey Knight pinning Saul Torqhuil brought his storm bolter back up. The second was stomping towards them. Dodging back behind the bolt-eroded obelisk the two inquisitors heard the reassuring blaze of storm bolter fire hammering into the masonry. To keep Saul Torqhuil alive, Czevak needed the Grey Knights' attention on them.

'What is that and how can it possibly be worth dying for?' Klute demanded.

'This is what is going to save our lives,' Czevak said then added darkly, 'but I want you to prepare yourself, Raimus. Nothing is without risk and there will be collateral damage.'

Klute snorted. 'Look around you – this is all about collateral damage.'

'You are more right than you know, my friend,' Czevak said under the gunfire. Then to his former acolyte, 'Last chance, you want me to save them?'

Klute thought of the impaled Torqhuil, the savaged Hessian and the blind warp-seer; even Steward-Sergeant Rourke and his remaining Savlar Chem-Dogs, criminals and deviants all. And all moments from death.

'Do it, if you're going to,' the inquisitor spat. Czevak nodded.

Czevak held the bell jar stasis casket up in front of him. The casket was made of a thin, matte-black metal shielding that Klute had never seen before. The inverse horse shoe symbol struck through in gold adorned a sliding panel that the High Inquisitor thumbed aside. The casket looked like a dark lantern, an enclosed lamp with a single opening that could be opened or closed to reveal the light inside. Except there was no light. Instead, Klute was privy to the contents of the stasis jar – automatically released from its suspended state upon the sliding panel release. Inside, the inquisitor saw a simple embryo, cradled in a tiny gibbet throne. It looked human but Klute found that he couldn't stand to look at it for too long. He instinctively backed away, almost taking him into the path of Grey Knight gunfire but settled for a stomach flipping wretch of irrational fear and loathing. The inquisitor vomited down the side of the Slaaneshi column before wiping the corners of his mouth with a lace handkerchief.

'What is it?' he croaked again.

Czevak tapped his thumb against the inverse horse shoe symbol, struck through in gold.

'An abandoned, heretical project – recovered from the Gorma moons by Inquisitress Perfidia Vong, no less,' Czevak told him, clearly impressed. 'Clone embryos, gene sequenced from blacksoul null-stock.' Keeping his handkerchief across his mouth, Klute pointed at the symbol.

'Assignment scale,' Czevak said to the inquisitor, 'Omega-Minus.'

Klute's eyebrows rose. The assignment scale determined the psychic ability of beings measured on a scale of psionic level and ability. Even seeming non-psykers like Klute himself registered as Pi on the scale, indicating some degree of ability – often manifested as luck or pretentions to a sixth sense. The more powerful the psyker, the higher up the scale they registered, terminating in Alpha and Alpha Plus individuals of freakish, world destroying power. The Inquisition preferred such individuals terminated upon sight. Klute knew that the scale continued well below his harmless level, however. The lower the assignment scale designate the greater the inert, negative psychic field generated by the individual. Some of these individuals had degrees of immunity to psychic powers and the energies of the warp; some – known as Untouchables or Blanks – had fields so powerful that their presence disrupted the powers of or wounded psychic beings. Czevak's *Atlas Infernal* undoubtedly harboured the flesh of such an individual. Omega-Minus specimens were virtually unknown outside of the secretive temples of the Officio Assassinorum. Its awesome nullifying power could be felt even by Klute, who had no psychic talents. The inquisitor couldn't imagine what it would do to an individual with such abilities. And then he realised he was about to find out.

'Czevak...' the inquisitor managed, coming out from behind his stained kerchief.

It was too late. The closing Grey Knight was upon them.

Light blazed through the phallic Slaaneshi obelisk as the Terminator cut the column in half with his Nemesis force halberd. The stone tumbled and crashed between Czevak and Klute, forcing both inquisitors back. The Grey Knight laid a colossal gauntlet on Czevak's gaudy-patterned shoulder and the High Inquisitor turned to find himself looking into the twin barrels of the Space Marine's storm bolter. Czevak swung the stasis casket around to meet his captor, holding it up at the Grey Knight Terminator helmet and allowing the full, unstoppable force of unbound psychic negativity to bathe the Adeptus Astartes warrior. The thick ceramite and adamantium of the Grey Knight's Tactical Dreadnought armour had shielded the Space Marine for centuries from a myriad of devastating weapons and foes but could do nothing to protect the psychic battle-brother within from the null field of the delicate Pariah embryo.

There was a momentary scream: unmanly and immediate. The blade of the warrior's Nemesis force halberd shattered like a glass tormented by the highest of sung notes, the psi-matrix interwoven metal fragmenting explosively in all directions. Klute and Czevak could only suppose that the same had happened within the Grey Knight's Terminator helmet because the huge suit sagged and became suddenly still.

Slipping out of the Space Marine's deathly grip, Czevak turned the stasis casket's beam upon the Grey Knight standing over Saul Torquhil. The Space Marine stumbled back as though caught in the shock wave of a distant but immensely powerful explosion. He brought up his force halberd only to have its flensing blade shatter like the first. The psyker dropped the shaft and fell backwards through the heretic collection of the reliquary before grabbing his helmet with both gauntlets and screaming his way to a swift death.

The two remaining Grey Knight Daemonhunters were rapidly coming to the conclusion that they were trapped with something far deadlier than Hessian in the chamber. Turning ponderously, the Adeptus Astartes warriors left the daemonhost to scream and smoulder against the cavern wall. Aiming the long shafts of their force halberds at Czevak, they found him theatrically stepping and skipping between dead bodies and wreckage. The Grey Knights intended to lance the man in the ridiculous coat with a full stream of warp-conjured soul lightning. Their powers failed to manifest however, and this gave Czevak the opportunity to turn his new toy upon them. The nearest simply fell to his armoured knees, put one gauntlet to his helmet before arching his inflexible suit and vaulting backwards – as though shot in the head from an execution pose.

The final Grey Knight abandoned the shattered stump of his force halberd and took solace in his training and his storm bolter's unimpaired ability to blast the High Inquisitor apart. The Space Marine also held his gauntlet to the side of his helmet but it was difficult to tell whether this was from pain or a gesture of vox contact with the Inquisitorial fortress above. The storm bolter's aim was wild, however, evidenced in the way it shredded the ancient artefacts about Czevak, suggesting that the psyker was suffering.

Blasting blindly at the pursuing Czevak, the Grey Knight staggered away, smashing his heavily armoured way through relics and damned archaeotechnology. An explosive miasma of boltfire flew randomly at Czevak, catching the pursuing High Inquisitor by surprise. Half skidding, half falling, Czevak went down on his backside, holding the stasis casket up out of harm's way. The path of the negative psionic beam's influence bounced haphazardly about the reliquary chamber, shattering cursed items and psychically charged materials. These small nullifications and detonations were dwarfed by an explosion beyond. A portion of the ancient, wraithbone warp gate shattered as it turned from a dilapidated structure to a supernova of rocketing dust. Getting a grip on the rocking stasis casket with a second hand Czevak held the Pariah embryo still.

As the cloud of desiccated wraithbone drifted back to the floor of the reliquary chamber, Czevak turned to an aghast Klute, still leaning against the base of the obelisk. One entire quarter of the webway portal was missing. The segment connecting the top and left hand bulbs and previously afflicted with the spiral crack was gone.

'Oops,' was all Czevak had for him at that moment.

Both men turned back to the remaining Grey Knight, who was beating a half-stumbling retreat back towards the fully retracted bulkhead. It was humbling to watch one of humanity's finest shamed by such an action. Klute and Czevak watched the mighty Adeptus Astartes scream his way up the chamber before slowing to a standstill, which almost immediately became a topple forward, the deep, colossal thunk of adamantium and dead weight reverberating around the cavern.

With the Grey Knight psykers dead but the screams continuing, Klute dashed across the chamber at the High Inquisitor.

'Czevak!' he called and he slid down onto the floor beside the High Inquisitor and snapped the opening on the stasis casket shut. The screams continued. As Klute scrambled to his feet and threw himself across the chamber in the direction of the torment, Czevak slowly stood up. Nearby lay Saul Torqhuil. The Relictors Space Marine was a mess. His armour was rent, sliced and buckled and doused in blood and hydraulic oils. His servo-harness was a tangled nightmare of decapitated tools and sparking stumps while the right arm he clutched to his ruined chest was missing his actual hand. This half masked his most grievous wound, a gaping hole in his fused rib-cage in which sat a butchered heart. Czevak watched like a morose ghoul as the Relictor's second heart kept the Techmarine alive. The High Inquisitor found that Torqhuil was looking right back at him. His ebony face was caked in his own blood, which cracked under a grim acknowledgement from the Space Marine.

'Thanks,' the Relictor said, which at first the High Inquisitor failed to understand, but the bodies of the Grey Knight Terminators said it all. Czevak had vanquished Torqhuil's mortal enemies and had saved the Relictor's life. Czevak's victorious euphoria was fading. He wasn't in the mood for congratulations and settled on an equally grim nod.

Klute reached Epiphani first. Father had descended from the safety of the cavern ceiling and was hovering above a collection of large storage crates near to the shattered webway portal. The warp-seer had crawled inside one of the archeocrates and was screaming to herself in the clutter and darkness. Creaking open the door Klute watched the girl feverishly scratching at the floor of the crate. The inquisitor gently grasped the prognostic's hand. She was like a small child, hiding from a monster. Pulling her into the light he saw that her face and body were splattered with rich, thick blood. Streams of the stuff had flooded from her nostrils and ears. Her hair and clothes were matted with gore and her cheeks were striped with tears of blood. The inquisitor sat, drawing her into a paternal embrace. Her red eyes were uncomprehending and her mouth wide open in a perpetual scream. Holding her to him, Klute fished around in his medicae satchel for a heavy sedative, which he administered immediately.

Klute could hardly imagine the agony the warp-seer was in. The inquisitor had seen the close range effect of Czevak's Omega-Minus experiment directly on the powerful Grey Knights. With the stasis casket's directed influence shone upon them, the psykers hadn't stood a chance. The unimaginably intense field of psionic nullity would have spread across the reliquary chamber, however, soul scorching those psykers and immaterial entities not even in the path of the Pariah's negativity.

As the screams continued and Klute's faith in the sedative waned, he saw what the warp-seer had been scrabbling for. She had been looking for her snuff box but in her half-mindless state had been sitting upon the object. Leaning over and scooping the tiny box up, Klute flicked open its lip and dabbed the tip of his finger in the jade crystalline powder of the Spook. Klute shook his head. The warp-seer was beyond instructions and her nostrils were still streaming with thick blood. Hooking her bloody top lip with the digit he proceeded to rub the psychic drug into the warp-seer's gums. Such intimacy would have ordinarily bothered Klute, but he was a doctor as well as an inquisitor and the professionalism of medical necessity saw him through the uncomfortable episode. Not a specialist in psykana medicine, it was all Klute could think to do.

The girl's response was almost immediate, the Spook's psychoactive properties cushioning the crippling blow the stasis casket's inhabitant had dealt her psychic being. The screaming stopped and the girl's eyes closed, the sedative finally having chance to take the soul-soothed warp-seer to unconsciousness. Checking her vitals, Klute laid her head down, satisfied. Father's missing lower jaw unspooled vellum. Standing, Klute tore off the scribbled message. He looked into the empty sockets of the servo-skull. The long, hang-dog skull that had belonged to Phalanghast – his mystic and Epiphani's actual father.

'She'll live. I think,' the inquisitor half-reassured the familiar. 'Watch over her,' he ordered the drone before moving onto Hessian.

On the way, Klute came across Steward-Sergeant

Rourke and the paltry remainder of his regrouped Savlar penitents. Only two Chem-Dogs had survived the massacre. Now that the battle had passed, the Guardsmen had preoccupied themselves with scavenging and stripping down the bodies of their fallen comrades for anything valuable or useful. The two ruffians looked up at Klute from behind their nitro-inhalers. The first was a shaven, thick-set brute that was more scar tissue than man; the second wasn't a man at all, but a sour-faced woman sporting a smashed targeter on a pair of half-goggles for what could only be sentimental reasons. The two were draped in recovered weaponry, hanging off their shoulders in the form of lascarbines, shotguns and autorifles.

Rourke, who was leaning against a smoked-crystal display case ordered, 'Jagger, Nashida, assist the inquisitor.' As they moved aside Klute could see that the steward-sergeant had taken frag through the gut. During the battle, the Grey Knight storm bolters had shattered the damned artefacts of the chamber, showering the Guardsmen with cursed shrapnel. Rourke clutched the ragged wound with one hand while holding onto an effigy of the aquila he carried on a cord around his neck with the other.

'Assist your sergeant,' Klute returned and tossed the penal legionnaire he assumed was Nashida a field dressing and saniseptic wash.

'Don't worry about me sir,' Rourke insisted through clenched teeth. 'I have my faith to sustain me.'

'We might need a little more than that today, sergeant,' Klute informed the Guardsman before moving across to Hessian.

The daemonhost's unnatural state, in the main, kept the thing from serious harm. Hessian, the daemonic entity, and the body of Phalanghast's boy-vassal were two separate parts of the same damned monstrosity. Bound as it was, the creature's powers protected its host's body from molestation from weaponry and environmental hostility. Klute fancied that this might even have included the soul lightning that he had watched the daemonhost endure from the tips of the Grey Knights' Nemesis force halberds. Already weakened, the daemon's defences dropped as the null shock wave of Czevak's 'solution' crippled the warp entity. Without its defences, the soul lightning torched the vassal-host's fine flesh.

Black and burnt, Hessian's body stank and smouldered against the coolness of the cavern wall. Everywhere flesh was raw and crisp. Gone was the daemon's unhealthy glow and doll-dead, oily eyes. Instead, the uncomprehending agony of a host back in control of a torture-wracked body caused eyeballs to writhe around in sickly, silent torment. Where Hessian exactly was, Klute could not know. The inquisitor assumed that the trauma of the Pariah's presence had driven the entity to some dark corner of the host's soul to recover, but for all Klute knew the beast could have been banished back to the warp.

To prevent the vassal-host going into shock and to alleviate the poor unfortunate's suffering, Klute shot him up with enough sedative to drop a grox. As the boy both burned and shivered into a coma, Klute directed Guardsman Jagger to improvise a drag-stretcher from what he could scavenge from the reliquary chamber – scavenging being the Savlar's particular speciality.

Checking briefly on Rourke and the ham-fisted job Nashida was making of his field dressing, Klute jogged over to Torghuil. As a member of the Adeptus Astartes, Klute well knew that the Relictor could weather even grievous injury with a greater chance of survival than his ordinary human counterparts. Torghuil was now up on unsteady feet, with blood and blessed lubricants from his ruined suit of power armour dripping down his torso and spattering the reliquary floor. His left gauntlet sat on Czevak's shoulder in an effort to steady his superhuman bulk and not topple over. Klute shook his head; this was beyond his talents. Torqhuil needed immediate surgery and the attentions of a full medical bay. Klute stared at Torqhuil but spoke to Czevak.

'We need to get him out of here.' It sounded like an accusation. 'We need to get them all out of here.'

Czevak bit at his bottom lip. He knew what was coming.

'Well our exit strategy's a little compromised,' Czevak replied.

It had always been a possibility but Czevak was still surprised when it actually happened. Klute might have been a man of medicine but he could still throw an angry punch. With a ringing jaw and mauled lip, the young inquisitor stumbled back and fell on his rump.

'Well you'd better come up with another one fast,' Klute shot back.

'This won't help,' Czevak said, but Klute had already turned on him.

'How could you do that?' he growled, the tension in his voice climbing. 'You knew what it would do to them.'

'A calculated risk…'

'You could have killed them.'

Czevak thrust a finger at the stasis casket he'd placed on a giant, toppled urn. 'I used it to save them. Without it Torqhuil would be dead. We'd all be dead. I distinctly remember discussing collateral damage.'

'Discussing?' Klute marvelled. 'How can we have a discussion when you only ever give me half of the facts? I had no idea how powerful that thing was. I had no idea where you were bringing us.'

'You wanted to come to Nemesis Tessera,' Czevak said, getting up and throwing his hands up in the air. 'Congratulations, inquisitor, you're home. How did you like your welcome?'

'Thought you'd teach me a lesson, eh? This was not what I had in mind, and you know it,' Klute said. 'You wanted your little toy; you said you'd been here before. You intentionally brought Hessian along to trip the alarms and give you access to the other chambers. You gambled with our lives, again, for one of your damned trinkets.'

'I deceived you, is that what you're saying?'

Klute nodded savagely. The weary and wounded Relictors Space Marine watched the exchange of accusations and insults fly back and forth across his ruined chest. 'Like you deceived me in bringing the *Malescaythe* to Nemesis Tessera? Didn't have much choice in that, did I? Raimus, you are my brother inquisitor and my friend – probably the only one I truly have in the entire universe. But you can be both a hypocrite and pompous ass.'

'And you, my lord, are death to all who follow you.'

The two men burned into each other with faces flushed with anger and disappointment.

'It's too late, Raimus. There's no going home,' Czevak told him with sudden tenderness. Klute looked on with glistening eyes. 'The Inquisition will hunt us down as the renegades we ultimately are. You know we have all crossed a line. You must accept it, brother. I know that wounds you but it is simply a matter of perspective. We wouldn't be the first innocents to suffer the persecution of the ordos, now would we? But where the Holy Inquisition in this matter are misguided and shackled to the inflexibility of their beliefs, we are free – free to act. Free to do the Emperor's work. Korban Xarchos of the Thousand Sons will use the psychic energy created by his orchestrated massacres to realise the existence of Mammoshad – King of Kings, Enslaver of the Craven Worlds and Keeper of the Vault Abyssal. He will deliver this immeasurably powerful Tzeentchian daemon to his master Ahriman on Melmoth's World. With Mammoshad, Ahriman could achieve the unthinkable. Whether we like it or not, Raimus, we have now made that possible.'

Czevak pointed once again at the ominous shape of the stasis casket. 'With the right tools we can stop this. And it does fall to us to stop this. Because if not us, then who?'

Klute was silent for the longest time but as the seconds passed, the inquisitor's hard face softened. He looked around the chamber at the dead, the injured and the shattered warp gate.

'How does talk of stopping Ahriman, Xarchos and Mammoshad half a galaxy away help us? Melmoth's World is on the other side of the Eye. We are trapped in a reliquary dungeon below a secret Inquisition fortress that is undoubtedly on the highest of alerts and about to come down on us with the wrath of the God-Emperor.'

Czevak smiled and clasped his former acolyte on the shoulder. 'Grim odds, I grant you,' the High Inquisitor admitted, 'but I've beaten worse.'

A little of the excitement and enthusiasm returned and Czevak skipped across the mountainous corpse of a nearby Grey Knight Terminator and released the pressure clasps on his helmet. Fishing around inside the gore filled helmet, Czevak tore out the Space Marine's vox-link. Shaking the blood from the headset, the High Inquisitor held it tentatively to his ear.

'What's happening?' Klute asked.

'Military traffic. This is not good,' Czevak said, tuning into the encrypted vox-traffic on the daemonhunter's comm-set. 'Nemesis Tessera is in full lockdown. Every inquisitor and team have been alerted to our presence. Inquisitor Cyarro is in charge of our purgation.'

'Cyarro is a Puritan pig,' Torqhuil said, 'but an effective one.' Klute nodded his agreement. 'He'll send everything he has.'

Czevak moved around the chamber with a strange kind of aimless purpose, picking up artefacts from around the chamber with interest before tossing them over his shoulder to clatter and smash on the floor. He inspected the Tactical Dreadnought suits of the Grey Knights and the silent, sleeping forms of both Epiphani and Hessian. Finally he ran his palms up the wraith-bone of the damaged webway portal, laying his hand on one of the protruding bulbs and pressing his ear to the osseous surface. Turning he looked vexed and shook his head, presumably to himself.

'Well,' Klute said to the High Inquisitor.

Czevak brought the Terminator headset back to his ear and trotted back over to them while new information came across secure channels.

'Four full squads of Grey Knights mobilising. In the meantime Cyarro has ordered down the Thirty-second Royal Waspica Allegiants.' Czevak frowned.

'Inquisitorial storm troopers,' Klute informed him. 'Ordo Malleus chartered. How many?'

'All of them.'

Klute nodded. 'Of course, and your toy will be little use against them.'

'So it seems,' Czevak said, moving suddenly across the chamber to reclaim the stasis casket and drop it down into the bottomless pockets of his Harlequin coat.

'How long?'

'They've been rappelling down the cargo elevator deepshaft ever since we set off the purity alarms, so any-time now.'

'You have a plan?' Klute asked. Torqhuil fixed the High Inquisitor with a cynical stare.

'Always,' Czevak replied, unconvinced and mind else-where. He looked up at the cavern ceiling. The klaxons had desisted at some point during the chaos of the battle but the red ceiling lamps were still snapping on and off with silent urgency.

'Sergeant,' Czevak called. 'Kill the lights and then your own, if you please.'

'As you wish, High Inquisitor,' Rourke acknowledged as he took an autorifle from the murderous-looking Jagger.

'On three,' the steward-sergeant instructed his remaining Chem-Dogs before the three of them went to work on the roof lamps, blasting them out with careful aim and a judicious mixture of las-bolts and auto fire.

As the chamber became darker and shadows closed in around them, Czevak motioned them all to follow.

'The warp-seer had the right idea,' the High Inquisitor told them, leading Klute and Torqhuil to where the inquisitor had left her with Father. Darkness stung the eyes as the Savlar Guardsmen finished off the last of the ceiling lamps with their target practice. As they pulled back, Jagger and Nashida carried Hessian on a makeshift stretcher and Rourke led the way with the beam of the lamp attached to his autorifle. As they all convened in front of the archeocrates, around the light of the sergeant's remaining lamp and the cold blue orbs of Father, Klute looked up at Czevak for inspiration. He was standing by the shattered warp gate with the Terminator headset to his ear once more.

'So?'

'What?'

'You said you had a plan.'

'They're here,' Czevak told them in a hushed whisper, dropping the headset.

'And the plan?'

'Hide,' Czevak said, sidling into a nook in the wraithbone architecture of the ruined portal. Klute looked to Torqhuil and the Chem-Dogs and then straight back at Czevak.

'Hide. That's your plan?' Klute hissed in disbelief.

'And wait for the signal,' Czevak added in a light-hearted, sing-song tone. He slunk down inside his Harlequin coat, the garment's alien Domino field helping to melt the High Inquisitor into the silky darkness.

There was no time for the further questions Klute had about the nature of Czevak's signal and what they were supposed to do upon receiving it. As the inquisitor crept into the empty gloom of one of the archeocrates – as Epiphani had done before him – he hoped that both would become obvious when the time came. In the meantime, like his companions, he had to content himself with cradling his sidearm and thumbing fresh shells into the breach in the eerie darkness of the crate interior.

A seeming age followed. An indistinct period of time in which all Klute could hear was the shuffling of boots and the occasional chirp of a vox-bead. Klute could sense bodies everywhere but could see nothing. The 32nd Royal Waspica Allegiants were devout soldiers of the Imperium and were infamous for carrying out their duties with absolute conviction and surgical precision. The Seven Star Hegemony, the Vilo Rouge Twist Cleansings and the Decromunda Hive Holocaust were all the work of the Waspica Allegiants. Their service record and iron faith had earned them the prestige of a garrison rotation, a five hundred year charter to secure and defend one of the most secret of the Holy Inquisition's strongholds. They were unlikely to allow them to escape.

Klute suddenly became aware of something in front of his archeocrate. Blinking through a crack in the lid he saw the blackness outside move. One form of darkness usurped another as a figure passed before him. Willing even his heart to stop beating in case it alerted the Inquisitorial storm trooper to his presence, Klute heard the scrape of grit under lightly stepping boots and the hum of nearby weaponry and equipment. How the storm troopers could be moving throughout the chamber without lamps and lights Klute could hardly guess.

As the seconds passed, several more dark figures drifted by the archeocrate, drawn to the area despite their best efforts to disguise their location. Klute's fingers sank into the grip and lever action of his shotgun pistol. Upon detection, the inquisitor wanted to be able to announce his discovery with a blast of silver scatter shot and Saint Vesta's salts.

Klute blinked. And almost missed the signal.

From the deepest darkness erupted eye-searing light. A
momentary crack of warp energy, leaping from one side
of the webway portal to the other, instantly followed
by a billion blinding others. The gate opening assumed
the choppy, glassy, jigsaw reality of its former function
– unaffected by the accidental damage and missing section. It blazed interdimensional illumination across the
reliquary chamber like a newborn sun.

The silhouette of a Royal Waspica Allegiant stood
framed in the portal's brilliance. Barging out of the archeocrate with his shoulder, Klute brought the barrel of his
Cadian street silencer around to meet the threat. Pent
up tension led the inquisitor to fire early, Klute having
little idea of the storm trooper's orientation. The Allegiant had turned to face the warp gate in understandable
surprise and Klute's close range scatter shot only served
to blast the storm trooper's backpack. Spinning in his
black Waspica leathers and greatcoat, the storm trooper
instinctively turned his hellgun on the inquisitor and
would have despatched him with an economical head-
shot had it not been for his shot-riddled power pack.
The Ordo Malleus storm trooper's telescopic psyoccula
goggles bounced around ridiculously on his head as
he abandoned his dead rifle and went for his hellpistol
instead. Klute thrashed the lever action and hammered
the storm trooper again, this time tearing up the black
carapace on his chest. A third blast lifted the Guardsman
off his feet and a fourth smashed the psyoccula goggles
off his face.

As the storm trooper hit the cavern floor and remained
still, Klute stared around the reliquary. The impossible
activation of the warp gate had thrown light and shadow
all around. Plain to see now were the midnight black
figures of the Royal Waspica Allegiants, swarms of them,
spread out among the artefacts in a sweep pattern. All
had hellguns already up with stocks snug into shoulders

and some were even firing but most had their leather-gloved hands up in front of their telescopic psyoccula goggles. As an Ordo Malleus chartered sentinel force, Klute guessed that the storm troopers had been issued with exotic equipment to detect warp traces and imma-terial entities hiding in plain sight, witches and daemons like Hessian that nestled in human form. This explained why the storm troopers had not required torches, a reliquary chamber of damned artefacts, through the psyoccula goggles, would be lit up like the galaxy across a clear night sky. The warp brilliance of the activated webway portal would have momentarily blinded them however, explaining to Klute why he hadn't already been blown apart by a combination of supercharged las-bolts and expert marksmanship.

The hulking, shambolic form of an injured Torqhuil lurched towards the warp gate with a blissfully uncon-scious Epiphani over one smashed shoulder. Lucky hellshot pranged with lethal insistence off the Tech-marine's ruined power armour and Father zigzagged behind through the optimistic fire. The Savlar Chem-Dogs unfortunately did what they were trained to do rather than what they were supposed to do. Like Klute and Torqhuil they should have run; instead they fought. Rourke, Nashida and Jagger engaged their blinded oppo-nents, allowing their advantage and swift kills to draw them into a firefight.

'Come on!' Klute screamed as he ran at the interdi-mensional brilliance.

The Chem-Dogs had proudly taken down three nearby storm troopers but the remaining legion of Royal Wasp-ica Allegiants almost immediately responded to their training and turned on the ragged trio of Guardsmen. Like a powerful magnet, the Savlar Chem-Dogs drew las-bolts down on themselves. Nashida had the back of her skull burned out by a precision shot, while Jagger was cut up in the converging path of las-fire. With his flesh still alight from the glancing wounds and rifle clutched in one hand, the struggling brute dragged Hessian's limp body out of the stretcher and up towards the glowing gateway. As Steward-Sergeant Rourke soaked up the worst of the barrage, the Guardsman span and tumbled into a pile of ancient Chaos relics.

'No,' Klute bellowed at Jagger as the Chem-Dog dumped Hessian's body and ran back for his sergeant and warden. Storm troopers were closing on the portal, yanking up their psyoccula goggles as they neared and showering the edifice with snake-eyed firepower.

'Go!' Rourke gargled through blasted lungs. Jagger seemed to change his mind and turned. The Chem-Dog would have made it but for the Royal Waspica Allegiant stepping out from behind the warp gate where he'd been carrying out his sweep for the heretics. At almost point-blank range the storm trooper blasted a hole through Jagger's throat before turning the muzzle of the hellgun on Klute who had snatched Hessian's dumped body up by one wrist and was dragging him up to the portal. Klute just gaped up at the merciless storm trooper and waited for an execution-style death.

Czevak was suddenly beside the Allegiant. Unsnapping the storm trooper's chin-clasp, the High Inquisitor knocked the helmet off the side of his head. Czevak brought the gilded cover of the *Atlas Infernal* smashing down on the soldier's crown. The Waspica Allegiant dropped like a corpse and could well have been one. As Czevak stepped out of his hiding place in the portal's osseous architecture he grabbed Hessian's other black and bloody wrist and helped Klute drag the torched body of the daemon's unfortunate host through the blaze of interdimensional static.

What Klute noticed immediately was the silence. The webway was strange and alien enough but the transition was like being submerged in another medium. Torqhuil was already through, having laid Epiphani's body down to attend to further wounds of his own. Father hovered above the unconscious warp-seer and Czevak fell immediately to closing down the webway gate now that they were on the other side. Sealing the portal was not instantaneous however, and the Waspica Allegiants had time to funnel their firepower directly after the escaping renegades, prompting Klute to fall down beside the comatose daemonhost to avoid the hail of las-bolts lucky enough to make it through the fragmented reality of the eldar gateway.

One insane storm trooper, not content with sending his firepower through the crackling egress, threw himself through. The Allegiant might have killed a stunned Czevak or one of his team but for the fact that the Guardsman was so distracted by the unique, alien nature of another dimension that he had little choice but to stare rather than fire. With one meaty, remaining gauntlet, Torqhuil grabbed the storm trooper by the back of the skull and pulled him violently towards his armoured chest. After slamming him senseless against the ceramite, the Relictor flung the Inquisitorial storm trooper back through the sizzling gateway. Seconds later the agitated space solidified, confirming that the gateway had been dimension locked and their reality was sealed off from the danger beyond.

'One for promotion, methinks,' Czevak observed, half-serious.

'I thought that the portal was damaged,' Klute said finally, giving voice to what Torqhuil was thinking also. 'You said that our exit strategy was compromised.'

'Compromised, but not broken,' Czevak said triumphantly. 'The shock wave of negative psychic energy released by the Omega-Minus knocked out the gate as it knocked out the daemonhost and your warp-seer. They all just needed to reboot, as it were. You should spend some time with the Bonesingers of Iyanden. Alien architects. They taught me much of runes and wraithbone.'

'I'm a little busy at the moment,' Klute came back mordantly.

'The wraithfield integrity of a dimensional threshold is not maintained by physical parameters,' Czevak explained with authority. 'They are merely a marker of the field's influence.'

'I'm sorry I asked,' Klute told him and looked at Torqhuil.

'The field is maintained by some property of the barbs and bulbs,' Torqhuil guessed.

'Irrespective of damage to the other parts of the wraithbone architecture,' Czevak smiled. 'He gets it.'

'Fascinating,' Klute said, his voice indicating that it was anything but. Hoisting Hessian onto his shoulders he started marching away. 'You can tell us all about it on the way.'

'We are a clunky, functional race,' Czevak continued. 'The eldar are the galaxy's aesthetes. It is in their flourishes you find their function.' It was going to be a long discourse.

Groaning, Klute said, 'Somebody, anybody, please shoot me now.'

Exeunt

ACT III, CANTO III

Archeodeck, Rogue trader Malescaythe, The Eye of Terror

Enter CZEVAK with KLUTE and FATHER followed by BROTHER TORQHUIL who carries EPIPHANI and HESSIAN

TO KLUTE'S AMAZEMENT the rogue trader's medicae team and chief chirurgeon were assembled on the archeo-deck waiting for them. The medics had been sitting upon a nest of crates and barrels to one side of the Lost Fornical of Urien-Myrdyss. As the medics went from dumb-struck amazement to sudden animation, Czevak and his henchmen were set upon with stretchers, instruments and dressings.

Uncomfortable with further medical attention, Czevak ordered the chirurgeon not to fuss and directed her to Torqhuil and their unconscious comrades. As the Techmarine deposited the lank bodies of Epiphani and Hessian onto presented gurneys, Klute fell straight back into medicae jargon and protocol, triaging the patients, directing the infirmary technicians and explaining to the ship's chirurgeon the more exotic aspects of both the wounded and the circumstances under which they were wounded.

Czevak, meanwhile, was rune-locking the Lost Fornical and attempting to place a strange sensation he felt in the soles of his feet and the pit of his stomach.

'Doctor Strakhov tells me you voxed through to the sick bay before we left and ordered a medical team to wait by the portal,' Klute said, wiping Torqhuil's blood from his hands with a clean towel.

'The warp-seer's garb,' Czevak answered, absent-mindedly. 'She knew she was heading for a battle even though she could hardly have predicted the part that she would play in it.'

'You're full of it,' Klute told him before adding, 'my lord.'

'Must we go over the same ground again?'

'You knowingly walked us into a trap,' the inquisitor accused, 'a trap you brought us along to spring so that you could get your hands on that damned stasis casket.'

'All true, and if you ask me if I would do it again then I would. I'm sorry if that disappoints you Raimus, but contrary to a glance at the stars the universe is not black and white. Decisions are not always right or wrong – they are difficult but sometimes simply must be taken in the service of some greater good.'

'My people had a right to know,' Klute insisted solemnly. 'I had a right to know.'

'I'm sorry, Raimus. I truly am.'

'The damned thing is – if you'd told us I think that there would have been a fair chance we would have accompanied you anyway.'

Czevak smiled. 'And you're all the more fools for it.

Walking into a top secret Inquisition fortress and pillaging their reliquaries for heretical artefacts? Even I'm surprised we walked away with our lives – and I'm usually pretty optimistic about our ventures.'

Klute shook his head, reliving the nightmare of Nemesis Tessera. 'I'd call it luck.'

'Well,' Czevak smiled, 'does fortune not favour the bold?'

Klute nodded, smiling also. 'You know, this is only going to work if you trust me. I know I can't be privy to every thought you have but you might grant me some of the more basic information you're tempted to keep to yourself, like where we are going and if we are likely to die there.'

'I'll try,' the High Inquisitor said whimsically. 'If you put an end to this fanciful notion that the Holy Ordos would want us back for anything other than the secrets they would tear from our skulls.'

Klute rocked his head from side to side in mock hesitation.

'I'll try,' he said finally, but Czevak had already walked away. 'Czevak?' the inquisitor called. As Klute turned, he took in the grandeur of the open hangar. He suddenly realised that the medical team hadn't simply been gawping at the Fornical in amazement before rushing to their aid. They had already been staring at something else. As Klute drew level with Czevak the High Inquisitor spoke.

'I felt it, as soon as my boots hit the deck. Couldn't immediately put my finger – or rather, my stomach – on it. The ship is moving.'

The ship was moving. A violent banking turn. Heinus Regula, a barren, rusty, crater-dashed orb of a moon fell away from them and the *Malescaythe*'s starboard side rolled around to face the ice world of Nemesis Tessera. A hidden sun peeped out over the horizon of the world's curvature like a diamond ring. While undeniably beautiful, the far sun cast the ice world's bleached slush fields and roving blizzards in an ominous darkness that seemed an appropriate hiding place for a top secret Inquisition fortress. It wasn't the scenery that bothered the inquisitors. It was the small fleet of equally dark vessels, glint-smeared by the burgeoning sun and closing on their position from a myriad of other secret sentry-docks in the system that demanded their attention.

The ship rocked forward as though shunted by some colossal force. Klute fell at Czevak who half-caught him and helped the inquisitor right himself. Alarms fired off all over the hangar, archeodeck and rogue trader, flooding the corridors with light and sound.

'Battle stations…' Czevak murmured before looking at Klute.

'Bridge?' the inquisitor said.

'Bridge,' Czevak concurred.

The run and brief elevator ride up to the command deck was a blur of ear-splitting cacophony and flashing deck lamps. Mercantile serfs raced past with frightened eyes but the determination and purpose of a well-drilled crew. Savlar Chem-Dogs, liberated from the detention decks, were assuming boarder-repelling formations while enginseers and technicians bolted aft to see what they could do in the damaged areas of the ship.

Klute nearly ran into Reinette Torres's ensign, the boy blurting out, 'By the Throne, there you are. The captain requests your presence on the bridge.'

Klute didn't wait and continued up through a throng of gunners heading for the *Malescaythe*'s port battery. As the boy looked from the disappearing Klute to Czevak, who had slowed, he was seized by the High Inquisitor who grabbed him by the shoulders. Under the jarring shriek of the alarms, Czevak pulled the side of the ensign's head to his lips and issued an order before pushing the officer off in the direction of his new objective. The ensign gave Czevak an uncertain look before a grave nod from the High Inquisitor sent him off.

When they arrived, the bridge was cloaked in an ominous hush. The rumble of a vessel pushed to its sub-light speed limit transferred up through the decking and transept architecture. The bridge crew, like their captain, sat in grim belief – as if raised voices or a status report might break the spell of possibility. The possibility of the *Malescaythe*'s escape. As Klute and Czevak walked across the bridge and flanked the captain's throne the rogue trader vessel soared across the pole of another dusty moon.

'Rear view pict feed,' Captain Torres ordered. The moon disappeared as the lancet screen displaying it dissolved into static before presenting a rear view of the ship. Nemesis Tessera and Heinus Regula were now well behind them – the *Malescaythe*'s thundering engines carrying her at maximum speed away from the site of the secret Inquisition base. A pack of system ships and defence monitors were bearing down on the rogue trader from different hidden locations. Their role was simple: dissuade uninvited ships from cruising anywhere near the secret Inquisition fortress-world. They were perfectly outfitted for such a responsibility. Without the bulk and inconvenience of warp engines, the defence monitors could afford to sport powerful sub-light equivalents, monstrously thick armour and grotesque lance weaponry that protruded from the prows of the vessels like ugly bowsprits and could cut another vessel in half with a single discharge. Among them were a plethora of other vessels of varied forms and patterns: recommissioned Imperial Navy frigates, armed freighters and the occasional vessel of xenos origin. These Klute recognised as the personal vessels of individual inquisitors who had clearly been eager to join the pursuit, desperate for the honour of bringing down heretic prey like the *Malescaythe*.

'Prow power signatures building again, captain,' a lieutenant in an eye-patch and Navy dress like Torres called across the command deck, from a bank of runescreens.

'Evasive manoeuvres!' Torres shouted. 'Pitch minus four thousand and a port yaw roll as we descend.'

The rogue trader captain didn't acknowledge the inquisitors standing beside her. She was too busy saving her ship. All Klute and Czevak could do was look on as fat beams of lethal energy blasted up the side and across the bow of the rogue trader. Klute grabbed the pulpit rail as he felt the ship answer and the lance blasts rage by.

'Torpedo lock!' the lieutenant called with fearful formality.

'Damn it, I need that freak witch up here, now!' Torres hissed at Klute.

'Epiphani's in the sick bay,' Klute said.

'I don't care if that warp-sow has broken a nail, I need a jump plotting like ten minutes ago,' Torres called.

'She's unconscious. And yes, it is my fault,' Czevak said.

'It usually is,' the rogue trader spat with disgust.

The rear lancet screen showed a pair of torpedoes streaking up between the converging monitors, adamanticlads and Inquisitorial Black Ships. The vessel that fired them blazed up in their path. The system ships and exotic ordo vessels parted to allow the larger craft through.

'I have a partial identification for you, captain,' the one-eyed deck officer announced.

'Spit it out, lieutenant,' Torres ordered, not taking her eyes off the closing torpedoes or the vessel that launched them.

'A-A-Astartes Hunter-class,' the officer stammered, 'designated *Justicarius* – Grey Knights Chapter.'

Torres grumbled something to herself, then said, 'The others?'

'Signatures are ordo encrypted, captain. We don't have that information yet.'

Torres clicked her throne vox to a different channel. 'Ready turret crews,' she called.

The whole bridge ground to stillness as the torpedoes raced across the lancet screen and careered towards the ship. A violent blaze of turret fire lit up the blackness of space around the *Malescaythe* which grew brighter still as a lucky shot detonated the second torpedo en route. The ship rumbled. The first torpedo seemed determined to reach the rogue trader and managed to streak up through the tangled maze of turret fire offered by the *Malescaythe's* gun crews.

'Brace for impact!' Torres called across the bridge and open vox channels. Czevak grabbed the back of the throne and Klute was winded by the pulpit rail as both men were thrown forward by a blast into the back of the ship. Logic engines and banks of instrumentation went crazy across the command deck, followed swiftly by a flood of chatter from servitors and bridge officers reporting damage and casualties.

'Lieutenant, damage report,' Torres snapped.

'Still coming in, captain.'

'What do you have now?' she demanded as the officer side stepped along the cogitators, attempting to collate a clear picture of the danger the ship was in. 'Is the hull breached?'

'Yes, captain. Impact and detonation has damaged the main cargo hold,' the lieutenant reported and he digested further data. 'Detention decks east, in fact most of the lower decks have been hit and have been ordered sealed off.'

'What about the sick bay?' Klute asked.

'I have no information about that, my lord.'

'The archeodeck?' Czevak added impatiently.

'Archeodeck intact,' the lieutenant confirmed after an agonising delay and consultation with a flashing rune-screen. 'Hang on,' the officer begged of them, tuning into his vox headset. 'Enginseer Autolycus has confirmed some minor damage to the warp drive. Mechanicus technicians are on scene.'

'I need that damn girl up here,' Torres stormed. 'We need to make that jump while we still can.'

'If we still can,' Klute said unhappily. 'What about an emergency short range jump – unguided?' Klute had known captains to do such things unaided when the distances were very short and immaterial navigation not required.

'The jump point seems calm enough but we're too close to the Eye for that. There's no such thing as a safe, short range jump here.'

'Torres,' Czevak called turning around her throne from behind. The elevator door was open to the bridge and the ensign Klute had almost run into on the corridor below was now wheeling a gibbet cage onto the bridge on a cargo trolley. Czevak had ordered the insane Navigator Rasputus Guidetti to be summoned to the command deck. 'We have another option.'

'The hell we do,' the rogue trader captain said looking from Guidetti to the High Inquisitor. Pursing her lips the captain thumbed a vox-switch on the arm of her throne. 'Enginarium, prepare for a short range jump.'

The harsh, metallic burr of Enginseer Autolycus came back over the vox but between the chaos in the enginarium and the tech-priest's mechanical voice it was hard to make out. Torres scowled at her lieutenant.

'The enginseer needs six or seven minutes to re-route power around the damaged sections and reinstate full power to the warp drive,' the officer translated, prompting Captain Torres to spasm in fury and slam her back violently into her throne. 'He can maintain the Geller field but regrets the void shield generators will also be down during this time,' the lieutenant added.

All Torres could manage was an incredulous gawp.

'You know, this was not exactly the welcome I'd hoped for inquisitor,' she told Klute, her words thick with accusation.

'Did you run across a patrol?' Czevak asked.

'No. Your idea of hiding behind Heinus Regula was a good one, but you weren't the first to have it. We ran straight into a defence monitor also hiding in the scan and comms blackout area.'

'What did you do?' Klute asked.

'What do you think I did, High Inquisitor? We were attacked on sight. I destroyed it.'

'*Justicarius* closing,' the lieutenant announced. 'They're arming torpedoes.'

'Torres, you've got to give the enginseer time,' Czevak said, kneeling down beside her throne.

'Those torpedoes won't wait,' she reminded him harshly.

'Then put something between them and your ship,' Czevak encouraged her. He pointed up at the swirling stormball of Gerontia, a gas giant spinning like a bad omen near the top of the main lancet screen. Gerontia supported an equally giant ring system, an expanse of rock, ice and celestial metal, all tumbling through space like a ragged belt around the host planet's colossal belly. Inclined as it was, the system looked like a vox-disc turned on its side, displaying messy rings and narrow divisions. As she followed the path of his finger she realised that he was talking about the ring system rather than the planet itself.

'Czevak,' Klute warned.

'Aren't we in enough danger already?' Torres said.

'Absolutely,' the young inquisitor agreed. 'All I'm suggesting is good manners. Let's not be greedy. Let's share some of that danger with our pursuers.'

Torres took a precious few seconds to think it over.

'Helm,' she ordered. 'Execute an immediate course correction. Make for Gerontia – zone equatorial.'

'How will we make a warp jump from within the ring system?' the deck officer panicked.

'With added danger and difficulty,' the captain replied bleakly.

The *Malescaythe*'s prow rose taking the rogue trader toward the lethality of the ring system debris field that orbited silently above. The ring haze was largely created by tiny particles of dust but as the vessel neared it became apparent that colossal bergs of ice and rock rolled and tumbled through the void at different angles and velocities.

'Torpedoes away,' the lieutenant updated the bridge. Two bright streaks rocketed across the blackness at the *Malescaythe*, but the *Justicarius* was slowing – the Space Marine captain of the vessel not enthusiastic about joining them in the orbiting maelstrom.

'Ready turret crews,' Torres ordered.

'Helm,' Czevak added. 'Take us in as close as you dare to the debris field.'

The captain rolled her eyes, then, 'Make it so.'

Once again it was the second torpedo that caught the worst of the gun crews' fire, the first slipping through the spider's web of turret beams. The second missile detonated a safe distance away from the fleeing *Malescaythe*. The first came in under the rogue trader's unprotected belly. Torres took the prow of her ship up through a curtain of ice and metal fragments, the rogue trader's armour plating awash with the sparks and tiny detonations of small impacts. The torpedo reared up for the kill but upon attempting to the pierce the same curtain slammed into a large shard of irregular nickel. Once again, the rumble of the detonation passed through the superstructure of the rogue trader.

As the *Malescaythe* settled into a division between two of the larger rings, several system ships attempted to follow. Undoubtedly their captains wanted to impress their ordo commanders back at Nemesis Tessera with their skill, faith and fervour. Two monitors, an adamanticlad and a heavily armed freighter followed the rogue trader on its insane route through the debris field, the chasm of open darkness between the canyon-like walls of ice, dust and spinning boulders a tight squeeze for the vessels.

With satisfaction, Czevak noted that the rest of the fleet, including the *Justicarius* and the personal corvettes, re-commissioned frigates and exotic xenos vessels, were deemed too valuable to risk and had hauled off – as the High Inquisitor had hoped. Only the sub-light system ships had commanders desperate or foolish enough to follow.

As an optimistic beam of pure energy lanced up beside the *Malescaythe*, forcing the vessel into a slight roll that could be felt on the bridge, Czevak pointed out a small moonlet, not four hundred metres across, making its slow, orbital way amongst the icy haze and floating rubble. Torres nodded, immediately picking up on the High Inquisitor's intent.

'Ready starboard battery,' she said, flicking the vox-switch on the arm of her throne. 'Target the moonlet, fire as you bear.'

The Trader serfs down below on the gun deck could have little idea why their captain had ordered them to fire their laser cannons at a by-passing moonlet but they obeyed, hitting the pock-marked miniature moon again and again. Smashing it out of its tidy orbit, it was blown into a hundred rocketing fragments. These collided with other fragments, shards and debris that threw the ring wall into chaos and collapse. The ada-manticlad was simply unlucky. A sheet of metal spun at the passing vessel and sheared through part of its port engine block, cutting the chase dead for the system ship. The lead monitor, who had been responsible for the optimistic lance blast at the rogue trader moments before, attempted an incredible manoeuvre, evading a still glowing, smashed quarter of the moonlet.

A succession of minor impacts hammered the defence monitor's heavily armoured prow and slowed the vessel down. The armed freighter was sprightlier than the monitor and found following in the vessel's wake an easier task. The second monitor following behind was

not so fortunate. A head-on collision between the ship
and the rolling moonlet fragment became inevitable
and at the last moment the monitor attempted to fire its
mighty lance. The colossal explosion resulted in nothing more than blasting the vessel and part-planetoid to
dust and causing further disarray to the silent discipline
of the ring system beyond.

A second lance shot from the remaining system
monitor was swift and seemed to proceed from anger
and frustration rather than disciplined gunnery. That
didn't stop the high-powered energy stream cutting
straight through the *Malescaythe*'s port flank. Klute was
thrown towards the throne this time and Czevak into
the screeching Guidetti's cage.

'Report damage! Enginarium – where's my bloody
warp drive?' Torres called in anger and frustration.
Enginseer Autolycus's indecipherable gabble filled the
bridge once more but the captain ignored it.

'Port stabiliser fin hit,' the deck officer reeled off.
'Port ether vanes hit. Long range scan array hit. Comms
hit. Port sub-light engine column hit. Losing power
and speed.'

The captain's face began to fall only to re-tense with
immediate fury.

'All stop. Turn to present port battery.'

'One hit from that monitor will cleave us in half,'
Klute warned, hoping to bring Torres, ever the Imperial
Navy realist, back to her senses.

Again Czevak turned to the furious captain, 'Weapon
to weapon we are outclassed. You know this. Do what
they won't be able to do.' He turned and leant over the
pulpit rail at a runescreen below. Czevak pointed at the
display. 'The rings are not continuous. Some segments
are dense and others sparse. We're coming up upon a
gap. Take us through to the next division. Make your
enemies do the same.'

Torres looked down at the deck officer for assurance

of the gap's existence but she didn't need to. The *Malescaythe*'s inertial velocity and starboard engine column were bringing them upon it and the captain could see the division for herself on the main lancet screen.

'Belay that order,' the captain said, settling back down into her throne. 'Make preparations for a sharp, full-speed starboard turn.' Then to Czevak, 'You'd better pray to the God-Emperor that you're right about this.'

'If I'm wrong, little good prayers will do us,' Czevak replied dourly.

'The enemy vessel is charged and ready to fire,' the lieutenant informed the bridge.

'Helm, begin your turn,' Torres commanded.

As the brutal swerve began to take its toll the rogue trader vessel started to moan and creak. The crew felt the centrifugal pull in their bones and the *Malescaythe* felt it in hers. A beam of energy passed harmlessly past their blasted bow and into the haze, leaving the defence monitor and armed freighter moments to decide if they would follow.

The commander of the heavily armed freighter had clearly had enough of the *Malescaythe*'s games and carried on, beginning their ascent, aiming for the top of the ring debris field. The defence monitor, although broader and less manoeuvrable, bulldozed its way through the narrow, ragged gap. Czevak reasoned that the vessel's commander was intent on making a further shot from the prow at the rogue trader in a place where the *Malescaythe* could ill afford to manoeuvre. He didn't get his chance, however. The monitor misjudged the turn and allowed its aft section to trail around and be caved in by several spinning bergs of ice on the edge of the gap. Propelled further around, the defence monitor fell into the maelstrom of the ring itself. It was pulverised by rubble and debris before exploding spectacularly within the haze. The vessel's remains were then shredded by smaller fragments hitting the decimated ship with the speed of bolt-rounds.

For Torres it became not an issue of manoeuvrability – her orders, instinctive course corrections and the answer of the vessel's helm were almost perfect. It was speed. With the *Malescaythe* down to one sub-light engine it became increasingly difficult to keep the vessel's starboard side out of the gap wall of savage debris and colossal bergs. Moments from the ring division on the other side the *Malescaythe* began to shudder. The thunder of an avalanche of light collisions hammered through the plating of the starboard hull as the rogue trader's slacking speed took it into the debris field. When the rogue trader did explode out into the open space of the further ring division she looked as though she had been roasted on one side. The starboard hull was both clean-shaven of antennae, vanes and architectural flourishes and scarred like a glacier ravaged valley floor.

Torres visibly sagged as the adrenaline coursing through her body crashed with the passing of their immediate danger.

'All ahead full. Lieutenant, begin the ascent and take us out of the ring system,' Torres ordered. Then to the throne vox, 'Enginseer – I repeat, where's my bloody warp drive?'

As the *Malescaythe* rose out of the rotating ice and debris field, Klute clasped the rogue trader captain by the shoulder.

'Excellent work, Reinette,' Klute told her with a smile. 'Honestly – first class.'

Czevak wasn't with them. He was back to leaning over the pulpit rail, attempting to get a better look at the runescreen upon which he'd discovered the ring gap. Meanwhile bridge personnel went about the business of congratulating one another and celebrating their narrow escape. Only the servitors kept their jaded, lidless eyes on their logic engines and instrumentation.

'Enemy vessel, dead ahead!' Czevak announced, drawing officers and serfs back to their banks and consoles.

As the *Malescaythe* surfaced and erupted from the debris field it found itself looking at the armoured, cannon-bristling side of an Inquisitorial Black Ship.

'They're firing!' Klute called. There was nobody on the bridge that needed instrumentation to confirm that; the Inquisition vessel's side crashed and flashed with high-powered cannons and a broadside energy storm flew at the rogue trader.

'Master Autolycus, do we have shields?' Torres screamed at the vox. 'Autolycus!'

The deck officer ran along the wall banks, searching for confirmation.

'We have shields,' he called, almost tripping over himself.

'All power to the prow screens,' Torres bawled.

The order could barely have been given and executed when the first las-blasts hit. The area of space before the *Malescaythe* became a blanket of white as the forward void shields soaked up cannon bolt after cannon bolt, launched from the side of the Inquisitorial Black Ship. A continuous shock wave rippled through the rogue trader from bow to stern.

'Shields failing,' an ensign announced from the other side of the transept. The captain would ordinarily have shot the officer down in scorn but it had been a miracle that the shield generator had stood up to such a merciless pounding in the first place. Like the *Malescaythe* itself, it would not survive a second.

Behind them, the rear view lancet pict screen showed an explosion. At first, Klute thought they had been hit by another enemy vessel but in fact the reverse was true. The armed freighter had been similarly ascending from the original ring division only to be caught in the broadside fire not absorbed by the oncoming *Malescaythe*. Unprepared for such a mauling, the ordo system ship was vaporised, its fiery hulk falling away to join the rock, ice and metal in the ring debris field.

'I know that ship,' Czevak mumbled.

'What?' Klute said.

'That ship,' Czevak replied, keeping eye contact with the Inquisitorial Black Ship, 'is called the *Divine Thunder*.'

Klute's mind raced to catch up. 'Valentin Malchankov?'

While Klute wrestled with what was happening, Czevak grasped the pulpit rail with both hands. He turned gravely towards Reinette Torres.

'Maintain your course,' he told her. His tone was unreadable. It was difficult to distinguish between advice and an order.

'Czevak, the shields won't take another beating. We have to begin evasive manoeuvres before their battery charges,' Klute said. All the while the *Malescaythe* flew at the *Divine Thunder*'s row of gaping cannon.

'Inquisitor?' Torres said and could have been talking to either of them.

'Reinette begin...'

'Maintain your course, captain,' Czevak told her. This time she was sure it was an order. She'd never been issued conflicting orders by the Inquisition before and it was proving to be a most uncomfortable situation, especially under enemy gunfire. She trusted Klute; but High Inquisitor Czevak was the ranking ordo authority on board the ship. Besides, Czevak invariably had some brilliant plan or tactic up his sleeve.

Klute turned his attention from Torres to Czevak.

'It's not Malchankov, its Ahriman,' Czevak said with feeling.

'Captain, their battery is charging for a second broadside,' the lieutenant informed her.

Torres got up out of her throne, 'Are you sure about this, my lord?'

'No, he's not,' Klute insisted.

'Captain, maintain speed and heading,' Czevak said,

his eyes burning into the lancet screen. 'I want you to ram that vessel.'

'It's not Ahriman,' Klute shouted. 'Malchankov's probably been working out of Nemesis Tessera for years.

'And you can be sure about that can you?'

'No,' Klute admitted, 'but I can feel it in my bones.'

'Like you felt it that day above Cadia?' Czevak shot back, his eyes now searing into Klute.

Klute had no answer to that. The accusation had a physical effect on the inquisitor. His head bowed slightly; his shoulder sagged.

'Do as you will,' he said and turned to leave.

'Captain!' the one-eyed deck officer erupted. 'The enginarium confirms full power reinstated to the warp drive.

Torres looked at Klute and then Czevak. They both had their backs to her and each other.

'Lieutenant, make a short range jump, no more than five light years in distance,' the captain ordered. The jump was risky. She had little care for what havoc the immaterial leap might cause the enemy ship but it was possible that they could take half the gas giant's ring system with them through the warp.

'Torres!' Czevak turned on her.

'Destination, captain?'

'Any bloody where but here.'

'Torres, no!' Czevak roared, then turned to address the lieutenant in the transept, 'Belay that!'

The *Divine Thunder* fired.

The *Malescaythe* jumped.

'You fools!' Czevak yelled across the bridge. The rogue trader gave a violent shudder and the warp engines gave a screech of mechanical agony. And then there was silence. Something was wrong.

Not satisfied with a view from the command pulpit, Czevak skipped down the steps into the transept. Here he took a closer look at the cogitators, runebanks and screens. The instrumentation was frozen, however, each bank recording the same data from a few seconds before. Czevak called for the deck officer but when he didn't reply Czevak slowed to stillness himself. A chill ran down his spine like a droplet of icewater. Lifting his eyes from the frozen runescreens, Czevak stared around the transept. The bridge crew were still. Threading his way through the ensigns, logi and servitors, all struck still like statues, Czevak stared around amazed. Looking up at the lancet screens – both those belonging to the bridge as those devoted to pict feeds from the vessel's stern – all Czevak could make out was a deep darkness, the darkest he'd ever seen. Gerontia and its magnificent ring system were gone. The *Divine Thunder* wasn't there. Czevak couldn't even make out the twinkle of stars. It was a blanket state of nothingness.

Running back up to the command pulpit, Czevak found Torres out of her throne; mouth open as in mid-order. Klute had been frozen still as he made his way to the elevator but had turned back with the grim, hurt expression that Czevak had put there with his harsh and thoughtless words. In the silence and motionless calm of the bridge, away from the desperation and dread of battle, Czevak got a glimpse of the damage his selfishness could wreak – etched into the weary face of his only friend.

Detaching interfaces from frozen bridge servitors, Czevak screwed the mind-impulse links into the back of his skull. Nothing. The ship was completely silent. Dead. Without instrumentation there was little Czevak could do to ascertain what had happened to the *Malescaythe* or why he was seemingly unaffected by it. The High Inquisitor's mind free-fell through a sky of possibilities; perhaps the damage to the warp drive had been more grievous than Enginseer Autolycus had predicted. Or maybe the *Divine Thunder's* gunfire had found the rogue trader before or as she made her immaterial jump, causing further damage to the drive. The jump itself could have placed demands on the drive that, in the middle of repairs, it simply could not handle – the jump would then have caused further critical damage mid-flight. Perhaps, Czevak wondered, this was some strange effect of making an ill-advised in-system jump too close to the gravitational pull of a planetary body. Perhaps Torres had been correct about even a short range jump this close to the unnatural currents and warped immaterial forces of the Eye of Terror.

Regardless of its cause, it seemed fair for Czevak to assume that either upon entry to the warp or whilst attempting to exit warp space, the *Malescaythe* had become trapped in a moment in time – somewhere between reality and the psychic realm. Why Czevak himself should be exempt from the effects of this strange, dimensional flux, he could not know. He knew he'd seen stranger things in the Eye of Terror, where of all places in the universe the rules of physics, reality and sanity did not seem to apply. Perhaps it was his long term exposure to the age-regressing effects of the alien webway or maybe the High Inquisitor was simply dreaming the whole episode.

Then something swept away his fantasies and rationalisations with stomach-wrenching horror. Something moved. There were figures down in the transept, slipping between the frozen diorama of the crew and cybernetics. Czevak swiftly detached himself and ran forward to the pulpit rail. They were there and then they weren't; phasing in and out of the reality – or unreality – of the bridge. The freakish circus were here for him. The Harlequinade, come to take him back to the Black Library of Chaos, to live out eternity as a prisoner. Or worse, Czevak's panic-addled brain came to realise, perhaps they were here to kill him. To take back the *Atlas Infernal* and end his existence so that he could trouble the universe no more with the dangerous secrets stored in his head.

The High Inquisitor no longer felt in control of his

feelings. Gone were the cold, analytical contemplations of moments before. His heart was thundering in his chest and the bridge reeked of fear. He felt like a caged animal, moments from execution and his mind was flushed with the simultaneous and damning desire to escape and the futility of expectation.

The spindly leader stalked forward, his gargoylesque helmet leering at Czevak with hungry intention and the desire to swallow his soul. From the helmet sprouted the furious, pink plume and in each hand the monstrous alien carried a lithe plasma pistol. Nearby, the half-mask appeared from behind a frozen lexomat, moving like a carnivalesque scorpion, the riveblades and tubular fist spike adorning each appendage flicked out like claws. Framed in the absent-darkness of one of the lancet screens, the Death Jester bored into Czevak with the empty sockets of its ghoulish skull mask. It clutched the obscene length of its shrieker cannon to the ribs of its carapace, holding the terrified High Inquisitor in its sights.

Czevak turned and ran. It was all his usually inventive mind could think to do. Dashing past the suspended Torres, Guidetti and Klute, Czevak streamed shape and colour at the elevator doors, the Domino field leaving a trail of after-images behind him. The doors were locked shut, however, as they had been when the *Malescaythe* made its interrupted jump to warp space. No manipulation of electrics or hydraulics would open them, Czevak realised with sickening dread. They were frozen in time. Slamming his clutched fist at the metal he spun around, his back fearfully flush to the doors. His eyes were everywhere, searching for the predatory forms of his eldar assassins. His mind clawed for possibilities but was flooded with irrational terror. He searched for the source of the fear, the hurricane epicentre of psycho-emotional manipulation in the chamber and found him in the corner of the bridge. The mirror-masked Shadowseer

sat balanced on the pulpit rail, one booted foot casually supporting him while the other dangled to the deck,
the rune-smoking witchblade draped across the eldritch
being's shoulders with fingers resting on both hilt and
blade tip. The Shadowseer dropped down and began its
advance upon the helpless Czevak. Its Harlequin coat
– very much like the one Czevak was wearing himself –
rippled behind it with natural drama.

As Czevak came to see his own face in the eldar's
mirror-mask, he realised how completely the Harlequin
held both his horror-crippled mind and dread-seized
heart in its hand. Spinning and backing towards the
captain's throne with the Shadowseer playfully stalking
after, Czevak brushed past Klute. A momentary spark of
survival instinct flared in the darkness of Czevak's mind.
Snatching Klute's Cadian street silencer from his friend's
robes Czevak turned the sawn-off shotgun on the Shadowseer. The Harlequin theatrically lifted the leaf-shaped
blade of its witch weapon. The sidearm felt strange in
the High Inquisitor's hands. He was not a natural marks-
man and usually abhorred personal violence, much
preferring to let others around him indulge their brute
predilections when necessary. Holding the weapon firm
and aiming at the Shadowseer, Czevak yanked on the
trigger. The expected barrel blast and kick did not come.
The trigger was stuck. Further panic washed through the
High Inquisitor, and fearing his inexperience had somehow jammed the weapon, he went to work the shotgun
pistol's lever action, only to find that jammed and inflexible also.

As realisation dawned and the Shadowseer towered
over him, Czevak let the heavy shotgun tumble weakly
from his fingers and thud to the deck. Like everything
else – the bridge crew, the instrumentation, the elevator
doors – the weapon was frozen in time and the inner
mechanism needed to fire would not move. Another
thought leapt into his fear-stricken mind. Thrusting

out his fist, Czevak activated his wrist-mounted stinger. He'd never used the eldar monofilament launcher as a weapon before but now seemed the most appropriate time. Like the sawn-off shotgun, nothing happened.

Czevak tripped backwards over a fat cable running across the pulpit, into the captain's throne. Thoughts of violence scattered like a disturbed flock of bats in his mind. He was on his back, arms held out in front of him with the mindless pleading of prey about to be slaughtered. The Shadowseer spread its long legs and stood directly over the High Inquisitor, the sword clutched tightly in both hands, ready for a downward thrust, the tip of the steaming witchblade hovering over Czevak's chest. Czevak was a nothingness on the command deck floor, feeble in the face of death. Crawling around, the inquisitor presented his back to the mighty Harlequin and buried his head in his arms like a child.

Solus

I

INTERREGNA

Pancratitaph, Battle barge Impossible Fortress, *Above Etiamnum III*

CHORUS

CZEVAK WAS IN several kinds of hell.

The inquisitor's aged and broken body had been dragged by sallow-faced serfs through the warped corridors of the Thousand Sons battle-barge. The vessel was a monstrous base of operations for the Chaos Lord Ahriman and every available space was used to store the fruits of the sorcerer's labours – his galaxy-wide hunt for dark lore and arcane understanding – so that one day the monster could unlock the secrets of immaterial immortality and achieve Chaos godhood. The traitor vessel was a floating museum of recovered artefacts, daemon weaponry, damned tomes, hexscript, alien technologies and emaciated prisoners – only kept alive for the information held in their tormented minds. As the serfs hauled him through the insane architecture of chambers and corridors, Czevak's shattered bones grated and his wounds gaped and bled leaving a gore smear trailing behind. The passages were crowded with maniacal cultists, drunk on dark understanding and minor powers, along with hordes of wan-faced serfs and cluttered relics; the vessel had the feel of a swarming archeomarket. All the while, sorcerous lieutenants orchestrated diabolical machinations in quiet, shadowy corners of the ship, daemons crept and Ahriman's Rubric Marines kept an impassive, silent, bolter-clutching watch over proceedings from sentinel vantage points.

Drifting in and out of consciousness, Czevak was taken to the pancratitaph, a huge pyramid-like monstrosity reaching out of the battle-barge's superstructure. It housed Ahriman's most prized relics, hosted and architecturally amplified the psyker's pre-cognitive communion with the warp and was the location from where the daemon-sorcerer conducted his intricate campaign of galactic terror.

Czevak was taken to a chamber situated below the pyramid's crystal apex. There he was bound to a sacrificial plinth that was decorated with cyclopean designs. About him an honour guard of Rubric Marines stood in death-defying silence.

Days passed on the plinth with intermissions of brutal but calibrated physical torture. These torments – from a myriad of otherworldly cultures and races – were barbarically practised upon Czevak's butchered form. The pain and its wretched continuance was about all that the inquisitor could bear and it was all the inquisitor could do to imagine that he no longer had a body upon which the terrors could be inflicted. He was but a mind and a soul. Unfortunately, they were the focus of the Thousand Sons' primary timetable of suffering.

Ahriman and Xarchos – armourless and dressed

in extravagant, Coptic robes – conducted the psychic aspects of the interrogation themselves.

Whereas Ahriman was the arch-prognosticator and illusionist whose skills had effortlessly helped to acquire the unreachable Czevak, Xarchos was the telethesiac and telepath. It was his job to commune their minds and bring interrogator and prisoner together in horrifying, spiritual unity and mind-perfect understanding. The sorcerers experimented with vivamantic puppetry, potions of exactitude, Nekulli songwashing, attempted daemonic possession, mind-rape psionica, pentagrammic thought transference, neural scourges and deepsoul truth mapping, among a hundred other violations of Czevak's being.

As the self-professed patience of the dark sorcerers became increasingly stretched, even a half-insane Czevak began to question how he could withstand such extreme torture and manipulation. While in the Black Library of Chaos, Czevak had become aware of the Library's own seeming psychic ability to bar the weak and corruptible from crossing its thresholds. It was one of the dark craftworld's many defences. Czevak began to wonder – between the agony and intrusion of his tormentors' efforts – if that otherworldly protection extended to knowledge concerning certain aspects of the Black Library itself. Could knowledge of the Black Library be protecting itself in Czevak's tortured and terrorised mind? When Xarchos and Ahriman pummelled him with test questions regarding his deepest, most embarrassing secrets – the inquisitor vomited forth truthful answers under the myriad tortures.

'What shames you, pawn of the False Emperor?' Xarchos put to Czevak as the inquisitor bit back his sobbing and suffering. 'What haunts your memories with its self-loathing and disgust?'

'Pissed my robes… on the firing range, at Schola Byblos.'

'Yes,' Xarchos hissed his insistence.

'Bolt pistol jammed and exploded,' Czevak gagged. 'Thought I was dead.'

'Another?'

'Mind is sharp,' Czevak said, 'but lived beyond my years. I am a tired soul waiting in a cadaver's body.'

'You have repugnance for this body?'

'Long time…'

'And repugnance for yourself,' Xarchos insisted. 'For you have not the courage to take your life, hoping that another may do it for you. The infamous Bronislaw Czevak – who fears no one – but himself.'

'Yes,' Czevak coughed, spitting blood and phlegm.

'One more,' Xarchos said. 'A deep disgrace.'

'I ache for a girl I cannot have,' Czevak admitted, tears streaming down the sides of his battered face.

The androgynous giant savoured Czevak's cruel honesties. Then his face changed to that of a concerned mother, then to a cardinal world confessor with prayers and homilies tattooed into his face-flesh. 'Czevak the deviant,' Xarchos said.

'She both disgusts and excites me.'

'Continue,' Xarchos urged, soaking up the inquisitor's squirming mortification. 'What is she? Xenos? Child? Mutant?'

'Bloodlover,' Czevak said. 'But that is not why I long for her.'

'Long for her?' Xarchos repeated, drawing out Czevak's dark truth. Callibrating the prisoner for further truths of greater significance. 'You love her. From afar. Why not take her?'

'I cannot defile a Living Saint of the Creed Imperial.'

'And why not?' the sorcerer repeated playfully.

'She must be pure. Her reason just. She is a Saint, for Throne's sake. It is by His Will she lives at all. She is His to do with as He will.'

'And what would you do?' Xarchos asked, looking

up at his master. The sorcerer's face morphed from one form to another with rapid excitement. They were getting closer to breaking him. Ahriman looked down on proceedings with the disinterest of divinity. To Czevak's further shame, he told them.

This went on. Even questions relating to the inner workings of the Inquisition and the intricacies of his life's work and investigations – questions he'd been trained by the ordo to resist under torture – he spilled when inflicted with the sorcerer's mind-invasive arsenal. When Xarchos demanded the rune designations for the eldar warp gate on Etiamnum III, however, Czevak seemed to find an inexplicable strength of mind that resisted the horrors committed on his person and soul.

Beyond this consequential resistance, inherited from the Black Library's alien architecture and defences, Czevak had wiles of his own. Xarchos bled insanity and insistence into the air about him. Under the cold, sapphire blaze of his master's gaze he had pursued detail after detail down the long corridors of the inquisitor's broken mind.

'My lord,' Xarchos advised. 'Our forces are on the ground. Mordant Hex has the warp gate. Let us end this, take what we need from this specimen and step through into eternity. The Black Library will be ours and then the galaxy.'

Instead of giving a lot of information about the few things the Thousand Sons desperately wanted, Czevak began feeding Ahriman a little information about a lot he didn't need. Long lost details and secrets, buried at the heart of the Black Library and unearthed by Czevak's in-depth researches: incantations, hidden artefacts, the true names of daemons, lost alien races, heretical technologies, dark tomes, legends and locations. Chaos and dark power in all its forms. The sorcerer hungered for detail, moving from one item and piece of information to another. For days the dark Adeptus Astartes questioned

him, pumping him for rare and antique knowledge
while all the time neglecting the true purpose in captur-
ing and interrogating the High Inquisitor.

Czevak saw in Ahriman's graven eyes the brightness
of the fever he had planted. An unquenchable thirst for
knowledge. The meme-virus. Czevak had spat into the
sorcerer's eyes just so he could infect the monster with
an affliction that in the already insatiable Ahriman
would become an undeniable and all-consuming obsession. An obsession that had kept Ahriman away from
securing the prize. And so Czevak had given the Chaos
sorcerer a thousand dangerous but time-consuming
facts in order to deny him detail of apocalyptic proportions. The Counter-Clock Heart, the Black Sovereign
of Sierra Sangraal, the *Corpus Vivexorsectio*, the location
of the Obsidoculus, the fragments of the Indiga Staff.
Hundreds of dark secrets – irresistible obstacles to the
Black Library's location. Xarchos began to realise that
something was wrong when his usually distant master assumed control of the interrogation himself. Both
questions and answers flowed freely, reducing Xarchos
to silent observer. The shattered inquisitor began to
draw strength from the respite his truths provided.
Ahriman seemed less than himself. He was there,
feverish in the moment rather than cold, controlled
and everywhere at once. His desire for knowledge and
answers an all-too-human hunger in comparison to his
usual cool omnipotence.

'My lord,' Xarchos addressed his master, 'all these petty
secrets and much more can be yours when you take the
Black Library as your own. There in the alien eldar's
ancient shrine of lore you can drink your fill of the galaxy's mystery and devour the feeble hopes of everything
that walks or crawls. There, he that is more than man
may become god!'

Ahriman halted his questions. Steam hissed from the
sapphire blaze of the sorcerer's skin. The unnatural radi-

ance was no random mutation – and Czevak had seen many among the followers of Chaos. It was the full power of the warp coursing through its chosen vessel. Ahriman was a conduit of awesome immaterial power – a walking crack through which the warp and the real world bled into one another. The steam was something else and this was not lost on Ahriman's apprentice. A silence descended upon the chamber. All the while the empty armour of the Rubric Marines looked on. Silent. Impassive. Mindless. When Ahriman did speak, the slightest trace of anger betrayed itself in the sorcerer's serene words.

'You think to tell me what I will and will not do, apprentice?'

'I live to serve you. But you are not yourself, my master,' Korban Xarchos told him, his face now remaining that of the androgynous giant. 'I fear this mortal has tricked or poisoned you with his weakling ways.'

The insult went home, as the devious sorcerer had intended and Ahriman calmed to statuesque contemplation. Ahriman of the Thousand Sons would not be toyed with by a thing of lesser existence. As both his unusual anger cooled and the warp ran to stillness within him, the steam stopped rising from his sapphire skin. Beads of sweat cascaded down his face, evidence of the fever that wracked his body unnoticed. The demigod looked upon the broken Czevak – powerless on the altar – in silent disbelief.

Rending a claw-like hand through his Coptic robes to reveal the withering curves of an ancient but still muscular chest, Ahriman began to ripple his fingers in a drawing motion. With some exertion, tiny droplets began to appear on his chest, blotching and collecting on the white hair of his body before drifting towards the mesmerising motion of his hand. As the last of the liquid was drawn from his enchanted bulk, Ahriman relaxed and held a fist out over Czevak's smashed form. The stringy secretion dribbled from between the knuckles of the ancient Adeptus Astartes' pulverising fist. Czevak had no doubt that the fell sorcerer had just used his powers to extract the raging meme-virus from his body. When he spoke, his words were as ice again.

'Men like you,' Ahriman said, 'and men like me – when I was but a man – are maggots in the False Emperor's putrefying flesh. You wriggle about, seeking out corruption and feeding on the rot – for your own needs and that the foetid carcass that is the Imperium may shamble on. Your defiance is no more than that of a maggot and I have seen its futility.'

'The girl?' Xarchos asked. Ahriman didn't have to say anything.

Czevak blinked up at the crystal apex roof of the pyramid point. Through it Czevak could see light-years of darkness and the filth-puce tendrils of dreadspace reaching out of the Eye of Terror. A blackened pulley chain ran across the chamber above the prone inquisitor. Czevak tried to turn the spasmed gristle and wrenched vertebrae of his neck. Xarchos thrust his palm at the warped curvature of a wall in the pancratitaph top-chamber. A furious wave of extreme heat rolled across the chamber as Xarchos imposed his telekinetic will upon the heavy door and it violently opened, revealing what Czevak assumed to be some form of oven. An all too natural inferno blazed within. The inquisitor could almost taste the tang of promethium. As the blasted chains of the pulley ran above Czevak's sacrificial altar, something appeared out of the blinding flame. A skeleton, manacle bound at the wrists, hanging from the running chain, bouncing and spinning as Korban Xarchos drew it towards them with a motion of the hand.

As the scorched, soot-encrusted bones turned, Czevak moaned. Not a moan of shock or pain but of stomach-pit despair. He instantly recognised the glinting adamantium cuspids set in the skull, the signature adornment of the Path Incarnadine Haemovore Death Cult.

As the sorcerer Xarchos brought the skeleton to a swinging stop with a flick of his finger, Czevak was forced to watch as the sickeningly incredible happened. The skeleton's bones blanched white, before sprouting a labyrinthine net of veins, arteries and capillaries that swarmed its female frame. Muscle blossomed from the bones like fungus on and around a fallen tree, blooming through the blood vessels. The twirling ribcage housed a nest of organs, growing amongst one another: intestines snaking around a liver and kidneys, lungs that inflated, the fist of a heart that began to pound and beat. The rawness of tendons and skinlessness enveloped the horror beneath, followed by the sheen of beautiful dark flesh that sculpted itself across her back and buttocks. Tiny, sausage curls cascaded down her shoulders and as she craned her neck around to see behind. Czevak could make out the divinity of her full lips and big, brown eyes. Once again, Joaqhuine the Renascent, Living Saint of the Creed Imperial had returned from the dead.

'Joaqhuine…' Czevak whispered.

The Idolatress looked down at him and with the finishing touches of her agonising regeneration complete, allowed a tear to roll down one perfect cheek.

'I know something of this, inquisitor,' Ahriman said. 'To destroy the thing you love. What were you trying to do? Harness the secrets of resurrection? Did she know that eventually she would be destined for a laboratory? That her gifts were meant for your Corpse-Emperor, in the vain hope that you might resurrect Him one day?'

Czevak seemed not to hear him. The old man's heart felt crippled in his chest. Crippled for the torment he'd suffered; crippled for the torment his enemies had made Joaqhuine suffer; crippled for the suffering yet to come for them both. Ahriman went on, 'Was that not why you involved yourself with the alien eldar, so that you might steal their secrets of soul transference technology?'

As Saint and inquisitor exchanged pleading glances, both engaged in silent longing for an escape that would never come, the pulley chain began to reverse.

'No!' Czevak roared, writhing feebly on the altar. Above him danced the hands of Xarchos, a pushing motion telekinetically launching Joaqhuine's thrashing body back toward the oven's open door.

'Czevak!' she screeched as the flames re-ignited and the blast wave of heat from the inferno rolled across the pancratitaph chamber. As the Idolatress's body was swallowed by the blaze and the incinerator door slammed shut under Xarchos's control, Czevak could hear her screams. The screams of a woman dying, slowly burning alive but pleading for a swift death. A finality that the Thousand Sons would never allow her.

'Release her!' Czevak howled. 'Release her! Now!'

Ahriman stood at the head of the altar, the azure blaze of his face upside down and hovering over Czevak's own. Grabbing Czevak's head with his claws, the Chaos sorcerer held it against the stone surface of the plinth with irresistible strength and power.

'What is sacrifice, inquisitor, if you've nothing to lose? What is loss without love? A brother's love? A father's? An Adeptus Astartes' love for his Legion? A subject for his Emperor? A man for a woman?' Ahriman asked. Omnipotent. Everywhere. 'I beg of you, inquisitor. This is all so unnecessary. Give me the runecodes to the warp gate on Etiamnum III and I can end this pointless suffering.'

'Fiend!' Czevak roared. 'You live for suffering.'

'Joaqhuine lives and suffers, inquisitor. Give me the codes,' the sorcerer whispered, like a prayer inside Czevak's head.

The quiet rumble of the Adeptus Astartes' words passed through the inquisitor, the plinth and the deck and with them came a stabbing psychic shock wave so powerful that the altar cracked beneath. Blood leaked from Czevak's ears, his nose, and frothed down his cheeks from the corners of his mouth. For the inquisitor, time seemed to slow. Thought was painful. All he could see was the oven door. All he could hear was Joaqhuine screaming beyond. In his shattered mind he saw himself before the incinerator. He reached out and opened it. The blaze beyond hit him like a physical force, igniting his hair, torching his ragged clothes and flaying skin from his ancient flesh. He stumbled through the inferno, his scorch-raw arms groping for Joaqhuine in the fires... and then suddenly it was gone. There were no flames, no Joaqhuine, no incinerator. Only the door, and that was more of an arch. The Segmentia Demi-arch of Bel-Etiamnum. He fell to his knees within the dark aperture of the webway portal. It was open and he had opened it.

'Master?' Korban Xarchos said. Some time had passed, with inquisitor and sorcerer staring deep into one another's eyes; the Idolatress's hollow shrieking all about them. Ahriman turned his head from Czevak's crestfallen features to face his apprentice.

'I have the runecodes,' Ahriman said with impassive triumph.

'Then the webway is ours,' Xarchos said.

'Assume your battle-plate, my apprentice,' Ahriman said, lifting himself from Czevak's defeated form and laying the clawed fingertips of a huge hand on Xarchos' shoulder. 'Land our troops in preparation for a cross-dimensional assault.'

'The eldar will resist us,' Xarchos said, his face once again assuming the pallor of the alien farseer.

'The xenos will try...' Ahriman said. 'Have Mordant Hex complete the ritual. I will be along shortly with the runecodes.' Ahriman looked back at the inquisitor on the broken altar. 'And the location of the Black Library of Chaos.'

Korban Xarchos exited the chamber calling for his wretched serfs and his armour. Silence descended upon the chamber once again. 'I'm sorry, inquisitor. I must have it all…'

Like a swollen channel bursting its banks, Ahzek Ahriman overflowed. Thrusting his palms at the altar, warp streams leapt at Czevak's limp body and seized it. Czevak's shoulders lifted from the cold, stone surface. His body flipped and flew through the air, drawn along the warp stream paths, until it arrived in the clutches of the sorcerer. Holding the broken inquisitor by his rags and chest flesh, Ahriman shook him at the crystal ceiling of the pyramid pinnacle. His cerulean face contorted like an angry god – all eyes, teeth and wrath. The psychic blast wave of his sorcerous insistence tore Czevak's mind apart, smashing through his memories, hopes and fears – stripping back the depths of the inquisitor's very being. Somewhere inside this maelstrom the Black Library of Chaos hid amongst the damage, falling through the cracks of Czevak's consciousness, needing to be unknowable. Through the mental desolation the sorcerer had wrought in the inquisitor's mind, Ahriman stalked its location.

And then the sorcerer seemed to see it. As his mind walked amongst the inquisitor's memories, his eyes stared up at the void beyond. The glimmer of stars out of place. Staring up through the crystal pyramid that formed the ceiling of the pancratitaph above, Ahriman recognised the physical falsehood of illusion. It was not the heavens above. The almost imperceptible drift of starlight and the crackle of the dread Eye's nebulous tendrils convinced the Chaos lord that he was looking at a lie, a technological masquerade far beyond human design. Above the *Impossible Fortress* was an alien vessel cloaked by some kind of mimic engine. The Thousand Sons battle-barge was being boarded.

Ahzek Ahriman took a moment to see the future before him but before the demigod had chance, the present was upon him. The sorcerer dropped Czevak's barely conscious body to the deck by his feet. He called for his armour and weapons but the interlopers were already there.

Falling into reality nearby, the half-mask Harlequin that Czevak had encountered with Klute in the Kaela Mensha shrine on Darcturus was suddenly among them. Flicking out her riveblades and tubular fist spike like some deadly arachnid, the female poet-warrior ran straight at the sorcerer. At the sight of the Harlequin, Ahriman beamed serenely. No urgency appeared on his cerulean face. A sunken-eyed serf appeared in the archway at the rear of the chamber carrying the sorcerer's ancient Black Staff. Narrowing his eyes at both Harlequin and serf, Ahriman drew the force weapon to him. Ripped out of the serf's grip, the long staff span horned-skull headpiece over shaft-spike. The staff flew like a giant arrow towards the sorcerer and up behind the blaze of colour that was the advancing Harlequin. As the shaft-spike surged for her back, the Harlequin leapt, bending and stretching, spinning through the air with her knees to her chest and weapons out like stabilising spindles. The summoned Black Staff passed beneath the vaulting alien and she landed gracefully in its wake before darting after the weapon.

As the Black Staff reached its master's hands the Harlequin threw herself at Ahriman, riveblades and fist spike coming at the Thousand Sons sorcerer in a blur. The eldar's weaponry sparked unnaturally off Ahriman's Black Staff, the Adeptus Astartes putting the length of the weapon between him and the deadly alien weaponry of his furious attacker. Throughout the desperate battle the sorcerer's skin blazed sapphire and his face maintained a cold composure. Smashing her in the half mask with the shaft of the Black Staff, Ahriman turned the horned-skull headpiece on the Harlequin, holding it like a form of firearm and blasting force bolts of immaterial energy at her. The Harlequin leapt like a cat, toes and fingertips to the ground as the close-range barrage came at her – but time and again the sorcerer's doom-laden warp blasts failed to find their target.

Mouthing a stream of silent incantations and curses, Ahriman lifted the arcane staff and span it about him with martial precision. A cyclone of warp flame erupted from the floor about the fell sorcerer and the prone Czevak, spinning and radiating outwards. As the rainbow wall of moving flame came at the Harlequin like an infernal tsunami she flipped backwards, soles of her boots to palms of her hands, before melting out of existence entirely.

As she disappeared, the shadows vomited forth the broad carapace and skeletal visage of a Death Jester, whose shrieker cannon began hammering heavy shuriken rounds across the chamber at Ahriman. With a wave of the sorcerer's hand the first shot began to slow, allowing the second, third and fourth to gain ground on it. As the rounds began to pile up and strike each other in mid-flight they ricocheted off in different directions, fanning out harmlessly around the sorcerer. Ahriman's honour guard of azure-armoured Rubric Marines began to march to life, their mindless, heavy footsteps falling into synchronicity. Their firepower was similarly disciplined and, while coordinated and lacking in imagination, was brutally accurate. As a hailstorm of inferno bolt-rounds descended upon the Death Jester, the shadows reclaimed him. A moment passed before the bark of the Rubric Marine bolters came to a simultaneous halt.

The Death Jester rose out of the deck behind the Chaos Marines with a crackle of materialisation. The first of the Rubric Marines to turn found itself facing the muzzle of the shrieker cannon's length. He was hammered from his feet by a point-blank shrieker round that, although it couldn't pierce the Space Marine's power armour, almost knocked the monster back boot over shoulder plate. Before the other Rubric Marines had time to complete their ponderous turns, the Death Jester had elegantly buried the scythe attachment on the end of the cannon barrel into several armoured forms. Even those that did complete their turns had the riveblades and fist spike of the half-mask Harlequin to contend with – the alien athletically dropping into reality behind them. With the murderous arc of the Death Jester's scythe in front and riveblades and Harlequin's Kiss caving in helmets and puncturing ceramite chest plates behind, the living suits began to tumble and collapse. With their sealed power armour breached and the Rubric of Ahriman broken, the disembodied spirits of the ancient Adeptus Astartes warriors erupted from their suits in a phantasmal rush of ash, dust and ethereal screams.

Behind the slaughter, a line of fearful cultist serfs began running across the pancratitaph with individual pieces of their dread master's ornate power armour: gauntlets, shoulder plates, even his extravagantly horned Crusader-pattern helm. As the archway bulkhead admitted the slaves and closed behind them, the Death Jester turned and fired off round after savage shrieker round at the train of Chaos servants.

One after another the heavy shurikens found their mark, blasting through the cultists' bodies and delivering their payload of virulent genetic toxin. Reacting immediately, the organs and tissue of the serfs exploded along the line, showering the pyramidal chamber with a bloody haze and fragments of rapidly expanded flesh. As Ahriman's armour thunked to the deck, individual pieces bouncing and rolling, the Death Jester and his half-masked companion turned to face the Chaos sorcerer. Ahriman was already in mid-incantation, however. Rubric Marines were getting back to their feet, the rends and punctures in their armour closing and sealing under his control. As the suits repaired themselves, the freed spirits of the Rubric Marines were drawn, screaming, back to their adamantium prisons and re-illuminated the empty helmet eye sockets with brazen, blue light. A fresh blaze of inferno rounds came at the Harlequins and the pair were forced to phase out of reality once more.

Ahriman stood over the broken body of Czevak like a crafted colossus. The fell sorcerer twirled his Black Staff in his hands defensively, his neck craning around to locate the source of his next threat. As he turned he found himself looking down the twin barrels of the Great Harlequin's willowy plasma pistols. The eldar had appeared right next to the sorcerer but the shock failed to register on Ahriman's serene features. He brought up the levelled shaft of the Black Staff, smashing both pistols' aim at the heavens and the troupe leader back. The gargoyle helmet of the eldar warrior leered at the sorcerer and the extravagant pink plume bounced about wildly as the alien fell backwards into a tumble that became a graceful, gymnastic roll. From his crouch on the deck the Great Harlequin brought the plasma pistols up, the sunfire twinkle in the darkness of their gaping muzzles announcing their intention to fire.

Clutching his Black Staff the Chaos sorcerer waved a palm at the Great Harlequin. The pistols suddenly exploded, their detonating containment flasks vaporising the surrounding deck in a ball of sun-furious plasma. Despite Ahriman's efforts, the raw, white heat of the detonation set alight his Coptic robes and melted the cerulean flesh from the tip of his nose and patches across one side of his face. The sorcerer brought his clawed fingers up to the exposed tendons and roasted muscle before tearing the robes from his ancient, muscular frame. As the bubble of plasma and destruction receded, it became obvious that the Great Harlequin had disappeared once again.

A silence and stillness descended upon the pancratitaph. Czevak bled. Ahriman radiated power through flesh that was at once his body and a conduit to the

warp. The Rubric Marines slowed to statuesque dor-
mancy. Then… the fizzle of a phase-field intrusion.

The Harlequins dropped into reality all about him.
The Death Jester's scythe arced at the sorcerer, riveblades flashed by his face and the thin, razored edge of
the Great Harlequin's power sword almost skewered him
through the gut. Allowing the dark forces of the warp
to surge through him and the force staff, the sorcerer
managed to turn each weapon aside with prognostic
speed and surety. Exposing himself to the Harlequin's
death-dealing dance, Ahriman pointed the horned-
skull of the Black Staff at the crystal pyramid tip of the
chamber ceiling. Blasting a puce beam of warp energy at
the crystal directly above him, the sorcerer watched the
beam bounce and diverge away into hundreds of weaker
beams that were reflected prism-like back down into the
chamber.

There were suddenly Ahrimans everywhere. All bare-
chested, cerulean giants, clutching identical Black Staffs,
swathed in the thick, illusory haze of the chamber. Rather
than wait to be attacked, the Ahrimans launched themselves at the Harlequins, thrusting shaft-spikes, casting
warp flame and blasting the alien intruders with doom-
bolts from the eye sockets of their horned headpieces.
The Rubric Marines had also had time to react and the
lumbering suits began pooling their firepower into one
raging storm of inferno bolts flying at the vaulting eldar
warriors. The Harlequins danced through the havoc with
martial poetry, twirling through the gunfire, flipping
between spear thrusts phasing out of the corrupting path
of deadly warp streams. In turn their weapons flashed
and darted through Ahriman's phantasmic selves, unsure
which sorcerer was the real Ahriman.

As the battle blazed, Czevak felt his battered body
dragged like some wretched spirit through the chaos. His
toes skinned the deck as his limp, cadaverous form was
telekinetically hauled upright and gently glided towards

the shadowy alcove of the closed archway. He drifted
into the darkness, away from the crash of bolters and
the clash of weapons and floated, held there by an invisible force. Then, out of the shadows, Ahriman emerged,
his superhuman bulk towering over the inquisitor and
cerulean muscle rippling with the coursing, damned
energies of the warp. His plasma-scorched face seemed
calm and at peace.

'Come, inquisitor,' the sorcerer said with a chill conviction. 'I foresee at my hand a similar surprise for these
alien interlopers on the webway.'

Ahriman jabbed the door stud, prompting the bulkhead to gently rise and reveal a Harlequin Shadowseer.
Ahriman saw his sapphire inscrutability reflected back
at him in the Harlequin's mirror mask. The eldar warlock's eldritch fashions were crafted from pure confusion
and his every step quaked with disintegrate reality. The
length of the Shadowseer's leaf-shaped witchblade sang
at Ahriman, forcing the Thousand Sons sorcerer back.
Ahriman barely got his Black Staff in front of the devastating sword sweeps. Immaterial energies spilled from
both weapons as the psykers clashed, forcing Ahriman
further back. The archway bulkhead crashed back down
at the Shadowseer's mental insistence and the metal of
the *Impossible Fortress*'s walls melted and dribbled down
across the seals, fusing the door shut and trapping the
sorcerer in the pancratitaph with his enemies.

With Ahriman's power and attention directed very
much on his unwelcome visitor, Czevak's levitating body
dropped to the deck. From his perspective on the floor
the inquisitor watched witchblade and force staff smash,
both physically and immaterially. Where they did, the
fabric of reality tore. The disciplined grace and furiosity
of the Shadowseer's assault would have carved a blood-
thirster of Khorne in two. Ahriman was more than pure
wanton destruction, however. The Thousand Sons sorcerer was not only an ancient and devastating warrior, he

was one of the most talented psykers in the galaxy. More important than either of these facts was the torrent of unbound ambition surging through the sorcerer's veins. He was the impossible made incarnate.

As his retreating heel caught on Czevak's ragged body, the sorcerer tripped and for a second, Ahzek Ahriman allowed the irresistible potency of the Shadowseer into his mind. The seed of a moment's doubt blossomed explosively, filling the Adeptus Astartes with unfamiliar fear. Enough to turn the trip into a topple towards the exposed vulnerability of the deck. The Shadowseer strode across Czevak and pressed his advantage, whipping his witchblade around in an apocalyptic arc that came up over the top of the Harlequin's mirror-mask helmet. On the floor opposite the inquisitor, Ahriman was forced to defend himself, holding the shaft of his Black Staff across him in ready deflection.

The witchblade never completed its arc, however. From the throng of battle the Great Harlequin sprinted, blazing a trail of chromatic possibility across the chamber. Leaning to the side, the spindly eldar skidded down onto one knee and elbow, the sheen of his coat taking him across the polished surface of the deck and down beside the fallen Czevak. The inquisitor felt the long arms of the Great Harlequin tighten around him and then the indescribable sensation of phase-field relocation flood his broken being. He could still hear the distant ragged screams of Joaqhuine across the chamber and in jarring, dislocated agony tried to reach out for her.

'No!' the inquisitor cried out in futile defiance. Despite the agony that they had shared in this damned place, he didn't want to leave her as Ahriman's plaything for eternity. Instead of cutting through the force staff and its owner with the witchblade, the Shadowseer vanished above Czevak, leaping out of the immediate reality of the chamber. The Death Jester and his female companion melted into thin air as the dance of death the pair had been weaving came to an abrupt, if elegant, end.

As Czevak began to exchange one reality for another, his eyes met Ahzek Ahriman's. With his claws still clutching the Black Staff in the desperation of a defensive pose, Ahriman – Thousand Sons sorcerer and demigod – broke the impassive mask of his divine features and roared his dark, wretched defiance as the most precious of all his acquisitions was snatched away before his unbelieving eyes.

Exit

I

ACT IV, CANTO I

Command deck, Rogue trader Malescaythe, *The Eye of Terror*

As before

DEATH DID NOT come to Bronislaw Czevak.

The clamour of reality returned and lifting his head from the cold metal of the deck, the inquisitor found the bridge of the rogue trader *Malescaythe* in full, glorious panic once again. With the ship freed from the temporal freeze, time had once more found its rhythm. The Harlequinade were gone – which was how Czevak preferred them. As the fear that had crippled his heart faded, the inquisitor felt suddenly elated. Rolling onto his back he folded his arms behind his head and beamed up at the bridge's lancet screens.

Beyond the huge command deck windows was a vision both beautiful and insane. The *Malescaythe* had dropped out of the warp into a highly disturbed and

agitated reality. They were a tiny, vulnerable vessel
plying a sub-light speed path across a zone of colossal devastation. Even the emptiness of the void seemed
affected, with streaks of vacant blackness and the helio-
tropic nebulosity of dreadspace rolling and crashing
into one another like a stormy seascape. The starlit
heavens beyond faded and blazed – blurred then magnified in drifting and distant bubbles of fragmented
reality. Whole systems of planets had been torn apart
by gravity squalls and vortex rifts.

The area was strewn with debris. Colossal chunks
of rock rolled with the perverse currents, major strikes
pulverising both bodies while more sedate collisions
bumped planetary shards off into the paths of other
astral wreckage. Sprinkled across the field of interstellar
flotsam and jetsam were smashed ships – both human
and alien. There were bodies, countless corpses in
streams, twirling and pooling in eddies and dragged in
the wake of rocky bodies – equally dead but insistent in
their gravitational pull. The lancet screens flashed lazy
whiteness as bifurcating arcs of warp energy cut across
the devastation like lightning. As each jagged discharge
faded, it left behind a path of colossal crystals – magnificent, intricate and bizarre. The raw, solidification of the
Eye's psychic energies. Dominating the scene, however,
was a single star – a nearby giant that had miraculously
survived the warp-spumed desolation and continued to
rage its deep blueness into the chaos of the void.

Captain Torres was at the pulpit rail, reeling off orders
and demanding information. Her eyes caught Czevak,
smiling to himself on the floor, and she scowled. She
had bigger problems than the lunatic inquisitor.

'Status report,' Torres barked. 'Steerage feels off.'

'We lost both the port stabiliser fin and ether vanes
in the jump,' her lieutenant reported from the transept
nest of runescreens, trader serfs and servitors. 'Helm
compensating. The comms...'

'Forget the comms. What about the enginarium?'

'Port sublight engine column confirmed as destroyed. The enginseer reports that the jump caused critical damage to the warp drive and they're trying to locate the source of a massive power bleed. Until they cap the leak, no shields and no weapons, captain.'

'What have I done?' Torres said, hands on hips, shaking her head slowly.

'What you had to do,' Czevak told her. He was up on his feet and still smiling like a smug buffoon. Leaning against the pulpit rail he was thumbing through the frame pages of the *Atlas Infernal*. Torres swallowed in the presence of the artefact, waves of physical and spiritual revulsion passing through her as she stood ibefore of the flesh pages. On the other side of the command deck, Rasputus moaned in his cage. Satisfied, Czevak snapped the gilded covers of the ancient tome shut. 'Klute was right and I was wrong,' he insisted, loud enough for Klute to hear at the rear of the command deck, where the inquisitor was now waiting for the elevator and staring at the grim wonder beyond the bridge's lancet windows.

Czevak started taking steps towards him. 'The jump was a necessary evil. You gave us options.'

Torres didn't seem to hear him, still lost in the catastrophic damage that her actions had wrought on her ship – her family's ship – the last hope of the waning Torres-Bouchier Mercantile Sovereignty on Zyracuse.

'Geller field?' she said, her Navy training irresistible, despite her great anguish. Survival first; self-pity could wait.

'Holding,' the deck officer replied, then cautiously, 'for now, captain.'

'Warp exit flux signatures?'

'Difficult to tell…'

'Well, try, lieutenant.'

'Captain, the entire area is in flux. If a fleet dropped

out of the warp beside us right now I wouldn't be able to tell you.'

'It's highly unlikely that we were tracked and followed. We had no idea where we were going – how could they possibly know?' Czevak announced as he crossed the pulpit. The inquisitor thought it wise not to bring up the subject of the Harlequins – who clearly had found them.

What had been imperceptible to everyone else had been several desperate minutes on the bridge for Czevak. It didn't really matter whether it had been the *Malescaythe*'s damaged warp drive or the perverse and unpredictable immateriology of the Eye that was responsible for their interstellar mis-step, or both. The rogue trader had certainly travelled more than the five light years that Torres had ordered. They could have dropped out of the warp anywhere. Anywhere in the Eye of Terror, that was, because staring out into the void beyond it became obvious to everyone on the command deck that the *Malescaythe* was still very much in hell.

'He has a point,' Captain Torres said. 'Lieutenant, get a fix on our position.'

'Don't bother,' Czevak intervened as he joined Klute by the elevator door. 'We're very much off the map here. Far from even the perilous stepping stone routes Epiphani relies upon to traverse the dreadspace of the Eye.'

'You know where we are?'

Czevak stared out through the command deck's lancet windows, his brow knitting and rising hypnotically.

'Sort of. Been here once before. Briefly. Wouldn't recommend it.'

'Does it have a name?' Torres pressed him.

'Not one that your mem-banks would recognise,' Czevak informed the bridge. 'It's called the Scorpento Maestrale. The Eye of Terror is a strange place, a very, very strange place. But some bits are stranger than others. In the Eye, the warp and realspace co-exist. Time has less meaning here; matter and energy are indistinct and raw, emotive power rules. In some places in the Eye normal planets and systems exist, upon which unreality intrudes. In the Scorpento Maestrale the opposite applies – reality is but a drop in an immaterial ocean of madness and right now we are that drop.'

'So what do you suggest?'

'Full stop and hold on station,' Czevak insisted.

'Here? What station would we hold? This place is tearing itself apart,' the rogue trader captain said with incredulity.

'This place is safer than you realise. I don't think anyone is going to find or follow us here,' Czevak assured her. 'Pick something big and slow moving,' the High Inquisitor said. 'But not that,' Czevak ordered, pointing out the raging, blue star. 'Whatever you do, do not approach that star.'

'Why not?' Torres demanded, she was not in the mood for riddles. 'The debris field is clear over there.'

'Trust me, do not approach that star,' was all Czevak had for the captain.

Instead he pointed out a smashed planetoid that looked like it had had one whole third of its mass ripped out at one of the poles. Magma dribbled out its exposed core like a grievous wound, leaving a zero-g trail of molten globules in its wake. 'Something like that. Something that can afford the ship some protection and upon which it can hold station.'

'What are we supposed to do then?'

Czevak grasped for something both sensible and reassuring. 'Repairs?'

'We need to dry dock for that,' Torres said, unimpressed.

'Just wait for me, I'll be back.'

The captain was full of alarmed questions. 'Where the hell are you going?'

The elevator doors opened and both inquisitors stepped inside.

'Somewhere considerably less safe than here,' Czevak called from within.

The doors closed leaving the two men alone. As the elevator descended, the rumble of the *Malescaythe*'s manoeuvres and minor impacts rattled the car in its runners. The inquisitors were silent.

'I'm sorry,' Czevak suddenly blurted, as though some kind of pressure had built up inside him. 'I truly am. There, I said it.' When Klute didn't reply he added, 'Apologies – becoming a bit of a habit. But then I guess I have a lot to apologise for.'

'You have nothing to apologise for, my lord,' Klute said, his eyes still on the black, matte of the doors.

'Raimus, I have everything to apologise for,' Czevak corrected him. 'I got you into this mess. I have spent a lifetime compromising your career and endangering your life. And I will probably go on doing that but don't think that I don't know your worth.'

'My lord I…'

'Can we cut the formalities? This is no time to play martyr. Raimus, I'm sorry. What I said before – that was the pain talking, not the circumstances that brought me to it. Ahriman is the galaxy's arch-deceiver. He fooled us then as he's fooled us now. But this, and Cadia. I bring it all on myself, on all of us – I know that. I must be an infuriating companion, but my travels over the years, across the Eye, along the webway, have been… empty. Full of hollow purpose. Something else we share. You spent years searching the Eye for me. Never giving up. I must be a pretty disappointing reward for your efforts. I never thanked you for them, either.'

The elevator doors opened and the sting of saniseptic rolled into the car from the sick bay.

'You still haven't,' Klute said as he stepped out and across the infirmary.

The suggestion of a smile curled on Czevak's lips.

'Thank you, Raimus. For everything.'

But the inquisitor kept walking up between the transparent, plas partitioned walls of his sick bay. His boots trampled mounds of bloody bandages and dressings outside the compartment in which Doctor Strakhov and six orderlies were attempting to stem the bleeding from an armourless Saul Torqhuil's terrible wounds. On the opposite side of the section, Epiphani Mallerstang lay unconscious on a gurney, her face seeming softer and younger than her usual sass and disdain would allow. Father hovered above her, monitoring her vital signs, obediently waiting for the warpseer to wake. Klute stopped outside the next compartment and ordered a medical servitor to tighten the restraints on Hessian's bed. Like Epiphani, the daemonhost's body was still unconscious, but despite the straps on its wrists and ankles, it was floating a handspan above the sheets, giving some hope that the daemon was still present in some dark corner of the boy's soul.

Looking about the sick bay, Czevak nodded.

'Their blood is on my hands, Raimus,' Czevak announced, prompting the inquisitor to look up from a data-slate he'd just been handed. 'I know your worth,' Czevak told the inquisitor, 'and now I know theirs. I won't squander it again.'

The two men looked at one another. Another rumble shuddered its way through the ship. 'Like I said,' Czevak admitted, 'it's been a lonely path these years. Despite the fact that you are all intensely annoying and a danger both to yourselves and to me, I have enjoyed your company. I've enjoyed sharing the risk… the burden. I'd like to go on sharing that burden.'

Klute nodded. To himself and to his master.

'I have a plan I'd like to discuss with you,' Czevak called across the open space. Klute smiled, remembering their conversation about Nemesis Tessera.

Czevak slipped his hand down into the inside pocket of his Harlequin coat and extracted the gleaming, golden covers of the *Atlas Infernal*.

'We're going to Melmoth's World?' the inquisitor guessed.

'*I'm* going to Melmoth's World,' Czevak corrected him. 'You're going to stay here with the ship and your – our – people.' The High Inquisitor bit at his bottom lip in consideration before tossing the heavy tome across the sick bay, where Klute caught it with some surprise. 'Father, with me,' Czevak ordered, prompting the servo-skull to drift out of the nearby plas compartment and into the elevator by his side.

Klute looked down at the beautiful text, running his fingers across the filigree and armour plating. The spine-pump sighed rhythmically in his hands. He knew what it must have taken for Czevak to give up the *Atlas Infernal*, to trust Klute with its guardianship.

'But…' the inquisitor motioned, holding out the arte-fact in front of him.

Czevak tapped his temple with two fingers. 'Route is all up here, my friend. If I'm not back in six hours, take the *Malescaythe* to safety and destroy the Lost Fornical of Urien-Myrdyss. Remember, with eldar architecture and technology…'

'…the function is in the flourishes,' Klute completed. 'What about this?' the inquisitor asked, holding up the *Atlas Infernal*.

Czevak thumbed the elevator door stud.

'Destroy it too, if you can.'

Klute looked down at the tome with an imperceptible shake of the head. Then to Czevak, 'This is no time to play martyr.'

'Oops,' Czevak said and the doors closed upon him.

Alarum

ACT IV, CANTO II

Greater Goylesburg, Melmoth's World, The Eye of Terror

Enter CZEVAK with FATHER

THE REEK OF corruption hit Czevak immediately. His exit point was an alleyway, at street level, in the midst of an urban nightmare. The webway portal had long been covered with other, native architecture that itself was clearly considered ancient, an archway of bitumen brick, formed by the walls of the tight alley, the slate-cobble street and a first storey walkway. Everything had the stygian lustre of coal and was similarly soot-smeared to the touch. The walls of the alleyway constituted filthy, cracked windows and tiny dilapidated balconies facing into one another, speaking of the dreadfully cramped conditions of a densely populated slum. Czevak's appearance and the portal's lightshow, however, attracted little in the way of attention. Groans of slow suffering emanated from several open windows and a cluster of ragged vagrants sat in rubbish-strewn gutters that ran off a murky treacle. The vitreous run-off glimmered an oily spectrum of colours that made Czevak want to touch it even less.

As Czevak reached the top of the alley with Father hovering at his shoulder, the huddle of vagrants moved. A blanket of blotch flies dispersed from where they were feeding and laying their eggs. One of the vagrants was sick over the others. They were sleeping amongst rotting waste and were surrounded by empty glass bottles that lay nestled between the cobbles where they had been abandoned. The retcher did not notice Czevak. Not only was he too busy vomiting up a reeking mixture of bad food and mouth-scalding gin, his neck and face were covered with cancerous growths, hanging like flaccid, dry bags of pustular flesh that obscured his vision. The vagrants all seemed similarly afflicted and Czevak moved on swiftly.

The alley opened out onto a larger but equally squalid thoroughfare. Stinking lamps, fuelled by some evil gas, lit the streets despite the fact that the planet was currently experiencing what might have been called a day. Rain fell in a constant drizzle of pitch droplets from a nicotine sky, the sluggish, oppressive clouds of which touched the tops of the precarious, black-brick tenement slums. Everything seemed to lean against each other like towers of cards or stacks of dominoes. The buildings ran storeys and storeys high, walkways and gas lines traversing the street below. Sheets of vile rainwater spilled from roofs and clogged guttering and blotch flies were everywhere, seeming to swim through the moisture of the clammy air rather than flying between the droplets.

The flies were feeding on the shift change. Ghostly horns were blaring in the distance and workers in course, ragged coats and slack caps were pouring languidly from crowded doorways. Their labouring garb displayed tatty badges sewn into the filth of the material, each bearing a symbol Czevak recognised. Three arrows pointing outwards from the badge centre, nestled between the fat circumference of three bloated circles. The symbol of Father Nurgle – the Great Lord of Decay. The denizens of the burg seemed half-asleep and just as horrifically afflicted as their homeless counterparts, each sporting some kind of growth or wretched skin condition that ate into the face and scalp.

Czevak followed diseased hordes of men, women and children that marched downhill along the cobbled streets and lines of bitumen-brick buildings. As one shift descended, another climbed and began filling the gin mills and street churches that punctuated the unstable cliff face of slum housing. While one part of the unfortunate population drank their woes away another went home to rot and whimper in private. The remainder crowded around priests with tall top hats and false promises. Throngs of the desperate gathered around these charlatans, who were both quacks and celebrants, offering cures to the afflicted in the form of faith healing and bottled tonics. The medicine looked no different to the chromatic, inky swill that was sleeking down the drains and gutters. Across the burg the palpable influence of Father Nurgle could be felt, in the lethargy of industrial slavery, in the pox-ridden, diseased denizens of the creaking metropolis and in their languid hope – their desire to live and continue serving their beloved, daemon-lord despite the misery of such degenerate lives.

Above them all the phantom moon of Auboron sat, shining its sallow, craven light down on Melmoth's World. Czevak knew of Auboron as an oddity, even in the Eye of Terror. Swallowed whole by some ravenous warp rift or favoured by some hellish quirk, the tiny world of Auboron and its ill-fated people had been thrown backward in time. While the moon could clearly be seen and had a presence in Melmoth's skies, it could not be physically walked or landed upon because what Czevak saw was Auboron, stuck fifty years in its own past.

With the swarms of sickly labourers, Czevak descended into the lower burg that sat under a perpetual cloud of smog and shadow. Factories began to replace the upper slums and brick, soot-caked chimneys reached up into the grubby heavens. The miasma on the ground was thick and noxious. Its stink was suggestive of the warp's malignity. The shuffling crowds around the inquisitor became swirling silhouettes lost in the street's soup of obscurity.

Czevak blinked and stumbled back as something large and uncompromising passed before him. He swiftly realised that he had been standing on rusty rails that crossed the thoroughfare and that the shadowy forms around him had ground to a trance-like halt. A caravan of wheeled bogies ran along the lines, the wagons hauled by an ugly steam tug that was all filthy pistons and hot chimneys. One of the burg's filthy denizens found her way under the wheels of the factory tram and was dragged sickeningly beneath it. The accident drew no attention from the crowd, suggesting to Czevak that it was a common occurrence and that it might not have been an accident at all but completely intentional. The engine pulled cargo trucks full of a black, mineral fuel, the coals of which tumbled from the wagons and bounced off the cobbled street. Picking up one of the rocks, Czevak inspected it. Although it seemed to have the dark, bituminous sheen of everything else in the burg, the High Inquisitor recognised the warp-lustre of something evil and affected. This was no ordinary fuel and if it was burned in the industrial mills, kilns and furnaces of the backwater industriascape, then its corruptive influence was everywhere: clinging to the cobbles and buildings, falling in the black rain and part of the toxic brume that everyone was breathing.

Diverting off down crumbling steps, crushed archways and alleyways, Czevak followed the rusty track in the direction from which the mysterious mineral and the steam wagons were trundling. Taking care to memorise his route, Czevak traced the track through the underburg and down into the subterranean tram-tunnels that not only transported the mineral cargo but also sheltered freakshow communities of the most deformed denizens – the dispossessed masses of those no longer of use to the burg or themselves.

The track came back out into the noxious open in a colossal black pit, a vast open-cast mine upon the edges of which the burg teetered. The mine was one of many ragged gashes in the industriascape. The one in which Czevak stood was an obscene, terraced expanse littered with mining equipment like chimney-festooned dragline excavators, steam-drills and bucket engines ripping mineral deposits out of the bowels of the planet. Through an abandoned survey-scope, Czevak took in the detail of the dark crater. Parts of the pit were flooded with cloudy lakes of rainwater upon which swarms of blotch flies bred in living twisters that danced across the murky surface. Thousands of afflicted workers were stomping down zig-zag paths cut into the cast-side in dazed throngs. Deep horns still reverberated across the burg announcing the shift change and labourers snatched up freshly abandoned pneumatic shovels, steam-hammers and drill-picks at the pit face.

The grid cross-hairs of Czevak's survey-scope suddenly fell upon a structure that seemed out of place. Everything that the inquisitor had observed of Melmoth's World so far had confirmed a backwater, industrial level of technology. Men were hacking minerals out of the ground and the most advanced examples of innovation Czevak had seen were coal furnaces and steam-powered engines.

The twisted bulk outline of a Dark Mechanicus realspace Geller lance, surrounded by pentagrammic vivisection frames stood out immediately and occupied a quiet area of pit. A bright, azure hue emanated from the frame's centre point and armoured shapes stood sentinel around the structure.

Pulling his eye away from the lens, Czevak called Father to him. The servo-skull obediently drifted over. Taking the drone with both hands Czevak triggered a stud-catch at the back of Father's cranium. Epiphani used the empty storage space beyond for spare items she thought she might need out in the field: an addict's back-up box-thimble of Spook, eyeshadow, lipstick and other assorted powders and rouges for her face, a small tube-canteen of water and an ornate, pocket autopistol. Dumping the hoard in the grit, Czevak extracted the stasis casket from the inside of his Harlequin coat. Detaching its handle from the matte black shield casing and securing the dark lantern-style sliding door, the inquisitor slid the bell jar up into the servo-skull's cranial compartment and thumbed the stud-catch.

Going briefly back to the survey-scope, Czevak jumped as he found himself staring directly into the grillepiece, headdress and searing eyes of a Rubric Marine. He turned to find two more coming up behind, bolters trained on the garish figure of the inquisitor.

'Not good,' Czevak admitted bleakly. Then with a flourish of his Harlequin coat, 'This way is it? Come on then. Follow me.'

Ignoring the inquisitor's tomfoolery, the hulking Rubric Marines prompted him down the slope with their weapons. Drifting behind at a distance, the servo-skull followed tentatively. Stumbling and skidding down the rock and grit of the dusty coalface, Czevak walked towards the pentagrammic vivisection frames, where a circle of sentinel Thousand Sons Rubric Marines were waiting for him. Two came forward, grabbed Czevak by the shoulders and forced him down to his knees.

Looking up, Czevak watched a further squad of Rubric Marines stomp down the nearby scree. Upon their shoulders the undead Adeptus Astartes carried a golden, pyramid-style palanquin, upon which sat an armoured, androgynous giant. He wore the gleaming, ornate armour of the Thousand Sons Traitor Legion and as he got up out of his warped throne and walked off the palanquin, his boots telekinetically carried him to the ground as if walking down invisible steps. The monster pressed his palms and dark-rune painted claws together and feasted his eyes on Czevak's fresh face and athletic, younger body.

'You are looking well, inquisitor,' Xarchos observed, his own features rapidly changing, every turn and angle producing a different face. He finally settled on an unsettling reflection of the High Inquisitor's own. 'Far better than when I last saw you. I see the eldar have been treating you well.'

'Their hospitality was better than yours, warp scum,' Czevak told the sorcerer.

'Or perhaps you have succumbed to the regenerative powers of one of the cursed artefacts that you have been reading so much about in the Black Library,' the sorcerer said.

'Damn you, Xarchos,' Czevak shot back with a smile.

'Erudite, inquisitor. But hardly surprising. A truly learned man would not have been – for the longest time – my puppet, his strings tangled in my web of intrigue.'

'Save it, spawn-fondler,' Czevak called. 'I've cut my puppet's strings and seen myself for the pawn I've become.'

'I very much doubt that.'

'The *Corpus Vivexorsectio* and the locations of the Daecropsicum artefacts you have used to end lives all over the Eye,' Czevak told him. 'You even had me destroy the last of them and release Mammoshad from that damned coin, so that you might raise him here.'

'Excellent, inquisitor but I think that it is a little late in the day to be second guessing me now.'

'This set-up,' Czevak nodded at the vivisection frames, 'is but a distraction. Just like leaving a copy of the *Corpus Vivexorsectio* in the crate on Arach-Cyn, you knew where it would lead me. Likewise, this rig – you don't have an energy source large enough to power the Geller lance. You won't cut up your prize like the Dark Mechanicus. You intend to unleash Mammoshad on the galaxy – its freedom in exchange for an eternity's destructive service to the Thousand Sons – a gift, to your cowardly master.'

The crater echoed with the slow clapping of Korban Xarchos.

'So now I suppose that you should do what you came here to do. Destroy Mammoshad and stop me.'

Nodding a signal to the two flanking Rubric Marines, Xarchos prompted the Space Marines to drag Czevak across the dust of the cast-mine bottom. As the Rubric Marines hauled him towards the Geller lance, Czevak came to realise at least one of his mistakes. The warped machine was not a Geller lance at all, although it was definitely a kind of Dark Mechanicus construct. Something incorporating exotic xenos technologies, a Gauss arc drill. Supra-magnetic weaponry of alien design, designed to strip away even the thickest armour, layer by molecular layer. Constructed here to break the planetary waters of an infernal birth.

The Rubric Marines dragged Czevak closer to the contraption and the inquisitor found his boots no longer skidding on the bitumous grit but sliding on a polished marble surface. As he was effortlessly lugged by the Rubric Marines across the speckled, cyan tint of the smooth ground, the azure hue grew, until he found himself held precariously on the ragged edge. It was as though a colossal egg had been growing – in size and material presence – under Melmoth's blighted surface. Czevak now stood on the surface shell of that gargantuan egg. Xarchos's dark drill had uncovered it and punctured through in readiness for a daemonic birth. The rift had been opening for a long time. Mammoshad had been growing in Melmoth's rocky womb, fed by the psychic screams of a hundred catastrophes, orchestrated by the maniacal genius of Korban Xarchos and his homicidal manipulation of the Daecropsicum artefacts, of which Mammoshad had ironically been part.

Through the broken shell Czevak stared into the unreality inside. Inside the egg below his feet – an egg the foolish Nurglites of Melmoth's World had been uncovering with their picks and drills – the Tzeentchian daemon Mammoshad was being reborn, in its glorious original incarnation. A gargantuan phoenix-like monstrosity, aflame with azure radiance and enveloped in fiery wings of change. Reptilian of limb, it streamed warp blaze from the nostrils of its cruel, massive, snaggle-toothed beak. As he looked down through the blaze of the world inside the egg, warp streams of psychic energy threaded through the sustenance of soulspace like a bloodied yolk. They held in place a stunted obscenity, already immense in dimension, with curled limbs and spine and bloated head. With its beak buried in amongst its unfeathered wings, a huge, black orb of a daemon eye stared up at the inquisitor with unbound hatred.

'Mammoshad is ready,' Xarchos hissed from above the excavation. 'It just desires one more life. Feel honoured, Bronislaw Czevak, it asked for yours specifically. So, do what you came to do – destroy the daemon or be destroyed yourself.'

Czevak swallowed. This was not going according to plan.

'Where's that sorcerous bastard master of yours?' Czevak asked, staring into the depths of the warp void below. 'I would have thought he would want to see this story through to the end.'

Xarchos smiled. 'He's watching.'

Like a pebble dropped into a still pool, Korban Xarchos' face sploshed and rippled. As the wrinkles radiated outward the face became still once more, but instead of Czevak's features, the traitor's face was now that of Ahzek Ahriman. The sorcerer beamed cerulean majesty and turned his demigod's eyes on Czevak.

'Inquisitor,' Ahriman greeting Czevak with cold civility. 'Still the maggot wriggling through the rotten flesh of galactic corruption, I see.'

'Until maggots devour yours, deviant,' Czevak replied.

'It seems of late, inquisitor, that you have become distracted,' Ahriman said, his stoic features glowing bright. 'Entangled in a fruitless campaign to deny me my treasures, while coveting the greatest for yourself. A rare artefact from the Black Library of Chaos. An ancient tome that you reportedly never let out of your sight. An atlas that details the labyrinthine pathways of the xenos webway, leading to countless warp gates and portals about the galaxy and showing the location of the eldar's hidden repository of dark lore. The *Atlas Infernal*.'

Before Czevak had time to reply, the sorcerer waved two casual fingers at him. The inquisitor's Harlequin coat was suddenly aflame. The enchanted blaze flashed through the garment, incinerating the item about Czevak's body until all that was left was ash on the breeze and the junk that the inquisitor kept in his pockets. Peering at the items piled either side of the inquisitor from his now non-existent pockets, Ahriman's eyes glowed and narrowed.

'Could I be so bold as to save me some time and you unbearable agony – again – by asking, inquisitor, where is the *Atlas Infernal*?'

'I couldn't tell you…' Czevak began.

'I really have no interest in occupying the narrow confines of your mind again, inquisitor…' Ahriman's voice was everywhere, bouncing around the open-cast crater and through Czevak's mind. The Rubric Marines tightened their deathless grip on the inquisitor's arms, holding him in place as their sorcerer lord gazed into him. 'But if you press me.' The speed and savage force with which the sorcerer attempted to ravage his soul surprised even Czevak. The invasive mind probe blasted past Czevak's feeble attempts to resist, stripping away his most recent memories. Like pages in a book the recovered images were torn out one by one, screwed up and thrown aside by the fell sorcerer. Czevak with Xarchos. His capture by the Rubric Marines. Peering at the vivisection frames through the survey-scope. The servo-skull.

The servo-skull.

Czevak came back to his senses. The pollutive presence of the Thousand Sons sorcerer vanished from his mind. Ahriman's blazing eyes took in the crater, looking for the servo-skull he'd seen Czevak tamper with in his memories. The Space Marine's perfect vision spotting the dull, blue bionics of the drone peeping through the crane arm of a silent, dragline excavator. Reaching out with a clawed hand, the mighty sorcerer drew the servo-skull to him. Father's anti-gravity drive whirred at full repulsive power but it did not stop the drone's cranium smashing against metal struts as it was pulled through the crane arm and across the open space to Ahriman's waiting palm. Father's eyes flashed cold blue alarm and his vellum spool dribbled panic-scrawled parchment. Ahriman held the tiny servo-skull.

Czevak thrashed against the Rubric Marines in violent protest but was held just as steadfastly in their supernatural grip. Ahriman beamed down on the struggling inquisitor with his divine, impassive features, the all-knowing, all-seeing calm of a god. Ahriman triggered the stud and unclasped the drone's storage section. The bell jar stasis casket fell out into his waiting hand. As the sorcerer's brow knotted in confusion he let the servo-skull go, allowing Father to shoot off across the pit, vellum trailing after it.

'No!' Czevak bawled at the sorcerer. Ahriman's uncertainty spilled over into anger.

'Is this it? What is this?' the sorcerer demanded. Czevak writhed. The demigod burned into him with his blazing, blue eyes. Sweeping the object with two fingers the sorcerer telekinetically stripped away the matte black shielding of the stasis casket, revealing the bell jar beneath. Revealing the embryo within. Revealing the Omega-Minus Pariah in all its negative psionic glory.

Czevak ceased his mock resistance and relaxed into satisfaction. His pretence had been enough to pique the sorcerer's insatiable curiosity. He wanted to eat up his enemy's suffering, to savour the sorcerer's surprise.

'Enjoy, you warp-spawned bastard,' Czevak spat.

The soul-scalding agony of the thing was so much that Ahriman could not unclasp his spasming claw. Pure, inexorable nullification blazed through the psyker's being, visiting upon the sorcerer agonies ten-thousand-fold what the beast had practised on Czevak. Even in the presence of such devastation, the psyker was not without resources. The raging torment of Ahriman's twisted face contorted further as it began to change. Like the pebble-splash in reverse, savage wrinkles rippled inwards and before Czevak had chance to fully enjoy the agony of his sworn enemy it was replaced by that of its original owner – Korban Xarchos.

The shock and feral suffering finding its way immediately onto the androgynous face was impossible to describe. The Omega-Minus embryo bathed the psyker in immaterial deadness. Korban Xarchos held on for as long as he could, the sorcerer's ears, eyes and nose streaming gore. The sorcerer's chin came up and he roared his anguish and pain at the heavens. Czevak watched the monster quake in his trembling power armour, before a thick fountain of blood and brains erupted from his mouth, as though he'd been shot through the back of the head. As the bodily fluids rained back down on the beast the Thousand Sons sorcerer collapsed in a heap of lifeless ceramite. The bell jar fell from Xarchos' dead claw and rolled down the scree slope.

Beside Czevak the Rubric Marines became similarly lifeless and stiff. Without sorcerers to guide them the mindless Space Marines became immediately dormant. Slipping his arms out of their statuesque grip, Czevak dived for the embryo, skidding through the grit and soot in his shirt. Through his chest the inquisitor felt the ground rumble. Perhaps Korban Xarchos had provided the daemon's last sacrifice or perhaps the daemon Mammoshad had felt the shock wave of the null entity's agonising influence and had sensed its own vulnerability. Raging against its captivity the daemon tore the rift open about it, wanting to be born. Czevak's fingers reached the bell jar, which was wretched even for him to touch. Czevak was no psyker but the thing was such raw negativity that even the inquisitor's latent psionic potential was roasted in its presence. His stomach churned violently and his thoughts ached. Resisting the urge to be sick or even curl up and die, the inquisitor did the unthinkable and smashed the bell jar against the rocky floor of the pit. The receptacle cracked and a section shattered. Amniotic-stasis fluid gushed onto the floor. Unable to even look at the thing, Czevak blindly thrust the remainder of the jar and the unbound Omega-Minus Pariah embryo down through the opening and into the egg.

There was no time to enjoy Mammoshad's suffering. All Czevak could think to do was scramble to his feet and crawl for his life. Past the burnt-out corpse of Korban Xarchos. Past the motionless Rubric Marines. Past the excavation and steam-powered mining equipment.

Czevak pushed himself to his feet and ran. He immediately came to miss the comforting blaze of colour his Harlequin coat used to leave behind and he felt strangely vulnerable without it. His legs were lithe, capable and bursting with youth and vigour, however, and made short work of ground that felt as though it were moving. Rubble rained down the sides of the pit face as tremors grumbled through the earth. Czevak could barely imagine what was happening below his feet. The raw negative nullification clashing with the awesome, immaterial power of the daemon. Risking a glance behind, Czevak saw the horrifying spectacle of the entity trying to be born. The warp rift had been severely compromised in the Omega-Minus's presence but the monstrous daemon still struggled for realisation. The creature's massive avian head was a parody even of its warped daemonic self. The colossal beak burst from the ground twisted and aflame, the monster's azure feathers on one half of its head melted into its flesh. With its beak mangled up into one eye, the other midnight orb bulged with cyclopean fury. An appendage surged out of the crater floor, creating a black gorge from which the deformed limb spasmodically sprang. Despite its atrophied appearance, being somewhere between an arm and a wing, the gargantuan reach of the thing came at the fleeing Czevak.

The inquisitor rolled to the side, allowing the three, spindly, malformed fingers to score grooves into the rock where he had been. As the limb retracted Czevak could feel the backdraft created by the row of twisted feathers. They had materialised out of the twisted bones of the abomination like a sail along its forearm. Bolting across the score marks, Czevak ran up alongside the wagons of the cargo tram. The smoke-belching engine was hauling its burden of bitumen trucks up the track and into the mine tunnels. Risking a further fleeting glance behind, Czevak watched the wretched perversity of the limb come at him again, the daemon attempting to drag itself out of the ground and into Melmoth's sickly reality. As Mammoshad extended its broken reach, tendons snapped and bones split, stabbing their way out of the daemonflesh. The remaining fingers of the creature's hand had grown wing-like and useless out of its forearm and elbow, the sparse, stunted feathers blazing with unnatural fire.

Desperate to be away from the giant, Czevak took several bounding steps before launching himself at the steam wagons. The black mineral fuel that the Nurglites had been so slavishly industrious about excavating crunched under his body. His leg dangled dangerously outside the truck but the inquisitor managed to draw the flailing limb in mere moments before the container he was riding entered the tunnels. Looking back Czevak watched Mammoshad snatch at the final truck and miss, instead settling for grasping and squeezing the locomotive's rails with its two gangly claws. As the rails closed the wheels on the rear three wagons began to screech. Czevak buried his head in his arms as the trucks popped right out of their railings, propelling the chassis and its mineral cargo up into the tunnel ceiling. Craning his neck, Czevak watched the toppled wagons, twist, roll and skid along the tunnel behind the fast-moving train.

Somehow Mammoshad had got the warped bulk of its gnarled and bone-skewered torso out of the hole and out onto the flat of the crater bottom. Horribly, the daemon's second wing had materialised inside its body, making what would ordinarily have been narrow hips and muscular stomach and chest a contorted nightmare of umbrella-splayed bones jutting out of the enormous entity's flame-wreathed carcass. To make movement even more agonising, its other arm was completely fused down its broken back. Shuffling its monstrous and malformed beak along the mine floor, one avian nostril twitched and flared allowing a stream of sapphire flame to blast after the steam tram and funnel up the tunnel.

Czevak watched the warp flame rage up the passage behind the trucks, rolling and twisting across the walls and ceiling before devouring the toppled rear trucks. Pushing himself up out of the black fuel, Czevak leapt for the truck in front. It had undoubtedly been part of Korban Xarchos's sick plan to have the Nurglite population of the burg mine their fossil fuel from around the growing daemon egg. As the warping essence leaked out of the Tzeentchian monstrosity into the surrounding rock, lending the black mineral its warp-lustre, the Nurglites would have burned it in their factories and slowly poisoned their denizens with its powerful, warp spawning properties. Evidence of the success of the sorcerer's plan was living in the tunnels in the form of the freakshow communities hacking out a deformed and desperate existence, too unsightly for even the scabby and diseased inhabitants of the burg.

Czevak leapt for the next truck, his head coming close to being taken off by one of the tunnel's wooden support struts. The warp flame kept coming, however, sweeping through the screaming monstrosities of the tunnels and enveloping the rear wagon. The contents of the container exploded. The bitumen was flammable enough but it was the warp lustrecence threaded through its glimmering blackness that caused the detonation. The bank of flame rolled further up the tunnel, chasing down the racing truck, igniting and blasting apart a second and a third truck. Czevak was forced to jump again and again, almost falling over the side of a wagon as the tug hurtled its train around a tunnel corner. The warp flame suddenly died and Czevak gave thanks to the Emperor that the stream had run its course. In actual fact, the repeated detonations along the length of the track had collapsed the tunnel. Tonnes of rock and earth were falling, cutting off the immaterial flames but also caving in above the steam tram. With several trucks still aflame but as yet to explode, Czevak leapt between two of the wagons and yanked the pin connecting them free. As the flaming trucks slowed the collapsing tunnel swallowed them whole, leaving Czevak in the rearmost wagon – the train bolting out of the crumbling tunnel entrance.

As the mining tram rattled through the black-brick factories, Czevak could hear the daemon Mammoshad, thundering through the smog. The burg could no longer hear the deep bass of the shift-change horn. Now the metropolis rang with the avian screech of a decimated daemon. The huge, malformed aberration must be on its feet the inquisitor reasoned. It must have hauled itself out of the open-cast mine and was crashing unsteadily through the chimneys of the industriascape. Even through the agitated fog, whipped up by the gargantuan movements of the mortally-wounded beast, Czevak could tell that the twisted carcass of the infernal creature was still aflame and setting fire to the bitumen bricks of surrounding buildings with accidental ease.

The factories ahead were already blazing firestorms through which the locomotive steamed. Czevak ducked beneath the flames and kicked burning masonry from where it had dropped into his wagon. The fuel in the trucks ahead was taking, however, and rather than be attached to a raging, runaway train, Czevak pulled the pin from out of the wagon attachment in front of him. As his container began to slow, the inquisitor watched the tug and its trucks get away from him. The engine came upon cobbled roads crossing its lines. Nurglites, fleeing the daemon crashing through their burg, ran straight across the track. Body after body smacked against the boiler and chimney, before going down under the mine engine's wheel. After the fourth or fifth body, the locomotive jumped the tracks, sending it and its piling cart train into the side of a blazing factory.

Czevak saw a taloned claw – like that of a titanic bird of prey – slam down on the demolished wagons, the mangled torso and head of the monster lost in the smog. Czevak tumbled his own body out of the slowing wagon, from the ground watching the daemon's scaly stump of a second leg hobble past on the intersection ahead. All about the daemon precarious buildings and leaning chimneys were blazing and falling. Getting to his feet, Czevak knew that he had to make it to the webway portal before Mammoshad trampled the tinderbox burg into an inferno. He was about to tear off uphill when a sickening spectacle caught his eye. After the daemon's legs had stomped by, Czevak had expected to see the creature's tail pass. This it did, despite being a ruptured throng of feather bundles imbedded in a knotted, scaly, muscular club. The horror did not end there, however. Dragged through the demolished burg behind the daemon was another warped mass, an unrealised twin of a monstrosity, a plucked, unformed, foetal deadweight, blinking its immaterial agony at the world.

Czevak turned to sprint away up a flight of steep, fractured steps but almost immediately ran into the floating form of Father hovering behind, returned like an obedient pet with its blue, bionic eyes waiting for instructions. Czevak only had one for it.

'Come on, this way!'

Vaulting up the steps and along twisted alleyways, Czevak shielded his face from the flames of freshly ignited buildings with the sleeves of his shirt. He barged his way through screaming Nurglites who, shocked out of their languor, could barely comprehend what was happening. Father weaved his way behind, dodging around, above and sometimes between the cancerous legs of burg workers.

Above, the fog glared bright with the city fires and the indiscriminate streams of immaterial flame snorted across the tenement rooftops by the wild and warped daemon. As Czevak's legs began to burn with the demand of an uphill sprint and his chest wheeze with deep lungfuls of smoke and exertion, the inquisitor bundled straight into a mob of burg inhabitants. The dense crowd was formed by gaping Nurglites drifting out into the main thoroughfare from both the gin mills and faith healers across the street. They stared at the destruction wrought upon the city by the dying, behemothic thrashings of a monstrous daemon on its last legs. They gawped at the collapsing buildings and the strange flames that devoured the slum with an appetite for destruction. As Czevak pushed through their diseased bodies – just for a moment – he fancied he saw the Harlequin half-mask of one of his hunters. Czevak slowed and shook his head.

'No, not now,' he heard himself say before surging on through the filthy bodies of the stunned bystanders. With an adrenaline-spurred spring to his step the inquisitor bolted up the thoroughfare with Father gliding behind. A stretch up the street he saw eldritch boots dangling from a balcony upon which the gargoyle-masked leader of the Harlequin troupe sat. Slamming his back against the doorway of the tenement block opposite – escaping denizens spilling past him – Czevak watched the Great Harlequin nod slowly, doffing his wild, pink plume at the inquisitor. The slum frontage suddenly exploded as one of Mammoshad's legs stumbled through it. Czevak instinctively backed into the doorway alcove with the other squirming bodies for cover. As the taloned claw staggered uphill, creating fresh havoc beyond, the dust of the demolished building began to thin and reveal that the Harlequin was gone.

Czevak froze. He didn't know whether to run or hide. The Harlequins were everywhere, stationed along his route back to the safety of the webway portal. If they were not there then he was indeed losing his mind, the inquisitor reasoned. If they were really there amongst the peril of the daemon-ravaged city, then that was even worse. Over the thoroughfare rubble of the smashed tenement building, Czevak spotted the skeletal mask and carapace of the Death Jester, leant against a black-bricked wall in his long, dark coat. He was holding his shrieker cannon at ease like an agri-world harvester with his scythe.

A gout of rolling warp flame torched the roofs above before wildly streaming through the thoroughfare, razing the demolished masonry and cobbled road. Czevak was forced out into the open by flame dribbling off the roofs and onto the street. Upon realising that the Death Jester had also disappeared, the inquisitor set out across the scorched rubble. Above, the agonised screeches of the wounded daemon had grown mournful and desperate. The monstrosity could clutch to reality no more and as its presence grew ever more unstable and the warped realisation of its encounter with the Omega-Minus Pariah crippled and killed the beast, the prodigious creature began to stumble and fall.

Czevak ran at full speed for the alley through which he'd entered the damned reality of Melmoth's World. As he cornered and bolted down the cramped alleyway's depths, past the still-sleeping vagrants, he came face to face with himself, reflected in the Shadowseer's mirror mask. The warlock stood between Czevak and the sanctuary of the webway. The warp gate already crackled with interdimensional activation, indicating that the Harlequins had followed him through. Czevak's mind whirled with the dark fear he only knew too well in the presence of the Harlequin psyker. Were the Harlequins there to take him back to a prisoner's life in the Black Library? Had some farseer seen that he had outlived his destined usefulness to the eldar and the Harlequins had come to destroy him?

Mammoshad's club-like tail and the obscene deformity it trailed behind smashed through the alley wall, causing an unfurling tidal wave of bitumen bricks to fall towards the inquisitor. Faced with the fearful Shadowseer and the certain death of being crushed by the collapsing slum, Czevak ran at the Harlequin. As the bricks showered and smashed behind the inquisitor, the Harlequin moved to one side to block Czevak's route. The daemon-demolished wall fell too fast for both of them, the falling masonry threatening to bury the alleyway. Instead of trying to run by, since the inquisitor knew he could never beat the reflexes of an eldar Harlequin, Czevak ran straight at the Shadowseer. As the bricks rained down, Czevak's shoulder struck the surprised warlock in the chest. At that moment Czevak felt something that he'd only known once before, the pit of the stomach fizzle of phase-field relocation.

As both inquisitor and Shadowseer dropped back into reality a few strides up the untouched section of the alleyway beyond their positions were reversed. Czevak hit the ground nearest the webway portal with the Harlequin reeling from the impact and falling backwards up the alley. Scrambling arm over arm, Czevak crawled for the sizzling webway portal. As he pulled himself up against the black bricks that covered the wraithbone arch he looked back to see the Shadowseer flip from his back up onto his feet and draw the leaf-shaped length of his witchblade. Dark dread found the inquisitor and Czevak was rooted to the spot with irrational terror. The projected fear was fleeting, however, as the psyker's concentration was broken by an object hurtling up behind. The warlock ducked as Father passed overhead, bringing up his mirror-mask just in time to see the servo-skull disappear through the portal.

The alley was suddenly bathed in blackness as the gargantuan form of the daemon Mammoshad – King of Kings, Enslaver of the Craven Worlds and Keeper of the Vault Abyssal – stumbled its last and toppled across the passage. Distracted, this time by the creature's descending, avian bulk, the Harlequin got two steps into a sprint he knew he could not make. As the malformed monstrosity's body pulverised the remaining buildings around the Shadowseer to grit, Czevak slipped in through the portal archway. The Harlequin disappeared under the immense dimensions of the daemon Mammoshad's twisted, fallen body. As the inquisitor backed through the warp gate into the interdimensional safety of the webway, the slightest puff of masonry dust followed Czevak through. This was accompanied by the immediate sealing of the portal. Since he hadn't rune-sealed the archway himself, Czevak reasoned that the gateway must have been crushed by Mammoshad's warp-spawned carcass on the other side like the Harlequin psyker.

Collapsing in an adrenaline-drained and exhausted heap under Father's cold optical orbs, Czevak could only hope that he had been that fortunate.

Exeunt

I

INTERREGNA

The Wraith Tower, The Black Library of Chaos, The webway

CHORUS

BRONISLAW CZEVAK HAD spent a life long-lived in the librariums, archives and reliquaries of the Imperium but never once had he expected to become an exhibit in one.

Following his rescue from the depraved clutches of Ahriman of the Thousand Sons, the mysterious mirror-masked Shadowseer, known to Czevak as Vespasi-Hann, escorted him – as he had done years before – to the hallowed halls of the Black Library of Chaos. Czevak had observed – with his limited, human insight – that the dark craftworld was not where it had once been.

Like a floating berg of scorched, crystal translucence, the Black Library drifted through the colossal, arterial channels of the webway. It was vast and impossible, keen-edged, yet angleless and covered in vanes and serrated flourishes that seemed to melt into one serene, silky form. Even if the daemon-sorcerer Ahriman had managed to wrench the secret of the Black Library's location from his fragile mind, the monster would have found nothing. Upon Czevak's arrival the darkling craftworld was elegantly negotiating the mind-numbing dimensions of a webway juncture, the living vessel allowing itself to gently drop and descend down through the chasmic mouth of the tunnel below.

Although situated in a labyrinthine dimension, the dark craftworld itself was very much its own maze of osseous passages, convoluted corridors and arched chambers. These were all devoted to protecting and preserving the perils of Chaos lore, as recorded in the innumerable tomes, scrolls and technologies stored there. Bubble vaults hung below the wraithberg superstructure of the Black Library, pregnant with the dark secrets of darker gods, the names and deeds of the Traitor Astartes and the truth of the eldar's inevitable Fall; above reared a jagged horizon of tear-drop citadels, obelisks, monoliths, spires and columnar steeples – each its own treasury of forbidden works. In one of these towers, long before, Czevak had studied the works of the Dark Imperium. The Wraith Tower held the mon-keigh's miserable contribution to the study of the Chaos Powers and their dark arts. It was here, in his glass prison, that Bronislaw Czevak had whiled away the hours of the occupied patient, buried in the piles of desiccated tomes and faded scrolls of his infant race, reading about – among many other cursed events, artefacts and people – Ahzek Ahriman, sorcerer, Space Marine and Chosen of Tzeentch.

The inquisitor looked down at the wraithbone desk. Like everything else in his cell – and Czevak was convinced that the term was intended in both its monastic and incarceratory sense – the desk was vitreous and crystalline clear. Czevak could see his age-spotted feet in his sandals through the alien material. It was here, in a glasseous chamber, that the ancient inquisitor had made his physical and spiritual recovery. It had taken some getting used to. The only privacy he had was a coiled curtain in which to toilet and bathe. Able to see through the flowing form of the furniture and even the walls of the cell itself, Czevak was forever bumping into objects, feeling rather like a trapped and foolish bird, attempting to escape its aviary. At first this had not bothered the largely immobile Czevak, nearly every bone in his body had been broken and his mind was shattered and frail. As the wondrous cares, technologies and magics of the eldar helped to repair his body and soul, motility allowed for the solace of study. His xenos hosts had been thoughtful enough to grow his wraithbone recess in the very area of the Black Library in which he had spent countless hours of research and contemplation – the Wraith Tower.

Czevak shuffled about the crystal-clear walls of his doorless, hermetic chamber in sandals and the Shadowseer's Harlequin coat – the garment in which he'd been wrapped upon being rescued from Ahriman's ruinous clutches. The inquisitor had come to realise that he had become an organic artefact, like the wraithbone prison itself. His knowledge of the Dark Powers of the universe had been captured and reclaimed by the eldar for permanent study and display. Outside the see-through walls lay the expanse of the Wraith Tower's minaret chamber. Here, some of the most ancient, heretical and incisive works ever committed to paper by human hand were crammed and collected on stasis-shelf compartments, in spiral stacks of translucent obsidian, which bobbed across the chamber on anti-gravitic fields. A galactically young evil literally ebbed from the sea of dusty spines and pages.

Damned like the texts about him, Czevak had been buried in arcana for all eternity, for his own safety and the safety of the galaxy. He never felt more like an artefact or exhibit than when colourful and unknown eldritch forms put their tall, tapering helmets and fingertips to the transparent wraithbone and stared inside. He once even saw a human, a gunmetal grey-haired member of some Illuminati or xenos sect, entrusted like the inquisitor had been with the craftworld's secrets. As the two men looked at one another, the pony-tailed visitor gave what the aged Czevak assumed to be grim pity with his spiky, furrowed brow and steely eyes. That was the day Czevak started talking the lunacy of escape.

It was the solemn responsibility of the craftworld's Guardian-Scribes to collate and transcribe the awesome knowledge of the Black Library, gathering and interpreting its collected wisdom for use in the eldar race's everlasting battle against the dark forces of Chaos. Whereas the enigmatic warrior cult of the Harlequins were the keepers of the Laughing God's Black Library, the hunters of Chaos in all its forms and collectors of the Black Library's dark lore, the Guardian-Scribes were the custodians and caretakers of the craftworld's treasures. This included Bronislaw Czevak, who had been allocated a sable-robed, argent-helmeted Guardian-Scribe to attend to his recovery and supply the Wraith Tower's prisoner with simple human sustenance, water and a neverending supply of requested tomes and tracts from the surrounding shelves that could be seen but not reached by the inquisitor.

With the light waft of the coil curtain and pages on the wraithbone deck, Adara-Ke's appearance was heralded by the static spiral of phase-field materialisation. The Guardian-Scribe had two long armfuls of gathered texts, which she deposited on the desk. Slipping out of her tall helmet the eldar allowed her blue-black hair to fall down the back of her long robes. Despite being several times the ancient inquisitor's age, her alabaster skin was still soft and tight over her high, elfin cheekbones.

The only betrayal of her age were the lines around her unsmiling lips and alien eyes.

'This wasn't on my list,' Czevak mumbled with a crabbiness born of old age and repetitive disappointment. Adara-Ke often brought him incorrect texts, although whether this was down to the Guardian-Scribe's misunderstanding or the fact that the inquisitor had dreadful handwriting was unclear. On the top of the pile sat a bulky tome amongst gilded casket-covers. Its snap-lock and the burnished radiance of its golden frontispiece and bulky spine grabbed Czevak's attention immediately. The spine contained some kind of rhythmic pump that sighed with gentle, hypnotic regularity. Czevak's aged fingers were immediately drawn to its gilded representations and aureate lettering. 'The *Atlas Infernal*,' Czevak translated from the High Gothic, and his fingers drifted towards the text's cover clasps. Adara-Ke's long, pale fingers found their way urgently to the inquisitor's and stopped him.

'Don't open that,' the eldar insisted with uncharacteristic urgency. The Guardian-Scribe's Gothic was perfect and such articulation appeared strange spilling as it did from alien lips. The marble smoothness of Adara-Ke's brow creased. The Black Library of Chaos was a place of silent study, of quiet research and reflection. Czevak had never experienced such insistence in Adara-Ke or the Black Library and the inquisitor was immediately curious.

'Why not?' he asked. 'What's wrong? Is it corrupted?'

Adara-Ke knelt down beside the wraithbone desk, her hands laid across the *Atlas Infernal*'s magnificent cover.

'Listen to me very carefully, mon-keigh, for I have little time. This tome is an Imperial artefact from the early history of your human empire. It is one of the most dangerous and powerful works to be housed in the Black Library, although no ordinary eldar can know this because no eldar has seen what is written between its covers.'

Czevak nodded uncertainly. He went to speak but the Guardian-Scribe placed the tip of one willowy finger upon his cracked and aged lips.

'I have no time for questions, son of man – only answers. Deep within the Black Library at this time is a gathering. Vespasi-Hann has returned and the Harlequins perform, for the pleasure of the Laughing God as well as an audience of the Black Council and the Guardian-Scribes of the Black Library. You have borne privileged witness to such an event, have you not?'

Czevak nodded, remembering his exquisite experience at Iyanden, where the delicacy of narrative and fabric of reality became as one.

'At this moment,' Adara-Ke continued with grave determination, 'I am one of very few that walk the Black Library's halls.' The inquisitor nodded his understanding, even through the crystal wraithbone of his prison walls he could see that the Wraith Tower's chambers were unusually devoid of scribes and seers.

'The Black Council have watched while you have slept and studied. It sat to decide your fate, Czevak of the Holy Ordos. The Black Council is made up of the most powerful farseers of our race, drawn here periodically, in secret and safety. They discuss their divinations and guide our people through disasters yet to happen and threats we have yet to face. Morcan Fiorinintal of Alaitoc, Eiladar Ys of the Lugganath and Ffaid Karhedra of Eyslk-Tan, all sit on the Black Council. My father also sits on the Council; the devastated people of Iyanden have always known you as friend. Eldrad Ulthran – a most gifted ancient of our race – and chief farseer among the Ulthwé, could not sit for he fights the forces of darkness during your Thirteenth Black Crusade, both amongst the stars and on the webway. The fell-sorcerer Ahzek Ahriman has used the secrets he stole from you and breached one of our sacred thresholds.'

The Guardian-Scribe looked through the glass walls of

the cell and about the chamber before continuing.

'I am here with this news because the Black Council is split over your fate. Some say that they have come to see the Laughing God's servants show them the path, to read the truth in their art and war. Many favour your perpetual imprisonment in these hallowed halls, for the security of both our races…'

'As another relic,' Czevak said miserably.

'But some speak of futures yet to come,' Adara-Ke continued in precise syllables. 'Ahzek Ahriman was not to have breached the labyrinth dimension. His successes have already surpassed what the Black Council saw for him. Many fear what havoc the Changer's Chosen will wreak with the damned secrets you bled him from this sacred place. Even from afar, Eldrad Ulthran of the Ulthwé lends them voice and calls for your execution. He claims that you are too dangerous to keep alive. He says that you will betray us and yourself and as the oldest, most gifted and influential of the Black Council, his word will eventually be heeded.'

'So I'm a dead man, that's what you're here to tell me,' Czevak put to the eldar, his blood turning to icewater.

'The Black Council struggles with its own visions. The future is fickle. Even Eldrad Ulthran has been known to be wrong about that which comes to pass.'

'So what are you saying?'

'My father alone feels you still have a role to play in the galaxy's tumultuous affairs. He always has, ever since he sent for you with Iyanden's dark invitation. He listens to the Black Library; he tastes the future of history's past mistakes here and drinks its thirst for the morrow. He sees for a people on the brink of extinction; as Iyanden, he feels without fear the fate of our race. He feels you have yet to prove yourself. And that is why he has instructed me to set you free.'

Czevak took a moment to digest the alien's words.

'You and your father risk everything.'

'My father's reputation and my own will be saved by the simplicity of a clerical error,' the Guardian-Scribe told him cryptically. She took the parchment list of books Czevak had given her and showed the inquisitor his blots and scribbles. 'You truly have abominable handwriting, Czevak of the Holy Inquisition.' The eldar screwed up the list and tossed it over her shoulder – evidence to be discovered – before taking her hand from the casket-cover of the *Atlas Infernal*.

'Why would you do this?'

'I am a father's daughter,' was the eldar's simple reply.

'You are sending me back?' Czevak whispered, hoping, fearing.

'The doors are locked, I can but give you a key,' Adara-Ke instructed bleakly. She pointed at the burnished cover in front of him. Czevak looked from the ancient tome to the Guardian-Scribe's face.

'How is this a key?' Czevak demanded.

'It's a map – the only one of its kind. It will show you the way. It will show you many ways.'

'You have seen this map?'

'Like I said, no eldar has seen what is between these covers. Its pages are death to my kind.'

'But…' The inquisitor didn't have the words. 'Why?'

'The Black Library has spoken. Suffering and sacrifice are universal constants, are they not inquisitor? You of all people should know that. Besides which,' she repeated, unclasping the lock on the *Atlas Infernal*'s casket-covers, 'I am a father's daughter.'

'Adara!' the aged inquisitor called but the tome was open. Both of them felt the irresistible pull of the pages. They stared down at leaves of ancient flesh, stretched to transparency across lightweight golden frames and scarred with antique notations. The spine pump sighed its beating rhythm, injecting oxygen and circulating the Sister of Silence's equally ancient lifeblood through the labyrinthine network of veins, arteries and capillaries. All were visible at the surface and represented the present configured insanity of interdimensional tunnels known as the webway, closest to the incredible text.

The eldar screamed, clawing at her scalp and skull with her long fingers. She fell back, away from the field of nullification that the open pages radiated around the tome. Czevak scrambled to the translucent jet of the wraithbone floor. He dragged the thrashing Guardian-Scribe away from the horrific influence of the artefact's warp-blankness. Adara-Ke, who had given the Black Library of Chaos three centuries of loyal service, died swiftly in its hallowed halls.

As the eldar stopped shaking, Czevak turned her over, revealing a pool of blood and Adara's soul-scorched face. Czevak sagged, soaking up the enormity of the alien's sacrifice.

'I'm sorry,' he told her. 'I'm so very sorry.'

He allowed himself the unadvised luxury of several more moments of guilt and pain before moving on the ancient text. There were other existences ending around the inquisitor. He could see pin-pricks of soulfire slowly burning their way through the lucent wraithbone walls of his transparent cell. The negative psionic field of the open *Atlas Infernal* was scorching the infinity circuit and withering the soul matrix of the wraithbone structure.

The wraithbone desk began to melt beneath the *Atlas Infernal*'s armoured covers. As solidified warp energy, shaped by the psychic engineering talents of eldar Bonesingers, the material lost its solid, supernatural state. Wraithbone dribbled and bubbled to a viscous resin about the artefact. As the tome slid to the floor on the liquefying sheen of the disintegrating substance it rapidly turned the floor of the cell into a vortex of melted wraithbone. It spumed and blistered to gossamer thinness before glooping down through the ceiling of the Black Library chamber below.

Czevak reached for the *Atlas Infernal* but the armoured

tome slipped through the scorched hole in the floor. As the opening grew Czevak could see the vast vault of books below, equal in height and size to the colossal hall in which his cell was situated. Immediately below the gaping wound in the floor and ceiling was one of the chamber's towering spiral stacks that were crammed with ancient texts and daemonic tracts and drifted around the hall on anti-gravitic fields.

Forced to make the most of Adara-Ke's sacrifice and the precious time and opportunity the inquisitor had, Czevak allowed himself to fall through the rapidly melting floor and land in the treacle-slurp topping of inert wraithbone that had begun to gather at the top of the stack's spiral staircase.

Czevak skid-slipped down the melting steps, following the tumbling path of the *Atlas Infernal*. Several storeys down, Czevak came across the corpse of another Guardian-Scribe, clearly on his way up the stack to investigate the strange phenomenon in the ceiling. His helmet was off and the unfortunate eldar had made the mistake of picking up the closed *Atlas Infernal* and opening it before his face. The tome sat open once more in the alien's death grip, the Guardian-Scribe's eye sockets now two smouldering pits burnt out of his skull.

Grabbing the open tome, Czevak hobbled down the rest of the steps in panicked exhaustion. Engaged in the creaking awkwardness of an old man's run, Czevak loped across the vast chamber. It was largely deserted, no doubt due to the performance of the visiting Harlequin troupe. As he approached the looming archway connecting the hall to an antechamber, his heart hammering inside the fragile bones of his ribcage, he ran straight into two further Guardian-Scribes, carrying piles of grimoires and forbidden volumes. The eldar immediately crashed to the ground shrieking, their coordination gone, spasming and slamming their helmets into scattered tomes and wraithbone floor.

Skidding to a sandaled stop at the arch, Czevak put his back to the obsidian lustre of the wall. As a long time resident of the Wraith Tower and frequenter of the halls, Czevak knew that each antechamber contained a sentinel, a largely ceremonial guardian armed with ceremonial weapon – a broad, leaf-shaped blade sat atop a long spear shaft.

Czevak desperately searched for a way to bypass the Black Library Guardian without getting skewered on the extensive reach of the weapon. Something suddenly clattered to the floor beside the inquisitor and Czevak was shocked to see the self-same weapon lying on the floor in the archway. Peering around the doorway fearfully, Czevak found that the Guardian too had toppled, the alien laying dead in a gently growing pool of blood leaking from his helmet.

Slamming the casket-covers of the *Atlas Infernal* shut, Czevak dashed across the antechamber. Not favouring the inconvenience of clunky elevators or legions of steps, all floors of all towers were equipped with sizzling wraith gates to aid swift and open movement within and between the craftworld's expanse of buildings, vaults and chambers. An interdimensional portal was all Czevak needed, however, and as the High Inquisitor clutched the *Atlas Infernal* to his chest, he turned and took one last glance at the dark magnificence of the Black Library of Chaos, before stepping through the crackling static of the portal to his freedom.

Exit

I

ACT V, CANTO I

Archeodeck, Rogue trader Malescaythe, *The Eye of Terror*

Enter CZEVAK with FATHER

STUMBLING BACK THROUGH the Lost Fornical of Urien-Myrdyss, Czevak had sensed something was wrong immediately. The ship was moving once again, not holding on station as Czevak had instructed. The inquisitor, scorched and soot-stained from his adventures on Melmoth's World, assumed that the *Malescaythe* had run into further peril in the stormy region of hell that was the Scorpento Maestrale. This was until the two magma bomb warheads streaked past the archeodeck's hangar at screaming velocity. The ship lurched with such force that the rogue trader's artificial gravity struggled to nego-tiate the erratic movement. Even Father's anti-gravity drive failed to anticipate the pitch and the servo-skull swooped at the deck before recovering. Once again, the

Malescaythe was under attack but from who or what, Czevak could not imagine.

The elevator ride to the command deck was a stomach-flipping cacophony as klaxons wailed and the car rattled up the shaft, unsure during the rogue trader's evasive manoeuvres whether or not it could reach the bridge. As the door opened, Czevak was treated to an apocalyptic vision of destruction as the smashed planetoid, already missing one third of its torn and rocky mass at the pole, exploded spectacularly. Magma bombs had continued to fly at the *Malescaythe*, one of which had found the already storm-ruptured planetoid. Fragments of rock and streams of molten core rocketed in all directions, turning the existing debris field into an inescapable tsunami of tumbling rock shards and accelerating rubble, ready to cave in the side of the tiny rogue trader.

Captain Torres was not her usual self. Gone were the frenetic questions, savage demands for data and shouting. Her ship was dead and the situation futile. The best she could do was keep the *Malescaythe* out of the lethal path of both asteroids and magma bombs for as long as she could and this she did with an accepting, professional calm. As she issued desperate but peaceful orders to the helm, Czevak stepped out of the elevator. Father immediately detached and drifted across the bridge. All eyes were on the devastation raining down on them outside the lancet windows. Rasputus still sat in his cage with Hessian and Epiphani holding onto the gibbet bars for support. They were still dripping with tubes and wires from the sick bay, where presumably Torres summoned them upon regaining consciousness. If there was a slim chance that the enginarium might be able to restore the *Malescaythe's* warp capabilities then the 'freak', as the captain had put it, was needed on the bridge ready to plot a new course through the maelstrom of the Eye.

As Father approached the warp-seer the girl turned and noticed the High Inquisitor's entrance. She gave him a blank look of empty ambivalence, neither blame nor forgiveness. The prognostic had known the fear of uncertainty and seemed the younger and more fragile for it. Hessian burned into him with the oily, black eyes of his daemon-self and gave Czevak a predatory face of handsome hatred.

Armourless, the Relictors Space Marine too seemed frail and vulnerable, despite his height and broad shoulders being buried under a mountain of infirmary blankets. The dressed stump of his forearm was trussed up against his slashed and stitched ebony chest. As he saw the High Inquisitor with his burns and torn, soot-stained clothing he nodded grim respect and mouthed something to Raimus Klute, whose knuckles were white on the pulpit rail.

The relief and recognition in Klute's eyes was powerful but brief.

'Is it done?'

'For now.'

'Welcome back,' Klute said with genuine feeling. 'We're in trouble.'

'So it seems,' Czevak agreed. 'Aft pict screen,' the High Inquisitor ordered. One of the bridge's lancet windows swam with brief static before displaying a view from the rear of the rogue trader. 'No…' was the only expression Czevak could find for what he saw.

The rogue trader blasted on, pursued through the debris field by a growing pack of rapidly closing vessels. Warp exit halos erupted across the semi-reality of the Scorpento Maestrale vomiting forth a continuous stream of reinforcements, adding to the torpedo and warhead hurling chase.

'Malchankov found us,' Klute announced, putting into words what everyone else was thinking. Everyone except Czevak.

'Which you said couldn't happen,' Torres accused between course corrections.

'What I actually said was that it was highly unlikely,' Czevak corrected, 'but this is academic – it's not Malchankov.'

'Is there anyone who doesn't want to blow us out of void?' Torres asked, her very real fear hiding behind a sardonic wit.

'In the Eye of Terror?' the High Inquisitor said. 'No, we're pretty much on our own out here.'

'Then who is it?' Klute demanded.

'Pict magnification,' Czevak said. The image flickered and then returned at full magnification on the forward vessel in the chase.

'Adeptus Astartes strike cruiser *Stella Incognita*, Excommunicate Traitoris. Gladius-class frigate *Rubrician*, Excommunicate Traitoris. Armed transport *Chimera*, wanted for mutiny and seventeen counts of piracy. Adeptus Astartes battle-barge *Impossible Fortress*, Excommunicate Traitoris–'

'We get it, lieutenant,' Torres stopped him.

The magnification blurred before sharpening on the strike cruiser's insignia, a ragged circle created by a serpent eating its own tail – a symbol of eternity and more specifically the Thousand Sons Traitor Marine Legion.

'It's not Malchankov,' Czevak repeated, echoing the reverse of his earlier conversation with Klute on the bridge. 'It's Ahriman.'

'And friends,' Klute added taking in the swarm of cultist craft the Thousand Sons had brought with them.

'He doesn't want to lose me again,' Czevak said to himself, feasting his eyes on the horrific, overwhelming pursuit.

'You think?' Klute said.

'I'm open to ideas,' Torres reminded the inquisitors as smaller rubble fragments from the destroyed planetoid hit, scraping and bouncing along the *Malescaythe*'s hull.

'How is this possible?' Klute asked, taking in the growing flotilla of Chaos vessels. Czevak nodded, turning the question – which he regarded as more than rhetorical – over in his mind. It hurt not to know how the daemon sorcerer had trapped him again. He thought of his meeting with Ahriman in the open cast mine. It was true that the *Impossible Fortress* needn't have been in orbit around Melmoth's World, nor Ahriman actually on the Nurglite planet – although Czevak reasoned to psychically wear Korban Xarchos's body as he had would require some proximity. 'I left you on the other side of the Eye,' Czevak muttered to himself. 'How can you be here? How can you be here?' The distance seemed too great to cover in the warp, especially through one of the most perverse and stormy regions in the rift. 'Why here? How could you know I'd be here?' the High Inquisitor asked himself.

Czevak recalled Melmoth's World, in all its dour and toxic detail. In his mind's eye he stared up through the thinning smog and into the night sky, fancying he spotted in his memory a large ship in low orbit. The *Impossible Fortress?* Then he remembered something else. Looking past the shape – that in the vagueness of his memory might have been a cloud of filthy, factory emission, a Space Marine battle-barge or a super heavy mineral transport – he saw the phantom moon of Auboron, there but not then. A world stuck fifty years in the past at the whim of the Eye's perverse forces.

'No, no, no...' Czevak heard himself say before spitting on the deck and shouting, 'Devious bastard.' The High Inquisitor tried to imagine how the Thousand Sons had found him in the Scorpento Maestrale. He re-lived the polluted presence of the sorcerer. How he had invaded Czevak's mind once again on the surface of Melmoth's World, with the Rubric Marines holding him still. In his feverish search for the *Atlas Infernal*, Ahriman had set upon Czevak's suspicious memory of Father, but Czevak hypothesised, what if the sorcerer had seen more? Travelled back further in his memories and only in the reflection of defeat had seen Czevak give the *Atlas Infernal* to Klute; had seen the Scorpento Maestrale and the deep blue star outside of the bridge lancet windows. An astrotelepathic message sent to Auboron – perhaps only the simplest of warnings and locations – forwarded to a confused Ahzek Ahriman, fifty years in his past. Would the daemon sorcerer heed its own garbled counsel? He might, with nothing left to show for years of intricate planning and failed entrapment than a vanquished daemon and an Omega-Minus level soul-scalding, high up above Melmoth's World. Czevak grunted. The Eye of Terror was certainly strange enough to support such a hypothesis.

'Czevak?' Klute said as the High Inquisitor thought on the Scorpento Maestrale, on the deep blue star and on his earlier consultation with the *Atlas Infernal* on the bridge.

'Czevak?'

'Turn us around,' the High Inquisitor suddenly commanded. It was time to stop blundering into the traps of others and start setting some of his own.

'Are you insane?' Torres said.

'I said turn us around,' Czevak insisted, trotting down the pulpit steps and scanning runebanks and screens for the *Malescaythe*'s current degree of declination and celestial ascension.

'Those cruisers will get a clear shot at our flank,' Torres said angrily, her naval training and common sense in evidence.

'Have any of the vessels hit us with their batteries or ordnance?' Czevak put to her, running back up the stairs. Torres stared back at him in silent defiance.

'No,' Klute supplied the answer for the captain.

'That is no accident,' Czevak said. 'They will not blow this ship to oblivion because there is something on the *Malescaythe* that they want.'

'You, I suppose,' Torres cut back.

'No,' Czevak said smugly and held out his hand towards Klute. Reaching inside his robes, Klute extracted the casket-covers of the *Atlas Infernal* and passed it to his master. 'This. Ahzek Ahriman wants this vessel, he wants the crew alive and he wants this precious artefact in one piece. Mark my words,' he told the captain. 'He will not destroy this vessel, but if he catches and boards us he will slaughter everyone on board, slowly.'

Once again, captain and inquisitor had carried out their contest of common sense in front of the crew on the command deck and Reinette Torres had lost.

'Lieutenant, make your turn,' the rogue trader captain ordered. Then to Czevak, 'Where are we headed?'

'The blue star,' the High Inquisitor said.

'You told me explicitly not to approach that star,' the captain snarled.

'Yes I did,' Czevak said, 'but that was then and this is now. Make your course, a stellar approach: equatorial east, axial declination –23°26".'

The bridge crew complied and the *Malescaythe* rolled into a savage turn, blazing for the blue star at sub-light speed. As the rogue trader presented its length to the primed bombardment cannons, torpedo shafts and lances of their pursuers, the entire command deck held its breath. As Czevak predicted, the ordnance stopped flying at the vessel and the pack of Chaos vessels threw themselves into a similar banking manoeuvre. With only one sub-light engine column functioning, Czevak could not hope to outrun his hunters. The inquisitor hoped he wouldn't have to.

Czevak watched Torres shiver. Klute's breath started to cloud and the inside of the lancet windows began to mist and rime.

'Tell me about the enginarium,' Czevak said sharply. 'While I've been gone, has the enginseer carried out his repairs?'

'We have a single sub-light engine column, no shields

and damage to the warp drive,' Torres notified him miserably. The *Malescaythe* was a wreck and Czevak had barely the heart to admit to her what he planned to do next. 'We have power for the engine column, life support, gravity and the Geller field.'

'Captain, what I'm about to ask you will likely shock and appal you,' Czevak prepared her, 'yet I implore you to believe me that what I am about to tell you is the only way to save your ship.'

'Go ahead, inquisitor,' Torres said with resignation. 'Shock and appal me.'

Czevak nodded. 'I want you to get on the vox with your enginseer and instruct him to run the sublight engines to critical.'

A stunned silence descended on the bridge. Torres laughed.

'You want me to do what?'

'You heard me, captain. And you do not have much time to make this decision. Trust me.'

The air about them was gelid and a light frost had started to form on the captain's epaulettes as well as on the bridge's runebanks and decking.

'How about you tell me what you're already doing to my ship,' the captain seethed with misted breath.

'I'll be brief,' the High Inquisitor said. 'This is the Eye of Terror – the laws of reality, let alone the laws of physics often don't apply here. The star that we are cruising towards is known as the Kryonova. It burns cold, captain. As a star, it saps heat from the void around it rather than radiating it like a regular star. The heat generated by a critical engine meltdown might be enough to save the *Malescaythe* but if you don't initiate that and I mean now, the hull of the ship will begin to frost-shatter and disintegrate around us.'

A moment passed.

Torres looked from Czevak to Klute and Klute to Saul Torquhil. The Relictor Techmarine nodded gravely.

The deck officer held a vox-horn on a spiralled cable above his head and up out of the transept. Leaning over the freezing pulpit rail, Torres snatched the mouthpiece.

'Enginseer Autolycus, this is the captain. I am about to give you an order, I want you to follow it. I don't want to hear what the Omnissiah might think about it or about the *Malescaythe*'s machine spirit. She's my ship, I know her better than any on board. This is not some warp fever or the product of an insane mind,' Torres said, staring at Czevak. 'We know what we're doing. Follow my order to the letter. I want you to intentionally send the starboard sub-light engine column into critical meltdown and evacuate the enginarium. Do that now, if you please. Captain, out.'

As Torres handed the vox horn back to her lieutenant the bridge could hear Enginseer Autolycus's apoplectic response.

'Very good, captain,' Czevak said. 'That was well–'

'Don't,' Torres growled.

Precious moments went by. The metal decking and instrumentation bled deep, benumbing cold. The lancet windows were completely caked in white and the bridge crew had begun to double over with crippling cold.

'Come on, come on, come on…' the High Inquisitor said.

'Czevak,' Klute called, retreating into the folds of his robes. 'Perhaps we should evacuate the ship. Get everyone out through the Lost Fornical?'

Czevak smiled at his friend's compassion.

'There's still time,' Czevak told him. 'Besides, I don't think that Captain Torres is quite ready to give up on her ship yet.'

As they waited, the Kryonova leached heat from rogue trader's hull, refrigerating the vessel's interior. Instrumentation began to fizzle and die. Klute looked up as the vessel superstructure started to contract and creak. The *Malescaythe* moaned like some creature of the deep.

The excruciating torment of metal echoed through the ship as architecture contorted and the armoured hull began to fracture.

Torres motioned for the vox-horn again, which the lieutenant passed her with numb-jointed difficulty. Torres rasped, barely able to catch her razorblade breath in the plummeting temperature of the bridge.

'Enginseer…' she managed but at that moment the command deck klaxons and sirens screeched to life. The bridge became bathed in red and steam started pouring from wall and floor grilles. All over the vessel, emergency systems started venting heat from the starboard sub-light engine column and the enginarium. Unbeknownst to the rest of the ship, the plasma reactors had been quietly building to super-critical meltdown. Catastrophic damage and the thermoplasmic chain reaction that was sweeping through the vessel was combating the deep cold of the Kryonova's awesome radiance.

As thawing moisture began to rain down from the frosted lancet screens and runebanks blinked back into life, chatter and movement began to resume on the bridge. Through the command deck windows the Kryonova blazed deep blue with danger.

'Look!' Czevak yelled as he drew the bridge's attention to the aft pict screen. The *Stella Incognita*'s blunt prow filled the screen; the swifter vessel had run them down and was almost upon the rogue trader. The sorcerer-captain of the vessel intended to draw alongside and board the *Malescaythe*. Czevak could almost imagine the gleaming rows of silent, unquestioning Rubric Marines, waiting to storm the rogue trader.

As the *Stella Incognita*'s bombardment cannon shattered and fell away it became apparent to the Thousand Sons Space Marines that the boarding action wasn't going to happen. The strike cruiser had over-reached itself and was stone-frozen from bow to tail.

The bridge windows cracked in the deep cold of the Kryonova's warped influence and portholes all over the ship imploded. Sorcerous lieutenants could not think straight or move their fingers to work life-saving dark enchantments and Chapter serfs and cultists were frozen pitifully to the deck. The Rubric Marines waited as the strike cruiser's armour plating split and sheered away, until piece by frozen piece the *Stella Incognita* and its crew complement of mindless Space Marines shattered like cheap glass and fell away.

Too late, the *Rubrician* observed the strike cruiser's fate and began to turn away. The frigate only managed to swing its starboard flank to the Kryonova and the cold star flayed the side of the Gladius-class frigate, fracturing its silent laser battery and stripping away the vessel's presented hull and armour plating. The *Chimera* was panicking also. Blinded by dead instrumentation and frosted screens the armoured transport's prow buried itself into the *Rubrician's* port side, driving both vessels deeper into the frozen deadzone surrounding the sun. Everyone on the *Malescaythe's* bridge watched the transport ram the frigate past them before, like two celestial ornaments freshly drawn from a flask of liquid nitrogen, the two ships shattered around one another, turning into a shard-swarm of disintegrating scrap.

Many of the cultist vessels and marauders – largely converted mercantile craft and freighters – had even less defence against the Kryonova's stellar freeze. The flock of Tzeentchian ships raced headlong into the star's raging cryosphere, intent on catching the slow moving *Malescaythe*. The supercooling solar wind smashed them apart like a shower of frozen teardrops. Beyond the handful of more manoeuvrable rearguard freighters that had managed to haul off, only the *Impossible Fortress* remained. She came at the rogue trader, her colossal hammerhead foresection sweeping across the *Malescaythe's* wake.

'She's going to try to ram!' Torres called through the warming air. 'Evasive portside.' Unable to launch her Swiftdeath fighters and Dreadclaw boarding pods into the void, the battle-barge's only remaining option was to ram the crippled rogue trader off its suicidal course and out of the Kryonova's malign influence.

'I have nothing,' her deck officer reported miserably after a flurry of activity in the transept discovered very little in the way of functioning runebanks and instrumentation.

'Just hold your nerve and your course,' Czevak ordered. They watched as the monumental bulk of the Thousand Sons battle-barge thundered for them. Her foresection and thorax were caked with ice and her ancient armour was beginning to split and crack.

Czevak watched the behemoth suffer in its desperation to reach them. Every once-broken bone in his body yearned for the diabolic, sorcerous genius that was Ahzek Ahriman to end himself at the heart of a raging Kryonova. Then he thought of Joaqhuine Desdemondra – the Living Saint, who still suffered for him at the fell-sorcerer's pleasure. A suffering Czevak vowed he would end as soon as he could for the immortal.

As fractures threaded through the snow-capped pyramid that grew monstrously out of the battle-barge's armoured abdomen, the mighty vessel's hammerhead foresection drifted past the *Malescaythe's* bulbous rear. Finally, she was turning. An antenna shaft of vanes and aerials even scraped the rogue trader's hull but shattered against its comparatively warmer surface. The bridge watched the withering giant continue on its failed path, away from the fierce retro-radiation of the warped star. Even Ahzek Ahriman and his accursed sorcerers would have struggled to combat the simple hostility of the Kryonova, the deep cold stabbing into their minds, incantations out of reach and hex-casting fingers stiff and arthritic.

As the dull glow of revived runescreens and instrument panels lit the rogue trader's command deck, Czevak ran over to check their heading; their degree of declination and celestial ascension.

With the *Impossible Fortress* beginning to drift away, Klute called out. 'Shouldn't we pull off also? I mean, how long can the reactor's plasma core last?'

In answer to the inquisitor's question the rogue trader suddenly rocked as an explosion rippled through her starboard side. Thrown across the transept and into the pulpit rail, Torres and her bridge crew grasped for handholds. Steam from the vents began to thin and die and the rumble of the plasma reactor was conspicuous by its absence in the frozen silence of the *Kryonova*.

'Damage report,' the Torres ordered.

'We just lost the starboard sub-light engine column,' her lieutenant said grimly. 'Enginarium critical but no casualties. Losing speed. Warp drive failing. Captain, the Geller field is collapsing.'

'Not this; not again,' Torres said.

'Hold your damn course,' Czevak roared as breath once again began to rime on the air and the lancet screens began to cloud.

'Czevak!' Klute called in desperation.

'Dropping,' the deck officer announced, counting down the vessel's doom. 'Sixty per cent... Geller field at fifty-five per cent.'

'Czevak!'

The High Inquisitor wasn't taking his eyes off the misting lancet screens. The *Kryonova* was so close now that the raging, blue surface of the star dominated the command deck's field of vision. Even where it didn't, the darkness of space was writhing with the airbrushed negative outlines of soul-hungry daemons and warp entities that thrashed in the void like swarms of fish in a vanishing, dry-season pool. The immaterial predators had hunting grounds here by the *Kryonova*'s cold trap. The creatures feasted on the crews of unwary vessels and the populations of unfortunate planetoids caught in the riftstorms of the Scorpento Maestrale.

'There!' Czevak called, pointing to a black ellipse situated in the star's equatorial east. It looked like a sun spot against the Kryonova's roaring, blue radiance but grew in size as the *Malescaythe* approached.

'Forty per cent...'

The rogue trader drifted through the angry void with inertial force, like a javelin tossed at a distant target. Once again, the *Malescaythe* began to creak and moan but it was impossible to tell whether the vessel was being ravaged by the crushing attentions of the deep, stellar cold or the diabolical warp entities pressing against the collapsing integrity of the Geller field.

All eyes were on the sun spot as it grew. Upon first sighting the blemish it had appeared tiny. As the frost-blooming vessel closed the distance, its actual dimensions were revealed. It was huge. Much larger than it had seemed. Much larger than the ship.

'Is that...' Torres began, amazed.

'It's a webway portal,' Klute said, barely suspending his own disbelief.

'Thirty per cent, captain,' the lieutenant informed Torres urgently. 'The Geller field is about to collapse.'

As the *Malescaythe*'s void-skimming prow drifted at the blackness the interdimensional energies of the warp gate blistered to life, arcing furiously across the portal's immense expanse and tessellating the reality of a cavernous webway tunnel beyond.

'By the Throne, it's opening,' Klute marvelled.

'And not by us,' Czevak said, almost to himself. 'Somebody's expecting us.'

The rogue trader pierced the transdimensional static of the portal entrance and drifted painfully inside. The *Malescaythe* was a certified wreck of a vessel, a dead mountain of metal aimed from an impossible distance at a target it could not have known existed. Its amazed crew stared through reinforced portholes in wonder and delight as the ship exchanged the terrors of the Eye – both environmental and daemonic – for the serene, immeasurable vastness of an interdimensional dry dock.

As the bridge took in the magnificent spectacle of the webway, Czevak turned and faced Klute and Torres. Of course, the High Inquisitor had seen such sights many times before.

'Captain, might I recommend commencing an extensive programme of repairs,' Czevak put to the astonished rogue trader captain. 'Can I suggest starting with life support and the heating? Is it just me, or is it cold in here?'

Flourish

![I] EPILOGUE

Hull exterior, Rogue trader Malescaythe, *The webway*

CHORUS

Enter CZEVAK, alone

HIGH INQUISITOR BRONISLAW Czevak slipped the goggles from his head to admire his handiwork. Dumping the spray gun, hose and heavy canister on the hull, he examined his paint job on the base of the newly erected, topside, forward-thorax-west ether vane. The High Inquisitor did not count among his talents artistry or engineering – he was far more adept at destroying things than fixing them – but conceded that he'd learnt a great deal about both over the past weeks.

Hanging in the safety of a webway dry dock, Captain Torres had made good on a guilt-ridden promise the inquisitor had made to help – primarily in using the

Lost Fornical of Urien-Myrdyss to acquire the vast array of parts, materials and specialist equipment needed to repair the horrifically damaged *Malescaythe*, but also in affecting some of those repairs and aesthetic improvements. Between them, the Techmarine Saul Torqhuil and Enginseer Autolycus oversaw the refit and the rogue trader crew's round-the-clock efforts to get the vessel both void and warp-worthy. The ancient vessel still looked like hell – even with her repairs and paint job – but Captain Torres didn't seem to mind. The captain was just happy to have steerage and propulsion systems back at her disposal, appreciating the implied honour of a veteran's scars.

Repairs were not restricted to the *Malescaythe* either. While Epiphani Mallerstang and the daemonhost Hessian recovered from their own soul-scars, the warpseer's gift slowly returning, Saul Torqhuil had started work on refurbishing the plates of his sacred armour and rebuilding his servo-harness and myriad of heavy-duty appendages. His first priority, however, had been a bionic substitute for his hand, which Czevak fancied was a thing of intricate beauty and more dextrous than the original. Dextrous enough to craft the bionic replacement for his primary heart that now thumped inside the Adeptus Astartes' mighty chest. The High Inquisitor didn't really know if any of them would forgive him for the trials and sacrifices of his acquaintance – but he was still alive, which was a good sign – and none of them had announced their intention to leave the rogue trader, which for most had come to represent a kind of a home in the unnatural hostility of the Eye.

Czevak dropped the paint gun and canister down a service hatch to an enginarium serf and told her to take them to Klute, who had been helping down below. He rubbed the paint from his hands on a set of robes Klute had lent him or that Czevak had stolen – he couldn't quite remember which. The High Inquisitor began to wander the hull exterior, taking in the colossal dimensions of the webway tunnel that tempted the traveller with the draw of its endless expanse.

He heard footfalls on the hull metal and turned. It was Vespasi-Hann. Eldar. Harlequin. Shadowseer. The warlock was going through the motions of lazy acrobatics, moving from the tips of his fingers to the toes of his boots, the kaleidoscopic chequers and stripes of his Harlequin coat and its Domino field creating a Catherine wheel of colour. His mirror-mask was the same, however, a silver, unreadable blankness that as ever, hid the psyker's face and intentions. The handstands, flips and carting continued with murderous agility, with Czevak standing still in its midst.

'That supposed to scare me, Harlequin?' Czevak finally called across the armour plating. 'Come to finish what you started?'

The Shadowseer continued his ominous performance. Czevak looked over his shoulder. He could tell the rest of the Harlequin troupe were there, the Great Harlequin playing with the stalks of his tall plume of pink, the half-masked carnival scorpion and the broad-chested Death Jester, leaning on the scythe attachment of his shrieker cannon. All sat about the hull architecture of the *Malescaythe*, just as indifferent as the Shadowseer. Czevak turned back to the psyker-swordsman.

'Are you really here?' the High Inquisitor asked him. 'Is this really happening and if so is it happening now? Sometimes, I swear I cannot tell.'

The Shadowseer jumped into a roll but by the time he was back on his feet he had produced his willowy witch-blade from a sheath on his back.

'Perhaps this is a dream,' Czevak pressed on. 'Perhaps it all is, but yours or mine? Or a performance – a piece of artifice, played out before the expectations of an eager audience. I was once privileged with a performance of the *Dance Without End*, at Iyanden. I'm told your masques only dramatise events that are significant to the destiny of your race. Am I a significant event?' the inquisitor said to the warlock.

The Shadowseer closed in predatory elegance.

'Is my story about to end, Harlequin?'

The witchblade sang through the air in practiced, leaping, back-arching flourishes, the psyker's grace both art and war.

'During the *Dance Without End*, Shadowseers like yourself used hallucinogenics and psychic manipulations to make us live their tale. We were as one with it. Is that what you do, Seer of Shadows, to make me fear you as I do?'

Czevak could feel it, like the closing of a ritual, the Harlequin moving in for the attack.

'Let me thank you, Vespasi-Hann of the Harlequinade, for saving my life on many occasions.' Czevak gestured at the webway around him. 'For opening the gate and allowing me in. I could not be sure, but I wagered you would want me back as much as Ahriman of the Thousand Sons, perhaps more. For that, I cannot give thanks. I will not return to the Black Library of Chaos a prisoner. And since I cannot live like a hunted animal – ghosted by you and your troupe – with a mind not my own, I think you know what I ask of you. What only you can deliver.'

Czevak turned his back slowly to the Shadowseer, resting his hands in his robes and closed his eyes. He heard the footfalls, the gymnastic prowl of the alien. He felt the darkness of a familiar fear creep into his heart. The Shadowseer was suddenly there behind him, his mirror-mask peering over Czevak's shoulder and the witchblade trembling with immaterial insistence, a hair's breadth away from the inquisitor's exposed throat.

'Is this what you came for, Harlequin?' Czevak whispered. In the inquisitor's hands, held at his chest, was the *Atlas Infernal*. The golden, lightweight armour of its casket-covers open. Its pump spine sighing rhythmically. The parchment-stretched flesh of the Sister of Silence on display – the blacksoul's ancient lifeblood coursing through the ever-changing labyrinth of arteries, veins and capillaries, winding through the pages.

Screams. Everywhere. Eldritch and involuntary.

The witchblade clattered to the hull and smouldered. The Shadowseer was gone. Czevak span around, with the antique Imperial tome held out in front of him. The Shadowseer was on the floor, repelled like a daemon from an icon of faith, writhing and squirming away from the inquisitor – unsuccessfully. As Czevak approached he looked about; the troupe had all been closing and had been stunned by the inquisitor's gambit. The Death Jester was doubled over; rich, red gore spurting through the teeth of his skull-face and onto the armour plating. The half-mask stumbled about the edge of the hull by the ether vane, gauntlets at her temples and riveblades and fist spike crossed above her head. Whether by accident or design, she slipped from the hull and fell off the side of the *Malescaythe*, tumbling past the rogue trader's cannon batteries and through the vast emptiness beneath the ship. The Great Harlequin was staggering at him, plume bouncing wildly and slender plasma pistols clutched in each quaking hand. The troupe leader dropped the weapons and hit the metal hull with about as little grace as Czevak had ever witnessed an eldar exhibit. Beaten and soul-scorched by the nullsphere of psychic blankness the pages of the *Atlas Infernal* radiated, the Great Harlequin and Death Jester phase-field jumped from the danger.

Vespasi-Hann was beyond such survival instincts. His burnt out mind could find no other expression of this than clawing at his mirror-mask. Czevak knelt down with the *Atlas Infernal* beside the afflicted alien.

'How does it feel, Harlequin? Fear?' Czevak put to the Shadowseer. 'Listen and listen well. I will not be a pawn

in some foreseen game of destiny, arranged by a vision-
ary farseer of your race. That's his Path. My path is my
own. I will stop Ahzek Ahriman of the Thousand Sons,
whether I am destined to do so or not.'

The High Inquisitor watched the Shadowseer scratch
at the clasps on his faceplate, gore bubbling and frothing
up from behind it and running down the silvery surface
of the mirror mask. 'It's over, Harlequin,' Czevak told
the dying xenos. 'I don't want to see your face. You will
always be just a masque to me.'

Czevak stood up. He could hear boots coming across
the hull towards him. Raimus Klute arrived, breathless,
robes flowing and shotgun pistol held up in one hand.

'I heard screams,' he said. Then he set his eyes on the
felled Harlequin. Not some paranoid distraction or
feverish hallucination, but a living, breathing menace
that had been stalking Czevak through time and space.
As the Shadowseer's fingertips fell from the mirror-mask
and a pool of blood began to gather on the hull under
the Harlequin's head, Vespasi-Hann lived and breathed
no more.

Czevak nodded.

Grabbing the sleeve of the Shadowseer's Harlequin
coat and pulling, Czevak tumbled the alien's body out
of it. The eldar's corpse rolled unceremoniously across
the polished surface of the sloping hull and then off the
edge of the ship. Slipping out of Klute's robes, he handed
the paint-smeared garment back to the inquisitor and
pulled on the Harlequin coat with the static crackle of
its Domino field.

'That's better,' the High Inquisitor said to himself.

'It's not safe to stay here any longer,' Klute said.

'Well, it's not safe to return to the Imperium,' Czevak
countered evenly.

'It's not safe for us "anywhere",' Klute concluded.

'And with us "anywhere", it won't be safe for Ahriman
either,' Czevak told his friend. 'Are they ready?'

Klute nodded and handed him a vox-bead.

'Captain Torres, you may begin your test run of the sub-light engines.'

'Affirmative,' the rogue trader captain returned and through his boots and the hull, Czevak felt the rumble of the sub-light engine columns coming to new life. As the *Malescaythe* gently pulled away from its dry dock moorings and the exotic brilliance of the webway's interdimensional walls began to drift by, the vox-bead chirped.

'Destination, inquisitor?'

Standing atop the magnificence of the battle-scarred rogue trader, the inquisitors gave each other wry glances. Czevak closed the *Atlas Infernal* and slipped it into the inside pocket of his Harlequin coat.

'Anywhere,' he replied.

Finis

ABOUT THE AUTHOR

Rob Sanders is a freelance writer, who spends
his nights creating dark visions for regular
visitors to the 41st millennium to relive in the
privacy of their own nightmares.

By contrast, as Head of English at a local
secondary school, he spends his days beating
(not literally) the same creativity out of the next
generation in order to cripple any chance of
future competition. He lives off the beaten track
in the small city of Lincoln, UK. His first fiction
was published in *Inferno!* magazine.

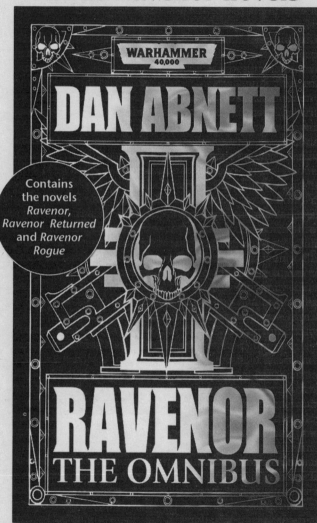

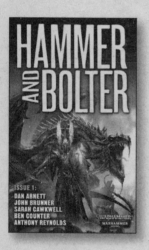
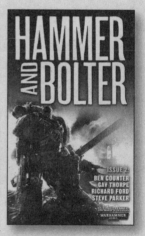

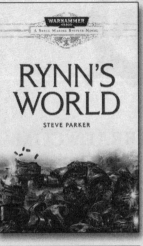

WWW.BLACKLIBRARY.COM

Join the world-wide community of readers who regularly discuss all things Black Library.

- Exclusives
- The latest news and event information
- eBooks

- Audio downloads
- Print on Demand
- Limited edition novellas

We connect with over 19,000 fans every day on our Facebook page, posting reviews, news, event updates and showcasing artwork from forthcoming novels.

Join us at *facebook.com/theblacklibrary*

You'll also find us on Twitter, where we're part of the large science fiction and fantasy online network.

Add us at *twitter.com/blacklibrary*

**Subscribe to our newsletter today:
www.blacklibrary.com/newsletter**